Other books by James Goodhand

Last Lesson

PENGUIN BOOKS

MAN DOWN

JAMES GOODHAND

MAN DOWN

PENGUIN BOOKS

Content note: this book contains the depiction of suicidal thoughts, coercive and manipulative relationships, and drug use.

PUFFIN BOOKS

UK | USA | Canada | Ireland | Australia
India | New Zealand | South Africa

Puffin Books is part of the Penguin Random House group of companies
whose addresses can be found at global.penguinrandomhouse.com.

www.penguin.co.uk
www.puffin.co.uk
www.ladybird.co.uk

First published 2022

001

Set in 12.5/14.75 pt Garamond MT Std
Typeset by Jouve (UK), Milton Keynes
Printed and bound in Great Britain by Clays Ltd, Elcograf S.p.A.

A CIP catalogue record for this book is available from the British Library

The authorized representative in the EEA is Penguin Random House Ireland,
Morrison Chambers, 32 Nassau Street, Dublin D02 YH68

ISBN: 978–0–241–38333–9

All correspondence to:
Puffin Books
Penguin Random House Children's
One Embassy Gardens, 8 Viaduct Gardens, London SW11 7BW

Penguin Random House is committed to a
sustainable future for our business, our readers
and our planet. This book is made from Forest
Stewardship Council® certified paper.

For Felix

Four's a Crowd

Will Parks is no longer alone.

This is the precise instant it begins. He is being watched. Followed. Everywhere.

And he won't be alone again until The End.

Will himself has not noticed anything change in these last few seconds. Why would he when there are so many more pressing matters to worry about? Not least that he's stuck in a confined space with a girl he doesn't even know.

He's wedged in the back seat of his brother's blue Fiat, the second car in the queue at the level crossing. The stereo plays way too loud, bassline pummelling Will's back from the enormous speaker behind his seat. Frowning eyes stare from the rear-view mirror of the car ahead. His older brother, Danny, plumes vape smoke through his open window into the September evening. In the front passenger seat, a girl. She's dressed up for a Friday night with Danny. Her name is April, although Will doesn't know this yet. He'd only dared to look at her for the briefest of moments when they picked her up. She's beautiful, though; that he knows. Of course she is. And she'll be gone in a fortnight.

'He loves them and leaves them' – that's what people say about Danny.

The train comes into view at last: an express scything across the marshes. It crosses in front of them in a blur, fast and close enough to make the little car rock on its springs. The flashing red lights switch to amber and Danny pulls away in his usual manner. Mr Unimpressed-Glare in front adds a small hand gesture to his expression of disapproval.

They rumble over the tracks into the part of town known as Patten's Island to drop Will off, his plans somewhat less stimulating than what Danny no doubt has in mind. But they make it barely a hundred metres beyond the crossing before Will feels several thunks from somewhere beneath his feet. The car begins to slow. The smell inside, candy-flossy vape smoke and April's perfume, is overpowered by the acrid whiff of mechanical failure. The stereo is suddenly silent as they come to rest, revealing a gathering chorus of horns from behind them.

Three times Danny twists the key. Four. Five. The engine cranks a little slower each time, the sound of his cool dying. He's furious, although you'd need to be someone as close to him as his own younger brother to recognize the signs: the reddening at the earlobes, the tremor in his right arm as he waves the traffic past, the sweat beading in the stubble of his skin-fade haircut.

In one movement, Danny is outside with the bonnet open. His muscle-fit jumper is rolled to the elbows, creating the illusion that he might have the foggiest idea what's gone wrong. That he might even *fix* it.

Unable to get out of the back seat without causing a fuss, Will instead stares out of his side window at the derelict shop they are stopped outside, with its peeling paint and cracked pebbledash. It was once a dry-cleaners, though the only evidence of that now are the rusted scars left by the signage. The sea is visible in the gap between this building and its neighbour. The light is fading fast, the setting sun like raging fire and smoke over the marshes. Will concentrates on the view, his head locked round at ninety degrees to his body.

I should have walked, he thinks. *I really, really should've fucking walked.*

'You see your nan every Friday night?' April asks.

Will's heels dig into the car floor. She's less than a metre away from him. *Way* too close for a conversation. At least she hasn't turned right round, instead just inclining her head to the side. Limited risk of eye contact.

'Sweet of you,' she adds, even though Will hasn't replied.

'Sometimes,' Will eventually says. A lie. He does see her every Friday night; spends most evenings round there if he isn't working, and he'd wish it no other way. He's only too well aware there will come a time, soon, when he won't be able to do so any more.

'What you reckon to sixth form?' she asks.

'S'OK.'

Will stares at his iPhone in his lap, smearing a wet thumb round in circles on the lock screen.

'Hear about the dartboards?'

He gives a snort of laughter. He *has* heard about them — how they didn't survive a week in the common room before being removed after Saul Caan had to be taken to A and E with a dart buried barrel-deep in the back of his neck.

'You're at ECS?' he asks. Three days into lower sixth at Ebbswick Community Secondary, he's sure he hasn't seen

3

her around. Though the fact that he hasn't yet set foot inside the common room has, of course, limited his opportunities for meeting his fellow students.

'I'm the new girl,' she says bouncily, turning right round to face Will and giving it some jazz hands. 'Got a kindly upper-sixther to show me the bright lights of the town, though.'

Will focuses on his brother, perched on the wing of the car, unsure whether April's sarcastic tone is in reference to the suggestion of Ebbswick-on-Sea containing even a single bright light, or that Danny's invitation could be in any way interpreted as an act of kindness.

'Where should we go?' she muses out loud.

Will smiles back at her for a moment. 'It's . . .'

April stares at him, waiting. But Will has merely succumbed to the pressure to begin a sentence, trusting that the rest of the words will follow. They haven't. This is always happening. When will he learn?

'It's . . .' he says once again.

At some quiet moment in the near future, he'll reflect on this exchange and carry out a post-mortem, running over every word and gesture in forensic detail, as he often does in the aftermath of a social encounter. At the heart of these investigations lies the big question he can never answer with any certainty: *What is it that I'm so afraid of?*

Saying something really fucking stupid, that's part of it for sure. But there's something deeper. It's a fear of being *seen*. Of being outed as *weird* – the hardest reputation to shift once gained. That's the furthest conclusion Will is able to reach. If he could only believe he might interact with another human being without the certainty they'll leave disappointed, amused – repulsed, even – by the encounter, if he could *know* that's not how it would end, maybe he'd be OK.

It's far from just conversations with girls at which Will falls short, although those are perhaps where the struggle is at its most acute. And it's not because Will fancies those girls, even if his maroon-faced appearance makes it look like he does. In truth, Will doesn't so much fancy girls as exist in awe of them, considering himself thoroughly unworthy of their attention. He's two weeks off seventeen, but he long ago accepted that it's exceptionally unlikely he'll ever have sex. Sometimes he wonders if he might, in the long-distant future, when he's thirty or forty perhaps, pay for it – just to find out what it's all about.

'What subjects you doing?' April asks.

'English, history, physics, photography,' Will reels off.

'Snap,' she says, grinning. 'Be seeing you in photography. One of my *five*.' She does a disgusted face.

'Five?'

'Beasting myself, aren't I? Figure if I keep myself busy, no one'll notice I've got no mates.'

You'll have friends soon enough, Will thinks. *You must be seriously clever*, he also thinks. But he doesn't voice either of these thoughts, for fear they'll sound like an attempt at a compliment.

'Sorry, kids, but this old bus ain't going nowhere fast,' Danny announces, kneeling on the edge of the driver's seat. His hands are remarkably spotless for someone who's been supposedly nursing a broken engine for the past six minutes.

'What's up with it?' April asks.

'Radiator, looks like.'

'Shit. Sounds expensive.'

'I'll slip a new one in tomorrow,' he says.

Will is always impressed by Danny's ability to speak with utter confidence on matters of which he knows little or nothing.

'You all right walking to Nain's from here, little bro?' he asks with a warmth he doesn't usually use to address Will.

'How come you call her nine?' April says.

'*Nain*,' Danny corrects, although it sounds indistinguishable from the number. 'Welsh for "Gran". It's where she grew up.'

Will is only too relieved to be squeezing past the front seat, unfolding his six-five frame into the salty air. He gives his brother a thumbs up, towering awkwardly over him.

'Don't forget to walk Beppo,' Danny adds with a smirk.

This is a running joke, entirely at Will's expense, but he laughs all the same because it's easier than getting annoyed.

'Got the lead?' Danny winks.

Will opens his rucksack and shows it to him.

'Woof woof,' Danny says, playfully jabbing his arm.

'Catch you in photography,' April calls after him, just as another train howls past the level crossing.

Will pretends he doesn't hear her.

She must think I'm so fucking rude, he thinks.

Shoulders rigid and hands jammed in pockets, Will walks away.

And he is followed.

That Friday Feeling

Will rounds the corner into his nain's road. The single working street light glows in the darkness, wobbling like a flower on a stalk as an onshore breeze kicks up over the beach in the distance. He passes an old caravan, slumped at the kerb on flat tyres that haven't turned in years. The bungalow over the road has its glass front door held together with parcel tape.

This part of town is known as Patten's Island, although it isn't an island, and Mr Patten – the businessman who built it – had the good sense to bugger off a long time ago. An area of reclaimed marshland, surrounded by sea on two sides, hundreds of chalets line its grid of roads. Once a half-fashionable holiday destination, in recent decades the buildings fell first into disrepair, and then into the hands of private landlords, who do as little for their tenants as they can get away with. Fifty years ago, you might have seen the neighbourhood depicted on postcards, but these days you're more likely to find it in one of those 'crap towns' sort of books, which a particular type of person is entertained by.

Will stops for a moment outside Nain's front door and takes a deep breath, as he always does. He knows that once he's pressed the doorbell or stuck his key in the lock, he's at the mercy of whatever might be waiting for him inside. There have been times when that fact has come close to making him walk away. He turns for a moment and looks at the few multicoloured flowers and stone squirrels that decorate her front garden. This small plot used to burst with blooms in every colour imaginable, a proper neighbourhood landmark. These days she keeps it simple.

'Let yourself in, Wilbo,' a voice shouts from inside.

Nain is in the kitchen, where she's half sitting on, half leaning against a wheeled stool at the worktop. In front of her is a mound of roughly chipped potatoes and a gin and bitter lemon in a half-pint beer jug.

'Look at the bloody state of them,' she says, pointing a shaking finger at the chips. 'Silly old fart.'

Will crouches to give her a hug and kisses her hot forehead. Beneath her silver woolly jumper she feels like a baby bird.

'I said I'd cook my tea,' he says, spotting the gammon and pineapple laid on foil and the beans on the stove. 'You've eaten?'

'Portuguese Louisa left ten minutes ago.' Nain has a protocol when referring to her carers, prefacing their first names with their country of origin. 'Cumberland pie. That makes it Friday?'

'Yup.'

'Don't get old, Wilbo. Working out the day of the week from what's on the menu! Bloody hell.'

She digs around in the fridge and Will helps her extract the chip pan from right at the back.

'I'll do my tea, Nain,' he says quietly but firmly.

'What use am I when I can't even feed you?'

'How are you?' he asks. 'Sorry, got called into work the last couple of nights.'

'You work too hard.' She rubs his arm.

'We kinda need the money. Been OK, though?'

'Fine, dear. Fine. Not buying green bananas, you know.'

Will tries to laugh, gripping his hand round Nain's as she attempts to light the gas rings.

'Go sit down,' he says. 'I'll join you in a minute.'

He guides her to her chair, arm linked with hers, lowers her by the shoulders into her threadbare mustard-coloured armchair and waits while she packs cushions round herself. As he steadies her, he looks at the wall over the fireplace. His grandad stares back at him, or at least so it seems from the sparkling life in his eyes. The framed portrait rests above a highly polished cherry-wood box on the mantelpiece.

'April 2018,' Nain says, wedged in position now. 'I was thinking about it the other night. He had no idea I was taking it. Last time we ever went out to a party. Worked out it was precisely a hundred days before, well, you know . . .'

Will nods. Like so many of Nain's photos dotted about the house, it's so beautiful that it's impossible to walk past. It's the sort of picture you can only take using an old camera with no electronics deciding you're wrong, because it breaks all the rules. Ninety per cent of the image is jet black, with slivers of white where his hair and the deep wrinkles in his Middle Eastern skin catch the low light. There is the quick-witted grin, the Sinatra cut of his suit: an entire person in a thirty-centimetre square.

'How you getting on with the camera?' Nain asks. She gifted her 1970s Olympus to Will a year ago. 'Shooting lots? Film's expensive, I know.'

'A bit. Here and there.'

He rarely leaves home without it. His wages allow him a thirty-six exposure roll every two weeks, together with the school darkroom fees so he can process it.

'I live in hope that you'll have something to show me one of these days. I know you have the eye.'

Will can't bring himself to show his work to anyone, especially not Nain, who he's certain he couldn't compare to if he practised for a lifetime. This is something Nain can't begin to understand, because while they may well share an eye for a good picture, above all they share a lack of belief in their own abilities. Someone need only glance around the walls of her small chalet, not just at the photographs but also at the watercolours of beaches and landscapes, the Indian-ink line drawings of animals, the scenes of fairies and picnicking teddies burned into slabs of timber, to realize that all those years spent working the delicatessen counter in an out-of-town supermarket were a waste of her skills. But Nain would never think such a thing. She can name scores of gifted people in this very neighbourhood; people who possess all the skill and flair to be master cake bakers, model makers, writers, who instead give themselves to jobs where someone makes you put your phone in a locker and tells you what time you can eat your lunch. There are professions that aren't open to people from places like Patten's Island; she's long known that.

'It's chilly in here,' Will says, flinching at the clank each time he prods the ignition button on the gas fire.

'Don't you bloody dare!' Nain laughs. 'It's September, for crying out loud.'

Will doesn't argue, instead unfolding a blanket and laying it over her knees.

'Least I can do is keep the gas bill under control,' she says. Her expression shifts suddenly, lips tightening against teeth. 'He was out there again this afternoon.' She points to the closed curtains, beyond which is her small back yard. 'Brazen, he is.'

Will's fairly sure he knows where this is going, but plays along regardless. Out of what – politeness? Duty? He's never sure.

'Who was out there?'

'What's-his-name. You know. Arbuckle! That Jonny Arbuckle next door.'

'Does he still live there?'

Will knows that the De Souza family live there, that Mr Arbuckle moved away five years ago.

'Stealing my electricity again. Making a racket all afternoon.'

'Maybe he was using his own electricity, Nain.'

'Drills, saws, sanders – all sorts. He thinks I'm such a mug.'

'I don't think anyone's stealing from you.'

'I can't afford it, Wilbo. As if things aren't bad enough.'

'Try not to worry. I'm sure –'

'It makes me so bloody cross.' There are tears in her eyes now as she slams a fist against the arm of her chair.

Will hugs her and kisses her head. Her soft white hair smells of the perfume she's always worn and, as Will closes his eyes, he realizes that it's him who feels safe now, even though he's the one doing the comforting. He thinks how bizarre it is that minutes ago she was remembering the exact day she took a particular photograph, and in another moment she's recounting something that never happened, or relying on a foil dish of Cumberland pie to tell what day it is.

As the moments pass, he feels the tension in her ease, and knows that she's either talked herself round or forgotten entirely what had wound her up in the first place.

'Gonna sort my tea,' he whispers, creeping back to the kitchen.

The chips are almost golden and bubbles rise slowly through the gloopy baked-bean sauce, popping and splattering the hob. Noise spills from the old medium-wave radio on top of the fridge. Through the whistling interference and the crackle of static, Will can detect two separate stations fighting each other to be heard. There's some sort of country and western song with swooping steel guitar, and then there's a radio play with cut-glass accents talking about a pheasant shoot.

Who are these people who listen to dramas on the radio, Will briefly wonders, and why don't they watch telly instead? He notices that if he concentrates on the music, the conversation fades into the background; if he focuses on the posh farmers, the song recedes till it's like the music in a lift. There's a great crack of interference as he sweeps the aerial to one side, finding a sweet spot where just the music remains.

He lifts the basket of chips to drain and switches the gas taps off. Before joining Nain, he stands for a moment and looks about the kitchen – at the irrelevant stuff that's been part of the scenery for every memory he's made here: the bar of hand soap no one uses, marbled green and white and split end to end; the London Olympics commemorative plate above the door, veined with superglue; the fridge magnets from places no one in the family has been.

He thinks about his first A-level physics lesson this morning. The law of entropy was the topic: how all things in the universe move over time from order to chaos. And he thinks how there was a time when his life existed in perfect order: when everybody who mattered was still alive, when no one had illnesses that would take them away, when both parents still lived under the same roof and divorce was just a word used in gossip about other families. His life once had order, and he was happy. As order moves towards chaos, Will thinks, so happiness falls to bits and becomes misery.

He takes a seat next to Nain, knowing that what little order that still remains will soon be chaos too.

But he's wrong. Unlike most of nature's known laws, there's room for a little negotiation where entropy is concerned. Things are about to get better for Will.

Although they might get worse first.

Work

Will stares at the folded trousers and the green and red striped waistcoat as his manager slides them over the bar to him. He feels nauseous. For a change, it's not because of the stench of stale beer and festering mops that always fills the pub until it gets aired out at opening time.

'Front of house?' Will asks. 'I'd maybe rather stay on pot wash.'

'Kitchen'll manage without you,' his manager tells him.

'I'm just not sure I'm –'

'High time we got you customer-facing – nice strapping lad like you. It's a cracking day. Be some tarts down looking for a bit of fun, mark my words. You'll be thanking me later.' He winks at Will. His name is Mick Touch, and there have been whispers from the younger girls on the staff that suggest his surname is not inaccurate.

Will keeps his hands clear of the uniform, as if picking up the pile of well-worn clothes will commit him to the gig. It's barely past ten on Sunday morning, but beyond the pub's glazed frontage the beach is already sprouting blankets and windbreaks, and the sea is fizzing with autumn sun.

'I'm kinda fucked since all the temp staff buggered off back to wherever,' Mick Touch tells him. 'That's the trouble. Give it a month and it'll be back to ghost town round here again.' He ploughs his fingers through his gelled grey hair. 'Tell you what: I'll let you keep some of your tips. How's that?'

He mimes spitting into his hand and holds it out.

With a choice only of agreeing or finding a new employer, the deal is sealed.

Mick locates a name badge from under the bar. 'Today, you shall be known as Mo,' he says, laying it atop the pile of clothes.

Will's been working part-time at Smugglers Pub and Dining for nearly two years. Like most of the staff, his is a cash-in-hand arrangement – four quid an hour with a fiver bonus if it's a public holiday. Ordinarily, he washes up, fetches ingredients from the fridges and cleans down the kitchen when the grill chefs are done. It's a job he rather enjoys; the pace and heat make him feel like he's working in the engine room of a cruise liner, and he creates his own fun by running a tally on every shift of how many times the C-word is used. He worked a double last Easter Monday when the current record of 412 was set.

'Now tell me, *Mo*,' Mick Touch says, 'do you want to know the secret to being a successful waiter?'

'I suppose.'

Mick stares at Will while nodding slowly.

'Erm, I don't get it,' Will says uncomfortably.

'It's almost witchcraft, Willy boy.' He's still nodding.

'What is?'

'I call it the Magician's Nod. You try it. Imagine I'm a table of punters. Ask me if I'd like another round of drinks. Go on.'

'Can I . . . get you some . . . any more drinks, maybe?'

'No, thank you!'

'OK. Sorry.'

'And now, Willy boy, nod while you ask me. Give it some Magician's Nod.'

Will does as he's told.

'Yes, I'm rather thirsty, now you mention it. Another round, young sir!' Mick grabs Will's shoulder. 'The power of persuasion, it's an incredible thing. Now ask me if I'd like any sides.'

'Any side orders?' Will has finished the sentence before remembering to begin the ridiculous nodding.

'Perfect! Onion rings, please. And, fuck it, let's have some garlic mushrooms while you're at it.' He thrusts the uniform into Will's chest. 'You're an absolute natural. Get yourself changed.'

Five minutes later, Will emerges from the gents. His trouser legs end several centimetres above his trainers. The waistcoat bulges between buttons like he's an illustration of a fat man in a children's book. He stands as if lost in this thoroughly familiar building, swinging his arms back and forth and certain he's glowing bright red, when Meera bounds over to him. She's well under five feet tall, not a day over fifteen, and she runs *everywhere*.

'Follow me,' she orders. 'Mickey Bum Touch says I've got to teach you everything I know.' She's also Smugglers' best waitress. 'Just you, me and Janice today –' a woman with crinkly blond hair waves with her back turned, laying up a table – 'and a hundred and twenty covers for lunch. That's just what's *booked*. Gonna be fun, washer-upper man.'

'Can't wait.'

'Be fine. Bum Touch given you the Magician's Nod talk?'

'Yeah.'

'Such a tit,' she says, and Will giggles along with her.

He tries to concentrate as Meera talks him through the touchscreen till and the card machine and the kids' menu and the Pepsi machine, but he's too busy panicking that he won't remember anything to be able to remember anything. Briefly, he entertains the fantasy of simply walking out, but he daren't; in a few weeks the wind and the rain will set in and Ebbswick-on-Sea will become deserted, and even jobs that pay as poorly as this one will become impossible to find.

The doors open. 'Love Shack' by the B-52s starts playing throughout the building, the first track of the playlist that's been on loop for the last year. As if walking in time to the drumbeat, early-bird boozers swarm to the bar. Mick Touch hooks his arm round Will's shoulder and guides him to a table of six seated in a window bay.

'Here he is, your server for today,' Mick booms as though he's compèring at a comedy club. 'It's Mo! Be gentle with him, folks – first-day nerves.' He ruffles Will's hair and struts away, laughing.

All the guests are over sixty and dressed smartly. This puts Will partly at ease, reminding him of the Christmas parties for the elderly held by the school community club, where he served turkey dinners and alcohol-free wine in the school hall. Although those events never involved *ordering*, and Will is suddenly at a loss as to how to begin this interchange.

'Drinks,' whispers Meera, whizzing past behind him.

2 Saint Clements, he shakily scrawls, *2 pints Creamflow*, *2 halfs Creamflow*, and just hopes the bar knows what any of that means.

The tables start landing fast, far too fast to remember where he's got to with each. But the little speech Meera wrote out for him – soup of the day is minestrone, special is steak and kidney pudding, no barbecue ribs left – quickly becomes well practised, and with Meera's and Janice's help drinks and food seem to be landing in front of the right people. The beauty of being so absurdly stressed, Will starts to realize, is that you don't have time to get stressed.

An hour in and he's mastered carrying three plates at a time and almost looking at the customers when they're talking to him. And most of Meera's advice has already proved accurate: everyone does order the second cheapest wine on the list; there's a wanker on every table who answers the question 'How would you like your steak cooked?' by replying, 'On a grill!'; and lots of customers don't waste time with please or thank you. This is the bit that Will finds most fascinating, as if by putting on a waiter's uniform he's been gifted the minor superpower of being able to see people's real character.

'Great work, mate,' Meera tells him as the restaurant begins to thin out in the late afternoon.

Will stands rigidly and gently pats her back as she hugs his torso. She grabs a wad of notes from her waistcoat pocket and peels off two tenners for Will. 'Redistribution of wealth, comrade. If Bum Touch sees this little stash, it'll be straight in his back pocket.'

Will scrunches the money in his palm. Sure, he's spent the day sweating like a marathon runner, and he was moaned at by a customer whose shouts of 'Mo!' Will had constantly ignored, and there was a complaint over a well-done rump steak that was too tough, which Mick Touch had to deal with, but Will is right now enjoying that brief window where he's happy with a performance he's given – before all the analysis has had a chance to begin.

He sinks a pint of soda water and begins the massive task of cleaning up the melted ice creams and dirty glasses that cover the vacant tables. Back in his own world, without people to serve and appear normal in front of, he doesn't notice the time pass, barely registers the beach falling quiet and the darkness setting in outside.

'Will!' comes a bark from the far corner of the building, where the restaurant gives way to the bar.

Will spins round, as if someone has woken him up.

'Need you, Will!' Janice shouts.

'What's up?' he mumbles, but she turns and hurries away, waving for him to follow.

He'll think about this moment a lot in the days to come. He'll wish he'd been harder to find, or that he'd told Janice to go and find Mick Touch instead – because it was his problem that Will was being invited to wade into. He jogs through the bar area, keeping Janice's bouncing mass of corkscrew hair in sight. In a low-ceilinged annex at the back of the pub, he steps into a load of trouble.

'Here comes the cavalry,' a red-faced man says, sniffing noisily and dragging his sleeve across his face. 'Big fucker, aren't you? How you doing, cock?'

'OK, thanks,' Will says, caught off guard and unable to forget his manners despite the tone of the question.

The room is open at one end into the bar, the other three walls forming a passage around the snooker table, which dominates the space. One guy stands in the corner, his cue gripped upright in his fist, his clenched jaw chewing at an invisible piece of gum. The guy who's speaking is shorter than his mate. He's perched on the far cushion of the table with his legs crossed. His disproportionally large bottom bulges over the edge on to the baize as if it's going to explode through the central seam of his trousers any second. Meera stands backed into the corner, hugging a stack of empty pint glasses to her chest.

Janice talks hurriedly to Will, moving her lips excessively as she speaks.

'Meera was collecting their glasses. The short one starts asking her to take drugs with them. Keeps trying to make her go to the disabled toilet with him.' She's talking quietly but Will's sure they're close enough to be overheard. 'The pair of them are off their faces on God knows what. Said some really disgusting things to Meera.' Janice looks round and flashes a dirty look in the guy's direction. '*Filthy* things,' she whispers.

Will nods. He's aware that the two men and Meera are all looking at him. He's confused. *Why the hell are you telling me?* is what he wants to ask. *What on earth has this got to do with me?*

'Meera asked them to leave,' Janice continues.

Will looks at her blankly.

'She asked them to leave, Will, and they won't. And they're being abusive.'

For the first time since this morning, Will's suddenly aware of his uniform, with its ankle swingers and silly striped waistcoat.

'Shall I call the police?' he whispers back, petrified he'll be heard. He's heard there are people who'll kill a man for reporting them to the law.

'Just get them out,' Janice says, shaking her head.

Will says nothing. He looks Janice in the face for a second. She's got to be the same age as his mum, older maybe. These guys are what – thirty? Why is he expected to resolve this problem? He may be nearly seventeen but he can't remember feeling more like a child than he does right at this moment. He wants to run home and cry in his room. He wants to be in the arms of his nain.

But a decision has been made that he is The Man. He is expected to fix this. It's not just Janice's eyes that drill into him, it's the two blokes' eyes as well. A stage has been set here.

A scene is expected.

I don't want to watch this.

Why do I have to watch this?

Why am I here if all I can do is watch? Watch and not help . . .

Why am I here at all? I guess that's the question I'm getting at.

Why am I following you around, Will Parks, every minute of the day and night?

Why you? Why can I only follow you? What's so special about *you*?

So many questions.

It was Friday night when it began. In the car, at the level crossing, with you, your brother and that April girl. So, forty-eight hours. Ish. That's the only way I can work it out – count the number of times it's got dark then light again. I can't *feel* the time passing.

But here's the odd thing, or rather the oddest thing: I can *see* it – I can see the time passing. If I look behind me, behind *us*, I see what was happening before what's happening right now started happening. And if I look forward, I can make out what's coming up next. It's like sitting between two mirrors, seeing copies stretching out to infinity in both directions. Only it's you I see, not me. And in one direction the image is lagging behind what's happening now, and in the other direction it's running ahead.

It's like I've traded one plane of movement for another. You, and everyone else, can move backwards and forwards and side to side. I can only deal in 'befores' and 'afters'.

How far ahead can I see? It's hard to be sure. Weeks, I think, maybe a month. And like looking at anything far away, the further into the distance I look, the less clear the detail.

Behind me, I can see no further back than my arrival on Friday night. Ever woken up certain you were having some crazy dream but can't remember what the hell it was about? That's what my before-Friday is like. If I knew where I was before then, I might have a clue what this is about. Who I am. *What* I am, even.

But among all these questions, there are things I do know. Things hardwired into me, instinctive.

I know I'm here for a reason.

I know I don't have forever.

I know I need to make contact with you.

Right now, it's that last one that's most pressing. Because if I'd already worked out how to contact you, maybe I'd've been able to prevent what's about to happen.

Because I've seen it coming and, like I say, I don't want to watch this.

Customer Service

'Can you please leave,' Meera snaps, eyeballing the guy perched on the snooker table.

'Me and my friend here are going to finish our frame,' he replies, 'and another round of drinks.' He stares at Will as he says it. 'Why don't you fetch us two Stellas, young man?'

'And couple of tequilas,' his friend mumbles, his face so taut he appears to have trouble speaking.

Janice's expression is one of disbelief, angled first at the two men, and then at Will.

'Where's Mick?' Will asks. 'We should get Mick.'

'Not a clue,' Meera says. 'Disappears when it gets quiet, doesn't he?'

'Come here, cock,' the guy says. His accent isn't local. It's London, almost posh. The sort of voice that gets what it wants.

Will looks at the cue lying across the table. If this was a film, he'd reach for that right now. He'd square up to this pair of arseholes, holding – no, *brandishing* – the cue, and they'd say something like, 'OK, cool it, mate, we're leaving.' But he's never had a fight, never been interested in how to punch, never thrown his weight around. There are people who somehow know almost instinctively how to do that, but Will is not one of them.

He walks round the table. The guy stands and blocks his path. Will's at least six inches taller than him but this gives him no sense of security, his height instead making him feel vulnerable, as it always has, as if he's towering above an invisible fortress that exists to protect all the normal people.

The guy flicks Will's name tag. 'Nice to meet you, Mo,' he says. His breath smells flammable. A halo of white dust outlines his nostrils. He grabs Will's hand and shakes it. And then keeps holding it. Will tugs a couple of times but it isn't released.

'Please leave now,' Will says. He's almost pleased with himself. There's unexpected authority in his voice.

'You ever had sex?' the guy asks.

'Yeah,' Will instinctively replies. It's a lie, of course, but he's very much in the mode of dealing with a school bully, which this guy almost is. Those people may grow up and blend in with civilization, but their old self is only too happy to be re-awoken with a few pints and some prohibited substances.

'Who?' the guy demands.

'Anyone,' Will replies. He doesn't know why he said that.

'Anyone? Fucking anyone?' He releases Will's hand, instead cupping his own on Will's crotch and squeezing.

Will grabs at the bloke's wrist but it's rigid as steel.

'You had a go on this?' he asks, nodding at Meera.

'No,' Will mumbles.

'*That?*'

Will follows his gaze to the far side of the table and Janice. She shakes her head. 'Hardly,' she mumbles, as if that's the most important issue to address right now.

The guy massages firmly between Will's legs. He grins. 'You're getting a hard-on, aren't you?'

Inexplicably, he is. He can't imagine feeling less aroused. But, yes, yes, he is getting a hard-on.

'Like the boys?' the guy whispers, lips millimetres from Will's, squeezing hard on the end of his dick, sending spears of pain shooting up to his abdomen.

'Fuck off!' Will shouts. He steps backwards. The guy steps forward, taking up the space.

'Fuck off, cunt!' Will shouts, trying to wrestle the hand from his genitals.

The guy's arm flies up from between Will's legs, grabbing him by the throat instead. In what feels to Will like one movement, he finds himself staring up at the ceiling. He's not sure how he's ended up there but he's laid on his back on the snooker table. His cheek is burning where it's been scraped along the baize. A cold blue ball rests against his eye socket. And a cue is pinned across his neck.

'Don't call me names,' the guy says.

'Sorry,' Will forces past his crushed vocal cords. He feels a hot tear running past his left ear.

'How sorry?'

Will says nothing.

'Sorry enough to kiss my feet?' The man adds a little more weight to his cue.

Will can hardly breathe now but gives a tiny yet emphatic nod. He slowly rises from the table as the cue is released.

'Don't, Will,' Meera says, not looking at him. 'You don't have to do that.'

Will looks at the balls scattered on the table. He could grab one in an open fist. He could swing it straight at this bloke's face. But he doesn't. He doesn't even seriously consider it. Will Parks is not the sort of person who can bring himself to really hurt somebody, to draw blood or break bone, and it would seem right now that there is shame in that fact.

He hears Janice muttering, 'Jesus Christ, Will,' as he drops to his knees and lowers his face to the floor. The navy suede slip-ons have an oddly musty smell, with a tang of what hopefully isn't dog shit. There's a mushroomy note to the taste of them as Will obeys the request for 'a bit of tongue'. The soles are grassy, crunchy with grit.

'Good lad,' the guy says after a good minute or more. He pats Will's head. 'Apology accepted.'

He sinks his remaining half-pint of beer in a single draught. 'We were leaving anyway,' he says, launching his cue so it bounces across the table. And the two of them are gone.

'My boys are your age,' Janice tells Will. 'They'd have sorted them right out.' She rolls her eyes. 'Call yourself a man?'

'Everything OK?' Mick Touch asks, bowling through the bar in their direction. 'What have I missed?'

Janice shrugs and leaves them to it.

'It's OK now,' says Meera. 'No biggie.'

She gives Mick a run-down of events, sparing the most demeaning details.

Once they're alone, Mick reaches an arm round Will's shoulder. 'Willy boy, Willy boy!' he says, roughly shaking him. 'What we gonna do with you? Not one for playing the hero, are you?'

Will looks at the floor, noticing how his hands are still shaking.

'You gotta act a bit braver than that when you've got an audience,' Mick says, his tone worldly-wise. 'Good old Janice was ready to give you a white feather there. You know about white feathers, Willy boy?'

Will gives an embarrassed nod. It's a reference he understands from GCSE history: how there were women who would hand a white feather to a young man who was slow to sign himself up to go to war.

Mick Touch is something of an enthusiast for military history, often to be heard expressing how 'they should bring back national service', or that what this country really needs is another world war, a chance for us all to come together and fight for death or glory. Although if anyone deserves that white feather, it's probably Mick Touch himself, who spent the last ten minutes rooted to his chair in the office upstairs, watching the snooker table incident unfold on CCTV, his finger lingering over the panic button next to his desk.

'If I'd have been here,' Mick says to Will, 'God knows what I'd have done to them.' He raises a clenched fist close to his chest. 'Wouldn't have been able to control myself.'

Starting Over

The sad truth is that Will Parks doesn't really have any friends. And so, as is not unusual, he's riding the number 83 to school, sharing a seat with a complete stranger. Who, unfortunately, doesn't smell great. Will breathes through his mouth into his own sleeve, desperate for the traffic to get moving as the bus crawls past Patten's Island on its way towards town. Still a complex aroma lingers in his nostrils: like the airless hoover cupboard in a holiday let, plus a touch of blue cheese. A raspy cough escapes from the old bloke and Will holds his breath till his vision swims.

It's not that Will is especially unpopular. Few of his fellow students would think twice about riding to school next to him. It's just no one would go out of their way to do so. Friendship was once such a simple thing. You throw a load of kids together in a neighbourhood or a classroom and you're done – everyone's friends and they all go round each other's homes on their birthdays. But then something weird happens. You hit your teens and suddenly it's necessary to be in a tribe, to gravitate towards people of shared interests, of similar ambition, of roughly equivalent financial standing. Will isn't a weed smoker, doesn't care especially for grime, couldn't give a toss about PC gaming or chess. He's a kid from a skint family in a nice road. He enjoys night-time beach walks in the pissing rain and taking black-and-white photos. He likes novels from the 1960s, films from the 1980s and dance music from the early 1990s – preferably on vinyl. His is a tribe of exactly one.

The bus is packed, mostly with ECS pupils. Will keeps his face turned from them. It's unlikely any of them know about yesterday evening's shoe-licking incident, but he can't be sure – who knows what details might have been shared and gone viral. There could be photos. What if there's a video? The more he considers it, the more sure he becomes that people know. That *everybody* knows. Why else would they all be having such a good laugh at this time of morning?

He cringes as he hears Mick Touch's words again in his mind: *Not one for playing the hero, are you? You gotta act a bit braver than that when you've got an audience.*

Will has long thought himself a wimp, but it's one of many secrets he keeps from the world: how he can't answer the front door at home, how he ignores the landline when it rings, how he finds things to do in the shed on Halloween to avoid being faced with someone demanding he answer the question 'Trick or treat?' But now it seems likely his cover is blown, that the truth is out: Will Parks is a pathetic little wimp.

The bus rumbles over the railway and pulls over at the stop in front of the library. As the doors hiss open, a fresh breeze whips in, swirls of dust turned to glitter by the morning sun. The man next to Will grapples with the seat in front, drawing himself upright. He turns to Will, gazing into his face.

Will forces a small nod. The guy stares harder, like he's looking deep into Will, and clean through him at the same time. His skin is waxy grey and his beard is stained brown from smoking, but he's a good deal younger than Will had assumed – too young for that death-rattle cough. His eyes glow in the golden light, as alive as the rest of him is nearly dead. A half-smile forms – a wistful, knowing sort of smile.

He begins a lengthy clearing of his throat. 'Thank you,' he eventually says.

Will's expression is asking, *Thank you for what?*

The man's eyes begin to redden, dampness welling in the left. 'Thank you so much.'

It's a growling whisper, impossibly earnest.

'Sorry, I don't . . . Maybe you've confused me with someone else,' Will says.

'Can we move along?' calls the driver.

The man raises a hand, his eyes not leaving Will's.

'Oh no,' he says. 'No confusion.' He flashes a broad smile and for a second he is unexpectedly handsome. 'Thank you. It won't be forgotten. Not ever.'

He staggers, bent-legged, towards the exit, looking back briefly at Will. 'Go well,' he says, tipping the brim of an invisible hat. 'Today it begins. Make the best of it.'

He stands at the kerb in front of the library and watches as the bus drives away.

Will doesn't dare to look back at him, pretending instead to check his phone. But he replays the interchange in his mind for the twenty-minute journey to school, rattled by how certain, how serious the man was, how heartfelt the misplaced thanks.

The questions of what it could be that begins today, and what could possibly warrant such thanks, are still nagging at Will hours later as he makes his way to period-four photography.

'Don't be shy,' Ms Calloway shouts across the room as Will hovers in the doorway. 'Join our circle of trust!'

She beckons him over with both hands raised like she's an evangelical priest. 'Breathe in – I'm not sure there's room for everyone.'

With insufficient classrooms to go round, photography lessons have been scheduled in the Walton Room – a smaller version of the school hall, usually used for parents' evenings and public exams. It's named after Ebbswick Community Secondary's most – perhaps only – notable former pupil, Jack Walton, a betting shop entrepreneur. A grinning portrait of him in trademark red blazer and check trilby hangs above Ms Calloway's seat at the far side of the room. Four chairs are arranged in a circle round her, enough for the entire class, Will now realizes, mildly panicked that there's no corner to stash himself in.

The chairs themselves are minimalist items fashioned from a single metal tube snaking from the floor to the top of the backrest, their contemporary style at odds with the faded blue carpet tiles and slatted window blinds. The seat springs backwards as Will lowers his weight on to it and he has no choice but to sit perfectly still till the rocking motion stops.

'Cool chairs, huh?' Ms Calloway says.

Will smiles and nods, accidentally setting the bobbing motion going again.

'It's driftwood,' she says, stroking the silvered dagger of timber hanging round her neck, giving Will the benefit of the doubt about where his eyes have come to rest. 'Jurassic Coast. So smooth.'

There are tiny tattoos on each of her long fingers, Will notices. Among a bland teaching staff whose personal histories no student could give a toss about, Ms Calloway is the source of much gossip. The billowing skirts, crazy jewellery and the regular mention of her wife add up to make her worthy of speculation. Rumours abound that she lives in the camper van she drives to school, that she once did magic mushrooms with her sixth-formers, that she was in a cult till her forties, when she swapped it for a life as an art and photography teacher. It's a reputation she's never been known to play down.

Two chairs remain empty, but already here is a guy called Kris Tring. He hasn't so much as looked at Will yet, instead sitting bolt upright clutching a massive Nikon, complete with flashgun and hooded long lens. His black-framed spectacles are what Will's dad would disparagingly call 'media glasses', and his air of nonchalance and the skinny fit of his clothes lend him the appearance of a conceptual artist in training.

The door rattles. Will feels his pulse quicken. He glances behind him and sees approaching the same black ankle boots that were in the hallway at home when he returned from Nain's late Friday night.

'Hey, Will,' April whispers as she takes her seat in the circle.

Again, Will nods. And again, the chair is off. Her perfume is familiar and it amazes Will that he can experience such a feel-good nostalgia from so recent and inconsequential a memory. He thinks about the closed bedroom door that night, and the noises beyond it, and the things he could hear Danny saying, and how he felt grubby and disgusted with himself for listening. And he thinks of Danny's brags on Saturday morning, and how they made him nauseous, and now he's glowing red and has an aching in his guts and he's glad of any distraction.

Alfie Lim, last to arrive, surveys the ring of chairs. 'What's going on here?' he asks. 'Meeting of Alcoholics Anonymous?'

'I like to think of it more as the United Nations,' Ms Calloway replies.

He pretends to sob. 'It all began when I had eight JD and Cokes on my first birthday . . .'

'Thank you for sharing,' she says. 'Now if you wouldn't mind.'

He drops into his seat and stretches his arms and legs out, lolling backwards and forwards as if he's on a bouncy castle. He hoots with laughter so infectious that it soon spreads to Will and April.

'Can you shut up, please?' Kris Tring says. 'Some of us are here to learn.'

'What is that motherflippin' bad boy?' Alfie asks.

'My camera,' Kris says matter-of-factly.

'Did they not have anything bigger?'

'They did, actually.'

Alfie turns to Ms Calloway. 'I said no press, Miss. If I'd known there'd be paparazzi . . .'

A scuffle follows as Alfie pretends to wrestle the camera from Kris, who slaps at his hands each time they venture near the enormous lens. Soon even Ms Calloway's chair is rocking, her shouts of 'Stop it now' delivered with less authority at each repetition.

This isn't the first time Will and Alfie have been classmates. Will's GCSE French lessons were regularly interrupted in much the same way as this, and it was Alfie's dicking about that meant Will left those lessons aching with laughter rather than bored to death as he otherwise would have been. Alfie's proudly one of the Rough Kids, and he spent his earlier years at ECS earning nicely from selling shoplifted sweets at a generous discount. These days his business is designer trainers and tracksuits, which are almost indistinguishable from the real thing. Something he's a lot quieter about is the fact that – despite never seeming to have paid a minute's attention in class – he aced his GCSEs.

Alfie tires of provoking Kris and settles back in his own seat, gently bobbing up and down as Ms Calloway welcomes the class and talks them through the course ahead. The room is warm and Ms Calloway's voice is soft and hypnotic, and Will finds it impossible to be anything other than calm as she talks about focal lengths and exposures and depth of field.

He allows his eyes to wander to April, who seems to be similarly entranced as she tucks her short dark hair behind her left ear. Side-on, he can glance wherever he likes now. He stares at her tiny earlobe and the grey heart-shaped ring threaded through it; at the profile of her slightly pronounced lower jaw, and at the shallow relief at the back of her bare neck. He imagines his cheek against her skin. Is it, he wonders, as impossibly smooth and perfect as it looks? He imagines the tip of his nose gliding over her neck and her back, how the heat would rise from her, how she'd smell that close, how her hair would feel, dusting over his lips. His chest hurts, like the thought of it could make him cry. And he snaps his attention back to Ms Calloway, struck by his own weirdness and filled suddenly with a sense of guilt, like he's been trespassing.

'So here's what I want from you this term,' she's saying.

'Homework?' Alfie whines. 'Come on, Miss. Back me up here, Will.' He slaps Will's knee, an action that instigates a Newton's cradle effect where both their seats rock equally and oppositely.

Will laughs, touched that Alfie knows his name.

'I want one photo from each of you,' Ms Calloway says. 'Which, as you'll realize soon enough, is a much tougher assignment then if I were to ask you for a hundred.'

'Tell me we don't need one of those,' April says, pointing at Kris's Nikon, which rests on his lap like a Bond baddy's cat.

'I don't care what you shoot on,' Ms Calloway says. 'Big ole SLR – Polaroid – iPhone – whatever. Photographers have a nasty habit of obsessing over equipment. It's to misunderstand the art. No one asks what brushes Michelangelo used to paint the Sistine Chapel, do they? And they certainly don't assume they could do it too, if only they owned the same gear.'

For the first time in the lesson, Will dares to reach into his bag, no longer embarrassed by Nain's vintage Olympus. He removes it from its tan case and catches a whiff of the reassuring smell – light oil, leather, hand cream.

'Mind if I take a look?' April asks.

Kris Tring huffs as she frames and focuses, treating it like a precious antique.

'Two photographs for your consideration here,' Ms Calloway says, standing an A4-sized image on each knee. 'All about the one on the right, isn't it?'

All four of her students agree. Will can't look away from the picture. It's a shot of a dandelion head, almost filling the frame, translucent and ghostly. Behind is the moon: huge and veined and glowing. It's haunting and it's beautiful.

'Now look at the one on the left,' she says. 'Boring, innit?'

It's a picture of the front at Ebbswick, shot from the marshes. There's some overgrown shrubbery in the foreground, a few people walking on the beach, a full moon just about visible out over the sea.

'What have these two pictures got in common, do you think?'

There's silence as everyone studies them in detail.

'Wow!' April says. 'They're the same thing!'

'Bingo!' Ms Calloway says. Even Alfie looks intrigued as she points with a pencil to the bottom corner of the boring photo. 'Here's the dandelion, if you look close enough. And up here, there's your full moon. Same scene, same time. Just a different way of composing the shot.'

Will feels a tingling in the back of his neck, and an urgency to be out taking pictures.

'This dull picture,' Ms Calloway says, 'is, I fear, how most of us see the world. We're surrounded by beauty, and we walk around like these folks on the beach, asking, "Where's the beauty?" And we think we'll find it if we just see more of the world, when actually maybe we need to see *less* of the world. This big, bland photo is just ordinariness, but it's made up of a million extraordinary details.'

'Deep,' mumbles Alfie, pretending to take the piss but clearly as enthralled as everyone else.

'If you dare to believe it's there,' Ms Calloway says, 'if you really look for it, you won't believe the magic you'll find going on around us.' She stares at each of her students in turn as she says it, Will feeling her gaze burning into him when she reaches him. 'So there's your assignment, peeps. One picture of one tiny, heart-stopping detail. You have the season on your side as well: harvest moons, long tides. Orange leaves and frosts before long.'

The class is quiet, the silence only spoiled by the squeaking of rocking seats.

'All so pensive. Any questions?'

'Yes!' Alfie snaps, leaning forward. 'Just one.'

'All ears, Alfie.'

'What the hell are these chairs all about?'

'I've no idea,' she says, her shaking head setting off an oscillation in her own. 'An attempt by our headteacher to appear *cool* to visitors, I fear.'

Alfie turns to Kris, who's chewing at the arm of his oblong glasses. 'Are they something to do with you, Tring?'

'What you talking about?'

'Did you design these chairs, Tring?'

'Fuck off, Alfie.'

'You did! You designed the shitty cool chairs, didn't you?'

Will looks at Kris, at his slicked back hair, his uber-cool specs, his tight trousers and winkle-picker shoes. It is impossible to imagine someone looking more like a designer of minimalist furniture. Will explodes with laughter. He laughs so hard it hurts to breathe.

'You might find it helpful,' Ms Calloway says, waving at her class to quieten down, 'to work as a group?' She casts her eyes between Kris's shaking head and Alfie's smirk.

April looks around. 'Will? Alfie?'

'Sure,' Alfie mumbles.

Will is silent, his expression adjusted to appear that he's thinking about it. But, behind the disguise, he's beginning to panic. Sharing a room for an hour with these people has been exciting and he'll long for the next lesson – he knows that. But to see them outside of school? A girl? And a guy like Alfie? It's like finding a secret passage to having *mates*.

'It'd be really cool to work with you,' April says.

But it's too much. Like jumping too many steps. The idea scares him. Briefly, an image of the three of them meeting up at a weekend plays in his head. He's dressed all wrong, and his ideas are shit, and then he runs into the guys from Smugglers, who kick off again and show what a total coward he is, right in front of these people he's so desperate to impress.

'Maybe,' he says.

''K,' she says with a shrug, passing him back his camera.

And they leave separately for their lunch break, Will mumbling it to himself over and over. 'Maybe. Maybe. Fucking *maybe*.'

But he knows, too, that it's better this way.

I've got it.

I know why I'm here.

I understand what this is about.

I may not know who I *am*, but I see now what I must *do*.

Here I am, following you. The time we've covered together reaches out behind me. A few weeks of future are visible up ahead. It's like scenery, only I'm seeing time stretching away from me, not distance.

But every now and then, without warning, something assaults me from nowhere. Like firing a camera flash into darkness. A horrific image. So many people. Twisted and dying. A picture of panic. I see it for an instant. I try to see the detail. But in the same moment it's gone.

Perhaps you'd call it a premonition, but it feels like a memory, too. Like some sort of flashback to a life I can't recall.

The vision is so real. Each time I see it, it brings with it an unmistakable certainty, awakening a truth that's been buried in me from the start: this is coming.

When? I have no clue.

Where? Same.

But it's coming. Something huge. Something devastating. A *tragedy*.

This is why we're here, you and I, isn't it? Why would I be seeing this awful thing, and be inescapably attached to you, if together we didn't have a chance of stopping it?

What other reason could there possibly be?

Right from that very first moment, in the car with you and Danny and April at the level crossing, a sense of purpose has nagged at me, a certainty that I have a job to do.

This is it, surely?

I need to make contact with you. How, I'm not yet sure . . .

I was seen, though. That's a start. That man on the bus, he knew I was there. In fact, it felt like he was looking for me. That he was somehow *expecting* me.

He saw me, and I knew I was real. What a silly thing to have ever doubted perhaps.

But it's one thing to be seen. It's quite another to change things. And change things I must.

There it goes again. A bright flash. Just milliseconds and gone. Vile, vile scene. Hell itself. So many people. I can't bear it.

I need to make contact with you, win your trust.

I have a job to do.

We have a job to do.

Sweet Seventeen

'Go easy, party animal,' Danny says as Will adds a glug of lemonade to his glass of Prosecco.

'Just don't like the taste of it much,' Will whispers, careful that their mum doesn't overhear. He knows the household budget has been stretched to pick up the three bottles.

'Well, happy birthday, Wilbo,' Nain says, raising her glass.

They've been through this ritual three times already but still Will and Danny chink her. She sits hunched at the picnic table in their back garden with Will's puffer resting over her shoulders. It's warm for late September, but still she shivers and sinks her wine and mumbles about getting her booze jacket on.

'Cheers, lads,' their dad shouts from behind a cloud of barbecue smoke. 'Life begins at seventeen!' He takes a gulp of beer, ejecting a belch from the side of his mouth.

Their mum slams another dish of marinated chicken down next to him. 'Already cooked through,' she says. 'Don't ruin them.'

'Get some flavour into these bad boys,' he says, finessing them on to the grill with long tongs.

'Looking forward to those homemade burgers and kebabs you promised us,' she says, sharp with sarcasm, as she turns for the kitchen.

'Traffic was a nightmare, Tori,' he says.

'Yup, you said. London, weekday rush hour, gridlocked. Fascinating.' She pats her hand to her mouth, miming a yawn.

'Well, it was. Still, nice to make it over eventually. You know, see my house . . .'

'It smells glorious, Mike,' Nain shouts from her seat. 'Fine teamwork.'

She winks at Will. It has to be the fifth time she's made this comment. Each time it looks as though Will's parents are about to break into a full-blown row, Nain starts jabbering away with compliments or another birthday toast to fill the airspace.

Will's mum takes her seat and brims her glass with fizz.

'Tuck in,' his dad says, laying a platter of steaming meat in the centre of the table. He slackens the straps on his *hilarious* woman-in-lingerie apron and slings it inside through the back door. 'I can't help feeling we should have invited more guests.'

'Thank you for that insight, Mike,' his mum says. 'I did ask him. No friends, just us. That's what he wanted.'

'Are you not having any bread, Danny?' Nain asks, looking in amused horror at his plate, piled high with chicken thighs. 'Or salad? Or pasta even?'

'Bulking up, aren't you, mate?' their dad says.

Danny smiles and tenses, his pecs leaping up and down like there are two rats having a fight inside his vest.

'The gym's become something of an obsession,' their mum says to Nain.

Danny beams, like someone might if they were being complimented on their charity work or groundbreaking scientific research. His commitment to working out – five

43

days a week, often at six in the morning – is something Will can't fathom. He's equally bemused by the pictures of Danny's mood-lit bare torso that are posted almost daily, with his slogan inviting his followers to 'Dare to be Great'. A passion for taking photos is one of the few things the brothers have in common, though Danny points his camera the opposite way round to Will.

'I just don't know how you can enjoy all that protein,' their mum says, as Danny grins.

Will watches as he rips chicken from the bone with his teeth, cheeks glistening with grease halfway to his ears. And he watches as his mum pushes pasta around her plate, washing down the occasional nibble with a gulp of wine. Tucking into his burger, piled with Stilton and onion rings, he thinks how he's the one who has fun poked at him for being 'weird', but he's the only member of this household with a healthy relationship with eating – what with Danny's food-as-fuel approach and his mother's just-enough-not-to-starve system.

'Bet the chicks dig it,' their dad says, winking at Danny.

'Shut up, Dad,' he replies, but gives a conspiratorial nod when he thinks no one's looking.

It's often said that their dad is 'where Danny gets it' – *it* being his charm, his way with the women, his credentials as a *heartbreaker*. All the stories from Mike Parks' past tell of a popular all-rounder, as at home on the rugby field as addressing a hall of people as head boy. From money and uni-educated, he was considered a catch for a girl who grew up in Patten's Island, and in the early years the boys' mum was often congratulated for marrying above herself. Mike, just like Danny, was a golden boy.

'Who you seeing this week, then?' he asks.

Danny smirks. 'No one special.'

'That's not really true, is it?' their mum says. 'Who's the young lady I've seen trotting off down the front path in the small hours twice these past few weeks?'

She grins at Danny, her eyes glazed from sinking a bottle of fizz on an empty stomach.

'Mum!' Danny whines.

'Aha! Up to his old tricks,' their dad shouts. 'Different days, though – you sure it was the same bird, Tori?'

Their mum laughs. For a few seconds there's no atmosphere between his parents, and Will experiences a shot of nostalgia, like catching the smell of primary school or hearing a long-forgotten Christmas song.

'Don't be shy,' their dad says. 'Tell the class.'

'I imagine she has a name?' their mum says.

'April,' Danny says. 'That's probably who you've seen.'

Will does his best not to react to the invisible point that skewers his lower gut.

'Nice. Pretty. Earthy,' their dad says. 'April. April. Like it.'

Why does a name feel like that, Will wonders, why does it *actually hurt* when they say it?

'Serious?' their mum asks.

Danny shakes his head. 'Don't be silly. Not up to my usual standards.'

Will turns away from his parents' grilling of his brother. Nain gives him a sad smile. 'Just listen to them!' she whispers.

'Anyway,' their dad booms, 'what about you, birthday boy? Anyone special?'

'Or at all?' Danny adds. 'Ever?'

'Now now,' says their mum.

'All those evenings walking Beppo . . .' their dad says. 'That's an elaborate cover, is it not?'

Will scowls at Danny.

'I didn't tell him,' Danny says. 'Must've been Mum. You spend a lot of time walking Beppo. What's the big secret?'

Nain looks pained. 'Don't listen,' she mouths at Will.

'So, not met any nice young ladies out dog-walking, then?' their dad says. 'Shame.'

'I have not,' Will says, conscious of how riled his tone sounds.

'Any nice boys?' Danny says, grinning at the table.

His dad stands and assumes a teapot stance, flapping his wrist around. 'Oooh, any nice boys?' he says, lisping. 'Nice boys out on the marshes?'

'Don't be revolting,' Will's mum says, sniggering into her wine glass.

'All the boys together,' Danny says, camping it up. 'Dogging on the marshes.'

Will feels his cheeks burning as he looks towards Nain, who rolls her eyes and tuts.

'Enough of that now,' Will's mum says to Danny and their dad, who are already in fits of laughter as they take it in turns to mince round the patio with ever-more-tightly clenched buttocks. 'He's not *one of those*, thank you very much.' She stares at Will's glowing face. 'Are you, love?'

Will says nothing. It seems it's a rhetorical question.

'Let's get some more bangers on,' their dad says to Danny. 'Help me at the barbecue, my man?'

Why was I so insistent on having a family birthday party? Will briefly wonders. Of course this is how it was going to be. Silly to imagine his parents could even pretend to be the people they once were.

As a kid, it had always been the thought of the house burning down that scared the shit out of Will. But three years ago, without a single flame, a blaze ripped through the family home and destroyed everything. There'd been no warning, not for Will and Danny anyway. Surely, when a home becomes broken, there ought to be arguments and thrown china and stormings-out, so you know it's coming. There were none of these things – just a decision by their dad that he no longer wanted to be married to their mum or living with his sons.

'There's nobody else involved,' he told them many times. It may have eased his conscience to say it, but it made things no easier for Will – they'd been walked out on because their dad would rather be on his own than with them. He didn't want them any more. And the worst thing about your folks parting company, Will has come to realize, is that they stop being Mum and Dad, and instead become *people*. In the case of Tori and Mike Parks, people he's not especially keen on.

With Danny and their dad absent from the table, Nain checks behind her before speaking quietly to Will and his mum. 'He's been at it again,' she hisses.

Will's mum rolls her eyes. 'Who, Mum?'

'Spanish Joe.'

'The nice young carer?'

'Looks can be deceptive.'

'What's he been up to?'

Nain lowers her voice further. 'Poisoning. Tried again. Thinks I'm stupid.'

'Arsenic? Cyanide? What's his, erm . . .' She giggles at Will. 'What's his poison?'

'You think I'm a silly old trout, don't you?'

'Never, Mum.' She tops up her glass, foam erupting over the rim on to the table. 'I just think you need to lay off the Agatha Christie novels.'

Nain tuts as Will's mum staggers inside the house. 'I'm not stupid,' she says.

Will puts his hand on hers. It's freezing cold, no meat between the jagged bones. 'Try not to worry about it,' he says.

Her face turns blank, the pink evening sky washing over her pale cheeks. As so often happens, her worry has passed, leaving no recollection of what was troubling her just a minute ago.

Danny brings some sausages to the table and retakes his place.

Nain's expression hardens once again and she jerks upright in her seat, sending an empty champagne flute to the ground with her elbow. It smashes into pieces.

'The library!' she whines.

Danny instinctively turns his back and busies himself on his phone.

'Oh, the library! Sad, sad day!'

'What is it, Nain?' Will asks softly. Danny's giving him a cut-it-out gesture, but Will can't ignore her when she's distressed, like everyone else can.

'All those books.' She's almost crying now. 'Shame. Shame.'

'The library's going nowhere, Nain.' He's not convinced this is true, what with the campaign to save it that's been running for a year or more.

She shakes her head. 'With your friends, Wilbo.'

'Defo lost it now,' Danny mumbles. *'Friends!'*

'Calm down now, Nain,' Will says.

'Your friend owed her life to that place. She owed her *life* to it!'

'Try not to get so upset.'

'Don't stress it,' Danny hisses at Will. 'She'll have forgotten all about it in literally thirty seconds' time.'

'It all comes down, Wilbo. You're up there, right up at the top of the Martello tower. With your friend. Watching it all come down.'

Will hugs her head to his chest and strokes her fine hair and waits for this to pass. There are cool discs on his T-shirt from her tears.

'She needs you. Your friend. So sad!' She looks up, locking her wild eyes with his. 'You're there for her, Wilbo. Thank God you're there for her.'

She bows her head and Will feels the tension in her melting. 'It's OK now, Nain. It's OK.'

Will's mum and dad return to the table and it's clear enough they've been waiting in the kitchen for the commotion to pass.

'Thank you,' Will's mum mouths at him, dishing out dessert, which they eat in silence. 'Back in the room with us now, are you, Mum?' she eventually asks.

'I'm not deaf. No need for the raised voice,' Nain replies.

'Had one of your little episodes, didn't you?'

49

Nain waves the statement away. 'I'm fine, dear. Fine. Don't worry about me.'

Will's mum gives a bemused shake of the head.

'Present!' Nain shouts, so loud everyone jumps. 'Clean forgot about it! All that talk of dear old Beppo, and I still didn't remember.' She passes Will a brown paper package. 'Silly old fart . . .'

The table is quiet as Will holds the frame up to the evening light. He feels a warmth building in the corner of his eyes. It's a picture, made of a mosaic of small, irregular pieces of broken glass, all perfectly slotted together. There are the deep hazel eyes, the ginger and white fur, the grey round his muzzle. His eternal scruffiness and lack of good breeding are slightly overplayed.

'It's incredible,' Will says.

His mum strokes at the collage of glass. 'It really is, Mum. Beautiful.'

'It's OK,' Nain says. 'I made it ages ago. Did the finishing touches these last few weeks. On the good days.' She holds out a shaking hand and looks at it with dismay.

Will studies the picture in his lap. 'How do you even do such a thing?'

'Just an idea I had,' Nain explains. 'I spent a lot of time at the bottle bank! Carlsberg for the ginger fur, Harvey's Bristol Cream for the sky. All great fun working it out.'

'I love it,' Will says. 'It's so good.'

'Well, I'm glad you like it.' She shrugs, uncomfortable with the praise. 'The better our art, the longer we'll live.'

Will looks up from his lap and feels a twinge of guilt that he didn't make nearly as much fuss over anyone else's presents: the white-label vinyl from Danny, the Levi's and hiking boots from his mum, the pre-paid voucher from his dad for a course of ten driving lessons and the fuzzy dice – a jokey down-payment on his promise to buy Will a car when he passes his test, like he did for Danny.

'Thanks, all of you,' Will says. 'Really kind. All of you.'

His mum and dad smile at each other and for once there seem to be no seeds of arguments waiting to sprout and ruin everything. As the plates are cleared away, Will enjoys a few precious minutes of the birthday he wanted.

But it doesn't last. As his mum emerges with a cake and a tuneless chorus of 'Happy Birthday' begins, a wave of sadness crashes down on Will.

Why can't he enjoy this? Why does he have to be blindsided at this moment by the certainty that this'll be the last birthday with all these people here?

No one suggests he make a wish. And he doesn't, because he knows how it works.

Like everything in the universe: order to disorder; happiness to misery.

The game is on.

Burn, Baby, Burn

The debate over exactly how it happened will rumble along for years. It could be argued that the fag ends that were left to smoulder through the night, or, rather, the rough sleepers who discarded them, are to blame. Or perhaps fault lies with the member of staff who left the fire doors propped open in spite of the warning notices. But then she, like her two remaining colleagues, is no longer paid a salary; instead she's merely a volunteer, imperfectly trained in health and safety. Perhaps the blame lies with whoever took all the money away and stopped maintaining the building years ago.

But all that matters right now, on this grey and gusty Saturday morning, is that the library is burning.

It's a coincidence. Will knows that. He had been walking on the marsh path alongside the railway, dog lead wound round his fist, when he saw the smoke – black and opaque and gushing horizontally inland. He'd headed in the direction of the front as the fire grew in intensity, the smoke flashing orange at its source. Only now, standing among a crowd across the street from the two fire engines, does Will even make the connection with Nain's ramblings two evenings ago.

The building's old, late Victorian, and it burns like a wooden stage set. Another two engines from a distant borough arrive as sheets of flame leap upwards and are knocked flat by the wind. Will stands away as two red rubber hoses are plumbed into a hydrant behind him.

'Look at it go, Willy boy,' a familiar voice calls. Mick Touch, like most of the crowd, holds his phone above his head and films.

Will nods but can't pretend to share his enjoyment. Sparks shower into the sky as a hole opens up in the roof. The audience coo like they might at a fireworks display.

'Popped up from Smugglers to put a bet on,' Mick says, pointing at the betting shop next to the library with his folded slip. 'Got turfed out by the fire brigade! So what do you reckon – charity shop or another bookies?'

'How d'you mean?'

'Where the library was – charity shop or betting shop? It's all that ever opens round here, isn't it? If you want a tenner on the three o'clock at Chepstow while wearing a dead bloke's trousers, Ebbswick's the place, eh?'

Will shrugs. He thinks of the Saturday mornings spent at the library as a kid, of the movies he used to rent for a pound. And he thinks of the Laurie Lee short stories and encyclopaedia of photography sitting in his room right now. For a foolish moment he wonders how he'll go about returning them.

'Shit!' Mick says, grabbing Will's arm. 'Where's your dog?'

Confused, Will follows Mick's gaze to the lead in his hand. 'Yeah, it's . . .'

'He's not missing, right? Don't know if you noticed, Willy boy, but hell of a fire going on over there.'

'He's OK, I'm sure. Maybe I'll go and find him.'

'Need a hand?'

'Be fine,' Will says, a little too quick, gifted a reason to walk away.

Back on the marsh path and alone, two hundred metres from the fire, Will reaches into his rucksack for his camera. There's a guilt that almost stops him raising it to his eye, like he'd feel if he were to take a picture of someone burying a loved one. But he knows anyone claiming to be a photographer has a duty to document this. Because he can't shake the sense that this is a moment of change: a town losing a piece of its soul. And in among the sorrow he feels, there's an inexplicable satisfaction too, like this is inevitable: a billion words, burning to nothing, just atoms now on this charred and sour-smelling wind. Order turning to chaos.

With a black-and-white film loaded, Will knows there's potential for a picture so dark with smoke and foreground, and so light with raging fire, that it could look apocalyptic. He frames and shoots three times. But it's not right. He's too low down and unable to position the watching crowd between him and the inferno. Without the digital camera advantage of being able to immediately judge his work, he'll have to wait for the darkroom to know for sure, but he suspects all he's got is a *snap*.

He grabs at the vegetation between the path and the railway line, drawing himself up to the edge of the tracks. There's no fence, despite it being part of the coastal mainline with express trains charging across the marsh every hour. Will looks both ways – once, twice, three times – before leaping across like a ballet dancer. He heads towards the beach and a vantage point for a picture that will do this story justice.

Will doesn't recognize the guy at the tripod straight away, nor the heavily embellished Nikon attached to it that really should be familiar to him, given the amount of classroom mockery that's been directed at it. Standing at the top of the beach, squinting through the viewfinder, Kris Tring is dressed all in black: drainpipe cords, rollneck sweater, three-quarter-length leather jacket.

'Find your own shot, Parks,' he says, not looking up. There's a machine gun rattle from his camera.

The shore is deserted save for one crazy old person having a swim in the rough sea, their orange cap bobbing in the haze of spray blurring the surface. There's a brief moment in which the wind doesn't whip and crack around Will's head and he becomes aware of somebody yelling his name. Fifty metres away he sees her, sitting on the stones with her knees drawn to her chest, her hair plastered across her face.

'Miserable, isn't it?' April says as Will approaches.

He nods. With a common spectacle for them to stare at, he feels comfortable enough to stop and risk a conversation, albeit at a distance.

'Kris messaged me to meet down here this morning.' She points over to him at his tripod and smiles at Will. 'Not sure what the point of me being here is. Not exactly teamwork, is it? Think he just wants a *muse*.' She draws out the word. 'He was shooting graffiti on the tower wall when I saw the smoke.'

Will stands rigidly with his hands jammed in his pockets and looks over at the Martello tower a hundred metres along the beach. Built in the 1800s and looking like a massive concrete pork pie, the derelict fort is an irresistible canvas for anyone who enjoys tagging public property. He thinks of Nain's rant, her suggestion of him 'right up at the top'. The building's been sealed up for decades, no way to reach the roof without some serious scaffolding.

'How's things with Danny?' Will asks. It's an emergency question because he can think of nothing else to say. He doesn't actually care how things are with Danny. It's possible he'd rather not know.

'Think he'll be popping the question any day now.'

'Right.'

'Maybe a spring wedding.'

'Cool.'

'I'm shitting you, Will. Lighten up, man. I'm not sure we're even *together*. Are we together, you reckon?'

'It's . . . We don't talk about that sort of stuff.'

This isn't really true. Danny likes to drop little brags. Just last night he kept making squealing noises while rolling his eyes back in his head and twitching his eyelids, insisting it was the perfect impression of April's come face.

'Not sure it's an exclusive thing,' she says.

Will shrugs but knows better than to confirm her suspicions, correct though he knows them to be. 'You like him, though?'

'Do I?' April says back.

Will smiles at the absurdity of her asking him.

'Well, I guess I must do, I suppose. People do, don't they?' She shrugs. 'Never mind that shit. Where's your dog?'

He unwinds the lead from his hand, annoyed that he neglected to put it away before walking over here. 'Yeah, he's . . .'

'I can hardly hear you,' she says over the quickening wind.

Will comes a few paces closer. 'He's OK. Round somewhere.'

'What is he?'

'Just a mixture. Nain calls him a Heinz 57. Lots of varieties, you see.' Will feels a moment's guilt for the untruth in what he's telling her, but knows it's easier this way.

The ground shakes as something explodes.

'Fuck's sake,' April mumbles, staring back over the town again.

'You a member?' Will asks. 'Of the library?'

She smiles sadly at him. 'Oh yes.'

'Me too.'

'I kind of owe my life to that place.'

'How so?'

'It was like my hiding place. Long story. Maybe without it I wouldn't be here now.' She shakes her head. 'Boring!' she shouts. 'Always rely on me to make –'

'Sorry, what did you just say?'

'That I used to hide out there.'

'Before that, about owing your life to the place?'

'Yeah, I'm a weirdo, aren't I? Who owes their fucking life to a library?'

'I suppose.'

'You look like you've seen a ghost, Will.'

A coincidence, Will thinks. It has to be. Yes, those were the words Nain used, almost to the letter. *Exactly* to the letter, in fact. But it's a coincidence. Of course it is.

'Will?'

'It's . . .'

April pats at the stones next to her. 'Sit down.'

Will slowly comes closer and takes a seat. 'You ever told anyone else how you owe your life to that library?'

'Erm, don't imagine I have. Bit of a dramatic statement, innit? Just spent a lot of time in there. They were safe walls, those. Look at them now.'

Will nods, silently ordering himself to shut up about it.

'Gimme your number,' April says. 'I can shout you next time we're going somewhere to get pics.'

Her phone feels like a priceless artefact in his hand. His fingers shake as he taps his number in. This isn't an exchange of numbers in the loaded sense, he knows that, but still he feels unable to ask for hers.

'What books you into?' Will asks, close enough now he no longer needs to raise his voice to compete with the weather.

'Depends what mood I'm in. If I want something crazy or absurd, you'll find me in non-fiction. If I want a hit of absolute truth, I'll find a decent novel.'

'I like what you did there. Favourite book, though?'

'So hard to choose. I'd say Plath's *Bell Jar* but I don't want to be a walking cliché.'

Will laughs and nods and pretends to understand what she means.

'So, maybe *Geek Love*. Heard of it?'

'Don't think so.'

'Will, it's nuts! It's a proper celebration of weirdos. Weirdos doing dirty things to each other. What's not to like? And here's the best bit: as of this moment, I own a copy.'

'How so?'

'Cos I must've borrowed it ten times, and now there's nowhere to take it back to.'

Will laughs. 'I've got some Laurie Lee of theirs, too.'

'There's a man who can write. You can smell the words, can't you?'

Will nods as yet more sirens race through the town.

'Wanna swap?' April asks. 'Read *Geek Love*, I'll have a go on your Laurie.'

'So why did you spend so much time in there?'

'Bad year, Will. Doesn't matter.'

'How come you left your old school?'

'What have you heard? Have people been saying stuff?'

'Not heard anything.'

'I just wanted the first-class education that only ECS can offer.'

'Now I *know* there's a story.'

'It's a shit story. I fucked up bad.'

'Sounds interesting.'

'It isn't, Will. Let me enjoy my anonymity while it lasts. The scandal will follow me here soon enough. You won't want to know me then.'

'Where did you used to go?'

'St Anne's.'

'Private! Very nice too!' Will grins.

'It isn't,' she snaps. 'It's a piss hole. You reckon just cos people have got pots of money they aren't total scumbags?'

'No . . . I guess not. Sorry.'

Another explosion rocks the ground, louder than the last.

'They're evacuating the centre of town!' Kris Tring yells over to them, his telephoto lens trained on the fire.

'Police taping everything off. God knows what they're expecting.'

'Probably time we got shooting,' April says, pointing at Will's camera on the stones between them.

Right now, Will has no interest in doing so, but he climbs to his feet nonetheless. He looks along the beach towards the Martello tower. That conversation with Nain plays again in his head. She did not predict the library's demise. She didn't know it was April's safe space. Or rather she *did*, in the same way someone who gets several numbers right on the lottery has predicted the result. Chance. Probability. She also reckons her carer is poisoning her, and that's definitely not true. And Mr Arbuckle is certainly not stealing her electricity because he doesn't even live next door to her any more. Not to mention the hundreds of other nonsensical things she's said in the last few months. It's coincidence – nothing more.

But still . . . Will looks at the menacing tower with its two narrow slot windows.

You're up there, right up at the top of the Martello tower. With your friend.

'What you staring at?' April asks.

'Reckon there's a way of getting into the tower?'

She sizes the place up for a moment, a grin seeping across her face. 'Love your thinking, Will.'

He follows her as she stamps across the stones.

'Only one way to find out,' she says.

They step up from the beach on to the thick wall that surrounds the building. Will follows as April lowers herself into the narrow gap between the wall and the tower itself. The ground is thick with seagull crap as they follow the curved path round.

'We breaking in?' Will asks, excited and petrified in equal measure.

'I think we owe it to ourselves to at least try,' April says. 'Don't you reckon?'

This is not the sort of thing Will Parks does. But everything's up in the air right now: the town's burning, he's chatting with a girl, and a tiny part of him is open to the idea that something even weirder than those two things is going on. It feels like a day in which the rules don't apply.

'Gimme a leg up,' she says.

Will looks up at an entrance that's not so much a doorway as a boarded-up slot in the wall, over a metre clear of the ground. He cups his hands under her foot and she leaps up to the ledge.

'Surprise, surprise!' April says. 'We are not the first.'

She bangs at the sheet of plywood and it wobbles, split along one edge where it's been jemmied open in the past. She helps Will up to the ledge and between them they manoeuvre the panel a third of the way open.

The air inside is wet and fridge-cold. Will stoops and advances slowly, with April so close behind he can feel her breath on his neck. Three metres in and they are through the outer wall and at a small landing. Ahead is a circular room. The floor is covered with cigarette butts and food packaging, a filthy duvet heaped at the far side. To their left is a concrete staircase. It curves gently out of sight as it follows the outer wall but there's a suggestion of blueish light seeping down from wherever it leads.

'What we waiting for?' April says, easing past Will and beginning the climb.

The walls are green with damp, webs of slime stretched from bottom to top. The narrow steps are greasy, each footfall echoing like a penny in a well.

'Now *that*, my friend, is a view,' she says.

Will emerges into the dazzling light behind her. The centre of the tower is recessed where a cannon would once have been aimed out over the sea. He follows April to the edge and peers over. He can see the coastline, undulating from cliff edges to sandy bays, for miles in both directions. And behind them the town looks to have been tilted for their benefit, giving a perfect view over the evacuated streets, crowds assembled at the cordons, and the blazing library at its heart.

Will smiles at April as she leans on the wall with her head propped in her hands and her hair jetting out in front of her. The salty wind blasts past his face and rips the breath from him. He swaps the lens on his camera for a long zoom and scans the town.

It will take some weeks, but fire officers will eventually conclude that the library's aged structure was weak long before the fire took hold. They will deduce that the upstairs walls and the front gable were only held in place by the timberwork of the roof and floors. Which, after burning for three hours, is all but gone.

At first, Will thinks it's a distortion caused by the long lens. He's zoomed in on the building. The top half seems to rock back and forth. He brings it into sharp focus. It's real. It's moving.

Watching it all come down . . .

He draws back the zoom for a wider shot. The crowd standing at the cordon come into view, phones aloft. People turn their backs and take grinning selfies with the inferno as their backdrop.

Back on the library now, and the front wall leans perilously towards the road below. The phones are raised higher, the excitement audible.

Will puts the camera down on the ledge. April is sitting on the dusty concrete behind him, wiping the back of her hand against her eyes.

'You OK?' Will asks.

'Get your pictures,' she says.

She needs you. You're there for her.

Will shakes his head at the thought of Nain's words. Why did she say those things? What the hell is going on here?

'This is hard for you, isn't it?'

'Silly,' April says. 'It's just a building. Look at the fucking state of me.'

'It's OK. The place means an awful lot to you.'

She stands, head bowed, arms limp at her side.

Will's never hugged a woman before, not one he isn't related to, anyway. But, on this day, when the rules are on hold, it's the most natural thing to do.

The tower beneath them begins vibrating a clear half-second before the noise starts – a sound like a quarry truck tipping its load. They hold each other and watch as the front wall of the library drops, folding along its middle as it goes. The side wall follows seconds later, a diagonal landslide of bricks. Like it's been riddled with a giant poker, the fire roars skyward.

Will looks at April from the corner of his eye. Her face flashes orange, glittering embers reflected in her wet eyes. It's the most raw and devastating and beautiful thing he's ever seen. There's a split second when he thinks how this would make the perfect photograph.

April hugs him a little tighter and the thought is gone.

A Turn

Will gnaws at the rim of his cup, washing down the nuggets of polystyrene with slurps of scalding hospital tea. Whispered conversations between medics are drowned out by sprung doors *phutt*ing closed and never-answered phones bleating at nursing stations.

'I could do without this,' Will's mum mutters, not for the first time. She huffs and drags her fingers through her long hair.

'Go home if you like,' Will says, sounding more irritated than he intended.

'It's not your problem to deal with, love.' She pats his knee. 'Want another Snickers?' She nods towards the vending machine and digs in her bag for change.

'I'm good.' He stops himself mentioning that, in fact, it was her who ate the first one, knowing the stress that will cause.

He had a free period after lunch and was bound for the darkroom when the text landed: *Nain been rushed to hospital. Nothing to worry about. Mx*

He bunked the afternoon's lessons and got the bus straight over. It's not the first time this has happened, of course. And she's always made it home again, even if she is invariably set back from where she was before.

The door to the room next to Nain's opens and a woman in a blue top with a white band at the neck steps

66

out, followed by an elderly man. She clutches a bible in one hand and holds his shoulder with the other. The stooped old guy thanks her and makes the sign of the cross on his chest.

'Be lovely to believe in something, wouldn't it?' Will's mum says quietly.

'S'pose.'

'Times like these. Must make things so much . . . *easier*. Nicer.'

The chaplain smiles at each of them in turn as she walks away.

'Maybe,' Will mumbles.

He'd been planning to go round to Nain's tonight. Extra shifts at Smugglers have kept him away all week, but he needs to talk to her.

The next morning, there had seemed something almost unreal about the day the library burned. Will found it somehow necessary to take a walk there and survey the damage. He was faced with mounds of bricks and hunks of timber blackened like coal. The sour stench of water-logged carbon could be smelt for several streets. The scene gave Will two things: the chance to take the post-apocalyptic photos he'd missed out on the day before, and confirmation he hadn't completely lost the plot.

He got to thinking about an article he'd come across some time ago about déjà vu. Scientists, Will had read, are unable to agree on what causes it, but a popular theory is that the brain gets its wiring muddled up for a split second and sends information to the wrong place – the part of the brain where memory is stored, instead of the place where current situations are processed. In an instant, the wiring error is corrected, but already a memory has been formed that is identical to what is being processed as the *now*, hence that spooky certainty that an exact experience has happened before.

Is that what happened? Will began to wonder. *Did I really have that conversation with Nain? Or have I built some embellished memory that's mixed up with things that have happened since?*

As he walked back from the ruins of the library, he knew who he had to ask. It was mid-afternoon before Danny's bedroom door was propped open. Will invited himself in. The room smelt of sex – cheap fragrances evaporated from hot skin, with an underlying hint of something salty. Barely five minutes earlier, a girl had left. Not April – Will was sure of that, having peeked under the door to check during the small hours.

'You know when Nain came round the other day?' Will asked. His voice was nervous. 'My birthday, you know?'

'You being odd again?' Danny grimaced as he rubbed his cock through his trackie bottoms. 'I do recall, yes.'

Will felt immediately stupid, struck suddenly by the absurdity of what he'd started to think. 'It doesn't matter.'

'What do you want to know?' Danny was watching a video on his phone – a rerun of what had taken place in this room, Will assumed, from the slurping noises and his brother's whispered words of encouragement.

'You heard what she said, didn't you?'

'Man, she's loving it,' Danny said.

'About the library?'

'I think I might have permanently damaged the old chap, you know. You ever had that?'

'About it burning down?'

68

'Course you haven't.'

'You heard her, right?'

'Might be seeing nerd girl later. Hope it's better by then.'

'Danny?'

'Bruv, she says all sorts. She's off her rocker. Sorry, I know you love Nain and all that. But she's crackers.'

Will nodded. For all the back and forth in his own brain for the past twenty-four hours, he had to accept that his brother had nailed it there.

Danny began ushering him out of the room. 'Reckon I can squeeze in forty-five on the weights first if no one holds me up.'

'Who's nerd girl?'

Danny grinned. 'What's her name? Tiny tits. You know. April! That's the one.'

Will had retreated to his room with something aching in his chest.

'Doctor's all done.'

Will looks up from his tea cup at the nurse.

'I told your grandmother you're here,' she continues. 'She's very excited to see you.'

Will follows his mum into the room with a fake smile fixed in place. Nain's wearing no make-up, her lips the same greyish-yellow as the rest of her. Her hair lies limp on her head. She looks like every other old person in the place. The nurse fiddles with the cannula in Nain's wrist and Will has a sudden urge to make a plea to her.

She doesn't normally look like this, he wants to say. *She's not old. Don't treat her like she's old. Don't treat her like she's ready to . . .*

He can't even think the word. And he doesn't say any of it. Of course.

'Why aren't you at school?' Nain asks, smiling weakly.

'Already had that conversation,' his mum says, standing at the end of the bed.

Will takes a seat and holds her cold hand over the guard rail. 'How you feeling?'

'Like I need to have a bath, put my face on and change into something less comfortable.' She runs short of breath as she says it, looking at her hospital gown with horror.

'You'll be home soon.'

'Not too soon,' his mum says. 'You need the rest.'

'I'll be getting lots of rest before you know it, dear,' she replies, her voice running out of steam again.

'What do they think's wrong?' Will asks.

'I'm falling to bits, Wilbo!' Her laugh graduates into a cough, which she struggles to clear. 'Minor heart attack, they think. I'm all out of rhythm.' She tugs at the bunch of wires attached to her chest. 'Look at the state of me. I've got a cardiologist coming to see me. They should send an electrician.'

'You'll be OK, though?'

She takes a deep breath, enough oxygen to see her through a whole sentence. 'I am hammering on recovery's door.' She picks up the volume. 'Don't go worrying about me.'

Will squeezes her hand. 'Do my best.'

'Never mind me. How are you? How's your week been?'

'Good. Really good.'

This is a lie. It's been a miserable week. Will's read an awful lot of novels over the years, and so had dared to believe that he understood roughly how love stories work. But since that day with April, he's realized he knows bugger all.

For a few hours after they'd hugged on top of the Martello tower, he imagined this might be the start of something, that each time they met from now on they'd fall a little further for each other, until – probably in some torrential rain – they'd lose control and confess their love and kiss hungrily and forsake all others. To that end, he'd even begun compiling a list of conversation topics, saved on his phone for future meetings. But when he next saw her in Ms Calloway's photography lesson, things were no different from how they'd been before. In fact, they were *worse*.

In the hours after he'd left her at the beach, he'd done something silly. Unable to think of anything but her, he'd looked her up online. And, as grubby as it made him feel, he locked himself in the bathroom for five minutes and propped his phone against the taps, a close-up of April's face on the screen. It was possibly the fastest, and definitely the guiltiest, of his wanking career.

Why could he not dismiss the thought that April somehow *knew*? It was illogical to believe that somehow his phone had accidentally filmed him and forwarded the video to her. Illogical, but another idea Will was unable to shake. These thoughts had taken him over so completely that, come photography, he couldn't even look at her when she handed him the library copy of *Geek Love*, as they'd discussed. His hands were shaking so viciously as he traded it for his Laurie Lee compilation he couldn't even keep hold of the thing. Mercifully, as he fumbled, a distraction was provided by the noisy arrival of Alfie Lim, who began a striptease in front of Kris Tring, ordering him to 'Shoot me like one of your French girls.'

How could he imagine anything could happen with April? She's beautiful, clever, kind, gifted. He's Will Parks: a loser with thoughts of hitting on his brother's girl; a wimp who licked a man's shitty shoes rather than risk a fight; a sex pest who tugs himself off to holiday selfies.

A love story? What was he *thinking*?

'Don't look so sad,' Nain says. 'I can't bear it, Wilbo.'

Will looks up from the bed to see his mum has left the room. 'Can I ask you something?'

'Anything,' she says, her face lighting up. She wriggles to get comfortable. 'Let's talk about art, creative stuff, *ideas*! I'm tired of talking about who's going to put the bloody bins out while I'm in here.'

'Just something else first,' Will says, feeling the same sense of stupidity wash over him as when he spoke to Danny. 'How did you know about the library, Nain?'

'Gosh, who told me? Someone did. Told me to go outside. I could see the smoke and the flashes from the back garden. Terrible.'

'Not on the day it happened, Nain. You told me about it before. At my birthday. You knew it was going to happen.'

She smiles, but Will's sure she's not digesting what he's saying.

'You said about it burning down.'

'Awful, wasn't it? All those books. Shame.'

'That's what you were saying. Don't you remember?'

'Oh, I remember it all right.'

'Who told you, Nain. How did you know?'

'Who told me? Wasn't it you?'

'No.'

'Well, it can't have been, can it? Or you wouldn't be asking me. Someone did. And I went out in the garden, and the smoke! The flames! Like it was right in front of me. Terrible!'

'Don't get her excited,' Will's mum says in a loud whisper, stepping back inside. 'She's had a heart attack, for Christ's sake.'

'We were talking about that awful fire,' Nain says.

Just let it go, man, Will tells himself. *Fucking let it go, you absolute dick. Think about something else.*

His pointless enquiries are still making him cringe as he waits at the bus stop outside the hospital an hour later. The doctor is with Nain and Will has reluctantly agreed to go home. Outside the ward, it's like the fresh air has woken him from a daydream, making him confront the things he'd been wondering this week, the daylight illuminating all the silly details.

A coincidence, Will tells himself once again. No more debate to be had.

He scuffs his feet over the green cubes of broken glass and shiny laughing-gas capsules in the shelter. Unfamiliar with this bus route, he scans the timetable. As he studies the minute print, he hears squeaking wheels and footsteps come to a stop immediately behind him. His eyes focus on the reflection in the plastic screen. Right behind him is an old-fashioned navy blue pram pushed by a woman wearing a fuchsia headscarf.

He doesn't know her name, nobody round here does. But everyone knows who she is, as they cross the road to avoid her, or nod hello out of charity.

'Will?' the woman asks.

He feels himself stiffen but he doesn't look round.

'It is Will?' Her voice is gentle, homely.

The pram is almost touching him as he turns to look at her. Her face is softer than he expected. For a moment, he's not wary of her. The wheels squeak as she rocks the pram gently back and forth. Will can't remember a time when she wasn't to be seen lapping Ebbswick, always pushing this same well-polished pram, always dressed the same way: blue jeans, white anorak, pink headscarf. The sight of her has always elicited the same reaction in him: a combination of the creeps and an unmistakable second-hand sadness. But up close, as she is now, she's an unintimidating woman of maybe seventy, who speaks nervously and smells of fresh washing powder and soap. Who, it seems safe to assume, has been derailed by unbearable tragedy in the distant past.

Will nods. *How the fuck does she know my name?* He's never spoken to her before – he'd definitely have remembered.

'How are you, Will?' She smiles and stares deeply at him.

He's willing a bus to round the corner. 'You all right?' he asks vaguely.

She nods, making cooing noises at the pram.

Forgetting himself in the awkwardness of the moment, he glances round the raised hood into the pram. It confirms what he, and everybody else in this town, has long known. There is no baby.

'Won't be long, I'm sure,' he says, gesticulating towards the road.

'I'm not here for the bus.' She puffs out her cheeks and giggles, putting on a show to amuse the mound of bedding in the pram, before looking back at Will. 'I'm here for you.'

He sidles towards the kerb.

'I have a message for you.'

Don't be afraid.

There's nothing to be scared of.

Sure, at a glance, she seems crazy. She isn't. These people we dismiss as mad see more than most. The looser their grip on the obvious realities, the more attuned they become to the quieter voices. She hears me. She *sees* me. She wants to help.

So listen. Listen to what she has to say.

Let's change things.

Because now I know we can. Already we've changed something. You, on the Martello tower, hugging a girl – that was me! Without my words being delivered by your nain in a fit of confusion, untethered as she briefly was from the here-and-now, it wouldn't have happened. This I know.

So why did I go to all that effort, just for you to make a friend?

The thing is, I know what you are prepared to do. And I know what you won't do. Because I can see it, up ahead.

Could I have got a message to you about the smouldering cigarettes? Perhaps. Would you have believed it, acted on it, saved the library?

You wouldn't. Too much to ask. Too much at this stage, anyway.

I have to win your trust first. Your *faith*. Help you become who you need to be.

Because we have a job to do.

It keeps taunting me, this end that's coming. I'm just peacefully following you, drifting in time, and – *bang*! The vision hits . . . shouting . . . screaming . . . death upon death upon death. Then black.

No detail, just an undeniable certainty that this is coming.

Together, we might change things.

Together, we must at least try.

Go-Between

'The buses round here are terrible,' the old lady says. She offers a pinkie finger into the pram and smiles as if a baby is sucking at it.

Will frowns at his phone. She's right: his bus is running late and no amount of urging it to appear and rescue him is about to change that.

'You're heading into Ebbswick, yes? The 403?'

I didn't tell her that, Will thinks. *Could she see where I was looking on the timetable?*

'You'll be waiting all afternoon – word from the wise.'

'Right.'

'Quicker to walk, actually. It's half an hour from here, no more.' She manoeuvres the pram out of the shelter and aims it up the road.

'OK, thanks,' Will says.

'Walk with me? We can talk.'

'Maybe I'll give it another couple of minutes.'

The old lady looks at the hospital building, ten floors of stained concrete set back from the road. 'She's in the best place. Your nanna. Your *nain*.'

Will shuffles uncomfortably. 'How –'

'Walk with me, Will. Just a few minutes. Let's chat. You'll wait all day for that bus.'

She nods slowly. A Magician's Nod.

'You know my nain?' Will asks as they take a left through some playing fields. He walks a good two metres from her side and prays no one from school sees the two of them together.

'By association, I suppose you'd say.'

'Got you.' He's no idea what she means.

The old lady points out flowers and birds to her pram as they walk. She coos at butterflies and insects.

This is a wind-up, Will thinks. *Someone's set this up.*

But he's too polite, too timid, to just ditch her.

They reach the town and are closing in on a turning Will can use as a shortcut home.

'Don't go yet,' she says. 'I haven't told you what I came to tell you.'

Will hadn't said anything about going. 'I live just –'

'Sure you do. Walk with me to the front, though. Just to the front? It's not far.'

'Got some things I've gotta do. For school, and, you know . . .'

Who's behind this, Will wonders, who's having a good laugh at him spending his afternoon with this crazy old dear? He's nearly at the turning now, ready to break into a jog. What if April hears about this? What will she think of him?

'She likes you, Will.'

'Sorry?'

'You *know* who I mean. Really likes you. You'll see. Don't be afraid to be yourself with her, though. Your greatest asset, that is – being *you*.' She repositions the pram so it's between Will and the turning. 'Just to the front, Will. I have a message for you. Listen a moment.'

'Who?' Will asks, an edge of irritation to the word as he accepts that he's carrying on walking with her rather than going home. 'Who from?'

'A friend of yours wants to see you.'

'I don't really have any friends.'

'Oh, you will. Soon enough. Lots. Too many to count.'

She natters away – how she loves this time of the autumn, what the buildings in the town used to be in her day – never leaving a gap long enough for Will to change the subject. Side by side they walk through the backstreets of Ebbswick and on to the marsh road. Visible now, the sea is grey beneath dark clouds at the horizon.

'This is where your friend will meet you,' the old lady says. They cross the tracks and are stopped beside the level crossing on the road that leads into Patten's Island, barely a hundred metres from where Danny's car broke down on that evening a month ago. Cars thump over the tracks beside them and once again Will hopes no one he knows can see him.

'Someone's asked to meet me here?' Will asks her quietly, but it makes the question no less absurd.

'That's right,' she says. 'Give it a few minutes. What have you got to lose? If no one comes, go home. Then you'll know you were right and I really am a crazy old bat.'

'I don't think that.'

He does. But there's something else, too. Something unsettling about her. The way she looks into him when she speaks, like she knows more about him than she has any right to.

'I'll leave you now,' she says. 'Thank you. For coming this far with me. It must all seem very strange, I know. But you've done the right thing. Wait a minute and you'll see.'

'See you around, I guess,' Will says.

She rocks the pram and squints at the sun, low over the marshes now. 'There's one last thing.'

'OK.'

'Listen carefully to this, Will, it's important.'

'I'm listening.'

'When someone tells you to move, you have to run. Fast as you can. You'll come to no harm, I promise you. But just run, yes?'

'Right.' He takes a step backwards, but he's already against the wire fence dividing the road from the railway line.

'You understand me? When you hear "*Move!*", yes? You run. No stopping to think. Run.'

'Got it.'

He feels his cheeks glowing. He'll wait long enough for this bonkers woman to be out of sight, and he'll be straight out of here.

She smiles, almost smug. 'You'll be fine.'

The level crossing alarm begins to sound.

'Take care, Will,' she says. 'Your friend will be right along.'

Rooted to the spot, Will watches as she turns back towards the town and hustles the pram over the tracks just before the barriers come down.

Joyride

Will stands back from the road, loitering in the passage next to the derelict dry-cleaners. He rocks his weight from foot to foot, waiting for the queue of traffic out of Patten's Island to begin moving. Reaching inside his school bag, he massages the rough leather of Beppo's lead. The ground vibrates as an express hammers over the level crossing. The barriers lift. It's been a few minutes – surely the old lady will be out of sight now, leaving him free to head home.

There's a squeal of brakes behind Will as he sets off, the traffic on the move again now. A scruffy BMW pulls over ahead of him, scuffing its tyres along the kerb.

'Willy Parks!' Alfie Lim shouts through the open passenger window. 'Wanna ride?'

Will says nothing.

'What do you think of the whip?' Alfie asks.

'Whip?' Will's voice is inaudible over the clacking of the engine.

'The car! Beaut, isn't she?'

Will glances at the wing and the bonnet. The matt black paint looks to have been applied with a toilet brush, the underlying orangey-red showing through in places. He gives Alfie a thumbs up. 'You passed your test?'

'Never been known to hang about. When you got as many fingers in as many pies as I have, it pays to be mobile. This is what freedom looks like, cuz! Where you headed?'

'Just home.'

'Where's home?'

'Westlands Way.'

'I know it. Jump in.'

'It's OK. Good walking, thanks.'

'Come on, Parks. We'll take the scenic route.'

Will takes a step closer and stops. Is this the friend the old woman was talking about? Did Alfie tell her to bring Will here?

'What's up, cuz?' Alfie says. 'You look confused.'

Will shakes the stupid thought away. Of course he didn't. How absurd. He was just passing. Nothing else.

'Let's ride,' Alfie says.

Will jiggles the door handle but it doesn't open.

'On my to-do list,' Alfie says, releasing the catch from the inside.

As he lowers his weight into the passenger seat, it occurs to Will that if they crash no one will be able to open the door to get to him. What if he needed urgent medical help? What if there was a fire?

'Relax, man,' Alfie tells him. 'Getting stressed just looking at you.'

Will smiles and slackens his white-knuckled grip on the seat bolster.

'Cruise along the front? Drop you back at yours after.'

Will nods.

'Oh, don't look so scared, cuz. I know how to drive. Promise.' He swerves left on to the cut-through that leads up to the coast road. For a moment they are dazzled by the evening sun, before Alfie flips down both visors. 'Fine German engineering,' he says, directing Will's attention around the interior with a flailing hand, like an exuberant salesman. 'BMW indicators – never been used.'

'Cool,' Will mumbles.

Alfie has begun frantically winding his window open and closed. 'Keep-fit windows. Don't see those on many cars, do you?'

Will smirks.

'Spanish gearbox.' Alfie presents the gear lever as if it's an antique up for auction.

'Spanish gearbox?'

'Manuel!'

'Stop it.'

'And the crowning glory, Parks – she has a bidet!'

Will's laughing aloud now. 'A bidet?'

'Come on, guess.'

'I don't know. Tell me.'

Alfie hits a switch on the dash and there's a buzzing and a scraping noise from behind them. 'Rear washer!'

It's a full minute before Will has stopped laughing. 'Where do you get all these from?'

'My dad used to trade a few cars. Used to go up the auctions with him when I was a kid. All the old geezers talked like that.'

They take a right turn and Alfie drives slowly along the front, scanning for people they know as they pass Smugglers and the amusement hall.

'Looking troubled, man. What's on your mind?' Alfie says.

'It's nothing.'

'Now tell your uncle Alf.'

'How come you were driving up from Patten's Island?'

'I live there, cuz. Lived there all my life. Lovely area. The Beverly Hills of the south coast.'

Will laughs. 'Yeah, know it well. My nan lives there too.'

'A woman of taste.'

'Funny question – you didn't, like, ask someone to tell me to, like, meet you . . .?'

Alfie's looking at him with a strange expression. 'Did I what now, Parks?'

'Sorry. Really stupid question. But . . . how come you pulled over? Back there, at the level crossing?'

'Could hardly miss you, could I? What are you, six eight?'

'Six five. And a bit.'

'Crazy.'

Will nods.

'I like you, Parks, you know that?'

'Cheers.'

'And I never know when I might need help with my photography coursework.'

'Got it.'

'So what's happening with you and April then?'

'What?'

'Cuz, you are crushing on her! Crushing on her *hard*!'

'She's kind of seeing my brother, I think.'

'I ain't judging, cuz.'

'I'm not into her. Not really.'

'Crushes are the worst things, man.'

There's a definite warmth seeping through Will's guts. Right now, a crush doesn't feel so bad.

'They make you feel like you're dull. Like no one could love you. Know what I mean?' Alfie says.

'Not really.'

Alfie reclines himself even further, surely struggling to see out over the dash. He steers with one outstretched arm on the bottom of the wheel.

'You're giving one person the power to decide what you're worth. You don't wanna go giving that responsibility to just anyone, cuz. Seen too many bros taken down, trust me.'

'Right.'

Alfie's eyes are off the road for several seconds as he gives Will a self-satisfied grin. 'I'm the fucking Dalai Lama, aren't I?'

'Is it, like, *that* obvious? That I, you know, like her?'

Alfie shrugs. 'Don't fret about it. I can spot these things. Sensitive soul, me. Don't go telling anyone.'

Alfie jolts upright. 'Fuck!' He cranks his seat back to a more sensible angle.

'What's up?' Will asks.

'Don't look now, but we have company.'

Will adjusts his position so he can see the road behind in the door mirror. A police car.

'What *you* looking so pale for, Parks?' Alfie asks. 'I imagine you have less to worry about than I do.'

The road splits into two lanes as they approach a green light. Alfie hangs over to the left and backs off the gas. 'Go past,' he mumbles. 'Fuck's sake. Go past.'

There are two peeps of siren.

Alfie looks ill as he comes to a stop. Both he and Will stare straight ahead.

'Nightmare,' Alfie keeps mumbling. 'Fucking nightmare. This can't be happening.'

'Mind stepping out of the vehicle?' the officer says, thumbs tucked behind her stab vest. 'The pair of you.'

A stiff wind gusts along the front as Will stands on the pavement. Beyond the low wall behind him it's high tide and the beach is well populated, people in coats with collars turned against the spray. Two kids wrestle with a stunt kite, its covering billowing as it swoops this way and that, straining against its line. An ice-cream van runs along the front, the notes of 'Greensleeves' bending eerily on the wind as it motors away into the distance.

'Car's all legit,' Alfie says, allowing the police officer to usher him round to the pavement where Will stands.

'A matter of opinion,' she says, running her fingers along the textured paint finish.

'Insured. Taxed. You name it.'

She smiles. 'I know that. Ran the reg before we stopped you.'

Alfie looks no less tense. His fingers shake as he tries to extract his licence from his wallet.

Will looks back at the police car parked behind them. In the front seat, another officer talks into a radio, his eyes flitting between Alfie and Will.

'I wasn't speeding, was I?' Alfie says. 'I thought I was watching my speed.'

'Not speeding,' the officer says distractedly. 'Although your driving position leaves something to be desired.' She begins reading his licence number into her radio.

'Just go if you want,' Alfie says to Will. 'You look fucking terrified, man. My problem, not yours.'

'Both of you can wait here, please,' the officer says.

Will forces a smile. He flinches at a loud slapping noise behind him. The stunt kite howls past them and climbs back into the air. There are hoots of laughter from the kids flying it as they dance on the stones trying to keep the thing under control.

The male officer is out of the patrol car now and checking the BMW's tyres with a pen torch. 'This one could use some air,' he mutters.

'It's only flat at the bottom,' Alfie says, trying to wink at Will, but his face is too taut.

'Joker,' the other officer says. 'Not heard that one before.'

She passes back Alfie's licence. For a second it looks like they'll be sent on their way. She paces round the car one more time, slapping a palm on the boot lid.

Will looks at Alfie. He looks ready to cry.

There's something in the boot, Will realizes. Something illegal, it's safe to assume.

Will scans the far side of the car. The male officer is crouched down and busy inspecting something. The female officer's hand slips ever closer to the boot release.

'Fucking hell!' comes a shout from the beach. They all spin round to see the kite skimming the wall behind them before gaining height again.

The officer takes her hand off the car and faces the beach. 'Can you two be careful with that thing, please?' she yells. 'Or we'll be taking it into custody!'

The kids shout their apologies.

She wanders back to the car. Alfie's lips are moving, like he's saying a prayer.

He's fucked if they search the car, Will is thinking. *Is there anything we can do to stop them? What the hell can we do?*

The officer is speaking on her radio, one hand resting on the boot handle once again. She signs off, concentrates on the job, pops the button. The boot lid rises a few centimetres.

What the fuck can I do?

He can't look. He gazes instead to the other side of the road. There's an alleyway almost blocked with wheelie bins next to the fish and chip shop. The fans above spew out cooking smells, which Will catches a whiff of. He feels suddenly sick.

There's a sharp snapping sound behind him.

'Shit!' yells one of the kids. Several people shout obscenities.

Alfie and the officers all spin round. The kite has broken one of its lines. Like a guided missile, it's aimed at where they stand. It's coming down fast.

'Move!' the policeman shouts.

Will turns round.

'Fuck's sake! Move!' the officer shouts again.

Will jinks to one side, the kite howling past him. The officer chases it down, grabbing it by the corner before it can cause any more havoc. The female officer leaps into the road, frantically stopping cars before they run her colleague over.

When someone shouts 'Move . . .'

Will feels a burst of adrenaline.

You'll come to no harm . . .

He is Alfie's only hope, he knows it.

Run as fast as you can. No stopping to think. Just run . . .

It's a snap decision, no time to analyse, apply logic. This is the right thing.

Will stares wide-eyed at Alfie. 'Later,' he mouths.

And he's off.

He's leaping over the kerb at the far side of the road when he hears the policewoman shout after him.

He's in the alley next to the fish and chip shop.

He squeezes through the tiny gap between the filthy industrial bins and the roughcast wall opposite them. Glancing back, he sees both the officers are only now crossing the road after him. The male officer shouts back at Alfie to wait where he is.

Behind the parade of shops now, Will sprints along the overgrown service road. Rusting scrap slows his progress, almost taking him down several times. The long, high wall to his left, capped with mounds of seagull crap, tells him he's behind the Palace Hotel now. Grabbing an iron drainpipe, and using it as a pivot to take a tight right turn into a narrower pathway, he looks behind him. No sign. There are shouts and the sound of bins being wrestled. He's made good ground on them.

Slowing, he looks for the two lock-ups with maroon doors. They're further along than he expected, but he knows where he is now. A stitch burns in his chest as he fights for breath. His mouth is like dust. He forces himself into the gap between the two scruffy units. His hair rubs along the wall behind him, his nose almost in contact with the dimpled asbestos of the facing wall. His heart thumps between the two like a pendulum. He sidles ever closer to the daylight at the far end, only confident he won't get stuck because he's squeezed through here before.

'Willy boy!' Mick Touch shouts. He draws on the stub of his roll-up, pinched between yellow fingertips. 'By my maths you're twenty-four hours early for your shift.'

Will feels faint as he tries to catch his breath. He's in the yard outside the Smugglers kitchens. Black sacks of food waste are heaped in one corner, split and oozing scraps on to the muddy ground, the fat tail of a rat poking from beneath the pile. The head chef and a commis are smoking with Mick Touch in front of a wall where a running tally of their football match results on quiet shifts is written in chalk. On several occasions, as the skinniest member of the kitchen team, Will has been sent down that passageway to retrieve their sponge ball.

'I'm sure there's some guests in the bar who'd like their shoes cleaned,' the chef says. 'Heard you do a good job.'

'Easy now,' Mick Touch says. 'Then again, these old brogues could do with a shine up.' He looks at his own feet in turn. 'How's about it, Willy boy?'

The three of them roar with laughter.

'Fucking pussy,' snorts the shaven-headed commis chef, who Will hasn't met before.

'What you doing coming in by the tradesman's entrance, anyway?' Mick asks.

Will leans forward, dizzy all of a sudden.

'Will?' Mick says. 'Willy boy?'

Will stumbles and grabs at Mick's arm to steady himself.

'White as a sheet,' the chef says.

Mick puts an arm round Will, lowering him till he's sitting against the wall. 'Go and have a word at the bar, would you?' he says to the commis. 'This man needs a brandy.'

In

For someone who thinks he must surely be quite unwell, Will Parks is surprised by how curiously alive he feels. Alarmingly alive, even. That could, of course, all be part of the condition, Will now realizes.

He cups a hand round the screen of his iPhone so no one in this morning's assembly can sneak a look, and searches for ailments that cause an excess of energy and upbeat mood. Having been wide awake at six a.m., and out of the door for a bracing Beppo walk along the beach soon after, he adds 'reduced need for sleep' to the list.

At the front, deputy head Ms Rizzo addresses the lower sixth, but after the events of yesterday afternoon Will has far too much on his mind to be paying her attention.

Hypomania, his phone suggests. Commonplace, it seems. From this morning's googling on the bus, he had reckoned that epilepsy was the most likely cause of the recent strangeness.

Will shoves his phone into his pocket and massages his temples, bored with staring at one website after another in an attempt to self-diagnose. Somebody to talk to, that's what he really needs. The opinion of someone who won't laugh him off.

But who can he possibly be honest with? How do you tell someone you think random strangers and close family members are telling you about the future before it happens? Who's going to diagnose *that* with a straight face?

Ms Rizzo is giving an impassioned speech about the loss of the library. Behind her, PowerPoint shows photos of the old building in its heyday, an oddly named Princess Michael reopening it after a refit in the 1970s. And then Ms Rizzo sounds choked as she flicks to a shot she's taken this week – the remaining structure being levelled by bulldozers. She explains how there's no public money to rebuild the place, how only local fundraising might save it now.

Brain tumour.

The words arrive without warning. It hadn't occurred to Will before now, but that could explain it. Something growing in his own head, muddling the wiring between his synapses, making him remember things in the wrong order, believe that conversations happened before they really did. A tumour: abnormal cells, multiplying unchecked. Order turning to chaos – how very apt. He's not been taking this seriously enough, Will now realizes, grabbing again for his phone.

'I'd love it if someone were to take ownership of arranging an event for the younger years before the end of term,' Ms Rizzo pleads. 'Get the fundraising ball rolling. Prove we can do this.'

There are groans and blank faces around the hall. The lack of interest turns to muted chatter.

'April!' Ms Rizzo shouts over the burble. 'Yes, April. Thank you!'

Will's attention is snatched away from his health worries. He half smiles, enjoying the feeling of his heart breaking out of its rhythm – the way it always does when a period of thinking about something other than her is interrupted. Of course she's volunteered, Will thinks; if anyone can do the impossible and save that place from oblivion, it's her.

April stands in the second row from the front and looks about for anyone else who might join her.

'Do come on,' Ms Rizzo shouts. 'If no one offers to assist April, it'll be press-gang time.'

Will watches her over the sea of heads, dodging her gaze whenever it sweeps towards him. Her smile is less genuine now, embarrassment creeping into her expression as she shrugs her shoulders, pretending she's not fussed.

Only fleetingly does Will consider offering himself. But it's surely a job for comfortable-in-a-crowd, not-petrified-of-failure people. Confident people. People like April. People unlike him, however close to his heart the cause of resurrecting the library might be.

'Well, if anyone has an attack of community-spiritedness,' Ms Rizzo adds, bringing her assembly to a close, 'I suggest you come and find me post-haste.'

'Parks,' a voice barks behind Will at morning break. 'Willy Parks.'

A hand wearing several chunky gold rings is waved in front of Will's face.

'S'up?' Will asks.

'Gimme a hug, you motherfucking legend,' Alfie Lim says. His voice is unusually subdued. He stands with his arms outstretched. His eyes are shining with sincerity and for a second Will wonders if Alfie might cry.

'Do I owe you one, or do I owe you one?' he says, slapping Will's back as they embrace.

'It's nothing. Don't mention it.'

'Don't mention it? Don't fucking *mention* it? You're a dark horse, Parks.' Alfie laughs. 'Common room?' he asks, resting a hand over Will's shoulder. 'Bought some Pop Tarts on my way in. Well, I say *bought* them . . .'

Will doesn't reply but allows Alfie to guide him along in the direction of the sixth-form common room – somewhere he's yet to set foot in.

'I'm guessing you outran them?' Alfie says.

'Of course.'

'Fat fucks! Couldn't catch a cold. You shoulda seen them, trying to get past the bins. There was like ten people laughing at them outside the chippie.'

'You're kidding.' Will chuckles, amazed that he probably could've walked to Smugglers and still evaded them.

'So I'm dying to know,' Alfie says as they head into the warmth of the building. 'What did you have about your person that made you leg it like that?'

Will shrugs. 'Nothing really.'

'Right-ho.'

A girl from upper sixth leaves the common room as Alfie approaches with Will hanging a pace behind. The double doors flap back and forth as they close. A cocktail of a hundred fragrances mixed with toast and instant coffee wafts into the corridor. Will's been this close before back in the first week of term, but no closer. He hears R&B pumping from an overstretched stereo, the rattle of a ping-pong ball on bats, a celebration over a video game win. Combined, it's a familiar sound to Will: other people having fun.

He crosses the room behind Alfie, particularly aware of his own height, of his stiffness. He feels hopelessly out of place, as though his very presence is going to kill the buzz any time now.

'Offensive weapon?' Alfie asks, spooning an absurd number of sugars into two coffees. 'Class A drugs? Warrant out for your arrest?'

'Sorry?' Will leans against the windowsill but the angle is somehow wrong and he can't seem to remember right now what he normally does with his hands and arms.

'You running off.'

'It's . . . yeah, nothing really. Did the police come back for you?'

Alfie does an exaggerated laugh and slaps his thigh. 'Good one, Parks! You reckon I hung about for them?'

'You buggered off?'

'Like Lewis Hamilton off the grid, cuz. Second they disappeared down that alley, I was out of there.'

'Good work.' Will takes a sip of the tepid and revoltingly sweet coffee.

'Mate, without that little disappearing act of yours, I'd still be in the cells now. They'd be throwing away the key.'

He extracts the Pop Tarts from the toaster by stabbing them with a knife, pretending to electrocute himself by writhing and making *zizz*ing noises. 'Breakfast is served,' he says, passing one to Will.

'What did you have in the car?'

Curiosity's got the better of him, but as soon as he's uttered the question Will panics that he's broken some unspoken rule on not quizzing people about their criminal activities.

Alfie checks around him before answering. 'I'm into more shit than people here realize.'

96

Will shakes his head. 'It's your business, mate. None of mine.'

Alfie waves his words away. 'Shoebox full of designer shades in the boot. Six or seven grand's worth at retail.'

'Fakes?'

'*Six or seven grand's worth*, Parks. Every pair absolutely genuine. And one hundred per cent stolen. Still with their security tags on, in case there was any doubt.'

'Shit.'

'Yup. It wasn't me that nicked them, mind, but I believe that's not much of a defence.'

'What you doing with them?'

'Selling them. What else?'

'Are there not less risky ways to earn money?'

Alfie wipes his sugary face on his sleeve. 'Cuz, I'd love the pleasure of being able to do a Saturday job on a fiver an hour. Sadly, that's not gonna cut it. My life's complicated. Very blinking complicated. Know what I mean?'

Will gives what he hopes will be interpreted as a *knowing* nod. He has no idea what Alfie means.

'Oh, and let's not forget the couple of ounces of greenery in the glovebox,' Alfie says. 'Just to seal my fate. Shit, Parks, am I glad I picked you up. Saved my skin, cuz. Saved my fucking life.'

'Right,' Will mumbles.

'No need to look so weirded out,' Alfie says, laying a heavy arm round his shoulder. 'Love you, man.'

Will nods, his brain running round in circles again. The bell sounds and the crowd in the common room thins as people head off to period three.

97

'Physics,' Will says, grimacing as he sinks the last of his coffee, gritty undissolved sugar sliding into his mouth.

'Fuck it off,' Alfie says. 'Come on, there's a pool table free.'

Will stops halfway through raising his rucksack to his shoulder. He's never skipped a lesson in his life without illness or emergency. 'I should probably . . .'

'Let's have a quid on it,' Alfie says, digging in his pocket. 'Easiest money you'll ever make, cuz. I barely know one end of a cue from the other.'

Will's grandad taught him snooker when he was a kid, and he sometimes plays – and usually beats – the chefs at Smugglers after hours.

'Yeah, let's do it,' he says, excited by his own decision, by the lack of thought used to reach it.

'Good man!' Alfie says, strutting to the table and slamming his pound on the edge. 'Rack 'em up. I never know how to do it.'

Will grabs the triangle. He looks over at the girl and the guy playing on the other table and he remembers to feel out of place, something that for the past fifteen minutes he'd managed to forget. But they both say hi to him, and right now he can't work out why he'd expect them to do anything other than that.

'Nearly forgot, cuz,' Alfie says. 'Got something for you.' He checks he's not being watched before pulling a soft leather case from his school bag. 'Very fucking least I can do.'

Again, there's that puffy-eyed sincerity in Alfie's expression. He shakes it away, his noisy bluster reasserting itself. 'Careful you don't burn your hands on them, mind.'

Will pops open the case and delicately examines the Ray-Bans.

'Aviators,' Alfie says, putting on his own pair and pouting. 'Just like mine. Even levered the security tag off so you don't have to.'

'They're so cool.'

'Try them on.'

'If anyone asks, I'll say I found them.'

'Good lad. You're learning.'

'I love them,' Will says, slipping them on. 'So kind of you.'

'Yes, Will Parks! Proper suit you.'

'Reckon?' Will says grinning.

Alfie grabs his phone and holds it up. 'Selfie,' he says. 'We're the Blues Brothers, man.'

Will forces himself to keep a straight face as he looks up at the screen, Alfie's chin resting on his shoulder. A picture is snapped in which he barely recognizes himself. For a moment he wonders if life could ever look like that.

'Oh, and one other thing,' Alfie says with a dangerous grin.

'What?'

'I may have made a little arrangement on your behalf.'

'What you done?'

'What have I told you about looking worried, Parks?'

'To not do?'

'That's right. So you know me as Alfie Lim, but I go by another name too. *Cupid!*' He mimes firing a bow and arrow.

'Fuck, really? What have you done?'

'No need to thank me.'

'Seriously, Alfie, what have you done? Fucking hell.'

'Relax. Just volunteered you for a bit of charity work. That doesn't sound so bad, does it?'

Will's panic subsides a little. 'I guess.'

'So you are now helping April with her fundraising activity.'

'Really?'

'You're meeting her after school today, to brainstorm ideas.'

'Alfie –'

'All arranged, Parks. Very keen she was, too. She suggested Al's. You know, down on the front.'

'Look, I don't think I –'

'Mate.' Alfie puts his arm round Will's shoulders. 'If you can do a runner from the police, you can definitely buy a girl a coffee, yeah?'

'Can I, though?'

'Certain of it.'

'I dunno . . .'

'Don't sweat it, cuz. You can thank me in the next life.' Alfie picks up his cue, fumbling with it and trying out different ways of holding it. 'Come on, let's play.'

Will breaks. The fact that he's wilfully skipping a lesson is the furthest thing from his mind. Instead, he and Alfie play five games of pool, all of which Will loses.

I've got complacent.

I was beginning to think I'd got a handle on how this works: I follow you, I watch what's coming up ahead, and if there's a chance to be taken to do some good and improve you into the bargain, then I do what I can to get a message through that will guide you towards taking that chance. The more we do it, the more you'll trust me. The more you trust me, and the more confident you become, the more I can ask of you.

But the rules, it seems, are changing. Or perhaps I never understood them.

When this began, that night at the level crossing – what, a month ago? – I could see weeks ahead. Sure, I couldn't see things in the distance clearly, but it was there all the same: a month of time stretched out ahead of me. But now, I can see a week and a half, at most. I'm getting shorter-sighted every day. The longer I follow you, the less I can see.

And that's not my only worry.

'You saved my life,' Alfie said.

A bit dramatic, maybe. But you did save him from a world of trouble. And you've made a firm friend.

But you haven't saved his life, I fear.

Because I keep getting hit by those flashes – everybody panicking, writhing, certain of their doom. But now there's another vision that keeps coming for me, too. I see the marshes. Ground fog. Early, barely daylight. It's normal, it's normal, it's normal, it's –

What is that?

The sickness in the stomach. The reluctance to look. The need to look.

I can't just see it. I can *feel* it.

Black, skeletal tree. Rope. Body. Limp. Hanging.

Familiar. All too familiar.

If you really have saved Alfie's life, why do I keep seeing this? Just like that scene where everyone screams, where everyone dies, why does this vision seem like a premonition and a memory, too?

I only hope I can work it out. Work it out in time.

I'm trying. Believe me, I'm trying.

If only we could talk, you and I. If only there weren't so many degrees of separation between us. One conversation might unlock it all.

It's not all bad news, though. You're doing great. Already you're so much *bolder*. In fact, right now, all you need from me is a tiny little push, no more.

Pay attention. Today, fate has done the hard work for us. All you need is a well-timed reminder that opportunity exists for one reason only – to be taken.

I'm here, I'll remind you.

Not a Date

'What a piece of crap,' April says as she jumps out of the broken-down bus.

Will reaches out a hand to steady her. She doesn't notice, leaving him at the kerb with a limp arm. A younger kid in an ECS uniform points and laughs at him as he disembarks. Steam is billowing from the back of the bus.

'Gotta be the fourth time it's packed up this year,' Will mumbles. 'Hardly surprising.' He gestures towards the rust that bubbles through the scruffy cream and green paintwork. The bus is specially laid on for the afternoon school run and has to be thirty years old, embellished with a generation's worth of seat stains and compass-etched declarations of love.

'What is it with you and me and breakdowns?' she says. 'Remember that time in Danny's car?'

'Oh yeah,' he says, like he's had to scan his memory. It was the night they met; if asked, he could recall every word they exchanged.

'So what's the plan now?' April says. A light rain has begun to fall. She gazes up at the greying sky. 'Long walk to the front from here.'

They were ten minutes into the ride from school when the bus ground to a halt, although the journey had felt much longer than that to Will. Why did sitting next to her bring with it so many tricky things to consider? Look forward when she speaks or turn to face her? Where should his arms be? Crossed felt rude, but when he put them to his sides he kept brushing against her, which surely felt like an attempted groping. And why had he allowed Alfie to mist him so heavily in Jean Paul Gaultier before he left school? Will had been burning up so badly he could almost see a haze vaporizing from his skin. Surely he was stinking half the bus out?

The crowd at the roadside has thinned now as ECS pupils wander off in every direction. Just a few remain, sheltering under a tree. And milling about behind the bus is the old man with the stained beard and the musty odour who, thanks to April's presence, Will didn't have to share a seat with today. He walks slow circles, drawing on a sagging brown roll-up.

'Another time, maybe?' Will says. He's spent half the day toying with the idea of cancelling, so he's surprised at his own sense of deflation as he utters the words.

'Shame,' April says. 'Be good to put some ideas together. That way we've got the weekend to think about them some more. All for a good cause, innit?'

Will has almost forgotten this – that on the face of it they're simply going for a coffee to brainstorm ideas for events to save the library. This is *not* a first date. So why has he been so insanely fucking nervous about it?

'It's not far to yours from here, is it?' April says. 'Shall we do that?'

'It's . . .'

April waits on the rest of the sentence, but it doesn't arrive. 'It's what – ten minutes from here? If that?' She hunches her shoulders, the rain falling harder now.

'Yeah, maybe. I don't know if that's –'

'I have been to your place before, you know, Will. A few times.'

Will is beginning to panic. He hasn't taken a friend home for years. He's *never* taken a girl home. Sure, April's been over with Danny, but *his* room is set up for such visits – designed with them specifically in mind, actually. Will's room is most certainly not. Inviting April in is a sure-fire way of revealing himself as a total weirdo. And anyway, what if Danny's home? He'd have something to say about it no doubt.

'Maybe meet up next week?' Will says. 'At school? Lunchtime or something?'

Will doesn't look at her. Instead his eyes have wandered to the scruffy old man. He's ten metres away but the acrid smell of his damp ciggie sticks to Will's nostrils. Head tipped forward, his deep brown eyes – so alive, so good-looking – stare deeply into Will. His expression is hard to read, amused slightly, but somehow disapproving too.

'Not even for half an hour, Will?' April says, half turned to get going. 'I won't take up any more of your time than that.'

Will grimaces. He's made excuses too many times now. Another straight *no* would be plain rude.

The old man is still staring at Will over April's shoulder. He's surely too far away to hear the conversation. But he's grinning now. The nod is slow but unmistakable. A Magician's Nod.

Will knows it's the only answer, that the time for resistance is gone.

The man adds a wink, like he knows it's enough to push Will into the right decision.

'Look, it can't be too long,' Will says. 'I've got some things I've got to –'

'This way, isn't it?' April replies, bounding several steps ahead.

'You got it.' Will glances back at the bus once more as he turns to leave, but the old geezer is gone.

'This street?' April asks, taking a left turn.

The wind whips down Will's road. Raindrops needle his eyes as he strides to keep up.

They shelter in the porch. The keys jangle in Will's shaking hands and twice he uses the wrong one before succeeding in opening his own front door.

'We'll go straight up,' he says quietly, guiding her like he's cabin crew. There are voices in the living room at the far end of the hall.

'This your nanna?' April asks, picking up the framed photo on Will's bedside table. It's a picture from two years ago, Nain and Will on a day trip to London, on the steps of the Tate Modern.

What sort of seventeen-year-old has a picture of his nan by his bed? Will thinks. 'That's her, yeah.'

'She looks great. Nice clothes, cool hair. Hope I look like that when I'm her age. How's she doing, Will?'

'OK. No change.' He feels a stab of guilt that he's been so occupied these past twenty-four hours that he's forgotten to allow his worries about her to dominate his thoughts as they usually do when she's been hospitalized. Nonetheless, he's been texting his mum every couple of hours, so he knows the situation hasn't worsened.

April gently repositions the photo. 'What's wrong with her, Will, if you don't mind me asking?'

'Parkinson's. She's a fighter, though.'

'I'm sure. She's lucky to have you, though. Bet she knows it, too.'

Will smiles. For a moment, this feels a tiny bit less like two worlds colliding. Will starts to scoot around the floor, gathering up clothes and socks and pants.

'Chill, Will! My room's much messier than this.'

He tosses the bundle on to his mattress and wraps it in his duvet, scanning under the bed for any crumpled tissues that might have escaped his morning tidy-up.

'So cool,' she says, moving from his oversubscribed bookcase, studying the walls now and stroking her fingers on the glass fragments of Nain's mosaic. 'Your dog, yeah? Beppo?'

Will's discomfort returns full force. Has Danny told her about Beppo? What an arsehole.

'It *is* Beppo, right?' she asks. 'Isn't that what it says on the lead? The little silver disc?'

'Yes! His lead, yes!'

'Is he not here?'

'He's out the back,' Will says, a statement that's not entirely untrue.

She drops her school bag on to his bed. 'I've never been in a boy's room where there are posters of *books* on the walls,' she says, smiling as she reads and rereads the quote from *The Catcher in the Rye*.

It's so weird to Will, hearing *her* in *this* room, the place where so much of his time is given over to thinking about her. This is the window he looks at the night sky from and wonders where she is, and if perhaps she's looking at it too. This is the bed where he greets sleep with a certain relish, knowing he might get lucky and dream about her. There are the old records, so many of their lyrics finding new meaning in these recent weeks. And now she's here. Her voice is in here. Her smell is in here.

'Fuck!' April says, making Will jump. 'I didn't know you had these! This is bloody perfect!'

'The decks?'

'Yes, Will Parks. The decks!' She's almost jumping around with excitement.

'I don't get it.'

'So when Ms Rizzo was talking about fundraising, straight away I'm thinking school disco. Get all the year sevens and eights, charge a fiver each maybe. Probably spend all evening with boys and girls at opposite ends of the hall but *whatever*.'

Will laughs unnaturally loudly at this. 'Should make a few quid.'

April is skimming through his records now. Mostly early nineties dance, it's a collection Will's picked up from boot sales and eBay. It's the music his mum and dad were into in what they cringily refer to as their 'raving days', which they were still listening to years after its time, providing the soundtrack to long car journeys when Will was a kid.

'I was thinking about a theme,' April says. 'Then I remembered the tunes I've heard coming from this room when I've been . . . you know . . . *round* here.'

The unsettled feeling in Will's guts worsens suddenly.

'And I'm thinking, let's make it a *rave*,' she says. 'Proper old school. I'm thinking glow sticks, air horns, loads of Day-Glo stuff. Cool, huh?'

'Sounds awesome.'

She picks out his Prodigy records and sifts through them, impressed. 'But I didn't realize you actually DJ-ed. This is *perfect.*'

'Steady on,' Will says. 'I don't DJ. One of my dad's mates was getting rid of the turntables and –'

'But you can do that blending one record into another thing?'

'I can mix a bit, yeah.'

'How's that different from DJ-ing?'

'I don't do it outside this room.'

'You're such a dick. Come on, Will. Just do a little set of old rave stuff.' She pulls out a couple of records as she speaks, loading them on to the turntables and making comedy scratching noises.

'I'll think about it.' He has no intention of taking the gig.

'Cool,' she says, grinning and turning dials back and forth on the mixer.

'Have a go if you like.'

'Awesome! Come on, show me how.'

Will talks her through the hardware, the pitch controls, the crossfader. They both laugh awkwardly as they try to give each other space, their hands bumping into each other's all the same. Will starts The Prodigy's 'Out of Space' on the right-hand deck. His rather tired speakers squelch a little with the bass, but it still sounds involving in this small room.

'White label,' he says over the music, lowering a record with no writing on it on to the other turntable. 'Very rare.'

'Let's see how it's done then,' April says, grooving to the beat.

'Record one's playing through the speakers,' Will says. 'Now cue up record two, which is hooked up to these.' He holds up one ear of the headphones. April listens in too. A loose curl of her hair sweeps against Will's cheek.

'Find the first beat,' Will says, short of breath. Her head rests against his. He drags the record backwards and forwards. 'And drop it in time with the one that's playing.'

April lays a hand on the record and Will directs her as best he can without holding it.

'And then we have to keep it in time using the pitch control,' Will says. Her fingers land gently on his and follow his movements. 'It adjusts the speed of the turntable.'

'That simple,' April says, taking control and displaying what Will can only assume is beginner's luck by getting a perfect beat-match almost straight away.

'It's not usually *that* simple,' Will says, keeping to himself the fact that he picked these two records only because he's well practised at mixing them. 'And once they're nicely in sync, we slide the fader into the middle, and we have both records together.' Will does that, still relishing the wonderfully analogue feeling of two records spinning in front of him, their sound in perfect harmony.

'So cool,' April says. 'What next?'

Will reaches beneath the counter and grabs another vinyl. April leans her head on his shoulder as he passes it to her. They do another mix together, their hands on each other's, Will's burning face centimetres from hers as they listen to the headphones. When April speaks over the music, Will can feel her hot breath in his ear.

For twenty minutes they play tune after tune. Will's assistance is required a little less each time, but still given, never refused.

The vocal intro to Baby D's 'Let Me Be Your Fantasy' fills Will's bedroom. The air is thicker than ever with his aftershave. The tip of his nose rests in her hair. His heart thumps like it's in sync with the bassline that shakes the floor beneath them.

She turns, her nose almost touching his. Her eyes fill his vision. 'So, Will Parks . . .' she says.

Will fights his inbuilt urge to take a step back.

'It looks like –' April begins to say. She is silenced by a thump from the other side of the room.

Will jumps away from her. It feels like having the duvet ripped from his bed on a cold morning. 'Who the fuck?' he mumbles.

For a second time, a palm is slapped hard against the outside of the bedroom door. Their visitor doesn't wait for an invitation. The door is flung open.

Will instinctively goes for the volume control, turning down the music as if he's remembered himself, realized that he's in his room with a girl, listening to loud music. This is not what he does.

'We were just working on something,' he says. Immediately he hates himself. His tone so reedy and defensive. His stance so weak, the exact opposite of his brother's.

'Hey, kiddies!' Danny says. 'Mum thought it was you,' he says to April, 'sneaking up here with Will.'

He saunters over to them. Still flushed from a gym session, his singlet is soaked, sweat and exertion radiating off him.

'Project,' Will says, less casually than he intended. 'For school.'

Danny laughs. 'Relax, little bro. Hardly worried about you and her, am I?'

'Been playing some old tunes,' April says.

'Talented boy, our Will,' Danny says, slapping his brother's arse.

Will laughs, but it's clear enough that Danny is riled about April being here with him – his words have jagged edges.

Danny stands between them, playing with the mixer and scratching records badly, as though he imagines he could be a superstar DJ if only he were to give the pursuit a little of his attention.

'Will's been showing me how to mix,' April says.

Danny stands behind her, reaching round and kneading her breasts through her shirt. She wriggles a little and slaps at his hands – playfully or not, it's hard to tell.

'Sorry,' Danny said. 'I thought you said, "Squeeze my stuff." That's what you said, right?'

'I said, Will's been showing me how to mix. How does that sound like "Squeeze my stuff?"'

'Shit, my mistake!' Danny's grinding his crotch against the back of her skirt now. 'What else's he shown you? His teddy bears?' He winks at Will, turning April round and pointing at the gathering of threadbare soft toys keeping watch over the room from the top of Will's wardrobe.

'They're really sweet,' April says, smiling at Will.

Danny noisily nuzzles the back of her neck and jabs her earlobe with the tip of his tongue.

Turning a deep red, Will shuts down the decks.

'Join me in the shower for five minutes, yeah?' Danny says to April.

'We kinda got stuff to do,' she says.

'Come on. Live a little.'

'I'm good here.'

Danny's still smirking. 'Geeks,' he says, irritation burning through his jokey tone – the sound of a man who believes he should have control over a room but hasn't.

April looks at Will and mouths the word *sorry*.

'Look, I think I'm gonna go home. I guess we're kind of done here. You reckon, Will?'

Will shrugs. 'Think so.'

Why can't she just tell Danny to fuck off? he's thinking. Why does she let him do what he wants to her, have his hands all over her, uninvited? But then, why can't *he* tell Danny to do one? Why are they both trying so hard to avoid upsetting him?

'Sticking the shower on now,' Danny says, releasing his grip on April's hips, a semi lolling in his tracksuit bottoms. 'Join me in two, yeah?'

'I'll –'

'You should, you know. Could do with scrubbing up a bit downstairs.'

April reddens. 'Shut up. No, I don't.' She giggles as she says it.

Danny winks at Will. 'She does,' he says in a stage whisper. He waves his hand in front of his nose. 'All a bit prawn cocktaily down there, innit?'

'No, it isn't,' she says, looking at the floor.

'You wouldn't want to go down there, bruv,' he says to Will.

Why are we laughing along with him? Will's thinking. *Why do I laugh when he's not funny? Why are we so keen to make him think he's amusing us?*

'Stop it,' she says. She slaps him playfully, despite her obvious embarrassment.

'I'm only joking,' Danny says. 'You know I'm just having a laugh with you.'

She punches his arm.

'I'm not joking,' Danny stage whispers again at Will as he leaves the room. 'Fucking stinks, it does.'

His sniggering is drowned out by the shower firing up beyond the open bathroom door.

'Suppose I'll see you Monday, Will,' April says quietly as she steps backwards on to the stairs.

'Sorry. He's a bit of a dick sometimes.'

Again, Will is laughing, like it's all a bit of a joke.

April's smile shakes at the corners. 'Don't worry.'

'Probably shouldn't say things like . . . He doesn't mean it . . . Just having a bit of a laugh.' He hates himself a little more with each excuse.

'It takes more than that to upset me, I assure you.' She says it too bouncily, backing down the stairs.

She spins round too late and Will sees the first tear fall.

He wants to hug her, like he did that afternoon on the Martello tower. But he knows it's too late now. Mick Touch's words come back to him, from the night of the shoe-licking incident: *You gotta act a bit braver than that when you've got an audience.* The chance to do the right thing is gone.

'Get rehearsing on those decks, Mr DJ,' she calls up to him.

He gives her a thumbs up.

'Counting on you here, Will. You can do this.'

Stop beating yourself up.

You're doing better than you think you are, trust me. The biggest single step to making a change is wanting things to be different. You *want* things to be different. *You* want to be different. That's the most important thing of all.

Stop your worrying.

I'm right with you.

Be ready for me.

Because an opportunity is coming up, a chance to get a message across to you. I don't claim to know everything, but I know these chances have to be taken.

Taken Down

'Five minutes, folks,' a nurse quietly tells Will, Danny and their mum. He positions himself right in Nain's face. 'Taking you down in five minutes, my love,' he tells her.

'I'm fine,' she whispers into her oxygen mask, looking Will in the eye. He hasn't said anything but evidently his expression is giving him away.

'A turn for the worse,' that's what the nurse had said when he rang the house before seven a.m. 'You might want to come and see her today.'

It's been a week now since she was admitted to hospital. She'd been making such good progress up until this morning.

Will has questions. Like, how serious does it have to be to ring someone's family that early? And, what is a turn for the worse, exactly? He'd ask them if he wasn't quite so scared of the answers. Another heart attack, that much he knows. And that a *procedure* is required, with some urgency.

The smell – that was the first thing Will registered when he arrived. Not unpleasant, but different from his previous visits to this side room. He doesn't want to compare it to the meat counter at the supermarket, but that's what it puts him in mind of. The scent of a human being reduced to the sum of their working parts.

Will sits beside the bed while his mum stares out of the window with crossed arms. He looks up at the clock and its jerking second hand, and wishes he could hold it still, make these five minutes last until he's ready to let go of Nain's arm and let her be 'taken down' – another phrase he's not certain of the meaning of.

Danny is at the other side of the bed, leaning on the guard rail. Nain lays a hand on the cling film wrapped round his forearm.

'What have you done to yourself?' she asks. The question leaves her two words at a time.

'His first tattoo,' their mum almost shouts, despite there being nothing wrong with Nain's hearing. 'Couldn't quite wait the three weeks till he's eighteen.'

'Can I see?' Nain says into her mask, her eyes twinkling with excitement.

Danny peels away the film as though he's unreeling an ancient scroll, revealing six symbols along his lower arm, the ink shiny and swollen and framed with red-raw skin.

Nain shakily grips his wrist. 'Fascinating.' She gathers her strength after so many syllables. 'Tell me what it means.'

Danny shrugs. 'Don't really know. It's Chinese writing, I think.'

Nain snatches a deep breath and pulls the mask aside. 'What made you decide on it?'

'The tattoo guy had this book. Found a design I liked.'

She takes a moment to appreciate it, her translucent fingertips hovering over the symbols.

Danny enjoys the attention, his expression bordering on smug. 'You love it, don't you, Mum?' he asks.

'I should probably be angry,' his mum says, 'but, yes, it's very cool.'

'She wants to get the same one,' Danny tells Nain.

'I only said maybe,' his mum says.

Nain turns her head and smiles at Will. He can't be sure, but it seems like a tiny snigger, a minute rolling of the eyes, a sharing of a private joke.

This is my family, Will thinks. And for the first time, on this desperate morning, he dares to acknowledge the fear he's never entirely free of these days but that right now feels like a living, breathing, *fat* thing inside his guts. Without her, he only has *them*. And his father, of course, but that fact offers little comfort. Will knows what a family tree looks like on paper, but the connections don't really work like that – not in this family anyway, not for him. Even now, struggling for breath, barely able to speak, skin grey and hollow, Nain is the centre of everything. This family isn't joined by sideways and descending branches. Its bonds are like the spokes of a wheel, reaching out and tethering each one of them, Nain at the centre: the hub, the one thing holding everything together.

'Be lovely if you were to come back in an hour or so,' a voice says. 'But if you wouldn't mind just now . . .'

Will looks up to see a staff nurse and a porter standing in the doorway. He and Danny step clear of the bed. The process of disconnecting various wires and tubes from a console on the wall begins.

The nurse speaks quietly to Will's mum. 'It sounds a bit dramatic, I know,' she's saying, 'but it's a safe enough procedure.'

Will's ears prick up at the word *enough*.

'She'll be awake throughout, more or less. Doctor's hopeful we can avoid anything more invasive if all goes to plan.'

What plan? What if it doesn't?

The brakes are released and Nain's bed is swung round. His mum and Danny are already at the door. Standing in the now empty room, Will makes eye contact with Nain. He swears there's a second of panic, a bulging in her eyeballs over the rim of the oxygen mask in lieu of a scream for help. But it vanishes as Will blows her a kiss.

Maybe she's calm now, or maybe all her strength is in use to not worry him – it's difficult to tell which.

Her hand rises a few centimetres from the mattress and she gives a queenly wave. She is whisked past them along the corridor and into a waiting lift.

Killing Time

The bright coolness of the morning seems exaggerated after the claustrophobic warmth of the main building. Only now, as the automatic doors seal behind him, does Will allow himself to really breathe. He dodges a slow-moving ambulance and a racing cab as he darts across the service road that joins the hospital's many different buildings.

Maybe I'd know.

The thought strikes him at the same instant as the low sun catches him in the eye.

Would I know?

If something bad was going to happen, and it didn't have to. If there was something that could be done; something to avert the disaster.

Would I know? In the same way I knew about the library burning, and about Alfie and the police? Would someone warn me?

The idea brings comfort to Will – too much comfort to dismiss it with something so dull as logic. What if he really has been one step ahead? He lets himself wonder. What if this universe isn't always free to rip away what's most precious at the drop of a hat? What if we can interrupt that eternal flow from order to chaos? What if this lack of warning is in itself a promise that nothing bad is going to happen? Not right now, anyway. No news is good news, right?

Will continues pounding a lap of the service road. He passes a small memorial garden. Someone sits on a bench, eyes closed in silent prayer. Fresh flowers decorate a plaque that records a life that began and ended on the same day. On the other side of the road is the chapel. Beyond the glass door, he catches sight of the chaplain he saw doing her rounds when Nain was first admitted. Will's was an upbringing that never featured religion, but right now he reckons he understands. He feels as though he and that woman in the dog-collared top share something: the reassurance of knowing there's some kind of plan, that there's more than this. That something stands between us and the worst fate can do. Why would anyone want to shun that faith for something so bland as common sense?

He's close to completing a lap of the site. It feels longer but a glance at his phone reveals that it's barely fifteen minutes since Nain waved him off. Forty-five to go. Sudden tiredness takes him by surprise as the adrenaline that has been keeping him sharp gives up the fight. He's been wide awake since *that call* landed, and he'd barely slept before then. These last few days, sleep has become hard work. His brain just seems a bit too busy.

He joins the queue in the cafeteria, ordering a mocha with two extra shots. Sitting alone at a table, he aimlessly thumbs his phone so as not to appear a weirdo. For a moment he glances upwards, catching sight of a poster opposite where he sits.

Seeing Visions? it asks in big purple letters.

Will looks away, a sense of something deflating in his chest.

Change of Mood? it asks as he glances back.

He's almost tempted to give the poster a resigned nod.

Feeling Isolated?

Will's not sure that last one is relevant, given that it's hardly a recent development.

Psychosis can happen to anyone.

Will shuffles his seat along to get a look at the smaller print. Alongside a helpline number, it implores him as someone under eighteen to make contact with his local adolescent mental health service.

Reading this poster, Will feels like a truant come face to face with a police officer. 'It's a fair cop,' he's tempted to say.

Will checks the time. Thirty-nine minutes still. He knows what he should do.

Reality

She realizes it almost immediately. Something has gone wrong.

There's no sense of panic, just a recognition of the plain fact that this procedure has not gone to plan.

'Cardiodenisine,' the doctor had explained before they started, Nain's pulse drawing an irregular line on the screen beside the bed. 'You'll notice the drug taking effect pretty much immediately.'

The nurse had gripped the syringe in two purple-gloved hands and awaited the order. 'Don't you worry, my love,' she said.

Nain hadn't been worrying. She gave up worry some decades ago when she realized it never had any bearing on the outcome.

'It'll take a few seconds for your heartbeat to begin slowing,' the doctor had said. 'There will be a brief period of time for which the heart will be asystolic.'

'Not beating,' the nurse had whispered.

'At which point,' the doctor had explained, 'the heart's own sinus rhythm will restart. Less than a minute from now, we should have everything back to normal for you.'

That was more than a minute ago. Much more.

'Any questions before we start?' the doctor had asked.

Nain had smiled. Even if she did have any questions, she wouldn't have asked them. Born to a family of farm labourers in rural Wales, she was brought up into a working class that knew its place. And she may have left that life behind at the age of sixteen, but certain habits die hard, not least the awe and unquestioning respect that she was always taught to have for men of the clergy, veterinary surgeons and, most importantly, doctors.

'Thank you,' she had muttered into her mask.

A nod had been given, the syringe unloaded.

And it has gone wrong.

She hadn't expected to feel her heart stopping, but she did. But then, she now peacefully thinks, of course she would. There it's been, like the pendulum in a clock, back and forth within her ribcage, for over seventy-nine years. Just as everything she's ever done can be measured in seconds, hours or months, so those years could be measured by beats of that heart. And now it beats no more.

Time has stopped.

She doesn't wish to rush to this conclusion. The final few beats were irregular, like the thrashings of a drowning woman. The very last one was a solid thump. Defiant. A bowing out. And she waited. And waited. By the time panic seemed appropriate, panic was no longer available to her. *At peace*, she thinks. *What a cliché, but still . . .*

There's no pain, she now realizes. It's not only the chest pain that's gone, though. Nor just the wading-through-treacle stiffness of the Parkinson's. It's everything. Pain that she only now knows was there because it's gone. How long has everything hurt for? A lifetime, it seems.

And how long since she felt so free? The restlessness of living has gone. The eternal sense of needing to be elsewhere, no more. That obligation to always hurry, move on to the next thing, gone.

Has she ever felt so content? A flashback to roughing it through southern Europe in the summer of 1960, lying naked under stars with a young Jordanian man her family would never approve of. Just a girl and a boy before they became man and wife; Mum and Dad; Nain and Grampy; names on a plaque. She swears the scented night air is in her nostrils now, that those million fireflies that so astonished them zip past her vision. Was that it – the closest memory of when life was made of just a *now*? Was that as close as she ever came to this peace she's presently feeling, the peace of time ending?

All of those nows *that my life was made of,* she thinks, *and I was so often stuck thinking about the past or the future. Does everyone do that?* she wonders. *What a waste.*

A sense of everything closing down, that's what she's expecting now. She has no idea how long she's lain here, but that she is still conscious in some way or another seems surprising. It's been a fair while, no pulse, no breathing. How long exactly? Surely an hour. Probably more. But the closing down doesn't come. In fact, the shift, when it does begin, is quite the opposite.

She hadn't appreciated how grey that hospital room was. Perhaps she hadn't appreciated how grey *life* was. Because everything's becoming so colourful now. It must surely be an illusion, but it looks so real, as if the world she's known is the illusion and is dissolving in front of her eyes. Replaced by what – reality?

Only for an instant does she experience the realization that she has been living in something that's not unlike a kind of prison. But as the awareness comes to her, so that prison starts to fall apart around her. She has a sense of walls crumbling, an enormous labyrinth of cells folding in on itself. The prison, it seems, was her own body. Her own *self*.

Only now that she can see everything, and hear everything, does she begin to see how her lifetime has been spent experiencing just a small fraction of what's really going on around her. Small nuggets of reality have been fed to her like food through the hatch in a cell door. The exact amount she's needed for her survival. But nothing more.

She has never felt so free as she does right now. Never so calm. So unfussed. So . . . knowledgeable.

Time passes. It's impossible to quantify how much — hours certainly, it could be a day or more.

A babble of soft words fills the air, reassuring like downstairs voices to a sleeping child. The landscape is more vivid than she ever could have imagined, more beautiful.

From the mix, one voice begins to cut through above all the others.

A face comes into view.

She might have imagined it was God if it wasn't quite so familiar.

The Long Wait

'How long ago were you referred to us?' the guy at the desk asks, tapping at a vintage-looking computer that is clearly not playing.

Will's face feels warm. 'How do you mean?'

'Your GP, when they referred you? This year or last. Do you remember?'

Will sips his mocha, unsure how to answer.

'Sorry, give me that name again, would you?'

'William. Joshua. Parks. Look, I don't think I'm . . . You see, I've not been –'

'Possible psychosis, you said,' the guy continues. 'I'd like to think we'd have got you here quickly.'

He removes his glasses and rubs the bridge of his nose while staring at the screen. He looks like a man in need of some time off.

'I saw a poster,' Will says. 'In the café?'

The child and adolescent mental health service reception at which he now stands was just a short walk away.

'That one,' Will says, pointing at a copy of the same poster on the waiting room wall. 'Thought maybe I should get, I don't know, checked?'

He's fast beginning to wish he hadn't bothered.

The guy stops scanning his computer and exhales noisily. 'You'll need to be referred. I'm afraid there's likely to be a wait.'

Will looks around the room. A couple of the green vinyl chairs are vacant. He's still got at least half an hour to kill. 'Can I take a seat?'

'Like, a three-month wait. Quite probably more.'

Will nods, blood flooding his cheeks. 'Sorry.'

'No, I'm sorry. It's a scandal,' the guy says. 'A . . . scandal,' he repeats, redacting his own swear word. 'A and E is your best hope if you're in a bad way.'

'Right.'

'System's screwed,' he says quietly as Will turns to leave.

Will is almost out of the door when the receptionist catches up with him.

'Take this,' he says, passing him a leaflet. 'Some helpful info, couple of helplines, that sort of thing.'

'Cheers,' Will mumbles.

'Sorry I can't do more. And remember, A and E if you're really concerned.'

Will pounds another three laps of the service road, his coffee cold in his hand. Fifty-eight minutes have elapsed when he reaches the landing outside Nain's ward. Two self-conscious minutes are wasted gazing out at the grounds through the chicken-wire squares in the glass before he presents himself, on the stroke of the hour, at the nursing station.

The Other Side

Will sits next to Nain's bed once again. His mum and Danny aren't back yet. For a moment, no lunch trolleys rattle through the ward and no phones ring. The quiet is almost eerie, the calm in such contrast to how frenetic this room felt earlier this morning. Even that odd fleshy smell is gone. The sun beats through the high window and cooks Will's shoulder, giving the misleading impression that it's the height of summer rather than mid-October.

The staff nurse from earlier enters and silently crosses the room. She pats Will's shoulder. 'She's comfortable now.'

Will gives her a thumbs up.

'Sleeping so calmly.' The nurse smiles and fiddles with Nain's pillow.

Nain stirs, moving the sheet away from one arm, but she doesn't wake.

'Everything go to plan?' Will asks.

'Fine. Fine,' the nurse says. 'Doctor said it took a few seconds for her heartbeat to return by itself. That's not unusual though.'

'She's going to be OK? You reckon?'

'You're doing fine, aren't you?' she says directly to Nain, receiving a single grunt in reply. 'It's good you're here,' the nurse says, addressing Will now. 'She was a little distressed straight after. Stay, if you can. She'll appreciate the familiar face when she wakes again.'

'Of course,' Will says. 'Not going anywhere.'

The nurse is leaving the room when she spins round. 'I almost forgot. It is Will, isn't it?'

'Yup.'

'She was so agitated. After the procedure, I mean. She kept asking for a pen and paper. "Have to write it down," she's saying.' The nurse does an approximation of Nain's voice. '"Before I forget. Before I forget." Keeps saying it to us.'

Will frowns. 'That doesn't sound good.'

'She was fine once she'd done it.' The nurse passes a folded piece of notepaper to Will. '"Give this to my grandson Will," she tells me. Wouldn't relax till I swore I'd make sure you got it. God knows what was so important.'

When the nurse has gone, Will peels the note open. He feels suddenly unwell.

Dropping In

Nine days have passed when it begins.

Will unchains his bike from the beach-front railings outside Smugglers. He'd been scheduled to work the evening shift, but it's half seven and the restaurant is deathly quiet so Mick Touch has sent him home.

Until this week, Will hadn't ridden his bike in five years. The tyres have been inflated and the chain drips with rust-infused oil, although it's comically small for him and the frame is speckled orange where the sea air has got at it. But the riding to work is for good reason.

Since Will took possession of Nain's note, he has resolved to make himself *unpredictable*. How can anyone possibly know what's going to happen to him, how can anything be *predetermined*, if even *he* doesn't know what he's going to do next? He'll disprove this thing if it's the last thing he does.

It's why he takes his Beppo walks across the marshes instead of the beach, or the opposite direction to usual, or takes an earlier or later bus to school, or no bus at all in the hope he'll see Alfie and hitch a lift. And it's why he cycles to and from work sometimes. Or he'll just walk the bike home. Always he makes the decision as late as possible.

With an unexpected evening off to kill, Will wracks his brain for a way to spend the time, feeling like this is a golden opportunity to be one move ahead of what – *fate*?

He rides along the seafront before swinging left and taking the path beside the railway. Dismounting at the level crossing, he pushes the bike over the tracks and follows the poorly lit road into Patten's Island. He stops outside Nain's. A table lamp on a time switch glows beyond the net curtains. Will had thought he might pop in, water the plants, check the place.

He reaches into his pocket, feels the paper balled at the bottom, soft from being unfurled and scrutinized so many times. Just touching the note is enough to push Will towards doing something more unpredictable, more *spontaneous*. He hurries down the road, knowing he'll get nervous and change his mind if he thinks about this idea for too long.

Will has read the short note a hundred times. One thing of which he was immediately confident is that this isn't some weird hoax – it genuinely was Nain who wrote it. Her handwriting, once so elegant and swooping, has become increasingly wobbly, adding an unexpected sadness to the opening of birthday cards. This note bears the most spidery iteration yet, but it's undeniably in her hand.

Hastily written in bullet points, it's as if she'd just scrawled down a bizarre telephone message.

Tell Will trust me. Have to trust.

Tell Will lights will go out.

Lights will come back on late at night.

When lights back on see Danny. Go to alley to find. Only talk to Danny.

V. important you only talk to Danny. You'll understand.
Will, keep looking for me. Trust me. People not die if you trust.
Tell Will thank you.

She'd underlined 'Only talk to Danny' three times. Whatever's supposed to be going down, that part is clearly not up for negotiation. As for the location, there's a scribble prefacing 'alley' – a word beginning with a D, maybe a B; that's the best Will can tell. Narrowing his search on Google Maps to alleys and passages with names beginning with those letters, he discovered over twenty possible candidates within a two-mile radius of home. Not that this matters a great deal to Will. Because, as mysterious and unsettling as he finds the message, he has absolutely no intention of acting upon it.

Nain's recovery since that day has been close to miraculous and she's expected to be going home soon. Will's mum and Danny have been fascinated by how it must feel having your heart deliberately stopped – 'being technically dead', as his brother keeps putting it. They've quizzed Nain on the subject but she can remember nothing from when she was wheeled out of her room before the procedure until she awoke after dark that evening. Will hasn't mentioned the note to her, certain that she'll have no memory of it.

Two roads away from Nain's place now, Will stands outside a chalet bungalow similar to hers but smaller, and in a far worse state of repair. Crossing an overgrown lawn littered with toys, he takes a deep breath when he reaches the front door. Isn't Alfie always telling him to swing by? Drop in, have a beer? Surely there's no need to be nervous – this is what people do, right?

A small face appears at waist height as the door jams open as far as the safety chain will allow. The little girl is dressed as Batman and has Nutella spread halfway to her ears. She gazes up at Will in fascination but neither of them speak.

'Who is it?' a voice calls from inside – a child, but older-sounding than the girl, who is surely five at most.

The chain rattles free and a young replica of Alfie looks him up and down.

'S'up, mate?'

Another two kids emerge from a side room from where a telly blares, both standing in the narrow hallway and looking at Will. 'Who's that?' one asks to no one in particular.

'Ask him,' the girl at the door whispers back before returning her smiling attention to Will.

'It's . . . I'm just here to . . .'

'Parks!' Alfie shouts, appearing in the kitchen doorway. 'How splendid to see you. Get inside, you lanky bastard! Mind your head on . . . everything.'

As Will sidles along the hallway, Alfie instructs each of his siblings in turn to say hello to him, including a fifth one who's sitting under the kitchen table reading some Terry Pratchett.

'Sorry. Dinner time,' Alfie says, flipping breaded chicken under the grill and buttering bread on the only small square of worktop that isn't piled high with food packaging and washing-up. 'You eaten?'

'Good, cheers. Had some chips at work.'

'Beers are outside. Chuck us one over?'

Will nurses a can of Red Stripe as Alfie dishes up, each one of the kids taking their meal and returning to what they were doing. 'Take this into Mum, yeah,' he says to the oldest, putting a plate on a tray together with a cup of tea.

'Fucking madhouse,' Alfie sniggers as he ushers Will towards his bedroom, stopping en route to break up a row over an iPad.

Alfie's room is tiny and so cluttered that Will is struggling to find a space big enough to stand in. 'How come you're in charge of dinner?' he asks.

'They'll just eat rubbish if I'm not,' Alfie says.

'Stressful,' Will mumbles, perching now on the end of his bed.

'It's no sweat.' Alfie fiddles with a Bluetooth speaker and puts some music on, loud enough to mask the racket around them.

Will looks at the stacks of ring binders and textbooks among the clothes and trainers and aftershaves piled high. How does Alfie study in a place like this? Will is wondering. How did he score all As and A-stars in his GCSEs living like this? Perhaps he really is gifted and never puts in any effort – that's certainly what Alfie would have everyone believe. But then why all the textbooks and notes everywhere?

'So tell me,' Alfie says, sniggering into his beer can, 'how's that disco project of yours coming along?'

'Yeah, we're designing posters,' Will says. 'April wants to sell it as this proper old-school rave.'

'Now I've heard a rumour that there's a special DJ performance for us all to look forward to.'

'Yeah, that.' He feels slightly sick as he always does when he thinks about it. 'Might be dodging that one.'

'Be fine, cuz. Only for a load of kids anyway, innit?'

'Yeah. Because they're the most forgiving audience, aren't they?'

'They'll love you, Parks. Stop your worrying. You're cooler than you think.' Alfie ruffles his hair.

Will feels instantly comforted, his scalp tingling beneath the weight of Alfie's big hand.

'You two still not got it on?' Alfie asks. 'I'm expecting to see results from my matchmaking.'

Alfie asks about this regularly, so looks unsurprised that Will has little progress to report. Sure, Will sees April most days, in photography lessons or to discuss the disco, but things aren't the same since that afternoon in his bedroom. Was the electricity that day just in his imagination? Was it only him who felt it? They're quiet with each other now. Neither of them have mentioned how that afternoon ended, how Danny behaved, how Will did nothing. When he's with her now, it feels like April is permanently embarrassed, surely on Will's behalf.

'It'll happen,' Alfie says, scanning through his phone. 'She likes you, brother. Promise.'

He begins replying to messages, texting at speed while muttering to himself.

'Who's that?' Will asks, a little too quickly.

'Hold on a min, cuz,' he replies absently.

No longer the focus of Alfie's attention, Will feels a sting of jealousy. Who are these other friends who are always bugging Alfie on his phone, interrupting their time together? Will forces his annoyance away.

'Got a bit of business to attend to,' Alfie says.

'I suppose I should . . .'

'You're fine, cuz. Don't go. Long as you're cool?'

Will nods.

'Bit of the naughty stuff, this.' A pile of books collapses as Alfie jiggles open an old built-in wardrobe. 'But if I can't trust you after that police business, then there's something wrong with me. Watch the door, yeah? Can't have the little people barging in.'

Will holds a stack of trainer boxes that Alfie passes to him. With the base of the wardrobe cleared, Alfie jemmies a strip of wood free. He tosses a handful of unopened letters out from the void, all of them official-looking, many in red envelopes. They are, Will notices, all addressed to a Mrs Y Lim, who he feels it's safe to assume is Alfie's mum.

'Out of sight, out of mind,' Alfie says, spotting where Will's looking. 'Always get to the post first, that's the key.'

'Why's that?'

'Long story. Boring one too.' Alfie retrieves the battered cash box buried beneath them. 'Nothing to see here, officer,' he jokes as he empties the contents on to his bed.

Will watches, fascinated and terrified in equal measure, as Alfie sets up the digital scales and peels cling film from a tiny, bright white block.

'That was one of my regulars,' Alfie says. 'Pays to be reliable.'

He flakes nuggets from the block till the scales show a little over two grams. Using a Stanley blade he trims the small pile, sweeping the excess off the side till the display reads two exactly. He wraps it up in a little origami envelope, repeating the process twice into a couple of single-gram packages, discarding the excess off the side of the scales each time.

'Where you gotta take it?' Will asks.

'Other side of town. Not far.' Alfie rolls up a fiver and wedges it up one nostril. 'Just the dust off the scales,' he says with a wink. 'Perk of the deal.' In one neat sweep he hoovers up the scattering of powder on top of the cash box.

Alfie turns round and puts his face up to Will's. Will flinches away.

'Relax, bruv!' Alfie says, laughing. 'Just check my nose, yeah? I'm not trying to kiss you!'

Will's face burns. 'Yeah, it's . . .' His laugh is the wrong volume.

'Any gear round my nose, cuz? Not a good look, you see.'

'Fine. Fine. Nothing there.'

'Cool. Won't be a min. Gonna sort the kids out,' Alfie says.

Will waits alone in the bedroom. Beyond the open door, Alfie gives out orders to finish homework, to shower and clean teeth, what time each one of them should be in bed. And then he slips into the bedroom opposite his, emerging again after a minute or two, telling his mum he loves her and to get some sleep.

He's been so distracted since he's been here that for once Will hasn't been thinking about Nain's note. And so, when it happens, he doesn't immediately appreciate the significance.

'Power cut!' a voice yells as the place plunges into darkness. The kids shout and scream with excitement.

'Fuck's sake,' Alfie says. 'Put money on the meter yesterday.'

'It's the whole neighbourhood,' his brother tells him. 'Street lights are off.'

Will creeps to the front door. It's so dark in the bungalow that the glass appears faintly illuminated from the outside. Stepping on to the front porch, Patten's Island is silent and dark. The distant seafront and Ebbswick town beyond that are pitch black too.

Lights will go out.

Is this what the note refers to?

Lights will come back on late at night.

When lights back on see Danny. Go to alley to find. Only talk to Danny.

If Will had any interest in obeying that note, he'd be looking for an alley right now – one with a name that begins with a B or a D. He'd be readying himself for some sort of incident that might be improved if he would *only talk to Danny*.

But he's not playing.

'The things they get excited over,' Alfie says, joining him in the front garden. 'Keep dazzling each other with torches. Little fuckers.'

'Power's out across the whole town,' Will says.

'Yup.' He gives a wild smile. 'Perfect conditions for some lucrative criminality. Coming, Parks?'

'Think I'll maybe head home,' Will says, more uneasy by the second.

Alfie gives him a fist bump before getting into his car and driving away.

Standing at the kerb, Will's heart thumps. This is it. What he's been dreading.

This is when he finds out for sure.

In the Dark

How long do power cuts usually last? Will is wondering as he mounts his bike. He mentally plots a course home that's sufficiently random; if ever there was a time to challenge the concept of his movements being predetermined, this is surely it.

The level crossing is unlit and silent as he leaves Patten's Island. When he reaches the seafront parade he dismounts and stops for a minute. It's a night of low cloud and no moon and, with every light out, it's dark in the way only the coast can be. He gazes beyond the railings and the stony beach into the blackness over the sea. The autumn tide is especially low, the shoreline a good hundred metres away. Will thinks how he might just as well be standing there with his eyes shut. But with the town behind him silenced, the ocean seems to have turned up its volume to fill the void. Every tiny wave that laps on to the sand all that distance away can be heard as clearly as if he's standing at the water's edge – the slopping where currents meet and lose their composure, the fizzing where water foams as it sinks through the sand. And all this over the hiss of the sea, itself louder than ever.

Will digs into the pocket of his jeans, feeling the note scrunched at the bottom. He considers pulling it out and taking another read by the light of his phone but stops himself. Like a love interest's text, it's been scrutinized for greater meaning a thousand times already. What's the point of looking again? He turns his back on the water. The darkness too severe now for riding a bike with non-functioning lights, Will instead wheels it the rest of the way home, zigzagging a route through town.

'Now what have you been up to, getting in at this time of night?' his mum says as he slips through the front door and eases it closed.

She's sitting with her feet up on the sofa. Her face flickers in the low candlelight, the air scented with lavender. Ice cubes clink as she swills the contents of a heavy-bottomed glass.

'Work,' Will says, neglecting to mention that he was sent home hours ago. He fumbles pointlessly with the light switch.

'We haven't been cut off again.' She's clearly drunk and the words bleed into each other. 'Before you ask.' She makes a point of pronouncing each word crisply.

'Power's out everywhere.' He tosses his coat on to the banister and turns to climb the stairs.

'Come and talk to me,' she says. 'We never talk any more. You're always able to chat with Nain.' There's an edge of hurt, or perhaps annoyance, in her tone; Will's not sure which.

'Hardly ever,' he says, feeling compelled to lie.

'I worry about you.' She adds a couple of glugs of convenience-store vodka to her glass. 'Burning the candle at both ends. Working all hours.'

'I'm OK, Mum. Just tired.' He can scarcely remember feeling more wide awake in his life. But, though he's got no intention of going anywhere tonight, he still feels a strange urgency to be doing nothing, to be defying the note's odd instructions, *alone*.

'Are you? This business of walking Beppo. First thing in the morning. Last thing at night.' She eyes him over the rim of her glass as she takes a sip.

Will looks at his feet. He's in no hurry to explain.

'Always were the sensitive little soul of the two of you.'

'Got something for you,' Will snaps, diving back into the hallway and reaching inside his coat. 'Payday. Some housekeeping.'

He peels off four tenners and deposits them in the biscuit jar.

'Sit down,' she tells him. 'You always look so jumpy these days. Have a drink if you want. Think there's some juice in the fridge. Takes the edge off.'

Will perches on the edge of the armchair opposite his mum, checking through the gap in the curtains that every other house in the neighbourhood is still shrouded in darkness.

'I'd rather you kept all your wages,' his mum says. 'If he paid his way . . .'

Will waves the point away, hearing the bitterness gathering in her tone. Booze coupled with talk of his dad is never a great combination, and he's thinking of how he might change the subject. He's too slow.

'If he paid his way,' she says, 'we might be in a better position.'

Will shrugs. 'It's –'

'One day I'll tell you what sort of a man your dad really is.'

'Rather stay out of it.'

'I know you would, my love.' She reaches forward to pat him on the knee but misjudges the distance and has to grab the arm of the sofa to avoid falling off. 'Find it all upsetting, don't you?'

'It's fine.'

It isn't. Never has been. Sometimes he almost forgets. He can be heading home and his mind will have tripped back a couple of years, reset to how things were. And then the remembering will hit him like a train – the realization that not only did his parents split, but somehow the people they used to be died at that moment too.

'He's been saying something,' Will's mum says. She leaves an overlong pause now she has Will's full attention. 'He's worried that you're . . .'

'I'm what?'

She leans forward and whispers, boozy breath wafting over Will, 'A *nancy boy*.'

'He said that?'

Will feels no offence at the suggestion of him being gay. It's the choice of words that bothers him, the contempt in the term; he can hear the distaste with which his dad would utter it.

'A few times. Sorry, I shouldn't have told you.' She appears to be almost irritated by Will's lack of reaction.

'Don't worry about it.'

'Are you?'

'Am I what?'

'It wouldn't be a problem if you were.'

'If I was what?'

'What I just said. What your father said.'

'What, gay?'

'Yes.'

'You want to know if I'm gay?'

Will detects an instant of panic in his mum's eyes, like maybe she actually *doesn't* want to know.

Is he gay? Certainly it's been suggested to him enough times that he is: by Danny, by people at school who play contact sports and obsess over their clothing and hair. But in spite of these people apparently able to assess someone's sexuality at a glance, Will has, in fact, always considered himself straight.

In recent weeks, though, a seed of uncertainty has begun to grow. Sure, the thought of April, of touching her bare skin, of breathing her in, imagining the taste of her, her body entwined with his, drives him wild. He's never known desire and desperation like it. But what, then, are those things he finds himself feeling around Alfie all about? Why is he so instinctively jealous of other people Alfie spends time with? Why does he feel like he wants to know everything about him? Why does his mysteriousness and secrecy excite Will? And why does his touch feel so nice?

He's never felt anything like it before. Why is he so *drawn* to this guy? How has he become so attached, so fast, to this person?

'What makes you think I'm gay?' he asks.

'Look at your brother.'

'What?'

'Out enjoying himself. Different girl every night of the week. That's what boys do.'

'Not all of them.'

'Boys are simple.'

Are we? Will wonders. Maybe boys are *expected* to be simple.

'What was it they used to say? Fuck 'em and chuck 'em.'

'Mum!'

'Well! You'll only regret it if you don't.' She's laughing, but it soon fades. 'You'll end up like me before you know it. You'll regret not enjoying yourself.'

It occurs to Will that his parents' concerns are actually more about him not being one of the boys – a *lad*, a *proper* man.

'Get out there and break a few hearts!' his mum says.

'Not sure I want to do that.'

Incredibly, given her level of inebriation, she picks up on the sorrow in his tone. 'There's someone, isn't there?'

Will shrugs.

'Thought so. No one knows you like your own mum. And it is a girl, yes?'

'Yes it's a girl, Mum,' Will shoots back. 'Not that it should matter.'

'It doesn't,' she says, her relief palpable. 'Well, don't hang about. Make your move.'

'Not that simple.'

'Oh, William,' she says, patting his knee. 'Girls don't want someone who writes them poems and treats them like a princess. They want a man.'

'I've never written a girl a poem. I've never written a poem full stop.'

She waves her hand, as if that fact is irrelevant, but doesn't get as far as expanding on her point.

The intensity of the lights coming back on is initially dazzling. Bleeps of varying pitch sound throughout the house, appliances and telephones resuscitated. Suddenly, discussing his embryonic love life with his mother seems many times more ludicrous than it did by candlelight. In any case, the shock of the power returning appears to have made her aware of her own drunkenness. Shading her eyes, she struggles to her feet, briefly lost in her own living room.

'Toilet,' she says matter-of-factly, successfully identifying it beneath the staircase.

Will steadies her as she makes the short journey.

And he heads upstairs, closes his bedroom curtains and locks his door, sleep the furthest thing from his mind.

Blind Alley

How long have the lights been back on? Half an hour, at least. Will doesn't check, his phone face down on the bookcase just inside his bedroom door. Initially he'd enjoyed the sense of defiance – Will Parks is definitely someone whose life has not involved enough defiance – but the guilt doesn't take long to start creeping in. Nagging, gnawing – that inbuilt compulsion to follow orders. Life, Will realizes, is made up of the people who do whatever the hell they like, and the people who hold everything together so that they can.

He's lying on his bed, reading April's treasured library copy of *Geek Love*. Even in his distracted state, he savours each sentence, digesting the words slowly. Is the prose as luminous as it seems, or has April's love of it corrupted his judgement? He feels excited just looking at the yellowed pages. He's sure there's a whiff of her hand cream about it. Enjoying the story's strangeness and filthiness as he is, it's a book he knows he can't review with impartiality.

How would I do it anyway? Will wonders. *'Only talk to Danny.' What am I supposed to do, phone him? He never picks up calls.*

If he needed anything, he'd have messaged and Will's phone hasn't vibrated once. And he can't just go looking, not with over twenty alleyways to check.

He can feel it, though – the compulsion to roll off his bed, grab his phone and put a call in. Just in case Danny answers. Just in case there's good reason. But that means believing that scrawled note has the ability to, what, predict the future?

Will shakes his head. 'Not playing,' he says aloud.

By way of keeping busy, he flicks through his box of old dance records, most so dishevelled that the album and artist names have worn away from the spines. Torn between The KLF and The Beloved, he settles on the latter, taking a second to appreciate the aged cardboard smell from the sleeve.

Crackles and pops beat out of time with the drum intro. The song's called 'The Sun Rising'. Will sits on the floor in front of the speakers and feels something slacken in him as the haunting chorus builds. A shaft of light shimmers as if it's dancing somewhere above the record as it spins. Will can't put his finger on why, but he knows it sounds better because it's on vinyl. The best he can guess is that he's listening to a perfectly shrunken sound wave, re-expanded for him in his own bedroom, not something that has, at some microscopic level, been reduced to zeros and ones. Surely nothing so natural as music can be made to conform to a choice of being just one thing or another, forced to assume sharp edges that have no business being there? Of course it sounds better on vinyl.

His relaxation is short-lived. In the freedom of thought that comes with listening to great music, he instinctively finds himself reaching once again into his pocket for the note. He wasn't even thinking about reading it again, not consciously.

Within seconds, the contents of his pockets are tossed on to the bed: coins, tissues, packet of gum, train ticket, a fiver. Will pointlessly scratches through them, the record player shut off and slurring to a stop as if silence might aid his concentration. But he knew it the instant his hand had first reached for it: the note is gone.

He retraces his steps through the house in a panic. He upends the chair he sat on when talking to his mum. But the pointlessness of the search doesn't surprise him.

With that piece of paper close to him, he'd felt almost like he was in control. Without it, he's lost.

Did he ever have it? Does it exist? Has he gone *that* crazy?

He sits on the bottom stair and wraps his arms round his head.

Think. Think, man! THINK!

It was there after his Smugglers shift, when he stopped outside Nain's before going to Alfie's. And again when he was looking out to sea. He'd felt in his pocket. Next to his phone. He'd thought about reading it again. What, two hours ago? Maybe three?

That's if it was ever real. If he hasn't lost the plot completely.

Will leaves the house, half walking, half running. It's a windless night. That at least is good, he thinks as he follows the beam of his phone's light as it sweeps from side to side over the pavement and along the gutter. Utterly focused now, he has no trouble recalling the route he took home from Alfie's, random though it was.

How many times did he check his phone on that walk? Surely that's when he most likely dropped the note. But it's an action like blinking, almost involuntary. Maybe he never checked his phone at all. He had other things to think about.

He's out of breath and sensing defeat when he turns right on to Coast Drive, the short drag down to the seafront. The street lights glow, the ocean at the end of the road silent now. Cheap hotels are fly-postered with adverts for Halloween parties and Bonfire Night events. The traffic lights on to the beach road run through their ghostly cycle of red to green and back again, for the benefit of no one. The shattered remains of a whisky bottle twinkle as they're caught in Will's searchlight.

He stops dead. It was pitch dark when he walked up here earlier. He remembers now how he hadn't seen the broken glass till he was on it, shards crunching beneath his trainers and the wheels of his bike. He'd stopped and checked the tyres for damage.

With the light of his phone.

Hope buzzes through him. Somehow, he knows he'll find it here, whole seconds before he spies its crumpled form in the grating of a storm drain. It quivers in the air current like a frightened rodent. Will hurls himself in its direction, seizing it like a cricketer saving a ball from the boundary. He unfolds it, taking a moment to enjoy its familiarity.

The voices are barely raised to begin with. Were it not for the quiet of a sleeping town, he wouldn't be able to hear them at all. Distinctively teenage, they sound initially like no more than a group enjoying themselves. Will can't see anyone between him and the seafront, the sound emanating from behind one of the large buildings lining the road to the right.

Voices are raised. An obscenity is shouted. Something's kicking off.

Will slinks up close to the concrete wall, out of the street lamp's glare. There's a panicked shout that cuts through the night. Female, almost certainly. Familiar, quite possibly. And then a guy's voice. 'Come on then,' it shouts. The preamble to every punch-up of Will's childhood, it is unmistakably Danny.

Will scans the buildings along that side of the road. There's a red-brick office building, a multi-storey car park, a Romanian bakery, a newsagent's, and finally a service road, before Brooklyn Mega Bowl with its neon blue-and-pink signs on the corner.

Brooklyn Mega Bowl. The note still rests open in Will's palm. Even by the low light, one word seems suddenly readable.

Bowling. Bowling alley.

It happens at the bowling alley.

Lights will come back on late at night.

When lights back on see Danny. Go to alley to find. Only talk to Danny.

V. important you only talk to Danny.

Will knows he can't just walk away. Yet he steps no nearer either.

Danny's his brother. If he's in danger . . .

Again, that familiar girl's voice cuts through, echoing off the building fronts.

April.

I should check on my brother, Will thinks, striding in the direction of the commotion.

It wasn't me.

The note disappearing. You going looking.

Nothing to do with me.

I wouldn't know how.

If someone, or some*thing*, caused you to drop the note – and let's be honest, that seems likely – it most definitely wasn't me.

Whatever forces might be at work round here, they're bigger than I am.

But you're in the right place now – that's all that matters. Because where would we be if I'd got it wrong?

You tried to beat the system. You didn't.

I saw it, and so it will be.

Although comfortable viewing it isn't.

Showtime

The Brooklyn Mega Bowl building is a cube of concrete, its ground floor a low-ceilinged car park glowing with fluorescent light and open on all sides. Only one car remains there: Danny's Fiat Punto. Will stands out in the open air, the car park so densely populated by pillars that a small movement this way or that allows him to disappear.

'Say it to my face,' Danny shouts. He's twenty metres from Will, unaware of his presence.

A parking bay's width away from Danny, a tall, skinny guy jitters from side to side, slamming his palms into his own chest. His head is shaved smooth and he's wearing a beige rain mac with a popped collar. 'What you gonna do?' he shouts.

'Just get in the fucking car, Danny,' April says, one foot already in, leaning on the passenger door.

'Listen to your whore,' Beige Mac says.

Danny shrugs his hoodie to the ground. He's wearing only a grey, skintight vest underneath, which exaggerates his swollen and shiny arm muscles. He steps no nearer his opponent. In fact, they both appear to be performing an odd sort of dance, never straying over the white line each of them stands behind, the vacant parking space between them a makeshift no man's land.

Three other people cluster round Beige Mac, all of them about sixteen or seventeen. A dark-haired guy in a tracksuit stands a half-step back from the battle line, eyeballing Danny and kissing his teeth. A girl wanders in sweeping arcs around the Fiat, drawing on a cigarette and looking April up and down with an expression that implies something doesn't smell too good. And there's the guy in the green parka, who seems somehow less invested. He looks mostly at the ground, but when Will does catch a look at his face he recognizes him.

Benji Sanchez and Will have been at school together since they were four, and were friends from day one. They'd remained on decent terms until the late stages of year ten. He'd been a fun, soft-edged sort of kid, who often brought home-baked goodies to school. But Benji, like a few other boys Will could name, had the overnight compulsion to reinvent himself, returning after one half-term break thinking it necessary to belittle most of the people with whom he'd once been friendly. An unpleasant, but not especially unusual, transition from boy to man.

'Apologize to my girl,' Danny shouts, his eyes reddening. 'Or I'll floor the fucking lot of you.'

'Let's just go,' April says over the roof of the car, her voice calm now, resigned.

'Girl's a slut, mate.' Beige Mac takes half a step towards Danny. 'What you got, Mr Muscle?'

Watching from such a distance, the night rendering him invisible, Will still shakes with nerves, but he's oddly fascinated by this stand-off too: the silly faux-menacing looks the guys wear, their puffed-up postures, the stock phrases. Is this how all fights work? Like tomcats arguing over who can piss where? Will thinks back to the shoe-licking incident. Did he end up on his knees just because he can't do the dance that these guys seem to so naturally perform? Maybe.

Or maybe he really *is* a coward. He's hardly rushing to anyone's aid right now.

Not one for playing the hero, are you? What Mick Touch said that night. *You gotta act a bit braver than that when you've got an audience.*

Danny slaps his chest. 'Fucking talk to my girl like that.'

Beige Mac beckons him to close the gap. 'Let's have it then.'

'Fucking come on!' Danny yells, his voice echoing from all directions.

A realization comes to Will. He'd never scrutinized those words of Mick Touch's. But now they make sense.

Play the hero ... Act a bit braver ... when you've got an audience.

This is all bullshit, Will realizes. This is all a *show*. That's all these guys are doing: putting on a performance.

Yet even as he recognizes that fact, still there's a part of Will that feels he should get involved. Inside, he still feels a wimp.

Why is this programmed into us so deeply? Will wonders. *Why do we think we need to put on this stupid fucking show? Who taught us that?*

'Apologize to her,' Danny shouts, wagging a finger in Beige Mac's face, as if his anger has anything to do with protecting April's honour.

'For what?' the girl with the ciggie asks, her eyes fixed on April. 'She told you why she left our school?'

'Fuck's sake, Danny,' April says, dropping into the passenger seat. 'Let's go. Please?'

'Told you about her best friend, has she?' the girl says.

For a second, Danny takes his eyes off his opponent, glancing into the car. Beige Mac strides forward, halving the gap between them. Tracksuit Boy takes up a position a step behind. Benji remains looking at the ground, the fur collar of his parka pulled high round his ears. The others barely seem to register Benji's presence. He's an outlier to this group of friends, that's quite clear.

'News to you, innit, bruv?' Beige Mac says to Danny with a laugh.

'Ask her about Lauren Hall,' the girl shouts, talking to Danny but staring at the side of April's head through the side window. 'Best friends since they were babies. Know what this little sket bitch did?'

Will stares at April. She seems emotionless, looking dead ahead. Beige Mac and Tracksuit Boy close in another step on Danny. No man's land is gone. Still Benji hovers a distance away: an actor in the wings, waiting to step onstage.

V. important you only talk to Danny. Underlined three times. Will's heart pounds. Soon he should make his move.

Will looks again at Benji, standing alone, silent, one hand fumbling in his coat pocket.

'Gonna tell him what you did?' the girl shouts at April, slapping the window.

'Can you stick a muzzle on that?' Danny says, his nose almost touching Beige Mac's.

'Her best friend!' the girl shouts, drawing the words out. 'Pretty little April here, clever, goody-two-shoes April . . . was *fucking her best friend's dad*!'

Danny glances round at April but she gives no reaction.

The girl puts her face against the windscreen. 'Daddy-fucking whore!' she screams.

'Bit young for her, aren't you?' Beige Mac says in Danny's face.

Danny leans back from the waist. In one movement, his hands fly up, grabbing the guy by the shoulders. Danny's head comes piling forward into Beige Mac's face. The aim of his headbutt is slightly off, the thump as he contacts cheekbone instead of nose audible to Will all that distance away. Tracksuit Boy piles in. He and Danny slap and grapple in an attempt to get each other in a headlock. Half blinded though he is, Beige Mac weighs back in, feet first.

Benji walks closer. He watches, waits.

And Will sees it. Just for a fraction of a second. The sharpened edge catches the light. Benji – he of the homemade cheese scones and the cherry chocolate brownies – is armed. He has a knife.

In the scuffle, Danny and Tracksuit Boy fall to the ground. Beige Mac goes to work, kicking Danny in the torso and the head. Danny scoots along the ground and reaches his car. He's able to grab the front wing and pull himself back to his feet. There's a moment of truce, the three of them breathless. Danny's face is a mess. But he's not about to back down now.

Benji joins the other two, a semicircle round Danny.

Will looks once more at April. She's curled herself into a ball in the front seat.

'What the fuck?' Danny says, drawing his arm across his face, smearing blood and snot over his cheek.

Will is walking through the gap between Benji and Tracksuit Boy, staring only at his own feet till he's centimetres from Danny.

'Please can we go now. I think we should go. Please?'

'Get out of my face, Will.' He says it with no aggression, just confusion, almost as if it's a question. 'Seriously. What the fuck are you doing here?' He shoots a mouthful of purple spit to the ground. 'What the actual fuck?'

'You're going to get hurt if we don't go.' Will's voice sounds like that of a frail old lady: wobbly, high-pitched, petrified. The three guys are close behind him. He knows one of them has a point to prove, respect to be won. A desire for a starring role. A performance that'll be talked about, remembered. And he has a knife in his hand.

'Listen to the wise man,' a voice says – Tracksuit Boy. 'Know when you're beaten, pussy.'

'Shut up, prick,' Danny retorts.

'Tell him you don't mean it,' Will says to Danny. 'Tell him that you're sorry. Please say you're sorry.' He vibrates with fear as he speaks, tears juddering down his face.

Beige Mac and Tracksuit Boy don't try to hide their glee.

'Don't be a fucking gay boy all your life, Will,' Danny snarls.

'Please, Danny. Let's just go.' He nods as he says it. A Magician's Nod.

'You don't walk away from shit like this,' he snaps, something whiny in his tone.

Will detects a shuffle of feet behind him. He moves himself, ensuring his back remains turned on all the attackers. But he can feel it too – what Danny's saying. Inexplicably, there's still a part of Will that wishes he could turn round and fight. That same sense of defeat, of cowardice, nags at him like it did that night in Smugglers. Even knowing now what a nonsensical bit of theatre this is, a part of him still wishes he could be involved – that he could Be A Man here.

'Please just get in the car,' Will whispers. Tears pour from him. 'Please.'

'Fuck off,' Danny croaks, shiny spheres bulging in the corners of his own bloodshot eyes.

Will pushes himself against his brother, half hugging him. 'No. Let's go home. We should go home.'

Danny remains rooted to the spot, his muscle-bound body resisting the weight that Will leans against it. 'I'll fucking do you as well, Will,' he spits. 'Don't think I won't.'

'I'm sorry,' Will whispers.

Danny shoots a look past Will. His attackers have moved away. Their aggression has melted into amusement at Danny and Will's expense.

'I think it's over,' Will says. 'Let's go.'

He's right. These guys have won. They smirk with satisfaction. The show is theirs. There's nothing to fight over now.

'Go on, fuck off home,' Beige Mac says.

Danny barges against Will, eyeballing the group.

But they only laugh in response, already relishing their victory.

'Please can we go home now?' Will says again.

'Nighty-night, pussies,' Tracksuit Boy shouts as Will scampers into the back of the car, clinging to Danny's arm. Danny's hand drips with blood as he fumbles with the ignition.

'I can't believe you,' Danny snaps. The tyres howl as they swerve through the pillars and out on to Coast Drive.

'Sorry,' Will mumbles.

He knows that what he just did saved Danny from being stabbed. It's possible he saved his life. Without Will's intervention, without *that note*, Danny would be in serious trouble right now.

'I fucking hate you, Will. You fucking gay boy! A man fights!' Danny thumps the steering wheel. 'And if he can't fight, he *stands*.'

'I know,' Will says. 'Sorry.'

'At least fucking *stand*!'

Why doesn't it feel *like I've done the right thing?* Will wonders. Danny's escaped largely unscathed. *Why do I feel like I didn't play the hero, when actually I've saved his skin? Are you a hero if no one knows what you did?*

'Can you stop the car please?' April says, looking at neither of them.

'It's all right, I'll drop you home,' Danny says, his tone suggesting he thinks he's being magnanimous. He's driving recklessly: engine screaming, sawing at the wheel, no seat belt.

'Stop the car,' she says, firm this time.

They're off the seafront and on to the marshes by the time Danny agrees to stop. He bounces the car over the kerb.

'Fucking state of me,' he says, pointing at his bloodied face. 'What I get for defending you. Shit . . .'

'Next time,' April says, already out of the door and staring back in at Danny, 'don't fucking trouble yourself. All right?' And she's walking away before Danny can answer.

'Think I might walk from here, too,' Will says, easing himself out.

'Fucking right you can. Haven't you forgotten Beppo, you little weirdo?' There's raw hate in how Danny spits the words.

Will says nothing, walking away in the opposite direction to April. There's a roar of engine and a squawk of wheelspin. Will listens to the rise and fall of exhaust as Danny accelerates flat out through the gears. He watches as the tail lights shrink to nothing over the marshes.

And he turns on his heel, and picks up his pace.

Straight Through

'I don't need walking home, Will,' April says. 'Thanks all the same and that.'

'Not safe. Girl on your own,' Will mumbles, struggling to keep up without breaking into a jog.

She scowls at him over her shoulder.

'Because I need a man to look after me?' She stops dead. 'Because that's worked out well so far this evening, hasn't it? Thank God! Thank *fucking* God I had a man to defend me! Where would I be without that? Let me think. That's right, home fucking hours ago, and nobody hurt. What a disaster that would be!'

'It's . . .' Will can't bear to return her stare. Instead he looks out across the darkness of the marshland behind her, the sea a shiny ribbon of black in the distance.

'Just let me be, Will. I'll see you around at school tomorrow. Or maybe not. Don't imagine you'll want to know me after what you heard tonight.'

'What a bitch. Why would she say something like that?'

'Oh, Will. Don't make me talk about it.'

'Did you leave your old school because she was bullying you?'

The question sounds silly to Will even as he utters it, childish somehow. He's doing what he hopes looks like an *understanding* face.

'Her? She's a nobody, Will. I wouldn't leave a *room* because of her, never mind a school.'

'Why's she making up shit like that, then?'

'Fuck's sake, Will. Let me just go home, yeah?'

Will stops and lets April walk away. His quickest route home involves walking the same way as her as far as the level crossing, but he figures he'll wait till she's got a decent lead before he starts moving again.

'Sleep well,' he says, almost laughing at how silly the words sound.

Thirty metres down the road now, April stops. 'Is it really so hard for you to believe?' she asks, marching back towards Will.

'It's . . .'

'What if it was true? What would you think of me then?'

Will shrugs. He's being speared in the guts, the way he is when Danny brays about the things he's been doing with her.

'Every word of it, Will. All true. I'm the little slapper who shagged her bestie's dad. What a whore, eh? What do you think of me now? Still want to know me?'

'It's . . .'

'What, Will? It's what?'

Something's on fire inside Will. A homeless anger. A fury that doesn't know who or what to attach itself to. 'It's . . . OK.'

'Thanks.'

'Why did you do it?'

'Aren't you listening, Will? I'm a wrong'un.'

'Shut up. I just don't understand . . .'

'Judge away, Will. Come on. What you got?'

'I'm not judging –'

'Why did *you* do it? That's what you just asked. Like everyone does.'

'Sorry, I didn't mean –'

'Can't you see it, Will? Whatever it is around me? Like my fucking *aura* or something.'

As it happens, Will *is* aware of a force field that exists around her – a sphere of influence that, although not visible, he knows he's within because he becomes somehow nervous yet free of worry all at the same time, and time races by yet his brain is filled with more memories than such a fleeting instant has any business generating. But he says nothing, because he doesn't imagine this is the sort of aura she's talking about.

'What is it?' she says. 'There must be something about me that everyone can see. Something dirty. You can see it, right, Will? Like I'm gagging for it all the time.'

'Please don't talk like that.'

'Want an example, yeah? Other day I'm on the train. Like eight in the morning. I smile at this guy when he lets me past. He's what, *thirty*? Wedding ring, *et cetera*. Just smiled at him, that's all. Next thing, he's squeezing my thigh, fingers like two centimetres from my vagina, Will. And he's telling me there's this place we can go. What can he see? What vibes am I giving out? You're a man. Tell me, please.'

'I don't know. Nothing. You're not –'

'Just once. Just *once* I'd like to be nice to someone. Be *warm* to someone. And for them not to assume it's because I'm desperate for them to fuck me. Is that a lot to ask? It doesn't sound like a lot.'

'I'm sorry,' Will says. He doesn't know where the words came from, but he means it.

'For what?'

'I'm sorry that happened to you.'

April looks a little confused. 'Why are you crying, Will?'

'It's . . .'

'Will, please.'

'I can't bear . . .'

'Don't walk away, Will. I didn't mean to . . .'

He's not sure why he's crying. Or why he's shaking so much. But he does know that it's not the sort of thing he should be doing in front of a girl.

'Come on, Will,' she calls out to him, her own voice faltering.

Will has lost face here. He's lost all semblance of manliness, of dignity. In this instant, with nothing left to lose, he forgets to censor himself. He forgets to find his own feelings ridiculous. He forgets to be an *actor*. He is, instead, accidentally real.

'I think . . . I think I love you. Sorry.'

'What?'

'I love you.'

'Don't be stupid, Will.' She's really motoring now, trying to keep up. 'That's ridiculous. You don't even know me.'

Will snivels, great strings of snot sagging like phone lines, joining his face to his sleeve.

'Don't tell me I'm wrong,' he snaps. 'You don't get to tell me I don't. Sorry. I don't mean to be in love with you. I just fucking am. All right?'

'Why?' She stands in front of him, halting his progress.

'Please don't laugh at me.'

'It's silly, Will. *Love!* It even sounds silly.'

'You're right. It is silly.'

'Tell me. How can you *love* me?' She shakes her head. 'That's crazy. No one could . . .'

'Yeah, crazy. Forget I said anything.'

'Will!'

'I don't even know what I used to think about. Before you. You're what I think about, like, *all* the time. Whenever there's nothing else to think about, anyway. Stop laughing.'

'I'm just fascinated. Go on. Please, go on.'

'And everything's kind of exciting now. School, walking to the beach, whatever. Just because you might – because I might, I don't know, run into you. Stuff's exciting because you fucking *exist*! That's so weird. I'm so fucking weird, aren't I?'

April passes a handful of tissues to Will from her bag. 'Not weird, Will.'

'I know you'll never love me back or anything. Don't worry. I *am* cool with that. I'm not a complete idiot.'

April looks at the ground.

Will noisily blows his nose, stopping himself passing the well-soiled tissue back to her. 'I should go. Before I make more of a tit of myself. School tomorrow. Well, today, really.'

'Fuck it, it's Friday now. Who cares?'

'Sorry for being such a weirdo.'

'Stop it.' April puts her arms round Will and squeezes, waiting patiently while he works out where to put his own arms. He hugs her back.

'Such a weirdo,' Will keeps mumbling.

'We're all weirdos,' she whispers in his ear.

How long is too long to hug someone for? Will is wondering, the perfection of this moment diluted only by the knowledge that he'll at some point have to let go.

'Thank you,' April says as she pulls away. 'For what you did tonight. Stopping the fight.'

'Yeah.'

'Brave.'

'Not really.'

'Danny doesn't deserve you.'

Will shrugs.

'Saved his skin, Will.'

You don't know the half of it, Will thinks.

'Do you really have to dash off home?' April asks.

'Guess not. Why?'

'I've got an idea.'

She doesn't elaborate as she climbs over the low wire fence and begins to weave through the marsh. Will follows silently, stumbling and grabbing hold of grasses and shrubs as they head in the direction of the shore.

The Martello tower is no better secured than on the day the library burned, but by the light of their phones it seems damper and spookier as they shuffle through its fortress walls and up the curved stairway.

'Always makes me smile when I think about us breaking in here,' April says, leading the way on to the roof. 'There was me thinking you were such a good boy.'

'You and me both,' Will mumbles.

'What a place to watch the sun rise,' April says, at the top now. She leans on the perimeter wall and gazes over the sea. The cloud cover from earlier has gone, a few stars piercing through here and there. In the east, a strip of sky glows a lighter shade of navy than the rest. 'Hour or two, tops,' she adds.

Will kneels next to her. For a moment he wonders if it'll be noticed that he's not at home in bed, before remembering how drunk his mum was and the mood Danny's in. He's sure neither will register his absence. Would they ever?

'Do you not find it a turn-off?' April stares out to sea as she says it.

'What do you mean?'

'What you heard about me.'

'Don't know anything about it.'

'You know I got it on with my best friend's dad.'

'Did he . . . you know . . . *force* you?'

April smiles in a way that feels patronizing to Will. 'No.'

'Were you, like, really young?'

'It was a year ago, give or take. Was sixteen.'

'Pretty young.'

'Old enough. It was Lauren, my best friend – *ex* best friend – who caught us. Me and her dad! Fucking hell.'

'What happened to him?'

'Oh, Will. Who cares what he did? No one was interested in *his* behaviour. Not for long, anyway. A month after the scandal breaks and they're all happy families again. He's so sorry, hates himself for being *seduced* – all that shit. It's me who lost all her friends and had to hide for months and move schools.'

'You don't have to talk about this. If you don't want to.'

'You'd rather not know?'

'Just don't think you have to . . . *explain*. Your business.'

'Is it, though? You see, Will, it isn't my business. Not really. What we do isn't our business at all, not when there's sex involved.'

Will takes a moment to imagine if Danny were to get caught with a friend's mum. It's a believable enough scenario, for sure. Would he be forced to leave his school, lose all his mates? The thought almost makes Will laugh. He'd have to do nothing of the sort. It would, in fact, serve only to reinforce his legend.

'What you shaking your head at?' April asks.

'Nothing,' Will mumbles, although that's not true. He's wondering why he had to transpose the situation – boy to girl, girl to boy – in order to make a moral judgement.

'What an idiot, huh?' April says.

'Did you not tell him *no*?'

'Sometimes things just happen, Will. They don't make sense. There's no reason for them. They just *happen*.'

'How did it happen?'

'I'd had a horrible row at home, been chucked out. Went to Lauren's. Had nowhere else to go. Was in a state. Me and her, we had a few drinks. She had to go out. Her dad was there. We were chatting. What's that expression, Will? *And one thing led to another*. Christ, what a slag.'

'You're sure you never told him *no*?'

'Fuck's sake, Will. Not everyone's a victim, yeah? Stop trying to make me into a sympathy case. No, I never told him *no*.'

'Sorry.'

'Why I didn't is another matter. Why didn't I, Will? Why the fuck didn't I?'

'Don't let this ruin things at ECS,' Will says. 'Please.'

April shrugs. 'Not sure that's my choice.'

'Well, I'm not about to tell anyone.'

'And Danny?'

'I'll deal with Danny.' He's impressed with how assured he sounds. How will he deal with Danny? He'll worry about that later.

'What the fuck was I doing out with him tonight?' April says.

'Was sort of wondering about that.'

'I promised myself, as well. After he was such a prick when I was with you the other week. He's been messaging every day – *let's do something, come over*, all that. Been ignoring him. Till tonight.'

'He's a dick.'

'Why do I do it to myself, Will? Fuck's sake.'

'Don't worry about it.'

'It's what I deserve, isn't it? Someone like him.'

'That's bullshit.'

'Thanks, mate,' she says with a smile. 'Well, fuck him. If you see me anywhere near him, Will, promise you'll shoot me or something, yeah?'

Will laughs. 'You got it.'

'Seriously, Will. Me and him, we're finished. Fucking over and done.'

'Understood.'

The darkness is lifting now. To their right, the sea is cool and grey where it meets the coming dawn, still black where it merges with the night to their left.

'Anyway, you've heard all about my exciting love life,' April says, jazz hands sarcastically in use. 'So let's hear about yours. Come on.'

'My what?'

'Your history.'

'Right.'

'Tell me about – I dunno – your first time. When you ditched your V-plates.'

He only briefly contemplates lying. 'Still firmly attached. The V-plates.'

'That's cool. Saving yourself for the right person . . .'

Will stifles his amusement at an assumption that's worthy of a thigh-slapping laugh. Instead, he goes for a swift change of subject. An enthusiastic discussion about *Geek Love* follows: how they'd write a sequel, who they'd cast in the film, what the soundtrack should be. Reflected in each other's eyes, the sky morphs from grey to white, to pink, until finally a shaft of gold pierces over the marshes.

Will thinks about earlier, how he was adamant he'd defeat the note, prove its predictions wrong. But somehow, it seems, the note came for *him*, and now Danny is safe and Will is alone with the girl he's in love with. It was just, what, five hours ago, that he was hiding in his bedroom? But it feels so distant now, like it was a different *him* almost. *So much can change, yet so little time can pass*, Will thinks. The memory of sitting in his room all that time ago reminds him of the record he left on the turntable. As the sun crowns on the horizon, he pulls out his phone and finds the song. Not vinyl, but it'll do in the circumstances.

'What is this?' April asks softly, normally invisible freckles dusting her nose in the light.

'Cool tune, innit?'

The harmonies build as the chorus kicks in.

Now the night is past it's just the sun rising.

'Yeah. Not heard it. It's cool.'

'They're called The Beloved.'

'How old?'

Will checks the date. 'Just the thirty-two years.'

'Amazing.'

'"Timeless" I think is the word.'

The sun seems to stop at halfway, as though readying itself for a final push to declare this new day begun. If he could choose a moment when time could grind to a stop, this would be it, Will thinks. It seems to be so negotiable right now – time – so unknown, so unknowable. Never mind what the clocks say; there are moments, Will now realizes, hours or maybe just minutes, that matter more than whole years. And he knows that this – this right now – is one of those moments. Because at this moment there is only *now*. There is nothing else.

The half-circle shimmers at its edges. Will glances at April. At the same instant, she looks at him. They're almost touching.

Will has no idea how to kiss a girl. No opportunities for practice have ever presented themselves. The thought of it is so exciting it pulverizes him with fear. But it's not just inexperience or nerves that stop Will from closing the small gap between them. It is as well a curious sense of losing something to look forward to, of having nothing left to achieve, that holds him back.

'Why you laughing?' Will whispers.

'We're being watched,' April says quietly, guiding Will's eyes with hers.

On the perimeter wall of the Martello tower stands a large white bird, its beak half open as if mesmerized.

'That's a *massive* seagull,' Will says, keeping dead still.

'It's an egret. They're a type of heron. They live on the marshes.'

Will returns the egret's stare, but it becomes apparent that it's not looking at Will and April at all but staring at the empty space behind them. Will scans the damp concrete for whatever food or animal might have taken its fancy. There's nothing there. The egret begins to chatter, its beak juddering as it remonstrates furiously with the empty dawn air.

Moving slowly, April extracts her phone and begins to frame a photo. 'One beautiful detail,' she whispers, sniggering at the bird. 'Remember Ms Calloway's assignment?'

'Yeah, not done it yet,' Will whispers back.

'Perfect opportunity. And she even told us to work as a team.'

Will reaches into his rucksack. By feel alone, he extracts his old Olympus from its leather case. 'Use this,' he says.

Turning his back on the sun, he aims at the space behind him and takes a swift light reading, accidentally taking a shot in his haste. The bird still chatters away, oblivious. 'Focus under the wing, I reckon,' Will says.

April takes the camera from him. 'Let's keep the sun in the middle of shot.'

Will watches over her shoulder and claps his hands together. The egret stares at Will for a moment before taking flight. It's barely three metres from them when its feathered wingspan becomes a silhouette against the risen sun. The camera clacks and whirs as April releases the shutter and winds on in as rapid a succession as the mechanism will allow.

'Did we get it?' April asks, looking at the back of the camera. She chuckles as she remembers there's no screen there to check.

'There's the problem with film, I'm afraid,' Will says.

'I need instant gratification!' April says, laughing. 'I was born in the twenty-first century. Don't do patience.'

Will checks the time. 'Maybe you don't have to.'

He chucks the camera back in his bag and helps April to her feet.

'Where are you taking me now, William Parks?'

'Where do you normally go on a Friday morning?'

'Erm, school?'

'Got it in one. Never let it be said I don't know how to have fun.'

'That is the last thing I'd say about you.'

Will stops for a moment, puzzled. It seems she's being serious. Ridiculous.

In those flashes, those visions that feel so like a memory, I see their faces. Sometimes I hear the screams. Unmistakable. Children. I'm sure of it.

Can you sense them at all? The clouds that are gathering? It is the shadow that falls ahead of a tragedy. And it's drawing over this town right now.

Why can't I just talk to you? Why can't we speak directly, work together? Why do we have to rely on these flaky go-betweens? Why does this have to be so *hard*?

Just one minute to talk with you. Is that really so much to ask?

It's down to five days now, the time I can see in front of me. These fields of time were stretched out for a month ahead of me when this began, but are shortened to under a week now. How long before I lose all foresight, before I just have the now? Before I become useless to you? I have no clue.

But while I can still see what's coming up, I'll do everything in my power for you and those around you. Keep on trusting me, that's all I ask.

Because if it's the last thing I do, I'll work out exactly what's coming. I'll work out how this ends, and how to stop it.

And then I will need you.

What Develops

'In use?' April says, staring at the sign beside the darkroom door. 'This early in the morning? How can it possibly be *in use*?'

'Wasn't that Calloway's Kombi van in the car park?' Will says.

'Figured she was asleep in it.'

'She doesn't actually live in the van.'

'Sure she does. Her and her wife. Everyone says so.'

'I think it's one of those urban myths.'

'Ever been to her house, Will? Ever even *seen* it? Haven't, have you?'

'Well . . .'

April's grinning now. 'She's an ageing hippy who lives in a van and has lots of lovely lesbian sex on a fold-out bunk bed. Playground always knows best.'

'Yeah, you're right. Reckon she's off her tits on LSD?'

'Literally twenty-four/seven.'

'You know she started a meditation club last year to help everyone with their exam stress?' Will says.

'Is that another joke?'

'Straight up.'

'Actually, that's probably a really great idea.'

'Didn't catch on.'

'Shame.'

'Miss!' Will says, leaping backwards as the darkroom door opens.

Ms Calloway holds a hand to her chest. 'God on a go-kart! Thought I was imagining things again!'

April raises her eyebrows at Will. '*LSD*,' she mouths.

'What on earth are you two doing here?'

'Film to process,' April says.

'Right!' Ms Calloway says. 'What else . . .' With her hair all over the place and her eyes bleary from a stint in darkness, she looks even more like someone who's been up all night than Will and April do. 'Fine. Yes. I'll just collect –'

'Finish what you're doing, Miss,' Will says. 'We can come back. No hurry.'

'No. Wouldn't wish to get in the way of two such keen students.' She stands awkwardly in the doorway, doing exactly that. 'Just get my bits together.' She turns and begins to gather up various sheets of photo paper.

April peers in. 'Blimey!' she says, diving back out into the corridor.

'May I have a moment?' Ms Calloway says, closing the door behind her.

'What?' Will whispers. 'What did you see?'

'Wouldn't want to corrupt your pure mind, Will Parks.'

'Oh fuck off.'

'Didn't see a thing.'

'Well, that's a lie.'

Ms Calloway emerges. 'Don't do anything I wouldn't do,' she says, looking Will and April up and down with a smirk as she hurries away, papers stacked scruffily under each arm.

'We'd fucking struggle,' April mumbles through smiling teeth as she waves after her.

The ECS darkroom is no more than a pokey storeroom with no windows. The bare brick walls and ceiling are painted matt black and the door has brush seals round it so no light can seep in. There's a metal sink, some very vintage-looking developing equipment, a few barrels of chemicals and a small desk – the simple layout all the better for navigating in total darkness. By the looks of the yellowed information posters on the walls, sponsored by Konica and Agfa, the room has existed like this since at least the eighties, preserved for the few students like Will who enjoy the drama of shooting on film, and for Ms Calloway to do God-alone-knows-what in.

'Ready?' Will says, barging the door shut with his shoulder. He sets the film down on the desk in front of April. 'Reckon you can trust me?'

'Yes,' she says, as Will flicks off the lights, submerging them in a syrupy blackness. 'Unfortunately.'

'Whatever,' Will says, cracking the film canister open and feeding it by feel into the developing tank.

'This is much easier than using your phone and having it printed at Boots,' April says.

'I'm not sure if it's the huge expense or the ridiculous inconvenience that makes it so appealing.'

'God, it's dark,' April says. 'I'm waving my hand in front of my nose and I can't even see it.'

It's a delicate and fiddly operation, yet Will finds the job easier in darkness. His eyes rendered useless, his remaining sensory organs up their game; he can smell the cement in the damp walls, the smoky acid in the developing solution, the chemical fizz from photo film. April's a metre away but he can feel her soft breathing, smell the cocktail of sea air and almond oil from her hair.

'Can you hear that?' April whispers. 'Church bells.'

It's faint, but Will can.

'Never noticed them before,' she says. 'Must be miles away.'

'Uh-huh,' Will says, detecting also the twin-tone of a train horn. It must be coming from the line along the seafront, the entire breadth of the town away.

It feels like being shaken awake when Will flicks the lights back on. 'All done,' he says, pouring the fixer down the sink and rinsing the negatives. He cuts the film into strips, interested right now just in the shots April took of the bird taking flight into the sun. Crouching with his chin on her shoulder, he offers them up to the light.

'That one, I think,' April says, pointing to a shot where the feathered lower edge of the wing seems to rise from the sea and slice right into the dazzling sun.

'Agreed. It's a beaut,' Will says. 'Let's run a print.'

The lights are switched off again, but this time the room is lit by the amber glow of the safe lamp as Will walks April through the printing process, evangelizing its merits over digital printing.

Ignored in a plastic sleeve is the rest of the film. It is shortly to be tossed into Will's rucksack and given no more attention. Which is a shame. Because enthuse as Will might about film photography, there is another advantage it has over digital imaging that he's not aware of. Like music, there are things in nature that cannot be reduced to a series of zeros and ones. The natural world is very much *analogue*, billions of shades of grey. Never just one thing or another. Not even the things that appear to be absolutely binary. Life and death being just one example.

That accidental photograph Will took an hour ago, of the empty space behind him that seemed so fascinating to the egret. A digital image wouldn't have caught anything. But Will's camera did. It's a shame that in his haste to run a print, Will hasn't scrutinized that particular negative up close.

Because it might begin to shed a little light on what's been going on recently.

Last Lesson

'Well, we've made it to half-term,' Ms Calloway says, 'without losing a single student from the course. Almost unheard of. And, what's more, you have some photographs for my delectation.'

It's the last period of Friday afternoon. Will and April occupy the centre two seats in an arc, Alfie and Kris Tring to either side of them. Will snatched twenty minutes of sleep in physics earlier, but still there is a cotton-wool quietness about everything. Their all-nighter appears to have had no effect on April, however, who bounces from her seat, thrusting their print into Ms Calloway's hand. She considers it, smiling and raising her eyebrows.

'The homework, yes,' Alfie says, popping the cap off a cardboard tube. 'Just a little something I snapped.' He passes a rolled poster forward.

'There's been a bit of a . . . delay,' Kris Tring mumbles.

'You haven't done the work?' Alfie asks in faux shock.

'Please, Alfie,' Ms Calloway says, not looking up. 'If we can just go through one lesson without you two . . .'

'Perhaps you need to buy some more equipment,' Alfie says, on his feet now.

Kris clutches his professional Nikon bag tight to him, bulging at its seams with an arsenal of lenses. 'Perhaps some of us aren't content to hand in any old shite,' he says.

Alfie smirks, Ms Calloway beginning to unroll his work.

'You haven't done it, have you, young man?' Alfie says.

'Have, as it happens,' Kris huffs. 'Needs a bit more Photoshop, that's all.'

Alfie's standing over Kris now, his hips beginning to gyrate. 'Remind us of the brief, Miss,' he says. 'One beautiful detail, wasn't it?'

'That's it,' she says distractedly, staring at his picture in her hands.

'One *beautiful* detail,' Alfie repeats, thrusting his pelvis back and forth so that Kris has to shrink into his chair to avoid contact. 'Well, you're in luck, Mr Tring. Get that camera out while I get *this* equipment out.'

'Will you please fuck off?'

Alfie's slackening his belt now and feeling up his own torso.

'Alfie!' Ms Calloway shouts. 'Alfie, listen.'

He spins round.

'This is . . . spectacular.' She pins the poster to the wall.

'Was just walking past,' Alfie says, retaking his seat. 'Got it on my phone. Is it OK?'

The picture is black and white. The dark, craggy shell of the library sprouts from a thick ground mist. And in the foreground, one torn page, wet and singed at the edges, bearing two words: *THE END*.

Will and April grin at each other, an unspoken acceptance that they haven't aced the assignment quite as they imagined.

Alfie slips on a look that seems to suggest how it was all so *accidental*. Will nods at him, suspecting that actually a great deal of effort went into producing such a perfect piece of work.

'A room of very talented people,' Ms Calloway muses, still gazing at the picture.

Kris Tring mumbles something about shot composition and a failure to obey the *rule of thirds*. He is unanimously ignored.

'While we're on the subject of this poor old library . . .' Ms Calloway says, looking at April and Will in turn.

'We're on the case,' April says.

'So I've been hearing. And it is a most vital cause.'

'Not sure we'll be saving the place single-handed,' Will says.

'Well, no, quite. Although I'm hoping I may have moved things in the right direction a little for you.'

'What do you mean?' April says.

'I've had a word with the head,' Ms Calloway says. 'And it seems, given the great groundwork you two have put in, that it might be possible to extend invitations for this disco of yours –'

'– *rave*,' April corrects her.

'Rave. Indeed. To extend invitations to this *rave* further than ECS. I've been chatting with some of my opposite numbers at other local schools, and our head is comfortable that we have sufficient room here.'

Will does his best to remain casual, in spite of the fact that April has just grabbed his hand. Alfie winks at him, proud as a father seeing his baby walk.

'More kids means more money,' April says.

'And I've also heard whispers that some local businesses might be interested in sponsoring the event. And if you could get the press involved too . . .'

'We'd make a killing?' April says, unable to sit still.

'My thoughts exactly.'

'This is perfect.' She squeezes Will's hand. 'A *killing*!'

'I hear, Will, that we might be getting a performance from you,' Ms Calloway says.

'He's not actually said yes yet,' April says, slapping his leg.

Will's actually been avoiding thinking about it, holding off committing for as long as possible. And what had been proposed as a gig to years seven and eight of ECS now involves a far larger audience. And possibly press, even.

'No pressure, cuz,' Alfie says. 'You'd smash it though.'

Will thinks back to when he first sat in this room with these people. An outsider. Not more than six weeks ago. It seems so much longer. Here he is now, sleeping in lessons after an all-nighter, best mate to one side, the girl he's crazy about to the other.

'Of course I'm doing it,' Will says. Just like that, as if the words are someone else's. 'Not going to let you all down, am I?'

Maybe it's the tiredness playing tricks, but imagining this gig doesn't scare him like it should. There's a moment of confusion in Will's fuzzy brain. He knows how order descends into chaos, how happiness resolves to misery. Yet, right now, the universe doesn't seem to be playing by the rules. Half a term has gone by and his world has become richer, more exciting. Right now, what lies ahead promises more than what has gone before. And that, Will is sure, is not how it's supposed to work.

'Not till the end of November,' April says. 'Lots of time to practise.'

Who knows who I'll be by then, Will thinks. 'Looking forward to it,' he says.

House of Horrors

It will turn out to be a night of firsts for Will. This is the first proper party he's ever been to. And most definitely the first one he's gatecrashed.

It is unseasonably warm for Halloween, the sycamore trees lining the private road still clinging to their deep orange leaves, a light scattering of them swirling around the busy front lawn, as Alfie and Will pull up outside the house.

'Now I see why you were so keen to join the party, Parks,' Alfie says, eyeing both the enormous residence and the girls of about their age dressed in leopard-print catsuits, Lara Croft hot pants, and Rocky Horror stockings and suspenders.

'Why let everyone else have all the fun?' Will keeps his tone as breezy as he can, hoping to dodge any grilling on the matter of why he's been so keen for them to get involved with this party in particular.

'I've created a monster,' Alfie says, jabbing Will's arm.

It's the end of the half-term break and the two of them have spent most evenings together this past week. Sometimes Will has kept Alfie company on his 'rounds', or, on slow nights, they've been to Smugglers, where they can get served at the bar without question. These things, which had once seemed so risky to Will, have lost their teeth now. A little faith has crept up on him – a belief that if he was putting himself, or anyone else, in danger, he'd already know.

'Not sure we're fitting in, though,' Will says, noticing how several of the revellers on the front lawn keep looking over at him and Alfie.

'They're just jealous of the car.'

'Yeah, that's it.' Will laughs as he checks out the row of brand-new Mini convertibles and white Audis in front of Alfie's ancient BMW with its DIY matt-black paint job.

'No one would guess *I'm* the drug dealer, would they?'

'Must be doing something wrong.'

'Something wrong? Me?' Alfie reaches under the passenger seat for his Tesco bag of merchandise, ready-packaged to fill the host's order plus a little extra stock for spontaneous purchases. He picks a small paper envelope open, tipping a little powder on to the back of his hand, which he noisily snorts. 'A livener,' he says.

'What happened to just doing the dust off the scales?' Will asks with a grin.

Alfie waves away the question. 'Even the air smells better round here,' he says as he swings his door open and sets foot on the immaculate lawn. 'It's like all the dead fish wash up in Ebbswick and these rich fuckers get lovely fresh sea air.'

The party is only three miles outside of town, but they are in a different world from Patten's Island at the other end of the marsh road. *These aren't houses*, Will thinks, *these are 'properties'*.

In the gap between this glass-and-golden-timbered residence and its neighbour, he can see the moonlit private beach, the immaculate sailing boats and speedboats anchored perfectly in line around the cove.

Partygoers with public-school accents are grouped on the front porch, smoking and taking pouting selfies. They huddle round one phone. 'Put it on Lauren's Story,' someone orders. 'Halloween Beach Party group,' she yells for the benefit of everyone out on the front lawn.

'I wonder,' Will says to Alfie, as they enter the double-height hallway with its gleaming granite floor, 'do you reckon everyone's too busy trying to look like they're having a good time to actually have a good time?' It's the sort of philosophical matter that they have recently been debating well into the night. 'I mean, if you were *really* having a ball, would you think to take any pictures?'

'One for discussion later,' Alfie says, glancing around for a familiar face. 'As long as no one starts posting pictures of this transaction on the Halloween Beach Party group, we'll be fine and dandy.' He points into the kitchen, where the central island is piled with beer in ice buckets and every spirit imaginable. 'Be a darling and fix us both a drink, would you?'

Alfie heads out of the back while Will sheepishly grabs a couple of cold Stellas, certain that he'll be rumbled any second as an uninvited guest, even though, as he's relieved to note, he and Alfie aren't the only people not in fancy dress. The kitchen is vast, running the whole width of the house, its back wall glazed and partially open. Outside, guests huddle round gas heaters in the decked garden, which steps straight on to the beach. On the left side there's a swimming pool, steam hovering low over the dark blue surface.

Will knocks back most of his beer without even thinking about it; without Alfie at his side, it's not taken long for him to start feeling out of place here. He leans against a fridge that resembles a bank vault, watching a noisy game of beer pong being played on the breakfast bar. Four of the participants are Will's age, while the other player is much older – forties at least. He's unnaturally tanned, a fact accentuated by his sleek skinhead and gleaming white teeth. The loudest of the bunch, he breaks off to mix a cocktail of random spirits in a pint glass, rewarding one of the young guys for downing it by very publicly presenting him with a fifty-pound note.

Will overhears two younger boys chatting nearby as they get beers. 'Lauren's dad is a fucking legend,' one says.

'Must be minted,' the other says. 'Just look at the place.'

'Anyone else want to earn a few quid?' the man bellows, waving a bottle of tequila.

'Just imagine how much pussy he gets,' one of the boys says to his friend admiringly.

The man begins a lap of his kitchen, topping up people's drinks with neat spirits. He flashes an expensive grin at Will. 'All on your lonesome?' he asks.

'I'm cool,' Will says. 'Just waiting for –'

'Join us for a game? Can't bear to see a man left out.'

'I'm all right. Thanks, though.'

The man winks, eyes glistening with charm. 'Don't want to hang with an old git like me? Understood. Good-looking man like you, house full of drunk girls – course you don't.' He chinks Will's empty beer with a rum bottle. 'Have a *smashing* night, young man!'

Will grins as he eavesdrops on the guy lapping the kitchen, bonhomie and banter for every guest. He makes it look so easy.

A heavy arm lands on Will's shoulder. 'Right then,' Alfie says. 'Business done. Time for pleasure. Let's sink a couple and get mingling.'

Alfie grabs his beer from Will.

'I reckon this is gonna be a good night, Parks,' Alfie says. His cheeks are flushed and he keeps sniffing and playing his tongue over his front teeth. 'Can feel it in my water.'

'Been at the gear again?' Will asks with a smile, knowing the answer perfectly well.

'I have a very generous clientele,' he says. 'They buy it off me then chop me one out. Be rude to refuse.'

'Of course.'

'Got something for you, too,' Alfie says, poking a tiny ball of paper into Will's palm.

'What is it?'

'Just a tiny bit to loosen you up, cuz.'

'MD?'

'You got it.'

Ordinarily, the idea of taking drugs would scare the shit out of Will. *It was the first time they'd tried them* — isn't that how all the tragic stories always begin? But tonight he wonders if he has the luxury of knowing it'll do him no harm.

Will rolls the nugget around in his hand. 'Mate, I kind of need to be on the ball tonight.'

'Not forcing you, cuz. It's only a tiddler, though. You'll be more on the ball than ever.'

'Yeah. I dunno.'

'Your shout. What you need to be on form for anyway?'
Alfie's grooving on the spot and making eyes at a
Wednesday Addams across the kitchen.

'Oh, it's . . . nothing.'

It was two days ago that Will saw the old lady with the
empty pram again. He'd spotted her trademark pink headscarf
from a distance. She was sitting on a bench behind the old
tenement buildings on the outskirts of town. As nervous
as he was at the thought of another bizarre conversation,
he didn't try to avoid her.

'How lovely to see you, Will,' she said as he drew level.
The afternoon sun was warm as she fed scraps to the
seagulls with one hand, rocked her pram with the other.

'All right?' Will muttered.

'Good news about your nain.' Her voice was gentle.

'She's home,' Will said. 'Doing well.'

'Of course. Do you have a moment, Will?'

Her soft smile put Will at ease, slowing his racing pulse.
'Yeah. No problem.' Uncomfortable towering over her,
he took a seat on the bench.

'People don't usually sit next to me,' she said.

'Sorry, I just . . .' Will mumbled. 'It's . . .'

'It's nice. A nice change.'

They sat in silence for a few minutes, squinting in the
autumn sun.

'You believe now, don't you?' she said eventually.

Will nodded. 'I think so.'

'You should. You have very important work to do.'

Will was sure he could detect a sadness in her
expression.

'Why me?' he asked. 'These messages, why are they coming for *me*?'

'I don't imagine you're the first person to find themselves in this situation. I'm sure you're not.'

'Don't think that really answers the question.'

'Why you?' she said to herself, mulling it over. 'Why you?' She was silent for a full minute. Will gazed at her, hanging on an answer.

'It's hard to say. I think you'll find out, though.'

It was the look she then gave Will that really haunts him. So sorrowful. Enough to make him wish he'd never asked.

'You must stay open-minded,' she said. 'Be open to new ideas. That really is most important.'

Will smiled, struggling to imagine how better to prove his openness to new ideas than what he was doing at that exact moment.

'Be open-minded,' she said again.

The booze is starting to make Will feel comfortable among this crowd of beautiful, carefree and careless people. He takes one last look at the ball of MDMA in his palm. 'Yeah, fuck it,' he says to Alfie beside him, chucking it down the hatch and washing it away with beer. 'Fucking open-minded enough for you?' he mutters to himself.

'Let's get mingling, wingman,' Alfie says.

'Right behind you,' Will says. He looks around as they move through the crowded place, knowing at some point this evening it'll be time to act.

*

The old lady and Will sat silently on the bench as a few people walked past. Only once there was nobody around to overhear did she tell Will about the Halloween party: how Alfie would be going anyway to deal, how he'd invite Will along, how Will should go.

'What do I need to do?' Will asked, sounding bolder than he felt.

'You need to go up to the top of the house.'

'The top of the house?'

'It'll all make sense when you're there.'

'Right. When?'

'You'll know when it's time to go. When you realize who the man is, that's the time to act.'

'I don't get it.'

'You will. I promise.'

And she told him what had to be done.

'Can I do anything for *you*?' he asked.

'Not at all,' she said emphatically, like an older relative batting away any suggestion that favours need be returned.

'I'd like to help you,' Will said.

She shook her head. 'I *do* know,' she said.

'How do you mean?'

She nodded at the pram. 'I do *know* she's not . . .'

'You don't need to say.'

'Those we love only die when we stop thinking about them.'

Sadness washed over Will. 'I guess.'

'I'm OK. It's nice to be of use.'

'Thank you.' And Will sat with her and talked about school, about his fundraising efforts for the library, about the girl he likes. She was easy to talk to. She understood what was in the spaces where he said nothing.

The party's in full swing now. Will hasn't seen Alfie for a while, although for once there's no pang of jealousy at the thought of him having fun with other people. Whether he's been gone ten minutes or an hour it's hard to tell – the evening seems somehow jumbled. And in any case, things that are now in the past feel oddly irrelevant, much as the future does. He hears someone utter the word *tomorrow* and he's struck by what a distant, abstract concept that is. It's now that really matters, Will is thinking. This unit of time is more valuable than any before or after.

An image pops up, in his fizzing brain, of a massive zip, weaving from side to side like a ski run. And everyone's standing on the slider as it zooms along, locking the separate sides of the zip together. That's us, Will thinks, pulling all the possibilities together into one solid track – the past behind us, locked together, the future waiting for the now to get to it, to pull all the possibilities into line. There we all are, in the now, at the very frontier where all that's possible is gathered in, reduced to one unarguable history. And the image melts away, and Will can't quite remember what it was he was thinking about.

He steps out on to the deck, gazing around for more people who he can drop into effortless conversation with, as he's been doing inside. A DJ pumps out house music. Will grooves to the beat as he wades through a haze of weed smoke, which flashes blue and purple in the disco lights.

'Hey, big man,' a voice says.

'Hey,' Will replies, his voice so warm he barely recognizes it as his own. He looks the guy up and down. He's eighteen or nineteen, smooth-skinned, hair set in a quiff. Maybe he's come as James Dean. Or perhaps that's just how he dresses.

He's so close his cheek almost rests on Will's shoulder blade. 'There's a steam room,' he says. 'By the pool.'

Will forces himself to focus. The pool is well subscribed now, the surface foaming as bodies dance and writhe against each other. Beyond, there's a log cabin, glowing in UV light. 'Right.'

'Want to join us?' the guy asks. A step behind him stands a girl with jet black hair, a stripe on the left side of her head shaved to skin. There's a faraway look in her watery blue eyes.

'Are you guys together?' Will asks.

The guy shrugs as if 'together' is an outmoded concept. 'We both think you're hot,' he whispers, his tongue brushing past Will's earlobe as he speaks.

Will waits for the surge of nerves, of self-limiting panic. It doesn't come. He feels nothing other than excitement. So what that he doesn't know these people? That *they* don't know *him* is surely a benefit. Because right now he's just Will, not son of Tori and Mike Parks, not brother of Danny.

'You're really hot, too,' he says to the guy. The thrill is electric.

The girl steps nearer. A hand rests on Will's navel, fingertips tickling his flesh. Instinctively he breathes in, a gap opening between the front of his jeans and his waist, an invitation. The guy hooks his thumb behind Will's belt. His lips contact Will's. 'Pleasure to meet you,' he says, their tongues briefly rolling against each other's.

Will feels fingertips exploring him. He's not sure whose they are. But he knows it's the best thing he's ever felt.

'Cerys,' the girl says softly. 'He's Tab. And you are?'

Will laughs at the absurdity of only now exchanging names. 'Will. I'm Will.'

He leans towards her. If what happened with Tab just now didn't count as his first proper kiss, this one definitely does.

'So how about it?' Tab asks.

'Maybe,' Will says, his heartbeat trying to hammer its way out of the vein in his neck. *Is this a chance to find out for certain?* he wonders. Whether those things he feels around Alfie really mean anything. To know for sure if he is or isn't gay – bi at least. These people probably won't even remember him in the morning. The stakes couldn't be lower.

Tab leans closer to Will's ear and whispers. 'Let me make you come, gorgeous.'

'Fuck it,' Will says, 'let's do it.'

Tab grabs his left buttock and guides Will towards the pool.

This is mad, Will's thinking. *I'm at a party, buzzing on Ecstasy, about to join a couple in a steam room to do God knows what. All because a batty old dear told me to be here.*

'How do you know Lauren?' Cerys asks as they weave their way through the crowd.

'Lauren?'

Tab chuckles. 'Lauren Hall. Girl whose party it is.'

'Lauren Hall?'

'You do know her, right?'

It feels like a spell being broken. That name. There's a few seconds when his fizzing mind can't place it. He feels a dull nausea all the same.

'You OK, Will?' Cerys whispers.

'Lauren Hall?' Will says, suddenly remembering those yelled accusations the night of Danny's fight. 'Used to be best friends with April . . .' He's talking to himself rather than asking them.

'Yeah, well, less said about that the better,' Tab says.

'Lauren's dad,' Will mumbles, an urgency to follow his instructions returning.

'Speak of the devil,' Tab whispers.

The very tanned man from the kitchen has just climbed out of the pool and glistens as he hugs a towel round his shoulders. 'Water's warm,' he says with a wink as he walks past. 'Get yourselves in there.'

'You seem like you're not in the mood all of a sudden,' Tab says to Will.

'Sorry,' Will replies. 'Mind if I catch up with you in a bit?'

'Don't be too long, yeah?' Tab says. Cerys blows him a kiss.

Suddenly awkward, Will gives a deflated thumbs up and turns away from them.

He strides back into the house. He knows what this is all about now.

Room with a View

Will bounds up the first flight of stairs. He strolls round the mezzanine landing, feeling suddenly light-headed. Beyond closed bedroom doors, people fuck noisily. One door rests half open, a discarded vampire cloak strewn across the threshold. Will catches sight of entangled limbs belonging to at least four separate owners. At the end of the landing he ascends another flight, steps of solid green glass with light refracting through them.

The master bedroom occupies the entire top floor, glazed along its back wall, giving a birds-eye view over the bay and the English Channel beyond. Will takes no more than a few seconds to appreciate the view before darting to the far side of the space. The floor surface changes underfoot as it becomes a wet room, a slalom arrangement of frosted screens lending some privacy. Will perches on the edge of the enormous bath, positioned so he has a line of sight past the screens and into the room itself, where the vast bed takes centre stage.

He dips in his pocket for his phone, killing time by looking at the photos of this very party being posted by the minute.

But he doesn't have to wait long.

'Now *that* is what you call a view, huh?' the man's voice says, closing the double doors to the staircase behind him. 'What do you think about that?'

Lauren's dad is still damp from the pool. The towel is bound round his waist now, his chest as gleamingly hairless as his smooth head.

'Wow,' the girl says. She's giggly, nervous.

He puts his arm round her shoulder, his head resting against her blond hair as he points out which boat is his, and says how he sails to France sometimes and how she should come along one day.

'That'd be cool,' she says vaguely. Again, the giggling.

Will's uncomfortable watching this. The girl is young – younger than he is. There's something off in her manner; she senses something's not right. But this guy knows what he's doing.

Will tells himself not to think about this man and April. He knows that won't help right now.

Lauren's dad backs away from the window, perching on the edge of the bed. He reaches beneath his towel and shuffles his wet shorts down his legs into a heap on the floor.

'Thanks for showing me around,' the girl says, standing at the window.

He smiles and stares at her. 'God, you're so beautiful. Everyone says that, right?'

More giggling. But no smile now. 'I should probably get back to my –'

'Sit here,' he says. He's slackened the towel behind him and now it rests across his legs. He pats the bed.

There's something about how he talks to her, Will notices, the expectation in his words, the unspoken offence that'll be taken if she doesn't comply.

She sits a clear metre from him, hand clasped between legs. But in one movement he closes the gap and goes in for a kiss. Will can see the tongue that prods in and around her mouth.

'I've been wanting to do that all night,' he says.

The girl's face is pure panic, but she's somehow frozen. Tempted to reveal himself though Will is, the old pram lady was very specific about timing. *A moment longer*, Will thinks. *Just a moment.*

'I think I'm younger than you think I am,' she says. 'I'm not here with Lauren. I'm friends with Holly, Lauren's little sister. You know Holly?'

He dismisses her point with a gesture, not mentioning that of course he knows Holly, given that he's her father.

She goes to speak. 'I'm only –'

'We're just two human beings,' Lauren's dad interrupts. 'Two people, *enjoying* each other.' He looks her up and down like she's a car for sale. 'Nineteen, I'd say. Twenty, at a push.'

She doesn't look nineteen or twenty at all.

'So tense,' he says, massaging her slender shoulders. A small hump rises in his towel as he slides one of her top's straps to the side.

'I don't think I –'

'Loosen up a bit. Tonight's a night for letting it all go. Just doing what feels right.' He nods as he says it. A Magician's Nod.

'I don't –'

'I know why you came up here. I know what you really want.' He kisses the nape of her neck, her back arching away from him. 'Don't overthink it. Just go with it.'

There's a fire inside Will. He wants to smash this shiny bullshit house to pieces. And he wants to cry. And he's not sure which of these desires is going to win out.

Will can see what would follow now if he wasn't here. A girl – confident, sassy – who climbed those stairs without a care, descending them with a life forever separated into before and after. Such a small unit of time separating the two, long enough for the world to change completely.

And if she complained, what then? All that make-up. The heels. The scarlet she-devil costume. The fact she's in this room. That she's not said no. *What was she expecting?* That's what people will say.

And maybe, Will realizes, that's what he might think if he didn't know better.

Why did I like this man when I saw him earlier? Will thinks. *Why do boys eat up that easy charm? He isn't like us; we don't want to be like him. So why do we look up to men like this? Why are we made to feel like we're on their team?*

Lauren's dad lunges to kiss the girl full in the face again. The towel falls to the floor.

If he was a different person, Will would start a fight right now. But his shortcomings in that area are already well documented. He's no hero. He's not about to play the hero. He's not going to act any braver than he really feels, audience or not.

'What the hell?' Lauren's dad says, jumping to his feet and scrambling for his towel.

Will blanks him, looking only at the girl. He has no idea of her name, but figures that doesn't matter right now. 'Jess?' he says.

She looks up at him confused.

'Jess! I've been looking for you all over.' He wills her with his eyes to play along.

Her expression changes as she appears to catch on. 'I was just –'

'Everyone's wondering where you are.' Will reaches a hand out and she stands on wobbly legs. 'Let's get down.'

'What the fuck are you doing in my room?' Lauren's dad hisses, face crimson as he binds a satin sheet round himself.

Will steps backwards, evading the guy's attempts to square up to him. 'Sorry, you know, was only . . .'

'I should call the fucking police.'

'Yeah, sorry.'

'Call them,' the girl says, stepping into the space between the man and Will.

'What?'

'Let's just leave,' Will says.

The girl brings her face close to Lauren's dad's. Will's interruption has offered her the little time she needed to climb on top of her fear. A few seconds for her to catch up, to no longer be one step behind this man and his intentions.

Lauren's dad freezes, no easy words of coercion now. A lug of spit hits him hard in the eye. He stands motionless, red-faced, as it oozes down his cheek.

'Call them,' she says. She's still shaking, but fear has given way to anger. 'I dare you.'

Will follows close behind the girl as she leaves the room.

'It's Dusty,' she says as they descend the stairs, 'not Jess. And I think I'd like to go home now.'

They speak no more as Will waits on the side of the road with her for her grandad to arrive. Twenty minutes pass before a car pulls up with an old guy in a dressing gown behind the wheel.

'I'm sorry,' Will says as she walks away.

'Night,' she says quietly.

'I'm so sorry.'

He turns and looks at the house. Someone is bent double, vomiting on the lawn. The party, as energetic as ever, is less inviting to him now. He wanders back in, looking for Alfie.

Party's Over

'On the comedown?' Alfie asks, looking at Will as he approaches.

Will's footsteps crunch on the pebbles. 'Nah. Just not in the mood so much.'

'The comedown,' Alfie reiterates. He's sitting on the beach, hidden from the view of the party by the ridge carved out by high tides. Hunched forward, he works a pile of powder with his library card on the back of his phone. 'See it in your face, cuz.'

'Been a weird night.'

'Party and a half, innit?' Alfie shoves a rolled-up fifty in his left nostril and snorts a thick line that stretches across the entire diagonal of his iPhone. 'Want one, Parks? Give you a second wind while you tell Uncle Alf all about it?'

'I'm OK,' Will says. 'You won't believe it, though.'

Alfie looks up. Even in the low light Will can see how crazed his eyes are, how his jaw looks like it's been drawn on with a set square, how his ears burn beetroot red. 'Maybe go easy, mate,' Will says. 'That is definitely not the dust off the scales!'

'Been a highly productive night, cuz. These St Anne's guys know how to spunk an allowance, I'll give them that. Be able to settle some debts with tonight's haul.'

'Not if you vacuum up all the profits.'

'Yeah, well, not sure you'd find me much fun without it, cuz. *I* don't find me much fun without it.'

'That's bollocks.'

Alfie waves the discussion away.

'Where you been all night, anyway?' Will asks.

'Just where the business is at.' Alfie grins. 'You're a good wife, Parks – always asking me what I've been doing.'

'Yeah. Sorry.'

'S'fine,' Alfie says, putting his arm round Will. 'Let's walk. Tell me all about your strange night.'

They stroll together round the gentle curve of the bay, Will relaying to Alfie what he saw in the bedroom. The party provides a thumping soundtrack and a light show into the night sky regardless of how far they walk. Reaching a jetty at the far end of the cove, they stop for a minute. The sea slops against the rocky wall below them. Will reaches for his phone. If he's going to do it, now's surely the time.

'What you doing?' Alfie asks, fidgety, unable to sit for more than a few seconds at a time.

'Just updating the Halloween Beach Party group.'

'Really?'

'It's a video I shot earlier. Probably deserves a wider audience.'

'Shit, Parks.'

'Yup,' Will says, a certain weakness in his thumb as he hits the *upload* button. He shoves the phone away, no desire to see how it's received.

They begin their walk back round the cove. 'Hear that?' Alfie says.

'What?'

'Silence.'

The music has stopped. Seconds later, the coloured columns of light that beckoned them in like a homing beacon are shut off.

'Looks like I've made my last sale,' Alfie says with a laugh.

'Sorry about that.'

They walk without speaking for a couple of minutes, just the full moon over the sea now and the rhythmic crunch of their feet. And, in the very distance, raised voices.

'All kicking off,' laughs Alfie.

'Fuck him,' Will says.

'Fuck him indeed.'

Alfie is suddenly distracted, leaping across the stones like a gymnast. 'No way,' he calls out gleefully, studying the inside of a small boat perched at the top of the beach.

'What's up?'

'Thought I saw something twinkling.'

'What is it?'

'Keys, Parks. One of these rich bastards has left the keys in it.'

'You're kidding.'

'What's that old expression? A fool and his boat are soon parted?'

'Pretty sure that's not how it goes. What the hell are you doing?'

'Where's your sense of adventure, Parks?'

'You cannot be serious.'

We're so close to each other right now.
   Almost touching.
   And you're coming closer. We're just minutes apart.
   At last.

At Sea

The outboard howls as they clear the bay. A stripe of foaming water stretches out behind them. No one interfered as they manhandled the craft down the beach, although both of them are now soaked up to the thighs after scrambling aboard in a hurry. In open water now, Alfie keeps the throttle nailed, piloting the boat with unexpected proficiency.

'It's called a RIB,' Alfie shouts over the din, 'this type of speedboat.'

The whipping wind and salty spray leave Will short of breath and dry in the mouth. 'Fascinating.'

'Almost impossible to sink.'

'Like the *Titanic*.'

'Yup. Exactly like that.'

It's not the safety of the vessel nor Alfie's apparent expertise that comforts Will right now. It's the confidence that if he shouldn't have involved himself in the borrowing of this boat, he'd have been forewarned.

Alfie shuts down the outboard. They bob gently on the inky water. Currents slap and thud against the boat's inflatable sides.

'How cool is this?' he says.

'It's nuts. I can barely see land.' There's a distant sparkle of orange light here and there on the coastline, but not nearly enough to navigate by.

'We'll be fine, cuz.' Alfie begins the process of rolling a massive joint, sticking two papers together at a right angle. 'Smooth the comedown,' he says. 'We're both grinding our teeth here.'

Will takes a long pull on it, fighting to hold the hot smoke down. When he exhales, it leaves his mouth in jerks and puffs.

'Saw you getting with that guy earlier,' Alfie says.

'Yeah, that.' Will grabs the joint back, a taste for it all of a sudden. 'What was that all about?'

'Don't sweat it.'

'I'm not gay. I'm pretty sure I'm not gay.'

'Who cares? Try shit out. See what fits.'

Will smiles into the darkness. It's creeping up on him. That way he feels when he's with April, where time doesn't count, where nowhere else matters. He looks at Alfie's profile as he gazes out to sea. *Am I in love with this guy?* Will wonders. *Do I fancy him?* These questions don't scratch at him like they usually do. For a moment, he feels cheated that duty dragged him away from the steam room; who knows what he might have learned about himself with those two beautiful people? But he knows Alfie's right: who cares? Who gives a fuck? 'I'm glad we're friends,' he says.

'Me too, Parks. Everything's more fun with you.'

'Really?'

'Fucking hell, look at us! On a nicked boat, out at sea, in the middle of the night, getting wrecked on skunk!'

'I think that was pretty much all you.'

'I only do this shit because you're here, Parks. You dig my shenanigans. Is something funny if no one's there to laugh?'

'Important philosophical discussion, that.'

'You make shit fun. That's what I'm saying.'

'It is fun.'

'Love you, Parks.'

'Love you too.' Will laughs. 'But I'm not gay, honest.'

'And I'm not a drug dealer.'

They both find this statement hilarious, close to a minute passing before they compose themselves.

'You're always earning,' Will says, straight-faced now. 'Where does it all go?'

'Where's the flash car and bevy of groupies, you mean? Keep asking myself that.'

'Serious, though.'

Cigarette paper crackles as Alfie takes a drag. 'My life ain't simple, cuz.'

'I sort of know that.' Will thinks of that messy, noisy house on Patten's Island.

'Got five little brothers and sisters. Gotta provide.'

'Surely that's not your job?'

'Who else is gonna do it, cuz?'

'Where's your dad?'

Alfie huffs as he jets thick smoke skyward. 'Cancer,' he says quietly.

'Sorry, you don't –'

'Had a bad back. Worked two jobs, three sometimes, all physical stuff. Keeps going to the doc's. Doc keeps saying he's pulled a muscle. Could hardly move sometimes, but he was in work every day all the same, shit-scared of getting the sack.'

'Wasn't a bad back?'

'Leukaemia. Got diagnosed in the end. Inside nine weeks he's . . .'

'You don't have to say the word.'

'I was twelve, Parks.'

Will holds Alfie's hand in his and borrows the joint. 'Sorry, Alfie. Really sorry.'

'Mum's never got over it. She has a day here and there when she's OK. Mostly she isn't, though. Still good to the kids and everything. But she ain't gonna be getting a job any time soon.'

'You must get some help, right?'

'This is Patten's Island, Parks. Single-parent family. Mental health problems. Not exactly unusual, is it? They give us enough pocket money to make sure we only starve slowly.' Alfie laughs, lying down on the boat.

Will does so on the opposite side. His brain is beginning to feel somehow less solid than normal, as if its filing system is being messed up. It's as though all his thoughts and memories are papers, and they are being removed from their indexed drawers and scattered randomly instead. It's a strange but not unpleasant feeling. As Alfie talks more, Will can visualize the scenes he speaks of, feel them as if he was there.

'Man of the house,' Alfie says. 'That's what everyone told me I had to be. And that's what I became. Last to sleep, first up, one eye open all night, and a baseball bat under my bed.'

'He's proud of you,' Will says. He doesn't know where the thought came from, just one of those random brain-files that's lying about.

'Sweet of you to say. But I ain't gonna be like him.'

'Go on?'

'He worked like a dog. Killed him. Fuck all that shit.'

'Grades like yours, you won't have to worry.'

'Not as easy as I like to pretend it is.'

'Really?'

'Trust me, Parks, I *work*. I really do work. My GCSE results weren't a fluke, whatever everyone says.'

'You always seem like you don't give a shit about anything. All that stress you're dealing with and you make out like everything's a big joke. Dunno how you do it.'

Alfie burns his fingers on the spliff's glowing tip as he sucks the last bit of life out. 'If you make people feel good, then it makes you feel good, doesn't it.'

'So, what, it's an act?'

'Dunno, Parks. Is it an act? A disguise maybe?'

'Is it a *show*?' Will says, thinking again of Mick Touch's words of wisdom, and the revelation that came to him when he watched the ridiculous posturing of Danny's fight. 'Isn't that what we're all supposed to do? Put on a show?'

Alfie nods slowly as he digests the concept.

'Like we're supposed to be action heroes,' Will continues. 'Gotta be seen to be brave. Be seen to not give a shit. Don't show weakness, whatever you do.'

'Fucking hell, Parks, ain't that the truth.' Alfie exhales noisily. 'Just putting on a show. Nailed it there, cuz.'

'Yup.'

'It's like the rules, innit?' His voice is mellow, the weed getting to work on him. 'Don't you dare be honest. Don't you dare look like you're not in control. Just put on the *show*. The fucking *show*. Fucking spot on.'

The substances that course through Alfie's brain have allowed him to drop his guard this far, but no further. He doesn't tell Will how there are days when his brain is like fog, when he doesn't have the energy to know who he is. He doesn't tell Will about the nights that pass without a wink of sleep, when he wishes he could cry out but can't, and, anyway, who would come if he did? He doesn't tell Will about the debts that he's amassed. He doesn't tell him because that would mean acknowledging them as fact.

'Why do we do it?' Will asks. 'Why do we have to play this part, do you think?'

'God knows, Parks.' Alfie kicks off his trainers and paddles a foot in the calm water. His expression lightens. 'Who are we anyway? Who are we *really*? I don't think we know, do we? We just try on outfits and play a role and see if it works.'

'How d'you mean?'

'I dunno. Like, look at Kris Tring. Are his photos any better cos he wears roll-neck jumpers? Don't think he's had an original thought in his life, but he decided to be The Artist. And I play Class Clown, don't I?' Alfie rolls on to his side and smiles at Will. 'And look at you.'

'Look at me?'

'Yeah.'

'Do I put on an act?'

'Don't flatter yourself – course you do.'

'I don't get it.'

'You, with your old camera. Your it-sounds-better-on-vinyl bollocks. Your shitty old bike.'

'What? That's just my . . . *stuff*.'

'It's a good look. Good act.'

'Oh, do fuck off.'

'What?'

'It's not an act.'

'No, of course.'

Will stares across the boat at him. 'Am I one of those *vintage* dicks?'

'One hundred per cent. You're a solid-gold Vintage Hipster Wanker. Sorry, mate.'

The two of them giggle uncontrollably for an impossible-to-quantify period of time. Every now and then a come-back occurs to Will, with which he can hilariously take down Alfie, but each time he begins a sentence the thought vanishes, a paper brain-file that has turned to vapour. Instead, as the laughter and the tears run dry, they lie opposite each other in silence, gazing up at the night sky.

The sea swells softly beneath them, the rise and fall making it seem as though they are resting on the chest of an enormous sleeping beast. The stars that seemed so faint burn brightly now, increasing exponentially in number as layer after layer reveals itself. At first, like dusty spores on the black atmosphere, they ignite and sparkle like fireworks. Is the sky coming closer to him, Will wonders, or is he rising to meet it? He supposes that it hardly matters, Newton's third law making a guest appearance in his scrambled mind to remind him that every action has an equal and opposite reaction. If he's moving, then so is the sky.

'I'm so baked, Parks,' Alfie mumbles. 'Baked to buggery.'

He's on the opposite side of the boat but Will is sure he can see Alfie's face close up to his as he says the words, reminding him of those times when he dozes in front of the telly but can still see the show in his head, matching up with the sound.

Shards of colour spear through the black night, purples and blues and emerald green. It puts Will in mind of that glass picture Nain made him for his birthday. The thought elicits a pang of worry, a concern reaching in from the ordinary world. But he knows she's OK. He doesn't know how he knows, but he's certain: Nain is safe tonight.

The filing system inside Will's head continues its disintegration. No longer is there a grid in which knowledge and memory and ideas are kept regimented. Instead they tumble and dance and make new friends with each other. Will has the sense of his mind needing to escape from a prison that he never knew existed. It seems so obvious now, how his brain is sealed inside his head – dark, quiet, protected. Caged. Fed only through tiny wires that connect to remote ears and eyes and nostrils. But his brain seems to be breaking free right now. It is out there, exposed to everything – unreduced, unfiltered.

'What was that?' Will asks.

'Baked,' Alfie says. 'I was commenting on how motherfucking stoned I am.'

'Not that. After that.'

'Didn't say a word.'

'You didn't, did you?' And Will knows it's true.

Did he hear anything? Maybe not. But he was aware of something. He *is* aware of something.

Of someone.

'Say something?' Will asks, although he's not sure any sound actually leaves his mouth.

There's something. It's distant, yet it's right in front of him at the same time.

'Who are you?' Will asks. He's not seeing with his eyes. Nor is he listening with his ears. But it's coming to him.

Faintly, barely perceptibly, a connection is made.

'Tell me who you are,' Will says.

We've come together at last. How I've longed for this moment.

I wish I could answer your question. *Who am I?* If only I knew . . .

What unites you and me is still a mystery. But we'll work it out. Between us, I'm sure we will.

I wish I could tell you everything I *do* know. About those flashes I can't escape. The children. The screaming. The panic. More vivid each time they come, a new detail added every time. I wish I could tell you about the noise, the exploding glass, the strange brightly coloured clothes the children wear. I wish I could tell you how their happiness switches to utter terror in a heartbeat. Perhaps you know what it means.

I wish I could tell you about that other vision, too – the marshes, the tree, the rope. And I wish I could tell you how I could once see weeks ahead, but now it's just days – how I worry that soon I'll not know what's coming at all, that I'll lose my chance to prevent a tragedy.

So much I wish I could tell you. But – one step at a time. The main thing is that we *feel* each other now.

There's a place where you and I can meet. Look hard enough, believe that I'm there, and you will find me waiting. Let me tell you where. Just one simple message, crossing over from my plane to yours.

You understand, don't you?

You do.

Fireworks

'You're always hiding out in the darkroom these days,' April says, as she leads the way across the beach. 'What gives?'

'I'm not there *that* often,' Will lies. He jumps ahead of her on to the perimeter wall round the Martello tower.

'Just fascinated to know what you're working on in there.'

'It's . . . this and that, this and that.'

Even though the light is failing fast, the two of them are familiar now with the way in. Shoving the plywood boarding away and climbing the steps to the roof, they emerge into the deep-blue evening, puffing steam into the cold air after the climb.

'I ran a few more prints of our egret photo,' Will says. It's one of the many things he's done to pass the time in the darkroom this past week.

'Last time we were up here,' she says. They both grin at a perfect memory.

'Is it weird that I brought a blanket?' April asks.

Will opens his own rucksack and pulls out a tartan rug he's brought from home. 'Yeah, I was thinking it might look weird.'

'Perfect,' April says. 'One to sit on, one to get cosy under.'

'Yeah, sure,' Will says, an unexpected swallow breaking the sentence in two.

'Ebbswick Park display'll be starting soon,' she says. It's still not fully dark but already distant fireworks can be seen and heard from all sides.

'Bonfire's gonna be beaut,' Will says, peering over the wall of the tower to a tall triangle of timber two hundred metres along the beach – a local tradition.

'Well, isn't this the perfect vantage point?' April says. 'A fine idea of mine, even if I do say so myself.'

Our place. That's what she'd called it. 'Want to go to *our place* and watch the fireworks?' she'd asked after their photography lesson yesterday, as if it was the most logical way for them to spend their Saturday evening. A couple of months ago Will would have instinctively reached for an excuse. But he agreed with barely a thought.

And he hasn't even benefitted from any strange instructions to boost his confidence; for all the time spent waiting in the dark for his mysterious messenger, he's established no contact since that night on the speedboat.

Is this a *date*? Will isn't sure. He dressed as if it is: pressed shirt, fresh jeans, going-out trainers. He showered for a solid half-hour and he's flammable with aftershave and hair products. As silly and unnecessary as he knew it to be, he even gave himself a once-over downstairs with Danny's beard trimmer.

He feels overdressed now beside April, who's wrapped in a wool coat nearly to the floor. Although he has noticed that her hair seems shinier than usual and she smells glorious, like a bar of soap.

'Hit four hundred ticket sales today,' April says.

Will sits on the rug opposite her. 'Wow.'

'Two grand in the bag and counting. Go us.'

'Go *you*,' Will says. 'The disco's your baby. I'm not taking any credit.'

'Bollocks, Will. Anyway, it's not a disco, it's a *rave*! Managed to bag us a thousand glow sticks today, for *nothing*!'

'Amazing.'

'Oh, it will be. Two weeks to go, superstar DJ.'

'Yeah, yeah.'

'Been practising on those decks?'

'Here and there.' An hour a night, without fail.

'I can't wait, Will. You're gonna be *so* good.'

'If you say so.'

April checks her phone and curses under her breath.

'What's up?' Will asks.

'Sorry. Promised myself I'd stay off this tonight, give you my undivided.'

'It's cool, don't worry.'

'Just a friend in need. Shouldn't moan. Been messaging me all day.' She taps out a reply.

'Anything I can help with?'

'I've mentioned Lauren, haven't I?'

Will pretends to rack his memory. 'Think so. Poor little rich kid?'

'Enough of that. She's having a time of it.'

'Didn't she drop you like a stone?'

'She did walk in on me . . . *with* her dad.'

Will bats her point away. Thinking about such things does him no good – an emotional black hole beckons, filled with a curious and unwelcome mixture of fury and arousal. If he lets himself be drawn in, he'll be unable to escape. 'Think she's probably mad at the wrong person about that.'

'Well, so she now realizes. Needs a friend, that's for sure.'

'What's happened?'

'Just a world of shit with her arsehole dad. And that's not a jilted ex talking, I assure you.'

'Got himself into trouble, has he? Fucking little sex pest.'

'Have you heard something?'

Will does his best impression of total ignorance. 'Lucky guess.' He's certain he looks guilty as hell.

'All kicked off after a party at hers.' Her phone buzzes again. 'He's got himself into trouble again.'

'You're too nice. She's lucky to have you. Really lucky.'

'Yeah, whatever,' April says, firing off a message and tossing the phone on to the blanket. She joins Will at the wall, snuggling against him as they look out over Ebbswick from their aerial position.

Night has set in now and the sky flashes, explosions echoing like faraway gunfire. There's a single boom close by, loud enough to shake the concrete beneath them. A dog howls somewhere, followed by another, until it's a thin, frightened chorus across the town.

'Beppo locked up all nice and safe?' April asks.

Will smiles sadly into the night.

'Beppo died,' he says.

'Shit, Will! Why didn't you say?'

'Yeah, I should have –'

'Will, I'm so sorry. How? When? When did it ... happen?'

Will turns to face her. 'Like, about eighteen months ago. Sorry, it's ...'

'Eighteen months ago? I thought he ...'

'Yeah, I know.'

'But aren't you always out walking him?'

'Sort of.'

'The lead. It's always in your bag.'

'It's not, actually. Not any more.' Will feels a hollow of sadness in his gut.

'I don't get it.'

'I should maybe explain.'

Will had never been sure why he still always took the lead with him when he walked anywhere. Was it to somehow keep Beppo alive? Perhaps. Or was it more to keep alive the life of which Beppo had been a part? Maybe that too. He'd been a member of the family since Will was six years old; he'd been present for the entire *perfect* era, before order began its inevitable slide into chaos. Of course it was too hard to let him go completely. And there was another benefit of carrying the lead, as well: it made Will less self-conscious, as if its visible presence in his hand gave him a legitimate reason to be out taking a walk, should any observer wish to know. Only very recently has Will begun to realize that no one has ever given a shit about why he's out walking. No excuses are required.

Since his last meeting with the old pram lady, before the Halloween party, the business of the lead had been playing on his mind. Is he like her? Isn't he, in his own way, pushing an empty pram around, refusing to let go?

Those we love only die when we stop thinking about them. Wasn't that what she'd told him? Will knew he'd never stop thinking about Beppo – did he really need to still cling to this physical reminder of him?

It was earlier today when Will had finally felt ready to resolve the matter. With Nain round at his, fit and on great form after they'd so nearly lost her, and with Will filled with the nervy excitement about seeing April, the *now* didn't seem such a poor relation to the past. It was an opportune moment to put things to bed.

'Hello, old friend,' Will had said, kneeling in front of the small stone dog in the shade of the cherry tree. It'd been Beppo's favourite spot in the garden on summer afternoons. 'Miss you. I'll always miss you, little chap.'

The ground was soft as Will jabbed it with the spade. Careful to dig alongside and not the grave itself, he was clammy with sweat by the time he'd got down half a metre.

'Goodbye, Beppo,' Will said. He kissed the tired leather of the lead. 'Love you, mate.'

He laid it to rest, scooping earth over it in small handfuls to begin with. The tears had come by the time he was beating the ground level with the back of the spade.

It was only as he turned back to the house that he saw Nain had been watching him from inside the patio doors.

'It's the right thing,' she kept telling him as they hugged and Will gulped for air. 'You've done the right thing.'

She held him and stroked his hair until Will's mum returned home, at which point they both pretended all was normal.

'I think we need to bake,' Nain said to Will. It was a fine idea.

'Well, I'm sorry anyway,' April says, raising her voice over the fireworks loosing off everywhere now, 'whenever it happened.'

'It's cool,' Will says.

'We should drink a toast to Beppo.' She grabs a Thermos from her bag. 'I brought hot chocolate. And marshmallows. Is that weird?'

Will grins and reaches into his own rucksack. 'Is it weird that I brought brownies?' He took them fresh from the oven before he left. 'Made them with my nain. Rock and roll!'

'Well, as long as Alfie didn't help you.'

Will laughs. 'They're not *those* sort of brownies.'

'I'm sure we can liven up the hot chocolate then,' April says. She produces half-full bottles of Cointreau and Irish whiskey. 'Grabbed these on the way out.'

'Nice.'

April pours two steaming mugs from the flask. 'What are we having from the bar?' she asks. 'Bit of both?'

She's already pouring indiscriminate glugs of each spirit into both cups.

'Cheers!' Will says as they slam them together, although it becomes more of a wheeze than a shout as the booze hits his throat. They fall about laughing as they sink them. April pours them each another, with similarly generous shots added.

'The brownies are incredible,' she mumbles through a stuffed mouth as they get comfortable on the blanket, sitting against the outer wall.

The display in town is well under way now and they gaze up at the night sky to the rockets that break right above them. April unfolds the rug Will brought and lays it over their legs. She undoes her long winter coat, slipping her arms out so it's just resting on her shoulders now.

Will turns to look at her. It feels like he's been winded.

'Overdressed, aren't I?' she says.

Will shakes his head. 'You look . . . incredible.'

She smiles, embarrassed, tugging a finger against the fine silver chain round her neck.

Will looks at her again, almost having to force himself to, having to remind himself that he's allowed to, that this is legitimate. Only for a moment does he glance below her neckline, at the silver-grey minidress that seems almost shrink-wrapped on to her.

'I feel silly,' she says, snuggling against Will. She pulls the rug up to their shoulder level.

Will pulls her into him tighter, holding her in both arms. *Is it the booze,* he wonders, *making everything so hot, so fuzzy?* He leans his chin against her smooth neck. He feels light enough to float away as he inhales deeply through his nose. 'You're so perfect,' he whispers, unsure if she can hear over the cacophony of explosions.

April turns to face him, her nose against his. He can taste her hot breath, chocolate, marshmallows. Her eyes fizz with sparks of blue and purple and orange.

If he was a man, he'd make his move. No messing. He'd take control, take what he wants. That's what he should do. But even with barely millimetres separating them and their bodies intertwined, he can't quite do it. His heart thumps. It scares the shit out of him, and he feels a coward for having to ask first. Lips brushing her ear, he whispers, 'Please can I kiss you?'

He can hear the smile in her soft voice. 'You certainly may, William Parks.'

Time is stopped. There is only them. There is no space around them. No cold night. No flashes or bangs. Only them.

How long they kiss for, locked together, absorbed – *dissolved* – in one another, it's hard to say. Certainly by the time they can bring themselves to be a few centimetres apart, the firework display has finished its noisy finale. Once again, there's just the background rumble, as if a battlefield is being shelled in the far distance.

'What took you so long?' April asks.

'Have you been, like, waiting for me to . . .'

'Only, like, forever.'

'Shut up. You serious?'

April adds neat spirits to one empty cup and they both take a swig. 'Since I met you, Will. Since that night we broke down at the level crossing.'

'You're such a liar.'

'Not a lie, Will.'

'Why've you not said anything?'

April shrugs. 'Nervous, I guess.'

'How can I possibly make you *nervous*? That's ridiculous.'

'Because you're *nice*, Will. And I'm not used to that. And you're fun.' She runs her fingers through his hair. 'Don't worry, you're gorgeous as well,' she whispers.

A crowd has begun to gather on the beach not far from the Martello tower. A cheer goes up as the bonfire is lit. Will and April hold each other as they watch the flames roaring into the night.

'Funny, isn't it?' April says. 'All those people down there, and they've got no idea you and me are up here.'

'Guess so.'

'Kinda hot, don't you think?' April moves the blankets from where they were sitting against the wall, laying them flat in the middle of the tower. Orange light flickers over her as she lies down and pulls the rug over her. 'Or is that just me being weird again?'

Not permitting himself any time to think about it, Will shuffles into the makeshift bed next to her. They kiss passionately again, their hands beginning to explore each other's bodies.

Will strokes his fingertips along the small of her back, her shoulders, her neck. When he finds the catch of her bra, he begins the process of trying, by feel alone, to work out how the hell such a thing is released. Soon both hands are involved, shaking and no closer to a solution.

April giggles as she kisses him. 'You give up?' she eventually whispers.

'Shit. Sorry. Yeah. It's . . .'

'Don't worry, Will.' She pulls away from him and releases it herself, slipping her arms from the straps of her dress.

'Fuck,' Will says. 'Fuck. You're so beautiful.'

Over and over again he says it, he can't stop himself. He allows himself to gently touch her naked breasts. April shudders as he glances his thumb over a hard nipple.

He feels his jeans being loosened. Cool air breezes over the most intimate part of his body. Just the very tip of April's little finger makes contact with him. For an instant he's harder than he's ever been. A surge of pleasure washes outwards from his groin to the tips of his fingers and toes. His body convulses, thrusting clear of the ground.

'Shit!' Will says. 'Fuck. Shit. Sorry. Bollocks. Fuck. I . . .'

'It's fine, Will,' April says.

'Sorry. I'm sorry.'

'Stop, Will. It's OK.' She discreetly wipes her forearm on the rug. 'I'm better than I thought, clearly.'

'Such an idiot.'

'It's all right. It really is.' April snuggles next to him again and tickles his thigh.

But it's as though Will's entire body has become one single nerve ending. He pushes her hand away, too sensitive, her every touch like being electrocuted. Self-conscious all of a sudden, he pulls his jeans up and backs away from her. The night seems cold now, what the two of them had been doing till moments ago absurd.

April reaches for her coat, sitting up and wrapping it round her.

Will thinks of the people she's been with: Danny, Lauren's dad, whoever else. Would her previous lovers have disappointed her like this? Of course they wouldn't.

April turns to him. She chuckles gently, about to speak.

'Please don't laugh at me,' Will says.

'I'm not laughing at you. Was just going to say –'

'I'm sorry, right. I haven't had sex with loads of people like you have.'

'Excuse me?' She's silent for a moment. 'What the fuck's that supposed to mean?'

'Well, you know . . . Danny, and . . . well . . .'

'What the fucking hell's that got to do with anything?'

'It's . . .'

'It's what, Will? Do tell.'

'I'm sorry, all right? Sorry I don't know what the fuck I'm doing. Sorry I don't know how to show you a good time. Like Danny can.'

She raises an eyebrow at him. 'I'll tell you this, Will, don't buy the hype. What, you think cos he talks the talk he's this . . . *great shag*? You're way off.'

'Really?'

'Seriously.'

Will kneels on the ground, folding but then unfolding the blankets repeatedly. 'So why keep going back? Why did you keep seeing Danny if he was so . . .'

'Shit?'

'Yeah, shit.'

'You think I don't ask myself that question?'

Will shrugs.

'Because I make bad decisions, Will. It's what I do. I made terrible decisions before Danny – why change the habit? I was starting to think it was different with you.' She stares out at the sea, refusing to return Will's gaze. 'Maybe I thought I could make a *good* decision for a change. Start something new, something *great*. Not doing the same shit again and again.'

'Have you seen Danny again?' Will asks. 'Since the bowling alley?'

'Don't do this, Will.'

'But you said – you said you wouldn't. That night, after the fight. You said.'

'Stop.'

'Why? Why the fuck would you –'

229

'Oh, Will. I'm a wrong'un. I told you that already.'

'Did you fuck him?'

She looks Will in the eye, her face hard with fury. 'Fuck off, Will. What possible business is that of yours?'

'Did you, though?'

'You don't own me, Will. We're not *together*. Why does everyone think they're owed every fucking detail of a girl's sex life? Fuck's sake.'

'Why? Why did you see him again?'

'Maybe it's just easier than the shit that comes with saying no, Will.' She spits the words. 'Did that ever occur to you?'

'Don't get it.'

'Maybe I wasn't in the mood for being insulted. Or shamed for being a shit shag.'

'What do you mean? Tell me, April. Please?'

She grabs her phone from the rug with a shaking hand, unlocking it and throwing it at Will with Danny's text messages opened on the screen. 'If it fascinates you so fucking much . . .'

Will skims past the muscle-bound selfies and dick pics Danny has sent, speed-reading instead his texts when April has not replied to his suggestions they meet up: the belittling suggestions of how to improve her appearance and performance in the bedroom, thinly veiled threats to out her at ECS about why she left her old school.

'He doesn't like it when I ignore him.'

'I can't believe –'

'Believe it, Will.'

'What a fucking . . .'

She snatches her phone back. 'Yes, I'm weak, Will. I know that. Seeing him because it's easier than not seeing him. How fucking tragic is that!'

Will wipes his tears on his sleeve. 'I just can't . . .'

'Maybe that's all I'm worth. Perhaps *he's* all I'm worth.'

'That's bollocks.'

'Maybe tonight I thought things could be different. How wrong I was!'

'Tonight was amazing.' Will reaches out a hand.

April backs away. 'Look at the state of me. Dressed like a cheap whore. Who am I kidding?'

'Please. You're beautiful. So, so beautiful. And incredible.'

'Give it up, Will.' She's at the top of the steps now, ready to go. 'I'm no good. We both know it.'

'I love you.'

'You don't love me, Will.'

'I do.'

'No one could love me.'

'Don't say these things. Please.'

She pulls her coat tight. 'I'll see you around, Will.'

'Don't go.'

'Let's keep things at a safe distance from now on, yeah?'

'No.'

'Bye, Will.'

And she is gone.

Will paces laps of the roof before eventually descending the long spiral staircase himself. He stops halfway. It is pitch black. His legs crumple beneath him.

The sound of his own wailing is deafening in the darkness.

The Turning of Tables

It is the following evening and Will is in the Temple Arms pub. He's been awake all night and spent the day in his room with the curtains drawn.

Danny sits opposite him, not speaking, occupying himself on his phone. Their table is in front of an inglenook fireplace; Will watches the flames as they dance and the logs as they vent – one thing, one person, on his mind.

'A hand, you two?' their dad calls over from the bar.

Seeing no reaction from Danny, Will draws himself away from the heat. Unlike Smugglers, this is no seafront tourist pub; the Temple Arms is the sort of out-of-town place that has *regulars*. Will steps over two sleeping dogs and sidles between their almost-as-comatose owners slumped on bar stools.

'Either of you hungry?' their dad asks, as he and Will return to the table with three pints of lager together with crisps, nuts and pork scratchings. 'We can order dinner if you like.'

'Might get steak and eggs in a bit,' says Danny, surveying the menu dismissively.

'Have whatever you like,' their dad says. 'Will?'

'I'm OK, Dad. Not very hungry, thanks.' He really isn't.

'Well, cheers,' their dad says, raising his pint and taking a long draught. 'Photo?' He puts an arm round each of them, snapping away with one hand and holding his beer aloft in the other. There follows a minute of silence while he updates Facebook, as he does on these pub outings, usually with a strapline like #QualityDadTime or #DadOfBoys or just #Lads.

Since their parents separated, it's been a regular fixture for their dad to drive down from London every other Sunday evening to take the two of them out. Although in his malaise, Will had managed to forget they were due to meet today.

'How's the driving going?' his dad asks.

'Gonna book some lessons soon,' Will says.

In fact, he's already had a few tries behind the wheel of Alfie's old BMW on the dock roads, late at night. He's taken to it naturally enough, although he's not convinced that his teacher's instructions of 'Put your foot down' and 'Only one hand on the wheel' are especially helpful.

'Well, just let me know. Money's sitting there waiting. And we'll sort you a car for your birthday, like I promised.' He nudges Danny. 'Something better than this reprobate tanks around in.'

'Never had any complaints,' Danny says. 'I only wear trousers in that car to keep my ankles warm.' He and his dad laugh heartily, clinking their glasses.

When Will reminisces, as he so often does, about when his parents were together, the mum and dad in his memories are almost unrecognizable compared with the people he now knows. Where, for example, did this generosity come from? As a married man, his dad was never one for overblown gifts, yet these days they can't make it through a round of drinks without an offer of financial assistance or three, even if Will's mum is forever saying how he contributes nothing towards the household.

Not that this is the only change in Will's dad since leaving the family home – far from it. The way he dressed changed almost immediately. The unbranded shirts and well-burnished wax jacket were gone in a flash, and it's safe to assume the tattered moccasin slippers for which he was legendary went straight in the bin. Barely a week after moving out, he was in his new uniform of skintight jeans and tweed waistcoat, a beard establishing itself. This sudden change left Will with an unshakeable feeling of hollowness, which he eventually realized to be a sort of grief, even though the person he was mourning was alive and well.

The fortnightly Dad Nights began soon after that. 'There's no one else,' he'd said again and again during the break-up, but on that first pub outing Will had been shocked to see an opened twelve-pack of Durex Fetherlite wedged very visibly in the door pocket of the car. How on earth did his dad not think to hide those, Will wondered for some time afterwards. It took weeks of dwelling on the question before he began to suspect that his dad hadn't left them on show accidentally at all.

'You two are very quiet tonight,' their dad says. 'Don't tell me you're still not talking to each other? Hoped you might've put that to bed by now.'

'It's nothing,' Danny says vacantly, his attention focused on the woman serving at the bar. 'Will being gay, as usual.'

Their dad shifts uncomfortably. 'That's enough of that.' He turns to Will. 'Care to tell your old dad what this atmosphere is all about?'

'Nothing to tell,' he snaps.

Since that night at the bowling alley a fortnight ago, the two of them have barely spoken. In passing, Danny occasionally calls Will a 'pussy' or 'an embarrassment', but that's the limit of their interaction. So intense is Danny's venom that Will has to regularly remind himself that he saved this guy's skin, possibly his life, and that it's that which his brother is so aggrieved about.

Will opens a pack of nuts and picks at them, despite his lack of appetite. His pint remains nearly full.

'Reckon she wants to know?' their dad says, turning round and looking towards the bar, where Danny's eyes have been fixed for several minutes now.

'She's being all coy,' Danny replies. 'Little tease.'

Will glances quickly in her direction. The young woman doesn't seem to him to be 'being coy' at all. Instead, she has the demeanour of someone who knows they're being watched and is finding it thoroughly awkward.

'Can we stop staring?' Will says. 'Fuck's sake. It's embarrassing.'

'You old spoilsport,' his dad says, turning back round. 'Slip her your number,' he tells Danny.

'Oh, I'll be slipping her something, don't you worry.'

Their dad snorts as he sinks the last of his beer. 'What happened to the girl you were seeing?'

'Which one?'

'That's my boy! What was it, Amber?'

'You mean April. Yeah, *her*.'

'Sounds juicy.'

'Think I'm a bit young for her, to be honest. Rumour has it she's into the older man.'

'Can you put in a word for me?' They both roar with laughter.

'She'd probably be up for that. Might need to grey your hair a bit, though.'

'Where would we be without the dirty little slags?' their dad says. 'Like mopeds, aren't they?'

'How d'you mean?'

'Fun to ride, as long as your mates don't find out!'

It's a strange feeling to Will, this ball of energy. It started in his guts, but now it's reached his head and his fingers. And still the pressure builds, like Mentos in a Coke bottle, an aerosol in a bonfire. There's wool in his hot ears. There's distortion in his vision. *Red mist, that's what they call it*, he fleetingly thinks. *That's what it is*.

'Cunts.'

The voice is barely recognizable as his own.

'What's that?' his dad says with a perplexed smirk.

'Fucking pair of cunts.'

The pub, quiet before, is silent now. The snap of a log in the grate is like a gunshot. His dad begins to speak. 'Sorry, I don't –'

'Fuck you!' Will screams the words. His arm sweeps across the table, launching his dad's empty and his own nearly full glass like pinballs up the table. They explode as they hit the stone hearth. Beer quenches the fire in a cloud of sour steam.

'Whoa, whoa, whoa!' his dad says. There's no trace of the smirk now. 'What's up with you, mate?'

'I'm not your mate.' Will's face is so tight his jaw barely lets the words out.

Danny is shuffling back from the table. He's not making eyes at the woman behind the bar any more. Nor is he looking at Will.

'Please, mate?' their dad says.

'I don't want a fucking mate!' Will yells. 'I want a dad. That's what I want. Not a fucking *mate*! Can't you understand that?'

'What's brought this on?' He reaches towards Will.

'Don't fucking touch me!' Will's screamed words are like a hand snatched away from a hot pan: automatic, unthinking. 'You're a disgrace.'

Dizzy with fury as Will is, he's aware of two conflicting reactions building in him. He wants to inflict physical damage. And he wants to burst into tears. Is it the desire to lash out or the need to cry that's making his eyes burn like acid right now?

'Who do you think you're talking to?' Danny hisses. 'Wind your neck in.'

'Don't tell me what to do,' Will shouts. 'You prick. Look at you, sitting there stroking your muscles. Do you think they make you interesting? All you ever talk about is what smoothie you're making and who you think you're gonna fuck next. Lucky you love yourself so much, cos everyone else thinks you're a boring cunt.'

Danny looks confused. 'Mistake, little bro. Made a mistake here.'

'Fuck off and die.'

'Let's all take a moment,' their dad is saying, on his feet with a palm held up to each of them.

Will doesn't know what to do. The urge to strike is stronger now. The urge to cry is stronger still. Why does it feel like it's easier to lash out? Is he programmed to unleash his anger that way? Or is this how he's been taught to deal with it? In the end, it's the easier option that wins out. *Why*, he'll wonder, when he reflects on this, *is it so much easier? Why is it easier to be violent, to smash stuff up, than it is to break down and cry?*

Will grabs the edge of the table. Glancing down, he can see the glowing whiteness of his knuckles, the strained sinews in his forearms. The table is heavy, dark and sturdy. But it's no match for Will's fury. His dad jumps clear as the whole thing rises half a metre from the floor as it spins. Danny covers his face as Will grabs the pepper shaker and hurls it at him like a baseball pitcher. It misses, exploding in dust against the far wall.

They lock eyes briefly. They haven't fought in ten years. Neither knows what to do next. Then Danny legs it through the pub and out into the car park.

Will tails him as far as the door. Danny, somewhere in the darkness, shouts breathlessly. 'Mental case,' he keeps saying. 'Fucking mental case.' His voice is high-pitched, constricted by shock.

'I don't understand,' Will's dad says, approaching cautiously. 'What's happened? You're the quiet one. What the hell's got into you?'

Without looking behind him, Will begins to walk away.

'Talk to me, William,' his dad snaps, suddenly assuming an authoritative tone he hasn't used in years. A tone dating back to a time when he was worthy of some respect.

Hands in pockets and shoulders tensed, Will crosses the main road. The further he walks, the fainter the shouts of his full name become. Soon they stop altogether. His face burns more than ever before. In his wet eyes, the orange lights of the street lamps become starbursts. He wishes he had Beppo with him. Even just his lead. The thought doesn't help.

Will leaves the road and tramps across the dark marshes. How long's he been walking now? It's hard to say – an hour, ninety minutes maybe? He reaches the main line that runs parallel to the coast. With few trains running at this time of night, he walks the track, striding between the sleepers. Only when he reaches the level crossing at Ebbswick does he stop.

He crouches on the grassy embankment. Beside him, the rails gleam in the moonlight. In front of him, the main road is almost deserted. A van passes, rumbling over the crossing. Will follows its tail lights as it passes the derelict shops where Danny's car broke down.

Are we going to speak ever again, Will wonders, *or is this it?* He gazes up the road as it curves into Patten's Island and thinks of Nain, at home right now. He knows there has to be an expiry date on her current good patch. Looking to his left, his gaze follows the road that leads to the front. Demolition fencing circles the rubble-strewn ground where two months ago the library stood.

A warning siren begins to bleat. The traffic lights flash red. Will steps a few metres back from the line as the rails hum and the barriers descend over the road. At eighty miles per hour, a ten-carriage express hammers past. The noise and the vibration and the rushing of the wind shake something out of place in Will, like a blockage from a pipe.

He drops to his knees and he cries. He really cries. So hard he struggles for breath. Not just because of the row with his dad and brother. Not just because he fucked it up with the only girl he's ever loved. Not just because he's been awake for forty hours straight. But because of it all. He feels as though his world is shifting beneath him, as if one era is being ushered out, a new one in. He cries for what's being left behind. And he cries because he fears the unknown up ahead.

'What now?' he says to the night, everything quiet once again. 'Tell me what I'm supposed to do now.'

I am right here with you. I am always with you.

Please don't cry. And don't beg for my help like that. I need you. You need me. But not tonight. The things you've done this weekend, they are important. And you did them all without a word from me – perhaps that's the most important thing of all.

Are you now who you need to be? With each message from me, with every change you've made, you have grown a little more.

You are changed. You are not the person you once were.

Stop your worrying.

I'm right here with you.

Home Time

The train shrinks into the distance and the level crossing barriers squawk open. Will has his back to the town as he dabs at his tears, casting a long, narrow shadow over the tracks and on to the marsh road beyond. Yellow light washes over him from behind. The irregular beat of an idling engine is familiar.

A single working headlamp dazzles Will as he turns to face the single car waiting at the crossing. He drags his sleeve over his face, hoping it's not obvious that he was sobbing uncontrollably moments ago. Forcing a smile, he walks round and taps on the side window.

Alfie stares at Will through the glass, a painful delay before his expression melts from confusion to recognition. 'Parks!' he snaps. 'How's it hanging?'

'Yeah, it's . . . good.'

'What you doing out?' Alfie speaks with his teeth bared, like their top edges are glued to his lips.

'Pub. Dad and Danny.'

Alfie eventually nods, eyes aimed past Will.

'Window?' Will says.

'Window?' Alfie echoes.

'Open the window?'

Alfie's shoulder jiggles as he winds it open. 'Right you are, Parks.'

The heater is on full blast inside, a wall of hot air slapping Will in the face. He's unable to stop himself baulking at the smell. There's a hint of aftershave, but it can't compete with what it's trying to mask: booze, body odour, narcotic sweat.

'You going home, yeah?' Will says. 'You should go home.'

'Yeah, yeah.'

'Is driving a great idea?' Will gazes into the passenger footwell, where a carrier bag lies open.

Alfie slowly follows his gaze to the opened cans of cider. 'Just need some sleep, cuz,' he says. 'Something to help . . .'

Will nods in solidarity, aching for his own bed. 'You been out all weekend?'

'Guess so.' Alfie rifles through the glove box, inspecting a handful of empty cocaine wraps with dismay. 'Fucking hell,' he mumbles, eventually licking one with a sandpapery tongue. 'Got any weed, Parks?'

'Erm, no. Only weed I've ever smoked came from you.'

'Right. Fucking need to sleep, cuz.'

'You said. You should get home, mate. Want me to come with you?'

Alfie holds up a palm. 'Nah, don't sweat it. I'm going. Just had to sort . . .' He points at the passenger seat. There are a few loose bruised apples, and two pints of glass-bottled milk – lifted from someone's doorstep or clean off the milk float, Will assumes.

'Late-night shopping?'

'Fuck all food in the house, cuz. Can't have 'em waking up hungry.'

'You sure you're OK? Not seen you . . . like this.'

Alfie takes a moment to assemble his composure. 'I'm fine, Parks. Thank you for the kind concern.'

'Don't take the piss.'

'How was your night?'

'Fucking dreadful.'

Alfie nods, but it seems he hasn't digested the answer.

'I'll tell you about it at school tomorrow,' Will adds.

'Shit, school. Really?'

'Sunday night, mate.'

'Course it is.'

'Don't worry. Bunk off.'

'No, no, no. I'll be there. Sure thing.'

'If you say so.'

'We'll be laughing about this tomorrow, Parks.'

'Sure we will.'

'Wanna lift?'

'I'm good. Could use the walk. Get yourself home, yeah?'

Alfie gives him a thumbs up and snicks the car into first. 'Love you, Parks,' he says.

'Love you too.'

Standing at the crossing, Will listens to the fading rasp of Alfie's BMW as it motors into Patten's Island. He smiles to himself, certain that his best mate will be back on fine form by the morning.

What is it about this place? Standing here with you at this level crossing, everything is so very familiar. Eerily so. Like déjà vu. I've been here with you before, of course, that night with Danny and April, and a hundred times since. But the familiarity runs deeper than that. I *know* this place. I feel rooted here. Why is every detail so well known to me?

So many questions. For the both of us.

We must meet again. We need to speak.

You've been looking for me, I know. I see you there every school day. Look a little harder, a little deeper.

Because there's something coming up that you need to know about. It's not the massive disaster that I've been seeing, not yet. But it *is* something enormously important.

And it's something you can fix.

Keep looking.

You *will* find me.

Our Little Chats

Will looks at the clock on the darkroom wall. Five o'clock. He'll give it another half-hour. The door rests half open. Sometimes he closes it, when he can bear to be in here alone.

He sits at the film-processing desk in the tiny room and glances out into the corridor, unfamiliar in its fluorescent light, night falling fast, the windows like dark-blue mirrors. The school has become a ghost town, the building somehow cavernous now it's walked only by overworked teachers and the occasional humming hoover.

On the wall outside the darkroom there's a poster advertising the disco. They're all over school now, complete with their promise of a 'Guest DJ'. Will shakes his head, glad he at least has this excuse to speak to April. It's a week and a half away now – ten days in which to make things right with her.

He picks up his copy of *Geek Love*, which he's reading for the second time. It's been less of a thrill-ride this time around, perhaps because he's now familiar with its wonky plot, or perhaps because it's been in his possession long enough to hardly smell of April at all. Double doors squawk in the distance, making Will jump, as every noise he hears in this room does. He shoves the book away. The offbeat clack of boot heels and costume jewellery approaching can only belong to one person.

'Burning the midnight oil again, Will?' Ms Calloway says.

He looks up from the sheet of negatives he's inspecting, kept to hand for this exact eventuality. 'Just going to run a print, Miss.'

'Of course,' she says, with the same smile she wears whenever Will lies about what he's up to in here. 'Always with the prints.'

'Should I be paying a bit more for materials? I don't mind.'

She waves the point away. 'God, no. Last thing we need is for the powers-that-be to know it's only you and me who use this regularly. They'll repurpose the room quick as a flash! Then where will we be?' She stares deeply at Will as she says it.

'It's . . .' He feels himself redden. 'I'm working on something for the charity disco.'

'Perfect,' she says bouncily, lifting her bursting-at-the-seams leather bag on to the table and drawing out a chair. Will smiles and nods along as she natters about the day she's had, the few year sevens she teaches who've yet to have their innate creativity crushed by the system.

She catches him in here most days, be it at lunchtime or during a free period, or after hours. To begin with, Will worried that he'd have to fabricate a reason every time she appeared, but she never asks. Instead she just casually stops by for a chat, or just to say goodbye on her way out of school, reminding him how long it'll be till the caretakers lock up.

It's fortunate that she doesn't grill him because he couldn't possibly explain. He doesn't know when it'll come, that's for sure. He just sits here and waits. He jumps when he hears voices approaching. Hairs stand on end when he spots a shadow on the walls. He feels sick when he closes the door and seals himself inside and shuts off the light for twenty seconds, just long enough to see if anything's waiting in the darkness for him. There never is. But this is the place. That night on the boat, the instruction was clear: this is where they next meet.

'How's that brother of yours behaving?' she asks vaguely, gnawing at a red biro. She's removed a handful of exercise books from her bag, which she's browsing through.

'His usual lovely self,' Will says. Some days ago, Ms Calloway quizzed him about his home life and he gave a sanitized summary of the falling-out.

'Well, you're two very different people. Danny used to be in my form group.'

'I know. You've said.'

'Sorry. I forget. Killed too many brain cells in my crazy youth.'

Will giggles, imagining how much April would relish that statement if she was here. The thought of having something to tell her brightens his mood. Silence falls again, but it's not awkward. There's something calming about her being here, like a grandparent next to your bed. Will glances over to find she's looking straight at him.

'Did you have a go with those breathing exercises we talked about?'

'Sort of.'

'It'll help. With the stress.'

'It feels kinda weird.'

She's been briefing him on the benefits of light meditation. He's tried a couple of times when he's been lying awake at night but he's sure he's not doing it right. It doesn't calm his thoughts in the least.

'Keep trying, Will. You'll get there.' She stares at him deeply again in that strange way she has, where she doesn't seem quite focused on him. 'I find meditation helps us to understand ourselves. To shut out all the noise.' She flails her hand around, as if to dismiss their entire surroundings as irrelevant. 'There's all manner of things going on around us, Will. But you have to take a step back to see them.'

Will nods. 'Did you find it difficult? Meditating – when you first started?'

'Sure. I was desperate. I'd have tried anything.'

'Why so?'

'It was when my husband was dying. I wanted to believe there was . . . *more*. You understand me?'

'Definitely. Sorry. About your husband.'

'Fifteen years ago now.'

'I didn't realize you were . . .'

Ms Calloway laughs. 'I was married to a man before I met my wife, yes.'

'Sorry, none of my business.'

'I loved him dearly. I still do. And I love my wife dearly.'

It's a turn of conversation Will was hardly expecting, but, like everything they talk about, it feels natural, comfortable. Who cares that they're a teacher and student? Her frankness breaks down walls.

'If we're on this planet for any reason at all, Will, it's to work out who we really are.'

Will smiles, memorizing the sentence so he and Alfie can debate the theory over a spliff sometime.

'You can discuss anything with me, Will,' Ms Calloway says, a throwaway cheerfulness to her tone that doesn't fit the statement. 'Anything at all. These walls don't just keep the light out, they keep the words in, too.'

Nodding, Will feels the heat across the bridge of his nose that precedes an outpouring of honesty.

'You're carrying the weight of the world on those shoulders,' she says.

Will exhales noisily. 'Do you think that we . . .' The words seem absurd before he's even uttered them. But Ms Calloway's unfazed air keeps him talking. 'Hypothetically speaking . . . do you think there's some way we could know things are going to happen? Like, before they actually happen?'

'Sure,' she says, like it's nothing. 'It's a well-documented fact.'

'Really?'

'You mean like premonitions?'

'I mean more like somebody, something . . .'

'Go on.'

'Like, do you think there could be something trying to get messages to us? To warn us about stuff?'

'Certainly.' An expression flashes on her face. Satisfaction, self-congratulation almost. And in a split second it's gone, her look of pensive concern wiping it away. 'And – hypothetically speaking – these messages they pass on, would they always prove to be accurate?'

He skims through the times it's happened: watching the library burn from the Martello tower; riding with Alfie and running from the police; saving Danny from being stabbed at the bowling alley; heading off whatever was going down in the bedroom at that party.

'Yeah, always right, I think. Hypothetically.'

'Of course.'

'We really don't need to talk about this.'

'I suppose the main thing to consider in such a scenario would be what they might want from the person they're communicating with.'

'You keep saying *they*.'

'Do I? Yes, I suppose I do.'

'You assume it would be a *person*?'

'I don't assume anything. Who knows?'

'You don't seem to find this weird. Surely what I'm asking is pretty *out there*?'

'I've heard much stranger things in my time, Will.'

'So you think it's possible?'

'Sure.' Ms Calloway closes her eyes and thinks for a moment. 'Not only do I think it possible, I think it probably happens all the time, and always has.'

As she speaks Will feels like his brain is being ventilated. 'But how, though?' he says.

'There's a massive question! The thing is, Will, what is *time*? Nobody really knows. The best anyone can guess is that it doesn't exist outside of *us*.' She holds out her arms as if to indicate everybody in the world. 'Without people to experience things happening, things *changing*, there is no time. So, to understand time and how it works, you'd have to understand the nature of consciousness, of what it really means when we say we exist.'

'Cool!' Will says, grinning. 'So you reckon time is something we've just made up?'

'Thousands of eminent scientists think along those lines, yes. Not *made up* exactly, but that the concept of time is all in our own heads.'

'Surely that's the same thing.'

'Not at all.' She delves through her stuffed bag, books and pens dropping to the floor. With no explanation, she pulls a claw hammer from the depths. 'Now, if I were to smash this down on your hand, Will Parks, would it hurt?'

'Very much so.'

'Yet that pain would be all in your head, yes? Without *you* experiencing it, it wouldn't exist.'

'I guess so.'

'Does that mean it's not real?'

'No.'

'Quite. So we can agree that things which exist only in our minds can also be very much real.'

'Not sure that explains how you'd know about stuff before it happens.'

Having been enthralled for a few minutes, Will is struck again by the stupidity of what he's dared to discuss with her.

'What time is it?' she asks.

'Just gone half five,' he says, grabbing his phone to check the clock.

'Well, so the machines tell us. You and I are sitting in this room, and we can both agree that we think it's five thirty. Or, to put it another way, we are both in the present moment, we are in the *now*, and we are sharing the experience of seeing a clock that reads half past five. Yes?'

'If you like.'

'Now imagine there's someone across town, say. Let's call her Jan. And Jan is also in the present moment; Jan is also experiencing the *now*.'

'OK.'

'Then tell me this: what time is it round at Jan's?'

'Five thirty. Five thirty-three, actually.'

'Prove it.'

'I don't understand.'

'How do you know that Jan's *now* is the same as your *now*? How do you know that, in Jan's mind, she is experiencing the same present at the same moment you are?'

Will digests the concept for a few seconds before a thought pops into his mind with which to shoot it down. 'Very good, Miss.'

'You're looking smug. What you got for me?'

'What if I phone this Jan up? What if I just send her a text? What ... she's going to tell me it's a week next Tuesday? Shall I ask for next week's lottery numbers? I'll split the winnings with you, Miss.'

'Ah, but if you speak to her, you and she become just like you and I are now. Connected, joined by a common experience. Your *nows*, your *present moments*, become intertwined. Your consciousness and hers are connected.'

'Right.'

'You understand?'

'Not really. Enjoying the conversation, though.' They grin at each other. 'I'll maybe accept that people could exist in different *nows* from each other. So what you're saying is that

253

if we aren't in contact with someone, how can we know they aren't experiencing an entirely different present moment?'

'I'm saying exactly that.'

'But if you communicate with another human, that moment unites you, and your *nows* must be the same.'

'That too.' She wears the sort of smile that suggests she knows where this is heading.

'But we were talking about messages that predict things that haven't happened. Surely that means someone has to be in a different *now* while also communicating, which according to your theory means they have to be in the same *now*. So it doesn't work.'

'Everything we've talked about up till now, Will, is widely accepted metaphysics.'

'Metaphysics?'

'The place where science meets philosophy. The place where, some day, the answers to the Big Questions will likely be found.'

'Understood.'

'But now we dip into something a little more . . . what's that word we keep using?'

'Hypothetical?'

'That's it. Let's be hypothetical. So, what if there was a special case of consciousness? A mode of existence that breaks the rules the rest of us abide by. Imagine a conscious being who could exist in one *now* while being able to communicate with someone in another *now*.'

'Is that possible, you reckon?'

'Oh yeah. I think beings with that ability certainly exist. There's a massive body of evidence to back it up, in fact.'

Will is about to quiz her further, but he stops himself, a more pressing question taking over his mind. 'You've looked into this?'

Her thoughtful silence seems to last a long time. 'Well, yes, I suppose I have. These sorts of subjects fascinate me. I'm always reading up on something or other. The ways in which we're all connected are fascinating, I think. All . . . fascinating. Wouldn't you say?'

That's a lot of 'fascinatings', Will thinks. Why has she seized on this subject? Why is she so well read about it? Bursting with her own theories, for that matter? Try as he might to disguise it, there's confusion in his tone when he replies. 'Really interesting, yeah.'

Again, she's quiet for a moment. 'Sometimes we get a feeling about things, Will.' She looks deeply into him as she speaks. 'Sometimes we sense things that are going on around us. Some of us do. Well – I do anyway.'

'Right.'

'And we do some thinking about what we can . . . *sense*. And some research. And perhaps seek out other people who may have . . . come across such situations. You follow me?'

Will nods. Her answer begs a thousand more questions, but he says nothing. He needs to let her talk now. He can pick what she just said to bits later. 'So who are they, then?' he asks.

'Who do you mean?'

'These special conscious beings who can communicate between *nows*.'

'In a way, Will, it's all of us.' Her look suggests she's enjoying waiting for Will to catch on. 'All of us, *eventually*.'

'Don't think I'm with you.'

'Think about it. For someone to move between varied *nows* and yet be able to communicate with people of a different *now*, they'd have to exist in a different plane from the one we are most familiar with.'

'Got it.'

'They'd have to be outside the physical constraints of themselves.'

'Right.'

'As we all will be. Eventually. It's one of the very few certainties of life, in fact.'

If he were in the cold light of day, if other people were around, Will would probably have laughed her implication off. But in this dimly lit room, with just this utterly compelling woman, after all the many strange occurrences that have led him here, he feels a fizzing in his veins. These things may *sound* crazy, but they *feel* like truth.

'With me?' she asks.

'I think I am.' There's heat in his eyes. 'Lots of people see ghosts, don't they? It's not even that unusual, is it?'

But he can't voice the question that this acceptance leads him to: why me? What do they want with me?

'You've maybe made a leap there that you don't need to.'

'You are talking about ghosts, right?'

'I'm not sure I am.'

'So what *are* you talking about?'

'Something far less supernatural, that's for sure. We're talking about a conscious state that is well understood by science.'

'By which you mean death?'

'Aha! No, Will! That's the leap too far. Not death. *Dying*. The strange business of dying.'

'Is it a strange business?'

'The very strangest, Will.' A shadow falls over her face. 'When you've been with someone as they die, you realize what a complex thing death is. It's not like a machine switching off, I promise you. Everything that life means, gone in a few moments of oxygen starvation? Does that seem right to you? Does it *feel* right?'

'I suppose not.'

'One day you'll perhaps find yourself holding someone's hand as they go. You'll see what I mean.'

Will can't help but think of Nain and the turn for the worse she's taken these last couple of days; barely able to leave her chair, memory shot to bits.

'You OK?' Ms Calloway whispers.

Will dismisses the thought. 'So what is it that happens when someone dies? What happens to this consciousness?'

'Gosh, you're hitting me with some terrifically huge questions, Will! I don't think anyone can answer that with any authority. But there are good theories.'

'Like?'

'Firstly, let's take a moment to appreciate that there is no "moment of death" as such. Things stop at different times – the heart, the lungs. The digestive system, for example, carries on doing its thing at a molecular level for weeks. But what concerns us here is conscious thought.'

'The brain.'

'Exactly. The *mind*. Thought; imagination; perception – when do these things stop?'

'No clue.'

'Well, nor does anyone, not for absolute certain. But the best we can tell is that brain cells remain active for quite some time after the heart stops beating. Where do these people go, Will? Where is their conscious self? What seems likely is that this period of time feels much longer to the dying person than it actually is, in much the same way as time seems to move slower when we're in danger. There's a strong possibility that these last throes of consciousness, which might last just minutes to an outsider, to the dying person could feel like weeks. Even months. A dilation of time, smoothing the shock of death.'

'Wow.'

'Wow indeed!'

'Is this the out-of-body experience people who've come back from the brink talk about?'

'It seems likely, doesn't it?' She nods solemnly. 'Maybe these are the souls we mean when we talk of ghosts. Who knows?'

'So you reckon that, in that period of time, their conscious self is able to be in different *nows*? But able to communicate between those *nows*?'

'Well, not communicate with just anybody. But if they could find someone to share the same frequency, then maybe.'

'You really think that could happen?'

She has the look of someone weighing up how much they should reveal. 'Recently, I've become sure of it. Only very recently.'

'So, if you could sense someone trying to pass on messages about things that haven't happened yet, it would likely be someone who's dying?'

'Well, they'd be technically dead. Medically speaking.'

'But when might they have died, do you reckon?'

'Think about it, Will. They are no longer bound by their physical form. Time has dilated and stretched, leaving their present different from our own.'

'With you.'

'Are you, though?'

'What am I missing?'

'So, say I have a massive heart attack right now, and drop dead on this very floor.'

'OK.'

'And, some minutes from now, my brain, my conscious *self*, will . . .' She fumbles for the right word.

'End?'

'Oh, I don't think it *ends*. No way. It just stops being my own. I suspect my consciousness returns to something universal. Like a fallen oak tree dissolving into the ground from which it grew. Not ending, just different. What's that Newton law?'

'Energy can't be created or destroyed?'

'Spot on, young man! Life is far too full of energy to be ended by something so insignificant as death!'

'I like that.' *Another one for Alfie*, Will fleetingly thinks with a smirk.

'But we digress. We were talking about the short time it takes for my conscious mind to close down. The process of dying, itself.'

'Which feels much longer to you – to the person dying.'

'You got it. That period will feel to me like – who knows – weeks, say. During which I'll be aware, conscious, somewhere or other.'

'Yes.'

'To eventually slip away, a few minutes or hours from now. From this *now*.'

'Shit.' Every square centimetre of Will's skin tingles, rough with goose pimples. He understands.

She smiles. 'You're with me, aren't you?'

Much as he feels he should be, Will isn't scared by these ideas. He's just oddly satisfied, his brain fed to the brim with heady concepts. In fact, it seems impossible to be anything other than calm in the company of this woman.

'So this messenger, this person in another plane, this *ghost*; they're not necessarily dead.'

'Not necessarily dead, *yet*,' Ms Calloway corrects him. 'They are *dying*, yes. But in a *now* that *we* have yet to reach.'

'Jesus.'

'Hypothetically speaking,' she says, grinning this time.

Will wrestles out loud with the concept. 'In the last throes of dying, someone's consciousness could re-experience the months or weeks that led up to their dying moment. And while they are doing that, make contact with someone in the real world . . .'

'Who's to say for sure?' Ms Calloway says.

'So, when would this person actually be going to die?' Will muses.

'Only they could tell you that. That's if they know themselves. You'd have to assume it to be in the fairly near future, I suppose.'

Will thinks of the desperation he could feel that night on the boat. He thinks of the pleading in that note taken by Nain. Time, as wonky as it may be, is very definitely running out.

'What do they want?' Will mumbles.

'All you can do is listen and be there,' Ms Calloway says. 'What more can anyone do?'

Someone shuts off the lights in the corridor. The hoovers are silent now. A classroom door slams somewhere.

'It's late, Will,' she says. 'We need to go or they'll lock us in.'

'Thank you,' he says. 'I've really enjoyed this.'

'Gosh, me too! We'll pick it up again tomorrow, I'm sure.'

'I'd like that.'

She hoists her scruffy bag on to her shoulder.

'Hypothetically,' Will mumbles one last time.

'If it makes us feel better to say it, Will, then OK. Walk with me?'

Will grabs his own bag and follows her to the door, his hand hovering over the darkroom light switch.

'So eerily quiet, isn't it?' Ms Calloway says, stopped a few steps ahead of him. 'You could hear a pin drop.'

Will listens to the empty vastness of the building for a moment. There's a gurgle of a drain, tree branches stroking a windowpane. He suddenly remembers processing that film with April after they'd been up all night, what they could hear in the dark: the church bells, the trains from miles away.

'You OK, Will?'

The realization brings no fear. He's ready for this. 'You go ahead, Miss. I'm just going to finish something off.'

She nods, like she understands. 'I'll make sure the caretakers don't lock you in.'

'Thank you.' Will waits for her to round the corner at the end of the corridor.

He seals himself back inside the darkroom. He places a chair in the middle of the room. 'I'm ready for you,' he whispers.

And he really is now. He flicks the light switch and wades through the rich blackness to the seat.

He's comfortable. He isn't afraid. It's deathly quiet, and perfectly dark. Soon his own heartbeat starts to quieten, his breathing becomes calm. And there Will waits: eyes open, ears open, mind open.

He doesn't have to wait long.

And, just like that, I know.

Should it be a shock? For someone to discover that they're dying? Dead, actually – technically speaking.

Because it isn't. It is instead a sliding of things into place. I'm heading for the end. It's so obvious now.

Whoever I am, death is coming for me, fast.

Yet I've been given you, and maybe a chance to change things.

Why?

Why that chance?

Why with *you*?

Where would we be without Ms Calloway? I always had a feeling she could sense me here. We aren't able to communicate, but her mind is receptive; she is *aware*. Why her? I wonder.

Now I know *what* I am, things make so much more sense. Those flashes, those horrific scenes I keep seeing, the screaming children, their strange bright clothes, the bright light, the noise – those are my memories. It's the moment that has just happened. The moment of my death. It feels so long ago, yet it was so recent. For you, for your world, it's not happened yet. But it will, sometime soon. Very soon.

But that isn't the only memory that's been haunting me. It's the most vivid, sure, but not the only one. As well, there is the vision of the guy, on the marshes, a shadow in the morning mist, the rope, the air beneath his feet. That is something I saw when I was still *alive*. A memory not even dying can erase.

And now, I can see that same event coming up. You are soon to be upon it. My peculiar ability to see what lies ahead for you has converged with my own darkest memories.

And right now, in the blackness of this darkroom, we have connected. And now you know too. About Alfie, about what's coming. You know how to stop it. And I believe you'll do it. You haven't let me down so far.

This has implications, doesn't it? If we can fix this, what else can we do? Can we head off the tragedy that's coming? The disaster that put me here, all those – what – *minutes* ago?

At some point, surely I'll be able to see this final event up ahead too, and we'll know together how to stop it. But I can't yet. I have two days in clear sight, no more, and shrinking . . .

One thing at a time, I guess.

Thank you for waiting for me, for looking for me, for having faith that I'd be here.

You know what you have to do.

We know what we have to do.

Why us, though? That's the question, isn't it? What has brought you and me together?

Why us?

How I wish I knew.

Out of the Blue?

It's not yet dawn as he steps outside. He closes the front door silently and double checks it's secure, that they are all safe. If he's forgotten anything, too bad. His keys are inside – no need for those now. He turns round at the end of the weed-strewn pathway.

That's my home, he thinks. *That* was *my home. All my life.*

Giving himself one last chance to prove he's human, he waits a moment. And another moment after that. One last chance to feel, to feel *something*. Nostalgia, sorrow perhaps. He doesn't. It's no surprise.

Patten's Island is perfectly quiet as he walks. The fog is thick, as grey and as salty and as freezing as the silent ocean that hides beyond it. The couple of working street lamps bleed into the mist, reminding him of Christmas lights bound with old man's beard. Again, no nostalgia. No feeling. He's dead already really.

He walks neither fast nor slow. No great hurry. No great fear. It's below freezing but only his face feels it. There's three hoodies beneath this puffer jacket and some fleecy trackie bottoms under his jeans – all knock-offs of expensive labels, of course. His choice of attire wasn't made to be on-brand to the very last, but to be sure he doesn't shiver and risk confusing the cold with nerves.

And actually, there are no nerves. He's thought about this too many times. Fantasized, even. Recently, his days have become a negotiation: *if nothing else gets added to this insurmountable wall of shit, maybe I won't end it today.* Just that simple promise takes some effort. Not that anyone else could possibly know how much it takes for him just to appear normal. His turmoil is entirely private, the devil-may-care attitude such a well-rehearsed show that surely no one could possibly see *him* behind the act.

He thinks of his old friend Rocket. Real name Laurence, although he only discovered that from the order of service at his funeral. Rocket was older, seventeen to his fourteen, apprentice mechanic to precocious year-nine student, but the two of them had hit it off nonetheless. Nothing bothered Rocket. He was a lairy long-haired loudmouth who lit everything up. Lived to laugh and fuck and fight – his words. The car was found parked up along the coast at Beachy Head. The coast guard found Rocket a little after that.

He wondered for months afterwards what Rocket was thinking of in those last moments before he jumped, toes overhanging the cliff edge, pale face in the moonlight, so desperate. Was he crying? Was he longing for someone to love him enough to talk him down? Did he see his funeral in his mind's eye?

And now he knows it wasn't like that at all. It's so simple, really. It's just that the thought of dying is less crushing than the thought of living. That the idea of ending your life brings less anxiety than having to admit to everyone the mess you've made of it. The lesser of two evils.

He imagines it for a second: his name in granite. Alfie Lim. Visualizing his own gravestone doesn't shock him like it once did. In any case, it's less shocking than other things he can imagine. Tomorrow, for example. Or the day after that.

The first light of dawn seeps whiteness into the fog as Alfie reaches the level crossing where Patten's Island meets the marshes. He weaves through the vegetation to the side of the road. The ground is soon firm beneath his feet as he walks on the stones alongside the tracks.

Something occurs to Alfie as he walks, neither fast nor slow. There's some sort of order to his thoughts. He can actually *think*. He can actually process why he's doing this. It's been weeks since any real thinking about the towering walls of problems that surround him has resulted in anything other than a crashing of his brain's circuitry. But now a hint of clarity returns. A suggestion of order in the chaos that has taken over his days and nights.

He thinks about that day, all those years ago, when they said goodbye to his dad. Was that when everything changed? Did that event make this one inevitable? He's always missed his dad, sure. But if there's anything he's really yearned for from the *before*, it's how he could be *real*. He could be honest back then. To only have to be yourself – what a wonderful thing that would be!

Man of the house, that's what people told that twelve-year-old to become. And he'd felt ready for it. Even back then, Alfie Lim was someone who, when given a job, would be bloody good at it. He and his dad had spent their Saturday nights watching Jackie Chan movies, the *Die Hard* franchise, all the *Batman* iterations. Alfie didn't just know how to be a man, he knew the gold standard.

For a couple of years they got by OK. But his mum was struggling, dark shadows growing ever larger around her. She battled on, but having five kids younger than Alfie to care for plus a fifty-hour-a-week job in a betting shop proved too much. Eventually, her boss's patience ran dry with the late starts and the absent-mindedness. With no money coming in, only Alfie stood between five young mouths and an empty table.

Charming and astute, at fourteen Alfie was passing for older than his years. Looking up old contacts of his dad's, he soon had a sideline going in fake-label clothes. Word got round in no time, kids approaching him in the playground, and Alfie stepping outside the gates to show off the stock from a Gray Nicolls cricket bag he'd nicked from a visiting private school team. His pride one mufti day when half the school turned out in knock-offs he'd supplied almost brought a tear to his eye. On good weeks, his hustle kept the household in breakfasts, a full complement of toiletries, even a takeaway here and there.

Alfie enjoys the memory as he walks in the fog, only the polished steel rails guiding him to his destination. He'd been busy, defined by his success. Activity breeds activity – not only was business booming but he found the time and energy for school, too, his grades better than ever. He had too much on to be constantly aware of the void his father had left. His little siblings, used to going without, wanted for less than ever, and that small fact made their own loss less apparent, too. Things were OK. Hard work, but OK.

There are firsts in life that are carved on to our brains. For Alfie, they are the spring Sunday afternoon, green and breezy, when, aged seven, he rode pillion on his dad's old Honda for the first time; the moment a softly spoken man with a pink pocket square told him and his mum that his dad wouldn't make it; the first time he was naked in front of a girl; the first time, aged fifteen, that he did cocaine.

There was a problem, Alfie realized, with how they educated you about illegal substances in school – all that 'drugs are bad' business. Because, ten minutes after vacuuming up his first line, it was apparent he hadn't been told the whole truth. Contrary to many a PSHE lesson, Alfie didn't slide into addiction within the week. In fact, prioritizing his financial commitments at home meant he only allowed himself to get on gear once every week or two. The highs might only have lasted for the few hours in which he and his new-found mates were holding, but Alfie found himself immune to this 'comedown' that everyone else talked of. Instead, in those early days, the benefit of a good session stayed with him for days after. It was a vision of himself on best possible form. Because the thing about cocaine, he was beginning to find, is that it makes you immune to all the right things. One sharp sniff and in minutes you are the person you wish you always were. For someone whose brief was to be The Man, it was wonder powder. No fears, no creeping self-doubt. A drug that makes you everything a man should be. What's not to like?

It's nearly daylight now, but visibility is no better. The fog seems even thicker, even icier to the touch. Alfie's left foot scuffs along the rail as he treads from one sleeper to the next. He hears a metallic buzz, like distant mosquitos. Resting his trainer on the metal, he feels a swelling vibration. Gazing pointlessly into the fog, he wonders how far away the train is.

A gale-force blast of air wallops into him, the frozen cushion amassed in front of the racing locomotive. At the very last second, Alfie sees the lights, exploding from two tiny dots into two massive glowing discs, like giant hands intent on grabbing him. He jumps down the embankment, rolling in the mud and weeds.

Five thousand tons of coastal express train thunder past his head at eighty miles per hour. It rattles his organs in their cavity. A sheet of wind cracks in the void after the last carriage passes. The driver must have seen him jump clear, a needless blast of horn Dopplering into the distance. And then quiet, just the fading buzz of rails again.

Alfie draws himself up to his knees. He feels light-headed. Mud is thick on his palms and elbows; they smell of school-football-field misery. There's almost a smile as he stumbles to his feet on the slippery ground. Close one.

Funny thing – the survival instinct. Even this near to the end, every synapse had been in use to save his own skin.

He's about to start walking again when he sees his phone in the weeds, ejected from his pocket when he jumped. He picks it up and polishes it against his hoodie. The lock screen reveals eight missed calls and five texts. Every message and call is from the same person.

'Not now, Parks,' Alfie mumbles. But, again, there's the almost-smile.

Their friendship has been a welcome distraction these past couple of months. Alfie has enjoyed how Will sees him, how he buys the act so completely. He smirks, thinking of the hour they wasted the other day debating whether a vegan is still a vegan if nobody knows. He feels a rare warmth recalling Will's relish when he taught him how to sneak stuff through the supermarket self-checkout, to then deposit the goods in the food bank collection on the way out, like a game laid on for them. He thinks about Will's laughter when he went up to the bar at Smugglers, returning with a pint of lager for Will and a schooner of sherry for himself. 'Just fancied something sweet,' he'd told a creased-up Will.

He looks down at his phone again. He doesn't unlock it. What good would it do now? No friendly words are going to make any difference. For a mate to be any use now, there'd have to be just one or two problems to fix. Things would have to be *solvable*. Alfie's so far past that now.

The light of the screen dims; Will's name fades to black. 'Only end up letting you down, cuz,' Alfie says. 'It's what I do.'

He scrambles up the embankment, listening carefully for trains this time. He places the phone on one of the rails, ready for the next express. And he moves on. Not far now.

There's a popularly held misconception about drug dealers: that they all make loads of money. Sure, somewhere up the hierarchy somebody's getting rich. Maybe the guy who sells the gear to the guy who sells it to Alfie. Maybe the person above him. For Alfie, it was certainly no ticket out of Patten's Island, just another hustle to keep his brothers and sisters in the comfort he'd not had. The margins were small but the company and the clientele made it fun.

Alfie knows what an addict looks like – God knows they'd spent enough time at school on the subject. Addicts start every day with their substance of choice, can't function without it. Alfie was adamant; he didn't have a coke habit. He could go days without touching the stuff, a week sometimes. And when he did get on it, it tended to be just a line chopped up for him by a happy punter, or the dust off the scales when he was weighing it out. But as time went by, there seemed to be more dust finding its way off the scales. And margins being tight as they are, the dust off the scales *is* the margin. Alfie may have chosen not to notice, but he was hoovering up the profits. And a bit on top of that.

Not an addict, though. Of that he was certain. He didn't notice that taking cocaine was all he really thought about. All that he looked forward to. Some pathway had got closed off in his brain. Nothing made him happy any more. Nothing could excite him. The simple pleasure of a natural high had been lost to him. Even when he laughed, when he might be close to enjoyment, it would turn hollow with the realization of how much better this moment would be with some gear.

And here he is. Now. A seventeen-year-old who's become numb to the joys of life, blind to its brightness. Unable to sleep or eat. Insurmountable debts owed on fraudulent loans in his mum's name. All those things he treated his family to now pawned: telly, video games, even the microwave.

My poor mum, he thinks. *My poor little brothers and sisters. How I've let you down. How much better off you'll be without this worthless piece of shit dragging you under. You deserve so much better.*

Alfie veers left. Never mind the poor visibility; he'd know this view anywhere. About thirty metres away stands a solitary horse chestnut tree. Its branches, newly stripped by autumn frosts, are like skinny black arms with a hundred elbows. Its shape lends itself to climbing and he's been up it countless times.

The trick to success at conkers, his dad had explained, was having the right conker to begin with. The mistake everyone makes, he reckoned, is to collect what he termed the *rejects* on the ground. No. The tree hangs on to the best ones. And the finest of the lot, they're kept well out of reach, right up the top.

He'd say this stuff like it was not only irrefutable fact but blindingly obvious as well. As each autumn rolled around, Alfie needed slightly less of a leg up to the lowest branch. His dad would follow right behind, steadying him whenever he stumbled, until they'd reach the highest solid branch. They'd sit awhile in the golden air, salty and crisp and always with a hint of bonfire. A bag of good-sized conkers, still in their husks, would be picked, ready for multiple cycles of oven-baking and freezing until they were invincible. An annual ritual, it would feel to Alfie like an era ended each time they embarked on the climb, a new one beginning when they dropped to the ground again. The world went on turning beneath them, but at that great height above the town and the sea, the two of them had somehow stepped off it for an afternoon.

It's no effort for Alfie to climb on to the first bough. No need for those solid hands round his waist now. *Was it always this low?* he wonders. He reaches that familiar high branch. The fog is thinning up here, faint headlamps visible on the marsh road. Alfie leans against the trunk where once he and his dad carved their names with a Swiss army knife. No trace in the bark now. But still Alfie has a strange sense that this tree, this hunk of living, breathing timber, somehow remembers him. Surely not many people have sat right up here and shared its view?

What have you become? That's what Alfie imagines the tree asking. *When did you turn into this?*

Alfie sidesteps his way along the bough. He's out far enough now, a clear path to the ground below him. The grease-stained tow rope is fixed round the branch in no time. And he ties the other end.

There are no trains now. No cars on the road. Just the thick silence of the fog and soft rattle of his father's old watch on his wrist. There's a snap somewhere below. Footfalls. An animal, no doubt.

His legs shake as he half stands, clutching a spindly branch above him. There's a twinge of panic. Like leaving for a school trip as a tiny kid and suddenly deciding he'd rather not be away from his family. But he knows it's too late. Far, far too late.

One last look over the curtain of icy mist. A stripe of granite sea is visible at the horizon.

This is the last light to pass my eyes.

I don't want to go.

The knot is tightened, in readiness.

You have to go. No choice. Not any more.

Please? Please?

The shaking's bad now. His feet slide on the icy branch. He grasps the twigs about him in his greasy hands.

Time to go now. Time to check out.

'Sorry,' he says out loud. It's not his voice. It's a whimpering child's. 'Sorry.'

274

He closes his eyes. He knows he's seen all he'll ever see now. His breathing slows. He's almost calm. Or numb.

I'm ready.

Jump.

Jump, you fucking pussy!

'Alfie?' The soft voice is surely in his own head. 'Alfie, my lovely?'

He's colder than he's ever been. *Have I already jumped?* he wonders. Opening his eyes, it takes a second to orientate himself, to see that, no, he's still standing fifteen metres in the air.

Jump, already. Jump, you useless cunt.

'Alfie? Talk to me, Alfie?' Her voice is warm.

He looks around. It's not his imagination – the fog really is flashing blue to white to blue to white. A radio crackles somewhere.

'I just want to talk, my darling.'

She's on the ground, almost directly below him. She looks barely older than he is, but her fluorescent jacket reveals her to be here in an official capacity.

'My name's Odette,' she tells him. 'Just like to have a chat with you, mate. Do you think that might be OK? Just a chat?'

Alfie's legs seem even weaker suddenly, almost buckling beneath him. He shakily lowers himself so he's sitting on the branch.

'I'm with the ambulance service. Just want to keep you safe, Alfie. Can we talk?'

Alfie nods. He clutches the branch tighter than ever.

No Capes

'Shit! Didn't see you there,' the fireman says, shaking off and tucking himself back into his trousers.

Will sits on a low fence, facing across the marsh. 'Don't mind me.'

'Too many cups of tea. Keeps me awake on a night shift, see.'

Will smiles, still gazing at the bare tree fifty metres away. 'Is he OK?' he asks. 'The guy you helped down?'

Twenty minutes ago, this same firefighter had scaled a ladder, cut away the rope, and steadied Alfie as he returned to solid ground.

'He's in the best possible hands. Lucky we got here when we did. Poor sod. What drives a young lad to do such a thing?'

Will feels a fizzing at the bridge of his nose. 'Thank you. You and everyone.'

He gives a shrug as if to say *it's nothing*. 'You know him?'

Will nods.

'When you see him, tell him to stop playing at silly buggers.'

'Dunno if it's that simple.'

The fireman gives him a sad smile. 'Course it's not. I know. Bit of male camaraderie bullshit there, I'm afraid. Just slips out.' He pats Will on the shoulder.

The ambulance bounces along the track and picks up the main road. At the wheel is the paramedic who sat on the ground and chatted to Alfie on his branch for half an hour. She beeps the horn and waves to the fire crew and the two police officers. The fireman standing with Will raises his hand to her.

Another life saved, Will thinks. Just a little wave as if to say, *Nice to see you. Catch you next time we need to head off a tragedy.* All in a day's work.

'So long, anyway. Give your friend my best.'

He nods as the fireman jogs back to his colleagues.

Will had never meant to brink this quite like he did. Since his encounter in the darkroom, he knew it was supposed to happen this morning. And roughly where Alfie would be. But that's all he'd been told – all that had made it through to him, anyway. He's been up all night, roaming the marshes. By four a.m., with the fog thickening and his calls unanswered, he knew his only option was to place an emergency call as soon as he located Alfie. Anything else was just too risky. What the hell do you say to someone who doesn't want to live any more? Will's asked himself that question all night and still has no answer. He's glad he made the call, that's for sure.

Did I save his life? Will wonders. *Without me, he'd be dead now, surely.*

It's someone who's dying, someone who's going to die very soon – that's what he and Ms Calloway surmised about Will's unseen messenger. Somebody who needs his help.

Has it been Alfie all along? Is this over now?

The fog has thinned and Will gazes across the marsh and out to the cold steel sea.

Think about it: Alfie jumps, he stops breathing, his heart grinds to a halt, and the process begins – of dying, of his mind fading away. That process feels to Alfie like many weeks, his consciousness looping back to early September. And in that extra time, Alfie decides he doesn't want to go after all, so he follows the one person who might be able to stop him. Builds that person's trust, makes them believe in him, in *themselves*, nurtures them till they are the person they need to be to stop him.

It was Alfie, Will thinks. *It must have been. He dragged me out of my shell, made me befriend his other self, showed me how to change things. And here we are, on a frozen November morning, with everything fixed.*

It's over.

Will thinks about the day of the burning library, how his prior knowledge brought him and April together. And he thinks about the afternoon in Alfie's car, when Will ran from the police, when – of course, it seems so obvious now – he saved Alfie's skin and they became friends. He thinks about saving Danny from being stabbed, and the girl at the party. Disasters averted. Will getting a step closer each time to becoming the person he needed to be, ever more confident that he could change the path of time.

Are you a hero if no one knows what you did? Will wonders.

Not one for playing the hero, are you?

You gotta act a bit braver than that when you've got an audience.

There's been no audience, no one to *play* to. No *show* has gone down here.

Yet a person has been saved. *What would Mick Touch make of that?* Will briefly wonders.

Are you a hero if nobody knows?

A tear trickles down Will's face, its wet track immediately icy in the cool morning.

I guess it's over now, he thinks.

Alfie is saved. The version of Alfie who's followed Will and instructed him must be gone. Or merged, perhaps, reunited with the Alfie who survives. A new Alfie.

It strikes him now for the first time: *he*'s a new person, too. He has a best friend. He knows how to have *fun*. He still hangs on to the hope that he might make things good with April. He is almost unrecognizable, and happy to be so.

It's over, he says to himself.

There is a nagging doubt somewhere in his gut, a sense that this is too simple somehow. Will shoves the thought aside, dismissing it as a desire to continue that dangerous thrill of being wrapped up in the unknown.

It's over, he tells himself, more firmly this time.

Order to chaos. He'd been so sure of this theory. It's the rule of the universe, right?

And yet, has he not disproved it several times over? Saving Danny, helping the girl at the party, facilitating Alfie's rescue. Scenarios destined for chaos. Yet Will's actions have created order. They've created life, potential.

Is order really destined to become chaos? Or are such rules, Will muses, in fact, open to debate?

He wanders across the marsh towards the road, busy with morning rush-hour traffic now. He's been up all night but he's not tired. Not that he much fancies heading into school. Instead, he decides to take a walk to Patten's Island. He should be in time to have a breakfast cuppa with Nain. Might even wangle a bacon sandwich.

Out on the road, the number 83 bus crawls past, belching soot from its back end, its cream and green livery thick with road grime. It's the bus Will should have boarded fifteen minutes ago outside the ruins of the library. If he hadn't been out all night, he'd be riding it to school right now, looking out of the window at the very marsh on which he now stands.

A face turns inside the bus to look at Will. It's the hobo with the hacking cough and hoover cupboard aroma. He smiles earnestly through the murky glass and gives a shuddering thumbs up. He mouths something as the bus passes. It looks like, 'Good lad', or maybe 'Good man'. Will waves back weakly and continues on his way.

He reaches Patten's Island at the time he'd ordinarily arrive at school. Nain doesn't answer the door, but that's not unusual at this hour. In his distracted and exhausted state, he's forgotten to worry about what might await inside this house like the old Will would have done.

He reaches for his key and lets himself in.

And there it is. I know who I am.

It's so obvious, of course.

The number 83, the bus you should be on right now, is the bus I *was* on. When I saw Alfie beneath the tree. Too late. Far too late.

Such a harrowing memory. It was me, and the others on the bus, who raised the alarm.

I wasn't best mates with him, like you are. Things ran differently for me. But I recognized him all the same.

But you've saved him. *We've* saved him. There is a long road ahead, sure, but today he lives.

And now I understand why I never see you in my memories. I know what brings us together.

Because you are wrong. This is not over.

A tragedy is still coming that involves many, many people. And it involves you. And me.

Because we are one and the same.

I am *you*, dying. Very nearly dead, in fact.

We've done a great deal of good together. Just one last challenge remains – to head off the disaster that put me here.

One last change to the path of time.

I can see such a short distance ahead now, a day at most. Soon, surely, we will reach my *now*, and I'll know exactly what took my life and so many others. And how we might stop it.

I don't know when, but I know it's coming.

It's coming very soon.

I am Will Parks. And I am dying.

Holding On

'How's she doing?' Will asks. He leans over the bed and kisses Nain's clammy forehead. There is no response, of course.

'The staff are amazed she's still with us.' Will's mum squeezes Nain's shrunken forearm. 'Fighter, aren't you, Mum?'

Will crouches next to the bed, one arm round his mum's shoulder, his other hand stroking Nain's hair. He gazes at his own reflection in the window, the glass blackened by the night sky. 'Fighter all right.'

'You must prepare yourselves for the end.' These are the hushed words that have been uttered by sincere professionals several times in the three days since she was admitted. She's been unconscious throughout, due to the severity of her injuries and something Will is unsure of the meaning of: *complications*.

But still she seems to hold on, restless, mumbling incoherently at times. Everyone knows she's nearing the end, except Nain herself, it would seem.

Will's mind goes back to the dark silence inside her small house, the second or two after he'd opened the door when he'd felt weightless, disconnected from his own senses. Her purple lips, grey face. Translucent limbs in a pile at the foot of the stairs. Motionless.

It was the second emergency call Will had made that morning. And the paramedics who turned out were the very same crew who'd talked Alfie down and taken him to hospital, not that they'd noticed Will earlier. He's been to see her in hospital at least once every day since.

'Spoke with the doctor earlier, Will,' his mum says. 'They're just making her comfortable now. No treatment any more.'

Will nods, stroking his thumb on Nain's delicate skin.

'Her kidneys are failing. Another thing to add to the list. Be a matter of days. At most.'

'I think I should stay here tonight,' Will says, reaching for his phone to cancel this evening's plans.

'You look smart,' his mum says. 'Very handsome.'

'Thanks.'

'And you smell . . . *delicious*.'

Will reddens.

'Who's the lucky . . .'

'Lady,' Will says firmly.

His mum grins. 'Lady! Of course.'

'I'll reschedule,' Will says. 'It's nothing important.'

He forces an upbeat tone, tapping out a text. So what that April's agreement to meet up felt like winning the lottery. So what that this might be his only chance to make things right. Nain needs him.

'You'll do no such thing,' his mum says, pushing his hand away from his phone. 'What do you think your nain would say about it?'

Will shrugs.

'Do you think she might tell you to get out there and live?'

'I guess so.'

'I know so, Will.' His mum leans against him and puts a hand on his knee. 'You're very good to her. And she loves you very, very much.'

Will is sure he feels Nain's hand tighten round his. He tenses. Even with such legitimate cause, he can't let his mum see him cry.

'Oh, here's something you'll enjoy,' she says. 'I had your father on the phone this morning. As if I don't have enough to worry about . . .'

Will counts back in his head to when it kicked off in the pub. It was the Sunday before last – he's due this weekend. 'Is he coming down?'

'That's why he rang. Said he'll be giving it a miss.'

Will gestures towards Nain. 'Because of . . .?'

'God, no! Nothing to do with this,' his mum says, almost gleefully. 'Told me all about the fun he had with you and Danny last time. Quite the ruckus, I hear.'

'It was nothing really.'

'Well, Will, your father won't be coming down until further notice.'

'OK.'

'All my fault, apparently. You boys running riot. Your lack of respect.' She rolls her eyes.

'Interesting.'

'He said you need to learn that family comes first.'

There's a silence as Will and his mum's eyes lock.

'He really said that?'

'Yes, really.' She begins to smirk.

'He said *we* need to learn that family comes first?' Will grins.

'I shit you not, Will.'

In the muted laughter that follows, Will feels sure that even Nain is enjoying the joke.

'Your date,' Will's mum says abruptly, just as he's beginning to settle back into his vigil-keeping, chin resting against the bed rail.

'You sure it's . . .'

'Just go, Will.'

'It's not a date. Not really.'

His mum stands, wagging a finger. 'Will you go already!'

Salvage

'It's . . . really good to see you,' Will says, eyes flitting from April to the beer he swills round his pint glass.

'Yeah. You too.' She smiles awkwardly. 'Didn't we already say that?'

'How you been?' As he says it, he realizes they've covered this several times already, too.

'Good.'

'Great.'

'Miserable actually, Will.'

'Shit. Really?'

'And you're not?' She sips from her glass of champagne.

She'd told Will to decide what to get her at the bar, but he's now embarrassed by his attempt to appear sophisticated. Mick Touch had been good enough to let him have it free, though. 'Don't get much cause for the good stuff in the Smugglers saloon bar,' he'd told Will.

'Course I am,' Will says. 'Fucking miserable.'

'I am glad you called. Been sort of hoping . . .'

They are seated in a booth in the window and take it in turns to gaze out in preference to meeting each other's eye. Beyond the cars that zip along Coast Drive, a stripe of moonlight sways on the choppy sea.

'Been so desperate to, like, *sort things*,' April says. 'Can't bear the idea of doing this rave of ours without –'

'Of *yours*, really,' Will says.

'Bollocks. It's our baby. And it's *this week*, Will. Can you believe it?'

'You still want me . . . involved?'

'Stupid fucking question, Will.'

'Right.'

'More than anything. I'm literally dying to see you play.'

'*Literally* dying?'

She clutches her heart. 'Oh yes. No pressure.'

Will notices behind April the attention the two of them are being paid by Mick Touch at the bar. He nods at Will and screws up his face in an expression that says, *Get in there, my son!*

'I was such a dick that night,' Will says.

'I was a bitch.'

'Bullshit.'

'The whole damaged-goods routine. What a fucking embarrassment I am.'

'Stop it.'

'Let's just not talk about it any more, yeah?'

'I'm so sorry, though.'

'Honestly, Will, let's forget it.' She mimes sweeping something under a carpet. 'Time to move on.'

'Sorry,' Will mumbles again.

'Not like you haven't got enough to worry about,' April says. 'Your nan, Alfie . . .'

'I'm cool,' Will lies.

'Righto. Any word on Alfie?'

Will shakes his head. 'Spoke to the hospital again today. He's been transferred. Say they'll let me know where he is, but . . .'

'I'm sure he's fine.'

'Sure he is.'

'Everything'll come good,' April says, laying her hand on his.

It's not only Alfie who's been weighing on Will's mind. Nor is it just the situation with Nain, or his misery over the fall-out with April. In moments when he can ignore those most pressing worries, he dwells instead on the bizarre events of these recent months.

Alfie is safe now, and Will is certain that it was dying Alfie who was the messenger. He is confident it's all over now. But that surety brings little peace.

Why me? asks a voice in lulls in the day and the depths of night. *Why did time bend for me, so I could save a life? What makes Alfie such a special case?*

But any attempt to analyse it all leaves him with a feeling that some time needs to pass. Trying to get to grips with the saga right now feels like he's trying to comprehend the entirety of the Earth with his face a centimetre away from the ground – a task as futile as looking for the secrets of the universe with a microscope.

'We're attracting some attention,' Will says, as Mick Touch begins thrusting his hips back and forth, shagging the air.

April says nothing, staring out of the window. Her grip on Will's hand falls loose.

'I *am* sorry,' Will says again.

'Yeah,' she whispers, not looking at him.

Will notices how her hand has begun to shake. 'You're still really angry, aren't you?'

'Fucking hell,' she mutters.

'You OK?' Will sees now that her face is bloodless. 'What's up?'

She looks back at Will, forcing some composure. 'Fine. Fine. You were saying?' Her voice is breathy. She grabs his hand again. Her grip is cold and greasy with sweat.

'Something's wrong,' Will says.

'Not at all.' Her smile wobbles.

Will glances out of the window. Just metres away, a car finishes parking at the roadside. It's a two-seater Mercedes, ivory with huge glossy black wheels.

'Nice!' Will says. 'Hundred grand right there.'

'Don't look,' April hisses.

Will does look. If the private number plate wasn't a giveaway, the sight of that familiar tanned, shaven head as it emerges from the car is.

'Fuck,' Will whispers. His eyes dart between April's white face and Lauren's dad as he pops the collar on his camel overcoat.

The last time I saw this bloke, Will thinks, *he was yelling threats at me and desperately trying to cover his tiny cock.*

April breathes noisily through her nose – the sound of someone wrestling to control their hyperventilation.

'Don't think he's coming in here,' Will says.

Tears track down April's quivering cheeks. 'Why the fuck . . .?'

'It's OK. It's OK.' Will watches as the man turns his back on Smugglers and waits to cross the road.

'Why am I . . .?'

'He'll be gone in a minute.' Will tries to still April's hand, which vibrates, rattling the table.

She sinks her teeth into her lower lip. 'Fucking look at me. Fucking state of me.'

'Stop it. Please.'

She turns and glares at Lauren's dad's back. He's still beside his car, taking a call now.

'There's a back door,' Will says. 'Sneak you out if you like?'

She looks at Will, blank, confused. She's dead still. Then her eyes widen, catch fire.

'You OK?'

She is silent.

'You don't . . . *look* OK.'

She nods her head and slowly rises to her feet.

'Let's just . . .'

Her voice is scratchy, barely audible. 'I'm done.'

'What?' Will's following her as she crosses the bar.

'I'm *so fucking* done.'

The door strikes Will on the shoulder as April barges outside and he tries to follow.

'Hello!' April yells.

Lauren's dad spins round. He's about to speak when recognition flashes across his face, robbing him of words.

'How the *hell* are you?' April shouts. 'It's been a while.'

He holds both palms up and smirks.

'Too old for you now, am I?' she says.

'Let's calm it,' he says. 'Don't make a scene, love.'

Will stands several paces behind April.

'Get in the car if you want to talk,' Lauren's dad says.

April stands, rooted to the spot. The man looks more uneasy by the second, the bluster evaporating. He backs against his expensive car.

Slowly, April turns, eyeing the alpine garden that frames the Smugglers frontage. She saunters over, wiggling a small boulder free from the rockery. Clods of mud drop from it as she approaches Lauren's dad.

'Jesus fucking Christ,' he says. 'What are you . . .?'

Will dashes ahead of April, blocking her path. He's got a clear foot of height on her but still she barges him away like he's not there.

'My battle,' she snaps. 'Not yours.'

Lauren's dad bolts, lurching into the road. A car slams on its brakes and honks as he flaps to stay on his feet.

'What are you doing?' Will shouts. He is ignored.

The rock comes down on the windscreen of the Mercedes, the crazed glass bowing inwards. The side windows are next, popping into millions of green cubes like gemstones, glittering over the soft leather seats.

Lauren's dad watches from the central reservation, his expression torn between fury and resignation. A crowd has assembled along the front. Cars crawl past. No one intervenes.

'Gonna stop me?' April yells at him. He looks out to sea. 'Not so keen to get your dirty hands all over me now?'

The wing mirrors explode as they are propelled downwards, their entrails of fine wiring hanging in their wake, as the Mercedes becomes a steel drum, a metallic beat ringing out as panels are reshaped and shucked of special-order paint.

It's many minutes before April's energy starts to wane. Only then does Will dare to step closer. A siren howls in the distance, but seems to be getting worryingly closer.

'You OK?' Will says.

She glares at him. The colour is back in her face. 'I'm OK.'

'Sure?'

'I'm fucking angry.'

'Yeah, it's . . .'

'I'm fucking *angry*. At last.'

The buildings along the seafront flicker blue as a patrol car slows.

'Go home, Will,' April says firmly.

'Don't want to leave –'

'I'm fine, Will.'

'You're not.'

'That's where you're wrong, Will.' Her grin is wicked, but it's real. 'I'm great. I'm going to finish this. Finish it alone.'

She looks around and the assembled crowd feign disinterest. Laying the rock on the ground she walks towards the police car.

She turns and blows him a kiss. 'Night, Will,' she shouts. 'Get back to those decks, yeah?'

Today.

The End

It's a Friday lunchtime, late November. The forecast promises snow, but right now the skies are summer blue, the cold biting all the harder in the dazzle of the sun. Will Parks, having missed this morning's lessons, arrives at the gates of ECS. He didn't ride the bus in today. It's been a morning of tears and he needed the long walk, a chance to set aside the sorrow of what's going on at home and shift into the right mindset for this biggest of days.

He took the route across the marshes, beside the railway and beneath the tree where Alfie so nearly took his own life; along the front at Ebbswick, where saltwater swirls above the high tide and sprays the road surface white; past the Martello tower where it all began with April, where they finally got it together for one perfect moment. And now he stands outside his school. That fizzing inside him would once have been dread, but today it's excitement. Ridiculous as it seems to him, there is nowhere – and no-*when* – he'd rather be.

These past few days, Will has been oblivious to the presence that follows him around as faithfully as it ever has. No longer does he linger in the darkroom or keep an eye out for the old pram lady. He saved Alfie. He's done.

At the main entrance he stops and grins at the floor-to-ceiling neon poster on the window. *Sold Out!* declares a recent addition to it. And right at the bottom, there is the days-to-go countdown. Today – a big, fat zero.

The plans for April's event have spiralled over the weeks, now involving kids from a number of schools and sponsorship from a dozen local businesses. It's not just a disco, not even a rave – it's a festival in miniature. The current total stands at over eight grand, raised for the campaign to save the library, more than triple what they'd aimed for.

Will is ushered out of the way by two guys wheeling a trolley of lighting equipment into reception and onward to the school hall. Behind him, a catering firm's van pulls up. He stands at the door and thinks how, when he leaves this building tonight, he'll have done it: become the sort of person who can stand up in front of a crowd, hold their attention and *perform*.

He takes a lungful of icy air and heads for the hall.

'Good of you to show your face, Parks,' Kris Tring says. He stands back from the stage backdrop he's been painting for days, adding the finishing touches with aerosols of car paint. 'Some of us have been here since the crack of dawn.'

'Long story,' Will says, suppressing the ache of sorrow that'll take over him again if he lets himself dwell on it. 'Much rather have been here.'

He scans the unrecognizable space and the hive of activity it's become. A team of year elevens hang heavy black drapes over the walls. Comically oversized disco balls sway overhead. A couple of volunteers work atop a scaffolding tower, assembling lighting rigs. 'Loving the mural. What is that, Glastonbury?'

Kris winces. Over his trademark drainpipes and rollneck, he's wearing a knee-length beige-leather jacket, which he's rolled to the elbows. 'Inspired by Jean-Michel Jarre's concerts in Berlin.'

'Jean-Michel who?'

'Only the godfather of electronic music, Parks. The King of Synth.'

'Right. You been to Berlin?'

'Have *I* been to Berlin? Have I been to Berlin, he asks me. Let me tell you about Berlin . . .'

April hurries over in their direction. She glares at Will, doing a throat-cutting gesture. 'Don't mention Berlin!' she stage-whispers through grinning teeth.

Kris mutters something and returns to assessing his work at ever more oblique angles.

'The place looks amazing,' Will says.

'So much still to do,' April says. They stop metres apart. Will swings his arms back and forth. She scuffs a foot in circles on the floor. April is a hugger, ordinarily. The fact bothers Will until it dawns on him that not being hugged is probably more significant than being hugged.

'What do you want me to do for you?'

There's a flash of wickedness in her eyes.

Will's face feels hot. 'What needs doing, I mean? Round here? Sorry. Sorry.'

'Let's pack it in with that word, yeah?'

'What word?'

'*Sorry.*'

'Shit. Sorry.'

April starts giggling.

'Sorry,' Will says again.

April takes a couple of steps towards him. 'Can you believe I had the police called on me?'

Will closes the gap so they're almost touching. 'Yes, I can believe that. What with a six-figure car being trashed and all.'

'You make it sound so . . . *vandalistic*. I *remodelled* it, that's all. In some circles it would be considered art.'

'It was certainly a thing of beauty.'

'Why, thank you.'

'Did the police think it was art?'

'Not so much.'

'Are you in trouble?'

'Would you believe it if I told you the car's owner didn't want to press charges?'

'How very strange.'

'Curious, indeed.'

She checks that no one's earwigging. 'You said something interesting, a while back.'

'Did I?'

'That time we watched the sunrise on the Martello tower. Remember?'

Will grins. 'Hmmm. *Vaguely.*'

She punches his arm. 'You asked me if I said no. To *him*. I've been thinking about that question a lot.'

'You said you didn't.'

'Yup. I didn't say no.'

'Right.'

'But I never said yes.'

'OK.'

'And I've only recently realized that.'

Will reaches out for her hand. She locks her fingers with his.

'I think I've been hard on myself, Will.'

'That's a fucking understatement.'

'It's time to move on.' She nods as she says it. A Magician's Nod. 'Things are gonna be different now,' she says.

'Different?'

She puts both of her hands round Will's. 'Better. Much better.'

'Right. Great.'

'You know something else?' she says, barely above a whisper. 'People *know*. At ECS. They know why I left my lovely expensive school.'

'How?'

'I dunno. Rumours get around, I guess.'

'Yeah, well, if I hear anyone saying anything . . .'

'Thanks, Will. Means a lot.' April suppresses a laugh. 'But here's the thing – no one really *cares*, Will. All this time I've been shitting myself about being outed. Turns out, people couldn't give a toss.'

'This is ECS. Everyone's life is complicated round here.'

'Yup.' She grins. 'My kinda place!'

'I'm happy you're here.'

They stare deeply into each other, both of them perfectly still.

'Fuck, Will,' April snaps, breaking away. 'Been so wrapped up in my own stupid world, I forgot to ask. Your nain. How was she this morning?'

'Yeah, so she's not really . . . Just trying not to think about –'

'Sorry to interrupt,' a reedy male voice says. It's Mr Leavers, music teacher. 'There's some gentlemen here with a bouncy castle.'

'Right, yes,' April says, ruffling her already dishevelled hair. 'In the quad, I guess.'

'Bouncy castle?' Will says.

'They were supplying the inflatables and asked if we wanted it.'

'Cool!'

'It's got a bit out of hand, I know.'

'It's fantastic.'

'I was just thinking, like, Boomtown Fair meets Burning Man, you know?'

Will nods. He doesn't know.

'So I'll tell them to put it outside in the quad, yes?' Mr Leavers interjects.

'Please,' April says. 'Like, touching the doors, so you step out of the hall straight on to it. We've got some propane heaters coming for outside.'

'What's Leavers doing getting involved?' Will asks, as the rather squat music teacher scurries off.

'Got told I had to have some staff supervision.'

'And you chose *him*?'

'God, no! Ms Simon offered, actually.'

'Aha! Of course.' Will scans the hall, spotting her nursing a coffee mug in the corner as she supervises the unrolling of a length of fake grass. 'And there she is. Either that or some more inflatables have turned up.'

'Fucking massive, aren't they? She must have a permanent backache.'

'Small price to pay.'

'Come on, Will. What would you even do with them? Are boys actually into that?'

'Not really,' Will says, his memory briefly alighting on just how much time was spent in his bathroom during year ten, replaying Ms Simon's English lessons in forensic detail. 'She's doing it for Mr Leavers, though.'

'One of the great mysteries of the modern world. I mean, I hate all that out-of-their-league shit. But Leavers and Ms Simon?'

The two teachers have been attracting attention throughout this term. She's a twenty-something bombshell in stiletto ankle boots; he's unhappily married and late-thirties with the sort of symmetrical haircut a well-meaning parent gives their toddler. They're always together when supervising break times, or else Ms Simon is to be seen poured against the piano, gazing into Leavers' eyes as he rattles off a Lloyd-Webber number. It's no surprise the pair have turned up to supervise today, an otherwise deserted building soon to be at their disposal.

'Maybe he's got a whopper,' Will says to April.

'Maybe it's made of chocolate and he jizzes shoes.'

Mr Leavers gives them both a wave when he spots them looking over. They both fall about laughing.

'Not there!' April shouts out, strutting over to the double doors into the quad.

On either side of the stage, a stack of PA speakers has appeared. A guy in an Ebbswick Sound & Light T-shirt wires them. It feels unreal to Will that in six hours this hall will be packed out with close on a thousand kids. And, at some point during the evening, he'll be DJing for them. Sure, there's other people sharing the gig, but he's doing the proper nineties rave stuff, mixed live on vinyl – the music the whole event's been built around. He watches as a bass bin the size of a water butt is extracted from its flight case. And it's going to be loud. Very loud indeed.

'Thanks,' Will says to the guy, 'for, you know, offering to support this.'

The man grabs a reel of cable off his shoulder. 'Don't thank me. Management's decision. Something for the community. I'm just the lackey.'

'It's good of you, whatever. This is awesome kit.'

'This old shite? Hardly. They ain't lending you the good stuff for free.'

'Bet it sounds good, though.'

'Oh, it'll sound OK. Too old to be rented out, mind. They'll probably bin the lot when you're done with it.' He points at a red sticker on the amplifier he's wiring. 'See?'

Portable Appliance Test: Fail, it says. *Do Not Use.*

'And that was, what –' he studies the label up close – 'four years ago?'

'Works OK, though?' Will asks.

'Tried it all out this morning. Half of it's been in the back of a shipping container since fuck knows when, see.'

Will looks across the hall at April, running around, getting everything just so. 'It's not gonna pack up halfway through the night, is it? Be a total disaster if it does.'

'It'll be fine. These tests are fussy. Nanny state, innit? Besides, size of this system, if anything packs up, just turn the stuff that still works up a bit. Be sweet.' He thumps a heavy palm on the speaker cab. 'Vintage!'

The word puts Will instantly at ease.

'It really is starting to look like a festival,' Kris Tring says, taking a break from fiddling with his backdrop. He sits with his legs over the front of the stage. 'I had my reservations, I must admit.'

'She's incredible.'

'Bless.'

'I mean she's done an incredible job.'

'Just need a massive bag of pills to sell the kiddies and we'll have completed the effect.'

Will laughs vaguely, his eyes not leaving April as she stands on a chair, directing various caterers outside in the quad.

'Shame Alfie isn't around. He'd serve up to a bunch of twelve-year-olds without a second thought.'

Will spins round. 'What are you saying?'

'Drug dealer, wasn't he?' Kris's assured demeanour looks shaken.

'Don't talk about what you don't understand, please,' Will says. He's surprised by his own tone of authority. It's new.

'Sorry. He was your mate, I know.'

'*Is* my mate.'

'Sure, sure. Any idea how he's doing? In *that* place?'

'You mean hospital?'

'Yeah, yeah. Facility, whatever.'

'He's fine, Kris. He's doing fine.'

'Good to know,' Kris Tring says, slinking back to his artwork.

Will heard nothing from Alfie in the days after he was taken away in that ambulance. He walked up and down Patten's Island daily, surveying the Lim family's bungalow on each pass, but Alfie hadn't made it home. He sent messages, but none were delivered, Will unaware that

Alfie's iPhone lay atomized in an embankment, having been obliterated by an express train.

But yesterday, Will had a text from an unknown number. Alfie was just saying hi and apologizing for not being around. He's an inpatient now at a psychiatric unit. It's over a hundred miles away, so visiting is out of the question, but Will managed to talk him into FaceTiming.

Will wasn't sure what he'd been expecting, but he was surprised when Alfie looked entirely normal. It was awkward at first – listing off what he'd been up to, while Alfie listened and nodded along politely.

'I don't have to be here,' Alfie said, when a lull in Will's monologue became too uncomfortable.

'Oh, OK. That's good.'

'No, seriously, Parks. That's not the delusion of a mental patient.'

'I didn't think –'

'But you did, though. You thought, *Whatever you say, crazy bloke. I'll just play along in case you get upset.*' Alfie grinned and it was like curtains being flung open on a bright morning. '*Don't let him get wound up*, you're thinking. *Someone'll have to stick an injection up his arse and it'll be all my fault.*'

'Yeah, OK, maybe I . . . sorry.'

'S'fine. What I'm saying is, I'm not sectioned.'

'So why are you there?'

'That's the point, Parks. That's what I need you to know.' He looked straight into his webcam, voice rock-steady. 'I'm here cos I don't want to die.'

Will smiled, heat in the corner of his eyes. 'You did want to.'

'I was done. Out the game.'

'I'm so sorry, mate. So sorry.'

'Don't be sorry, cuz. I fucked up. Fucked up royally.'

'We could've fixed it,' Will said.

Alfie shook his head. 'Thing is, that morning, when they found me. They put me in the ambulance and I'm just – I don't know – *cold*. Like I've been pumped full of anaesthetic, can't feel shit, don't care that I'm alive, don't care that I'm not dead. Just *nothing*.'

'You were in a bad place.'

'Sure, sure. But this weird thing happened. We park up at the hospital, round the back where the ambulances go. And the back doors are open and I'm just sitting there like a jacket spud with a sheet of fucking Bacofoil wrapped round me. And I'm on my own for a few minutes cos the paramedics are booking me in or having a fag or whatever. I'm just sat there and there's this noise. I look out the back and there's a cat taking a stroll round the yard; she's all ginger and stripy, like one of those iced biscuits. So I call this cat over and she's rolling around at the back of the ambulance, and I sit on the ledge and I'm stroking this little thing. She's bloody loving it, meowing and purring and nuzzling up against me. Eventually, she lets me pick her up and she's all warm and soft and I'm stroking her as she stamps her little paws on my lap. And then I have this weird thought.'

'Go on.'

'I start thinking to myself, *I don't want this to be the last time I ever stroke a cat.* How stupid is that?'

'Not stupid.'

Alfie swatted away a tear like it was a fly. 'And I'm thinking, if I want to be able to play with a cat again, then I must not want to die. Not really. You know?'

'Totally.'

'So they come and get me to take me into the hospital, and I'm giving this cat a hug and its fur's kinda gone spiky cos I've been crying a bit. And they take me in and they do this psychiatric assessment. The thing they keep asking is, "Do you think you'll try again, Alfie?" And you know what, Parks? I told them the truth. I told them, yes, I will again, because nothing's changed. Send me home, I'll try again. But I don't want to die, I say. And I begged them to keep me in hospital, cos I knew it was the only way.'

'I'm so pleased to hear it, mate.'

'And that's what I mean, Parks. I don't actually have to be here. I'm here cos I want to live. I'm fucking desperate to live.'

Seeing each other cry felt oddly freeing, although neither said so.

'I love you,' Will told him as he wept. A life without Alfie was unimaginable to him.

'I fucking love you too,' Alfie said, barely able to get the words out.

It was some minutes before they were able to speak again. 'Are you getting on OK there?' Will eventually asked.

'Working through stuff. They're helping me get my shit in order. Gonna repeat the year at school, I've decided. One less thing to stress on.'

'Great idea.'

'Not gonna miss your old mate, cuz?'

'Got a feeling we'll be best mates whether or not we're in the same year at school.'

'Yeah, I got that feeling too. And I owe a lot of fucking money, Parks. Pay-day loans, credit cards and shit.'

'How do we fix that?'

'*We!* I like it, Parks! You're a great man. I've already sorted it, though.'

'What you done?'

'Owned up to it. It's all in my mum's name. And if it's fraud, the lender writes it off, see? Serves them fucking right for sending out so many application forms, making it so fucking *easy*.'

'And what happens to you?'

'Yeah, don't sweat. Court date, criminal record, community sentence maybe.'

'Shit.'

'Scrubbing graffiti off walls and mowing a few lawns? Do me good, Parks!'

'Guess so.'

'The people here, they're gonna help me with . . .' Alfie looked uncomfortable for the first time. 'With my enthusiasm for the gear.'

'Addiction?'

'Yeah, that's what they call it.'

'No shame in it, mate.'

'They say that as well. You should come and work here. You'd be good at it.'

'You're doing great. You'll be fine.'

'I *will* be fine, cuz. I promise. Just everything got on top of me, you know? I needed to, like, step off the world. To stop time, you know? So I could work things through.'

'I know.'

'And I thought I couldn't step off. But it turns out I can.' He smirked. 'And in such plush surroundings, too.' He lifted his laptop so Will could see around the ward: the barred windows, the Perspex-protected telly, the plastic plates and cups.

'You got a piano, though.'

'Yeah. Some old woman donated it, I'm told. Maybe I'll learn to play while I'm here.'

'You should.'

'Fuck me, man,' Alfie said. 'Am I glad they found me that morning.'

'Defo.'

'Anonymous call, apparently. Someone saw me acting strangely!'

'How unusual.'

'That's what I thought. Wish I knew who to thank, though.'

Will shrugged.

Are you a hero if no one knows what you did?

'Saved my fucking life,' Alfie said, his voice wobbling.

Will smiled as they brought the call to an end.

Yes, perhaps you are.

It will happen today. I can *feel* it.

And yet, at this eleventh hour, I still don't know what's coming.

When this began, I could see weeks ahead. It became just days. My foresight is now measured in hours. This evening is only just starting to come into clear view.

But this day *is* familiar to me. I lived it just hours ago, of course, even though it feels so very, very distant. And as I follow you, knowing now that I *was* you, my memory of this day is coming back.

Very shortly I will know *exactly* what happened to me – what is soon going to happen to you.

I have a plan for getting the message across when the time comes. Everything is in place. As soon as I discover what I need to know, I'll get the information to you.

You'll see.

Be waiting for me.

On a Promise

'You got this, Will,' April says, standing in front of the stage holding two ice-cream cones.

Will lays a hand on one of the turntables. 'Sure. Cometh the hour, as they say.'

'That's the spirit.' She bounds up the wooden steps. 'Pistachio or honeycomb?'

'You choose.'

April offers him the pistachio but not before she's gouged out a chunk with the tip of her tongue. Will has no appetite but gets stuck in anyway. *You know it's gone on too long,* he muses to himself, *when sharing an ice cream is a turn-on.*

'Cool idea, the stall.' Will gives a thumbs up to the guy manning the timber pop-up in the far corner with *Gelato* across the top in pink and blue letters. He feels his phone vibrate in his pocket and discreetly looks at the screen.

Danny.

It's the third call he's ignored in the last hour. Not a word has been said between them since the Temple Arms. Will's not about to distract himself from this big day by having another row with him now.

'I've gone too far, haven't I?' April says. 'I think I've been enjoying the distraction a bit too much, and totally fucking overdone it. Is everyone just gonna laugh at me?'

'It's incredible,' Will says. '*You're* incredible.'

She reddens and sticks out a honeycomby tongue at him. 'Are the decks OK?'

Will looks over the pair of Technics turntables, the CDJs, the Pioneer mixer, the pair of Sennheisers.

'Literally never used equipment this good before.' He wiggles the fader from side to side. 'Shit, I've never *touched* equipment this good before.'

'Glad I got that right, at least,' April says, looking pleased.

It's gone four now and it's nearly dark outside. The event's due to start at seven but right now the school is almost empty. April's team of helpers have gone home, just a handful of sixth-formers here now. Outside in the quad there's a barbecue being set up, a smoothie factory, the multi-room bouncy castle, a chill-out room of al-fresco sofas. The temperature is dropping ever closer to zero; there are space heaters dotted every few metres and a wall of spare gas cylinders just outside the hall doors. There's a howling noise from beneath the stage and a cloud of smoke jets into the open space, dissipating and fogging the entire room.

'Check this out,' Kris Tring shouts from somewhere in the wings. Coloured laser beams scythe through the white smoke. Even with the main lights switched on, it looks spectacular. 'Now that's what I'm talking about!' He emerges on to the stage, arms outstretched like a classical conductor expecting applause.

'Lovely work, Kris,' April says.

'Solved the smoke issues, then?' Will asks.

'Got there eventually,' Kris says, waving a roll of gaffer tape.

Will looks above the stage, able to make out a taped-up smoke detector above them. Kris's work this afternoon has been dogged by triggering the fire alarm.

'Had to cover up all four,' Kris says, pointing around the hall through the murk.

'Is that a good idea?' Will asks with a smile.

'Covering smoke detectors? If you want a smoke machine, it's a bloody brilliant idea.'

'True enough.'

'Had to wait for Simon and Leavers to clear off, though. Not sure they'd sanction the health and safety breach.'

'I wonder where they are.'

'Cleaning cupboard's my guess,' Kris says.

'Darkroom, I reckon,' April shouts. 'Which reminds me . . .' She retrieves a cool bag from the pile of coats behind the stage. 'While we're unsupervised.' She tears the foil from the neck of the champagne bottle, launching the cork across the hall. 'Why let the kiddies have all the fun?'

She pours a plastic tumbler for Will and Kris, and for a couple of other sixth-formers nearby. 'Bottoms up, peeps,' she says, swigging straight from the bottle. 'Here's to a successful evening. Let's set this place on *fire*!'

Bubbles singe Will's nose as he takes a gulp. He's no fan of champagne, but today it tastes different: ice cold and delicious. 'Three cheers for this one,' he shouts, prodding April and giggling as foam trickles off his chin.

He feels a buzzing in his pocket and glances down just long enough to see it's Danny again. *FUCKING CALL ME*, the text says. Just reading those three words feels like a perfect song on the radio being interrupted by an advert.

'No,' Will mumbles, returning his full attention to this moment.

'Shit, hide the booze!' April says over the last of her three cheers.

'Too late,' Ms Calloway says, cool perfumed air fanned across the stage by her long skirt as she strides towards them. 'But worry not – I won't tell.'

'Would you like a swig, Miss?' April asks.

'Very kind, but no thanks.'

'You hanging about? You could do a DJ set with Will.' April makes scratching noises on a turntable. Her voice is unusually loud after necking a third of the bottle.

'Wish I could,' Ms Calloway says. 'I have a weekend away with my wife. Christmas shopping. Although I don't like the look of this weather.' She glances towards the quad, where snow has begun to fall, settling on the awnings of the food outlets and the giant bouncy castle. 'Long train ride ahead, I fear.'

'Shame,' April says, burping into the back of her hand.

'Just wanted to wish you all well for tonight. What a fantastic job you've done.' She studies Kris Tring's mural. 'Berlin?'

'Thank you!' Kris says. 'Yes, Berlin.' He looks smugly at Will and April.

Ms Calloway grins. 'Make sure you get lots of pictures. Event of a generation, this is.'

'Already on it,' Kris says, grabbing his giant Nikon, flashgun and long lens attached.

'And you, Will? Your work's always so good. So *evocative*.'

'Probably won't get a chance tonight,' Will says. 'Kris'll have it covered.'

In truth, Will's not been taking many photos of late. He often leaves the house without his camera, which he never used to do. It's not that he's lost interest; he just seems a bit too busy to think to take pictures of things.

'You must keep on shooting, Will. Don't think I haven't noticed your absence from the darkroom this past week or so.'

'Will do.'

She holds his stare. 'And everything's OK, yes?'

'Absolutely fine.'

'I assumed they must be. As I haven't seen you.'

'No worries at all,' Will says dismissively, keen to avoid having to explain to April what Ms Calloway is talking about.

'Right. Right.'

'Hope you have a lovely weekend away, Miss.'

Her expression doesn't appear to register what he's said. 'I think you should stay vigilant, Will.'

April is not far behind Calloway, doing something on her phone. 'Of course,' he says.

Ms Calloway stares vacantly past him. 'Stay open-minded, Will. I think that's important.' She looks uneasy, like she can't quite lay her hands on the right words. 'I have a sense . . . that now's not the time to . . . *relax* is the wrong word . . . stop being *aware*.'

'Understood,' Will says breezily. 'I'll stay vigilant.'

'Do. I'm sure you'll be fine.' She shakes away her serious demeanour. 'I must be making a move.'

'You know what?' April says after Ms Calloway has left. 'I think she might have a bit of a thing for you, Will Parks.'

'She's just looking out for me.'

'So I see.'

'It's nothing weird,' Will lies. 'Just stuff we used to talk about. She got a bit of a vibe about something.'

'Your aura was the wrong colour? Chakra eye in the wrong place?'

'Don't take the piss. Doesn't matter now, anyway. It's all sorted.'

There's yet another vibration in Will's pocket and he snatches a glance at the screen.

'Someone's keen to get hold of you,' April says.

'Just my darling brother. He can wait.'

'Ah, yes. Danny. So . . .'

'Is there something I should know?' Will's heartbeat quickens.

'Had a chat with him this morning.'

'Right.' The gas from the champagne makes him feel bloated.

'Hadn't spoken to him in a while till today, actually.'

Will's sure his relief is obvious.

'I mean, his charming booty calls have continued unabated, of course. Almost nightly, in fact.'

'Of course,' Will echoes.

'Together with the insults when I ignore him.'

'Prick.'

'Well, quite. But I *have* been ignoring him, Will. I've not been back there, since . . .'

'None of my business.'

April eyes him suspiciously. 'So it isn't, Will Parks.'

Will notices his hands have begun to shake.

'And today,' April says, 'I decided I was done with his shit. So I rang him.'

'What for?'

'I told him, Will, to leave me alone. That I've no wish to see or hear from him ever again.'

'Why today? What changed?'

She takes a deep breath. 'Because there's someone else, Will.'

Will's face is burning. 'Oh, OK.' He does his best to look unfussed, even though it feels like his internal organs have been steamrollered. 'How did he take it?'

'He wanted to know everything about this new guy, like he'd lost some sort of competition. Keeps asking, "Have you fucked him yet? How big's his dick?"'

'Have you?' Will's voice wobbles. 'You know . . .?'

April grins. 'I told him I haven't yet. But that I think I'd like to. That maybe it's gonna happen soon. Like, very soon.'

'Cool.'

'Yeah, he didn't like it.'

Will stares at April. She's perched on the edge of the DJ table. She's kicked off her shoes, black tights covering her feet. Her hair's all over the place. There's an empty champagne bottle in her hand, her cheeks flushed from the booze. She's the most perfect sight Will's ever seen. 'Who is it?' he asks.

'Fucking hell, Will! Keep up!'

'How d'you mean?'

'You, Will! Obviously, *you*, you total dick!'

'Really?'

'Sorry – assuming you'll still have me.'

'Fuck. Thought you were talking about someone else.'

'I know. I was enjoying it.'

'Bastard. That was awful. Like, an actual nightmare.'

'Do you reckon we can just forget *that night* ever happened?' April asks, putting her arms round him.

'Definitely,' Will says. He feels her hands on his hips, a touch that he's yearned so hard for these past weeks that it's caused physical pain. 'Though maybe I don't want to forget *all* of that night.'

'True.'

'I'm so . . .' Will braces against the urge to cry.

'I've missed this, Will. *Us*.'

'Same,' Will says, forcing the word out.

'Think I've made sense of a few things.'

'How d'you mean?'

April breaks the eye contact. 'Maybe there comes a time when we start to see what *love* looks like. And when we do, we see everything that came before for what it really was. Does that sound a bit . . . cheesy?'

Will shakes his head. They're pressed against each other now, so they both feel it when Will's phone vibrates again. 'Did you tell Danny it was me?'

'Maybe he's worked it out,' April whispers centimetres from Will's face. Her hot breath is sweet with the champagne. 'He can do one.'

'Right. So, were you serious, you know, about what you said? About wanting to, you know, with this new guy?'

April sniggers awkwardly and doesn't look Will in the eye. 'If that's what he wants.'

Will leans forward till their lips meet.

'Oh get a fucking room, you two,' Kris says, stamping across the stage. 'Leavers and Simon can point you in the right direction, I'm sure.'

'Patience,' April whispers, pecking Will on the lips. 'Let's get this done, and we'll have all the time in the world tonight.'

Will reluctantly takes his hands off her. 'Can't wait.'

Once again, the spell is broken by his phone demanding attention.

A worrying thought occurs to him: maybe Danny's got urgent news about Nain. He reads the text that just landed.

Stop fucking ignoring me.

No. Clearly he's just spoiling for a fight.

Mum would call, he thinks. *If it was Nain, Mum would let me know.*

Standing alone with no one needing his help, Will dwells on his visit to Nain first thing. Pumped full of morphine and muscle relaxants and God knows what else, she was still fighting on.

She's been unconscious for a week now, but Will was sure he could feel the tension in her as he held her hand, winter sun bathing them. He didn't dare ask the nurses for a time frame, knowing too well she's outlived their predictions already.

He talked to her about school and photography and books – don't they say hearing's the last thing to go? – and told her about the disco, how he was playing tonight. He mused aloud that perhaps he should be here today, instead of there, a sense of duty gripping him. As much as he told himself it was his imagination, he was certain he felt Nain's arm flinch at the very suggestion.

'OK, OK,' he said with a smile, knowing he was attributing a signal to someone who'd long lost the ability. 'I'll go. Let me sit here a little longer, though. Promise I'll bugger off soon.'

I've been petrified of this for years, Will thought as he held her cool hand in that hot room. *And now it's here.*

And I'm not scared. Not like I should be.

He realized that what he's been feeling in recent days, that ache in his middle, isn't sorrow. It's guilt. It's guilt that this isn't killing him like it surely should be. He's guilty because he shouldn't be able to deal with this. But he can.

He could see now how he's spent these past few years desperate to cling on to the things that had made being a child so perfect: happily married parents, the joy of being home, the adoration of grandparents. And he's watched as, bit by bit, it's all been taken away. Order to chaos. Happiness to misery.

Will thought about these last few months since that night he met April in Danny's car. Somewhere along the way, he forgot to hold himself back, forgot to limit himself with the belief that all the good things he'll ever experience have already happened to him.

Happiness, he has begun to realize, is not this precarious thing. It is not an imposter, destined to be rooted out and crushed. It is not a stepping stone to inevitable misery. Happiness to misery; order to chaos. Like all rules of nature, they are based only on the evidence so far gathered.

Will wiped his damp eyes and looked up at the time. He'd been there well over an hour. Having promised April he'd be at school by lunchtime to set up, he needed to get moving.

He leaned over and kissed his nain's forehead. 'Gotta run,' he whispered. 'Back soon.'

More than ever, he could sense that tension in Nain, the clinging on to life. The fight.

Will stopped himself halfway to the door.

This isn't fair, he thought. *I'm not being fair to her.*

The top of her head was hot against his face. Her downy white hair tickled his cheeks.

'When you're ready,' he whispered, 'you must go. Please, Nain.'

Did he imagine that noise from her, the shift in her breathing?

Will hugged her harder and breathed in that happy smell that still clung to her. 'It's OK to go,' he said. 'We'll be all right.'

She seemed even more rigid beneath him. Defiant.

'It's OK, Nain. It's OK.'

He stepped out of the hospital into the freezing air feeling older, and curiously lighter, than when he'd arrived.

Armed with his bag of records, Will began the long walk to school.

She holds on for me. We are in contact.

She'll go nowhere till you and I have done what we have to. This she has promised.

I can so nearly see everything now.

And she tells me she is ready.

Disco Inferno

'That is a *lot* of kids,' April says.

She, Will and Kris Tring are in the foyer between the school hall and the outside. 'This is nuts! I can't even see the end of the queue.'

'Stretches clean out the gates,' Will says. He feels a spritz of goose pimples at how successful the publicity has been. 'Looks like Ebbswick's gonna be getting itself a new library.'

April high-fives him.

'How many tickets you sold?' Kris asks.

'Seven hundred and something, across all the schools. Eight hundred maybe.'

Will looks outside again at the snaking line. Kids swig from passed-around bottles that probably don't contain what the label says. Snowballs cannon up and down the queue. It's hard to imagine they'll all fit inside.

'Everyone ready?' April shouts to the sixth-form volunteers around the hall.

Mr Leavers checks his watch and nods authoritatively to Ms Simon. They reappeared half an hour ago, having been 'missing, presumed shagging', as April put it, for the bulk of the afternoon.

As they file in, Will is surprised by the effort the kids have made – neon stockings and eye shadow, Keith Flint mohawks and fluorescent framed shades. Every one of them looks blown away as they round the corner, past the enormous inflatable baubles and into the dark, smoke-filled hall. A year eleven girl kicks off the first DJ set of the night – chart stuff together with a bit of *Saturday Night Fever* era disco. The volume is staggering, with the sort of bass that rumbles around inside your chest.

Will works the door with Kris till even the foyer is jam-packed with bodies. And still they come. A poster on the door invites attendees to surrender knives, alcohol, cigarettes, lighters and illegal substances. Will has so far amassed an empty packet of Superkings, some spent laughing gas capsules, a snowball the size of a basketball, and a Smirnoff bottle that someone appears to have been sick into.

'Who's got some more old shit for me?' he shouts into the crowd.

The place looks more like an Ibiza superclub than a school hall. If Will had been expecting a disco with a void down the middle of the room separating boys and girls, he would have been mistaken. Under the darkness and darting UV lights, these kids have forgotten their inhibitions. Will's almost jealous of them as he squeezes through the crowd like he's chest-deep in the sea. It's not yet eight, but already a boy in a highlighter-green singlet and a girl in pop socks are snogging aggressively against the wall. The hand in each other's pants seems inappropriate to Will but he doesn't feel qualified to intervene. So what that these thirteen-year-olds are more sexually experienced than him? He hopes to have overtaken them by the end of the evening.

'This is ace!' Will yells when he eventually locates April.

She's standing next to the stage beside a five-metre-high billowing flame graphic that appears to be made from the sort of shell suit material that you're not allowed to wear at firework parties. She looks stressed, doling out orders as best she can over the music.

'Be glad when it's over,' she shouts at him.

'So will I,' Will says, grinning, but she doesn't hear.

'Can't find Leavers or Simon.'

'*Quelle surprise!*' Will says, realizing he can't shout in a French accent.

'Yeah, well I need them. Kids smoking up in the staff car park.'

'Just ciggies?'

'Weed. Can't leave it, Will. We're supposed to be keeping some sort of order here.'

'Want m

'Would

'Bunch of stoned children? Think I'll manage.' He's far from certain he will, but darts off regardless.

In the cool and relative quiet of the corridor, it occurs to him that his phone has been vibrating non-stop. 'Later,' he snaps, seeing the missed call total from Danny now stands at twenty-eight. Not to mention the scores of unread texts.

The snow creaks under Will's feet but the group of six pay no attention to his approach. They stand in a tight circle, wearing baseball caps or with hoods pulled forward. Snowflakes settle on the backs of their heads. None of them – four boys, two girls – look to have reached puberty. The sweet bonfirey smell reminds him of the inside of Alfie's car and he enjoys the memory.

Twenty metres away, a group of older teens climb over the perimeter fence, dashing across the grounds towards the building. More gatecrashers emerge from behind the sports hall. Will thinks better of intervening, focusing his attention on the smokers.

'Sorry, guys,' Will says.

There are sniggers from the group. 'Why, what you done?' a girl asks.

'Come on, this is obviously against the rules.'

'Call the police, then,' an unbroken male voice says, breaking into a giggle halfway through.

'Want a toke, bruv?' asks another.

A curl of dense smoke passes Will's face. It puts him in mind of that crazy night on the speedboat. He actually does want a toke, not that he's about to accept the offer. Right now, he needs to be assertive, as unnatural as that may be.

'Don't rip the piss, all right. This is school property. You're well aware this is bang out of order.' The blanketed snow makes his voice seem muffled, robbing it of authority.

'Not doing no one no harm, bruv. Just smoking a bit of ting.'

Will breaks the circle open. Despite their youth, a bunch of kids like this would've scared the shit out of him a few months ago. But up close he can see them for what they are – bored children trying everything out till something makes sense. 'Take your *ting*, and piss off somewhere you can't be seen, or smelt for that matter. Understood?'

There are grunts and giggles as they reluctantly turn to leave.

They all look to their left at the sound of a revving engine. A pair of headlights at the school gates cut through the falling snow. The driver's clearly in a hurry, wheels spinning as they accelerate on the slippery ground. The car is almost level with them when Will realizes who it is. The brakes are applied, the car slewing sideways to a stop ten metres away.

'Great driving, wanker,' one of the girls says.

'Fucking hell,' Will mutters as he ushers the kids and their spliff away. 'This is all I need.'

'Lost your fucking phone?' Danny shouts, clinging to his open door as his feet slip on the icy ground. He pigeon-steps over the snow to Will, leaving his car diagonally across the car park, engine running, lights on, wipers at full chat.

'It's not a good time,' Will says.

'You're a pain in the arse, you know that?'

'If we're gonna have another fight, can we get on with it? Got things I need to do.' Will flaps his arms, palms facing Danny.

Danny takes a step backwards. 'Why would we have a fight?'

'April,' Will says. 'Guessing that's why you've got the hump.'

'April? What about her?'

'You don't fucking own her, you know.' Will leans closer and Danny shuffles backwards once more.

'Spare me, Will, yeah?' he says. 'Spare me the fucking do-gooder bit. It's fucking boring.' For an instant, he meets Will's glare. His eyes are wide and wary, breaking away within a second.

'She's not into you.'

'Yes, thank you, Will. If you want to have a go on her, be my guest. You'll wanna wash your mouth out with soap after you've been there, though.'

'Shut up, you dick.'

Danny holds up a hand. 'All right, all right. Keep your tits on.'

Is he scared? Will thinks suddenly, out of nowhere. *Scared of me kicking off?* Impossible.

'You're not here because of April?' Will asks.

'No, Will. I haven't ragged it over here, nearly crashing, like, fifty times, because of her. If you answered your fucking phone, you'd know that.'

'What's up, then? I can spare literally a minute, max.'

'It's Nain,' Danny says. He and Will lock gazes again. The red-eyed intensity in Danny's expression is not anger, as Will at first presumed.

'What's happened? Is she . . .? Fuck. Tell me what's happened, Danny.'

'Stop panicking.' Danny reaches out and grabs Will's forearm. 'She's not dead, all right.'

'What is it? What is it, then?'

'Just calm down and listen a minute, yeah?'

'I'm listening,' Will snaps. Danny glares at him and Will takes a deep breath. 'OK, OK. I'm listening.'

'I checked in on her at the hospital this afternoon, expecting her to be out of it.'

'She wasn't?'

Danny shakes his head.

'She's woken up?'

'She thought I was you. Trying to grab my wrist, all out of breath. "Wilbo! Wilbo! Listen to me," she's hissing, trying to pull me in close. I told her I'm Danny. She glares at me, saying how I have to go and get you. Hence the fucking phone calls.'

'She's awake! I thought she . . .'

'She's stronger than everyone thinks, bro.'

'Fuck. That's incredible. Do you think, like, she might be . . . pulling through this?'

'Steady on, yeah? There's more.'

'Tell me.'

'Couldn't get hold of you, obviously, so I go home. When I get there, Mum gets a call from the hospital. Nain's going fucking *berserk*. They're saying they're gonna have to up the sedation cos she's a danger to herself.'

'Jesus.'

'I take Mum up the hospital. Nain's screeching your name, Will. Trying to roll out of bed, tearing out all the wires and shit. Can't hardly recognize her – face all angry, bulging eyes, the lot. Like she's been possessed by demons. And we're telling her to calm down and she won't have it. "Where's Will?" she keeps shouting. "Where's Will?"'

'Why?'

'Fuck knows. We keep telling her you're not answering your phone. But it just makes her worse. "Find him," she's saying. "Tell Will it happens tonight. Promise you'll tell him. Tell him it's happening tonight."'

Will bites his lip. Are these the ramblings of a confused old lady, one who's close to the end? Or is it possible there's more to it?

'She said you'd understand,' Danny says. 'It's why I promised to come and find you.'

'Shit.'

'So do you? Do you understand what she means?'

'No. Well . . . I don't know. Maybe. No . . . no.'

'She wouldn't let anyone touch her till I swore to God I'd find you and give you the message.'

'Thanks. For coming to tell me.'

'Yeah, well . . .' Danny shrugs.

'Is she OK now?'

'Mum just texted. She's calmer.'

'Should I come and see her, do you think? I should, shouldn't I?'

Danny looks at the school building through the snow. 'Big night for you, this, isn't it?'

Will nods.

'Had to listen to you practising the same mixes for weeks, haven't I?'

'Sorry.'

'Look, she settled down when I promised I'd find you. Worn herself out, I expect.'

'Yeah, but if she needs –'

'Will,' Danny says, grabbing both his wrists. 'You're very good to her. But tonight you gotta do your thing, yeah? I'll let you know if there's anything else.'

'Thanks. That'd be really good.'

They look at each other in silence for a moment. Behind his brother, Will sees another group of uninvited guests scurry towards the hall.

'We cool, yeah?' Danny asks. 'You and me?'

Will nods, heat in his eyes. 'Sorry. About the other night.'

'Yeah. What was that shit all about?'

Will turns his palms outwards.

328

Again Danny flinches, eyes flitting to Will's hands. 'Out of character for you, bro,' he says.

'Sorry.'

'Yeah, well . . .'

'Won't happen again.'

'Let's get back to respecting each other, yeah?'

Will nods, even though he has no recollection of ever having been respected.

Danny reaches out and they hug weakly.

'I'll call, bro,' he says, walking gingerly back to his car, 'do me a favour and answer this time, yeah?'

You need to listen to me. One last time.

At last I can see it – what happened to me. What happens to *you*.

You have to act very, very soon. If you don't, many people will die. And you will die. I will die.

Trust me.

And listen.

Please. Listen.

Lockdown

'What the hell are we gonna do?' April shouts.

'Do we call the police?' Kris says.

'And tell them what? We've lost control of a children's disco? Not a great look.'

Will, April and Kris have convened in a storeroom behind the stage, squeezed in among the boxes of props. Outside, a grime and hip-hop set shakes the building, but in this small room they can hold a shouted conversation. Will got April's text moments after Danny drove away, ordering him to meet her here. But it's taken him ten minutes just to fight his way through the crowd from one side of the hall to the other.

'Look,' Will says, 'it's nearly nine o'clock. We're due to finish in an hour. Maybe it'll be all right.'

April shakes her head. 'It's already a proper crush out there, Will. And we don't know who all these people are. What if it all kicks off?'

Will gives an exasperated shrug. He's due on the decks in half an hour. All he wants to do now is get it over with.

'She's right,' Kris says. 'These aren't year sevens getting in. They're nearer our age. And half of them are off their faces.'

With so many gatecrashers, the hall is so heavily populated that people nearest the front are having to climb up on to the stage if they want to get out of the crowd. When Will was in among it a moment ago, forward surges kept coming like waves. Some of the kids looked like they were loving it, some looked distressed.

'How many other sixth-formers you got here?' Kris asks.

'Seven, not including us,' April says. 'Dunno where half of them are, though. Only a couple are answering my texts.'

'That's the trouble. No way we can cover every door. The bastards are opening fire exits and letting their mates in. The grounds are crawling with people trying to get in.'

The storeroom door is barged from outside, opening twenty centimetres before crashing into Will's shoulder. Will squeezes against the wall and lets Mr Leavers in.

'This is totally out of hand,' he snaps. He blinks in the fluorescent light after the smoky darkness of the stage.

'We did try looking for you,' Kris says.

'Not very hard, obviously,' Leavers says. His expression is wild. 'Hoped you might have kept a little better order than this.'

April scowls, ducking flecks of spit. 'Rather hoped we might have had a bit of assistance.'

'Well, right now Ms Simon is with one of your fellow students, manning the main entrance. More use than hiding.'

'We're not hiding. We're here to work out a plan,' April shoots back.

'Well, I've saved you the bother,' Leavers says, waving a packet of industrial-size cable ties.

'Nice!' April shouts with a grin.

'What are we doing with those?' Will asks. 'Tying up all the gatecrashers?' He inspects the fat strips of black plastic. 'They'll never escape, that's for sure.'

Leavers rocks from foot to foot like a child desperate for the toilet. 'For the doors, you twerp.' He hands a fistful to each of them. 'We need to get this place locked down. And we need to do it fast.'

'Is that a great idea?' Will asks.

'Or we'll shut the whole thing down. Want to step out on to the stage and tell this baying mob to bugger off?' He waves a cable tie. 'If it's open, zip it shut. Any questions?'

'Just one,' April says, winking at Will. 'Where did you get them from?'

Leavers shakes his head. 'They were by the lighting rig. Fitters left them. Is that relevant?' He turns his back to leave.

'Fifty-shading Simon, more like,' April shouts when he's halfway out of the door.

'Felicity Simon is a dear friend,' Leavers barks as he motors towards the stage, Will and April smirking as they follow.

Will forces himself off the stage into the mass of dancing bodies. Leavers shouts something, but even this close behind Will can't hear a word over the music. It takes all of his strength to keep any forward momentum. There are moments when his chest – level with most of these people's heads – is compressed and it's almost impossible to draw breath.

The smoke is so dense he's becoming disorientated as he wades diagonally across the room. He's soon lost sight of Leavers, who can only be a metre or two away, his vision filled instead with beams of UV light that slice through the darkness and the glowsticks which occasionally whack him in the face.

What did she mean? Will wonders, thinking about his nain's words. *'It's happening tonight.' What's she on about?*

Is this about this morning, when he said that she could go? Is that what she means? That she's going to *go* tonight?

Will feels a surge of claustrophobia, a sudden desire to be free of all these bodies holding him back, to be in free air, able to run wherever he's needed.

How could she possibly know her number's up like that? But what else could she mean? He thinks of his birthday, when she said about the library burning, days before it happened. And that note she wrote in hospital about Danny at the bowling alley, how he would have been stabbed without Will's intervention.

But all that's over with now, Will thinks. *It has to be.*

It was Alfie. Dying Alfie, getting messages across where he could.

And I listened, Will thinks. *I was aware.*

And now Alfie is OK and normality has returned. Surely?

A deep bassline pummels Will's back as he makes a final push through the crowd, catching sight of Leavers weaving up ahead. Will is passing the doors out to the quad now. The outside space, enclosed on all sides by the school building, is almost as jam-packed as the hall itself. Still the snow falls in a neon-lit flurry, but the heat of the crowd, the flaring barbecues and the propane lamps keep the ground clear. Will ploughs on through the hall, enjoying the cool breeze from the open doors. Beneath his feet, a lake of water advances across the dance floor from the melted snow in the quad.

It's over, Will thinks. *It's been over for the past week.*

Unless. *Unless* . . . Could there be any way it *wasn't* Alfie? That it was someone else?

But, in that case, why has he heard nothing since the moment Alfie was saved?

Will shakes his head. He's not been looking, of course. He's not been *expecting* any contact. Is it possible, then, that it's *not* over?

Will finally reaches the back entrance of the hall. Mr Leavers is wrestling with the double doors, a guy of about fifteen on the other side trying to force his way in. Will glances at his phone, finally in enough space to reach his pockets. No more missed calls. Whatever's going on with Nain, it's not significant enough for Danny to ring. He looks at the time; he's due on stage in under fifteen minutes. There isn't time to think about this right now.

I'll work it out, Will thinks. *As soon as this chaos is over, I'll be able to think about it. Maybe I'll talk to April; maybe she'll understand.*

'Some help!' Leavers yells.

Will jams his shoulder against the door and pushes, slamming it into its stop. Leavers wraps a cable tie between the two handles and yanks it tight, adding a couple more for good measure. 'I've already done the side doors,' Leavers shouts, crimson-faced, pointing across the hall.

Will nods and follows him into the main school corridor. A group of teens swigging from cans of Strongbow bowl past them. He shoves Leavers, pushing him to keep walking when it appears he might tackle them. 'Pointless,' Will says. 'They're already in. Let's concentrate on stopping anyone else.'

Leavers grunts and speeds up to a jog, eventually reaching the wide-open fire door at the far end. He slams it shut and cable-ties the push bar. Will heads into the school library. From the big windows he has a good view of the grounds. Groups of teens, most laden with carrier bags of booze, circle the building looking for unsecured ways in. Will hears a noise behind him. The lights are off in the room but it glows in an amber sodium light reflected from the snowy landscape. He turns to see two boys, thirteen at most, locked in an embrace. The pair of them look petrified, clearly having been involved in some intense snogging till they spotted Will.

'Anyone in there, Parks?' Leavers shouts from the doorway.

Will holds up a palm to the two boys. 'There's a bunch of blokes trying to get in down at the humanities block.'

'Right!'

'Have a nice night,' Will whispers as he steps outside and quietly closes the door. He thinks of April and himself, and how this evening will soon belong to them, too.

He follows Leavers. Together they seal off the last remaining routes into the ECS building.

'One way in,' Leavers says. 'One way out.'

Will's heart thumps as he begins the walk back to that packed-out hall. This is it now. He'll be due on stage as soon as he gets there, playing the biggest set of the event. The set that will end the night.

Will Parks' Big Moment

These are the last moments of the before, the swansong of the normal. These are the times people will talk of with fondness before the story turns to sorrow.

The hall seems quieter than it's been all night. Sure, a thousand or more people hold their hands in the air and shout themselves hoarse, but it sounds almost serene in this lull in the music. From his vantage point on the stage, Will can see the first two or three rows, no more. Everyone else is lost to the ever-thickening smoke and the orange and purple lights that strobe through it.

An anglepoise lamp glows over the decks and mixer, casting just enough light for Will to work by. His record bag is arranged in order, every mix pre-planned and practised to death. Nothing's been left to chance. He's even rehearsed how to make his performance look spontaneous: expressions of surprise when tunes complement each other neatly, a contemplative look to wear when skimming through the records for what's next.

On the left turntable, he loads Liquid's 'Sweet Harmony', a record that might be close to thirty years old but which has the sort of euphoric piano intro that'll bring any dance floor to life. On the right, in readiness for the first mix, 'On a Ragga Tip'. He's slipping on the headphones when the noise ramps up from the crowd. Next to him, April hurls aerosol-powered air horns off the stage for people to catch. She grimaces as an orchestra of klaxons strikes up.

'Donated by the hardware place,' she yells into Will's ear. 'Got a hundred of them.'

Will gives her a thumbs up, no point trying to say anything over the racket now.

Half an hour, Will thinks. *Maybe forty minutes.* Fourteen classic rave records. And then it'll be over. He'll have done the thing that's frightened him to death ever since April first suggested it.

The air horns reach a crescendo. Will turns the master volume on the mixer till it's almost on the stop. And he drops the needle on the first record.

The kids go wild. The sound system is so loud Will's eardrums feel as though they're buzzing against his brain.

Straight away, he starts cueing the next track. It's near impossible to hear the headphones but he's familiar enough with these records to get by on the little beat he can detect. The Technics turntables are a pleasure to use, reacting instantly to every tweak of the pitch control, so much easier than the tired equipment in his bedroom. These past few weeks have been plagued by nightmares of him cocking this up, of breaking into his first mix and it being a calamitous clashing of beats. Nothing sounds worse than a bad mix. It's like a drum kit falling down the stairs. And he's been worried that these kids will dismiss this music, think themselves too cool for a genre their parents might have raved in a field to. But Will needn't have worried on either point. He's nailing this, and the audience are crazy for it.

Straight away, the two tunes are synced and the fader is moved to the centre. Another huge piano intro blasts out over the beat. And, again, a chorus of air horns tears through the place.

He looks across at April. She's in a world of her own, flailing two glow sticks above her head. Her neon orange vest top rides up, a jewelled ring in her navel twinkling in the coloured lights. She's oblivious to Will's gaze, lost to the music. With his set finally under way, the dull sickness that has dogged him all day now gone, Will reflects on the last few minutes before he took to the decks.

We kissed. At last, we kissed again, Will thinks.

'Knock 'em dead, gorgeous boy,' she'd said. And it happened. She was softer, wetter, than he remembered. Her fingertips on his neck and face fizzed with static. Their bodies once again slotted so perfectly against each other, like an external force was squeezing them together. And then, her mouth against his ear, she'd said it.

'I love you.'

Her kiss, those words. Ten, maybe fifteen seconds total. But a moment in time that matters more than most years do. The sort of fleeting instant around which entire eras are built. Another reminder of the thoroughly disorderly way in which time behaves.

Grinning, with pins and needles in his guts, Will focuses on his job. One mix down, he clears the left turntable and loads another record: a white label with the words *4 o'clock in the morning* scrawled in marker. It uses an unauthorized sample of a classic love song that, when the tune drops, it seems some of these young people are familiar with. Less than a minute of that before he's in the mix again, into The Prodigy's 'No Good'. Still no cock-ups, still no sign these kids aren't loving every minute.

But something's creeping up on Will. Unease. Doubt. Realization that this is going well. *Too* well. These past months may have changed Will, but no such transformation leaves someone totally different from how they once were. And so, still there's a part of Will that greets success as if it's only a visitor. Things can't go *this* well. And if they do, that success exists only to put you in a dangerous position, from which you can only go one way. Like everything in the universe: from order to chaos. He knows he should just enjoy this moment, savour it. But as the moments pass, it becomes harder and harder. It's all too precariously perfect. Such worries seem hardwired into Will's DNA.

With utter concentration, he brings in the next mix. Despite his faltering confidence, it's spot on again, hours of practice paying off. Next record on to the deck. Nearly halfway now.

The smoke is so thick Will can't see the front row. Can no longer see April, just a few metres from him. The rigs of bright lights suspended from the ceiling have no definition now, instead just diffusing into the dense atmosphere. When Will looks up from the decks, his vision is blanketed by one colour at a time, like he's facing the sun with closed eyes.

The sheer volume, so stirring to begin with, has beaten his eardrums into retreat. As the minutes pass, it becomes more and more of a muddy throb. His next mix might be in, or it might not; he's fast losing the ability to tell. Although, if Will can't hear the details, surely this crowd can't either. If he could see even a single one of them, he might be able to judge a reaction.

Will feels oddly alone now. He knows he's in a building with a thousand other souls, but what good is that if you can't see those people, can't hear them, or touch them? He has a sense of becoming exposed, of everything that exists to protect him being stripped away. Like he's standing on the very edge of a cliff. One tiny push and he's going over.

Visibility is so poor he has to use the torch on his phone to see what he's doing. His next mix, the hardest yet, Will keeps as short as possible. Just a couple of bars of overlapping beats before slamming the fader to one side.

It's as though he's no longer quite within himself, as if he floats a few centimetres off the stage, hovering in this dazzling fog. It's not dissimilar to how he felt in the darkroom, except now his senses are muted through overload rather than deprivation.

A sense of impending doom. He's heard people use that expression. And that is how he feels. He very definitely senses impending doom.

It's happening tonight.

Nain's words come back to him now.

Tell Will it happens tonight.

A certain clarity comes to his thoughts now, as if the peripheral worries of the day are shed, leaving behind just the stuff that matters.

Ms Calloway. How concerned she looked this afternoon.

Stay vigilant . . . Now's not the time to stop being aware.

Why would she say that?

The black smoke licks orange and red.

His mixes are becoming an afterthought now, he's only thinking to cue the next record each time the current track reaches its outro. He flicks hastily to Josh Wink's 'Higher State of Consciousness'.

He can't hear the voice, but Will's aware of something. Of someone. A *presence*. Less clear than that night on the boat, much less clear than it was in the darkroom. But still, there's something. Up above him. In the lights and the smoke. The song reaches its climax, synth screaming through the place.

He can smell something. At first he thinks it's barbecue smoke. But it's too synthetic. Like hot plastic. Like overworked electrics.

The song has almost ended before Will has thought to mix the next. He doesn't bother bringing the two records into sync, just switches from one to the other.

He thinks of the ropey amplifiers they've been loaned, working flat out for hours. The taped-up smoke detectors. The meltwater spilling in from outside, soaking the tangles of cabling all over the place. The wall of gas bottles in the quad. The crush of people in this overcrowded building. The sealed exits.

A disaster is just something that happens when several improbable events occur in the same place. That's all it takes.

Above him, a sheet of red light flickers across the blackness. Is that a face he can see? Like a giant. Enraged. Yelling at him to act? Or is it just disco lights, synced to the beat?

Will is paralysed by fear. He doesn't trust his senses.

Words are coming to him. Just like they did in the darkroom, on the speedboat before that. A voice that bypasses his ears, that speaks directly to his mind. The voice is familiar. It is the *same*.

This is *not* over.

That is what he's being told.

343

Something unspeakable is about to happen. The information bypasses the part of his brain where thoughts are processed, weighed up. Instead, it is etched into the corner of his mind that deals in certainty.

This is the end.

It becomes obvious now. This strange messenger, of course it wasn't Alfie. Will wasn't being readied to prevent just a suicide. This was always going to be about something bigger. Time hasn't yielded and distorted and folded back on itself just so *one* person's life can be saved. Saving Alfie was just a bonus. A training exercise, even. Of course it's about more than that.

Will gazes deeper into the smoke and the light. The less he focuses, the clearer it becomes. The face. The source of these words, of this certainty.

Why is this face so familiar to me?

No sooner has he constructed the question than the answer is clear to him.

It brings no shock. It is like he's known all along but only now chosen to look at the information.

It is me.

The messenger.

It is me. Dying.

Am I too late? Will asks. *Please. Let it not be too late.*

He loses focus on the face that bears down on him, that great magnifying mirror above his head. Instead he tries to see the crowd. Nothing. He spins round but he can't see across the stage either.

His chest feels heavy. Is it panic that makes it so hard to breathe? Or smoke? He's sure he can taste it now: bitter, toxic.

344

He has to do something. He knows he's condemning himself and all these hundreds of people if he doesn't.

There must be a break-glass fire alarm somewhere. But where?

He considers leaving the decks and feeling along the walls for such a thing. But then he thinks about the panic an alarm might cause. This many people – one way in, one way out.

The key, he realizes, is to keep this as calm as possible.

And he *is* calm, he realizes.

Amazingly, he's ready.

Will chucks his record bag to the floor. There are four records left inside, never to be played. The set was supposed to finish with The Beloved's 'The Sun Rising' – a nod to that perfect night he and April spent on top of the Martello tower. But he needs to close this down right now. He fades the volume on the mixer and dives blindly across the stage, scratching his hands along the wall. Somewhere here there's a bank of switches. He needs to get the house lights on. And he needs to get some doors opened.

'Please, don't let it be too late,' Will says out loud. 'Please. Please let there be time.'

With the sound system killed, his ears feel like they're stuffed with cotton wool. But from the ringing silence, the sound of the crowd starts to rise. It sounds different to Will from how it did earlier.

Because now the crowd are screaming.

The Calm

The snow falls gently, six inches blanketing the ground. Will stares upwards, each snowflake sizzling as it lands on his burning forehead. He's standing at the edge of the school grounds, the car park and playground separating him from the building. It's all but empty inside now.

The cold air is doing the trick. He can feel his pulse slowing, his breathing finding some rhythm. The urge to vomit strikes from nowhere. He spins round to face the fence and retches, but nothing comes up.

'What was all that about?' he mutters to himself.

The sweat that breaks all over him is reassuring. He's wearing just a T-shirt and, for the first time since he's been out here, he can feel the cold.

'What the fucking hell was all that about?'

'Bangin' tunes, bruv,' a voice shouts.

Will nods at the kid, a growth-spurting year eight with arms and legs like pipe cleaners.

'Cheers. Yeah. No worries,' he says absently.

The kid starts windmilling his arm, ready to launch a long-distance snowball. 'Bangin'. Should've played longer.'

'Always leave your audience wanting more.'

'Bangin',' the kid says again before releasing the snowball, his massive feet scrabbling in the snow as he scarpers.

The building emptied out fifteen minutes ago but nearly everyone is still on the school grounds. Most are messing around noisily in the snow. A small group smokes weed in the bin store, another shares laughing-gas balloons in the lobby outside the changing rooms. Couples disappear hand in hand in search of privacy.

Did I save these people, Will wonders, *or did I go a bit crazy for a moment?*

Are you a hero if no one knows what you did?

Am I kidding myself? Was it just some massive wobble?

It felt so real, though. It really, really felt like the end.

As soon as he'd switched on the house lights, Will had pulled every plug on the stage, killing the amplifiers, the lighting rigs, the air pumps to the inflatables, the smoke machine. The noise from the crowd, which had sounded so hysterical, was, in fact, nothing more than a thousand people screaming for more.

Unable to see Leavers or April or anyone else on the stage, Will had jumped into the crowd. Finding strength he didn't know he had, he'd barged his way to the back of the hall in seconds. Ms Simon and two sixth-formers were manning the doors; Will yelled at them to get everybody outside. He was relieved to see people spilling out from the side doors near the stage, Leavers at least having had the sense to start cutting the cable ties off the doors he'd sealed.

Inside a minute, the crush had eased. After five, the hall was nearly empty, the smoke just a light mist. Will stormed through the place, first the hall itself and then the wider building – a man looking for vindication. Was the place really moments away from an inferno?

The vintage amps with their *Do Not Use* labels were warm to the touch but nothing more. The melted snow had left the fake grass squelchy, but had soaked no electrics. The barbecue flamed low outside, twenty metres clear of the spare propane bottles. A search of the rest of the school revealed nothing more untoward than some underage sexual contact in dark corners, including the two boys in the library, whose clothes were by now mostly draped from the medieval history shelves.

No fire. No imminent danger.

Did I save anyone from anything?

Was it my own face, my own dying self, ordering me to act? Or am I just nuts?

Will doesn't see the snowball coming till it explodes between his eyes.

'Sorry, Mr DJ,' a voice screeches. The stinging cold is like a necessary slap in the face. He dries his face on his T-shirt.

'Just calm the fuck down now,' he orders himself. And he walks back towards the school hall.

'Now where the hell did *you* get to?' April says.

'Just checking on . . . a few things,' Will says.

She puts her hands round his waist. 'There I was, thinking you were giving me the slip.'

'No chance.'

There are no kids left in the hall now but there's activity all around them as the catering stalls are dismantled and carted away.

'Your set was wicked, Will. Made the night.'

'You reckon?'

'Everyone fucking loved it.'

'Cool.'

'Did think you might have stayed on a bit longer, though.'

'Did it sound weird? Ending when I did?'

'Not at all. Just everyone was loving it, and then you stopped. Guess we didn't want it to be over.'

'Yeah, think maybe I forgot to play one or two records. Shit . . . you know, performing like that, easy to lose track. Sorry.'

'I'm not criticizing, Will. It was awesome.' She holds his face in her hands. 'Always want more, that's my trouble.' She pecks him on the lips.

'You ever had a feeling like something bad's about to happen?' Will asks.

April makes a show of pondering the question. 'Only two or maybe three times a day. On the good days.'

Will laughs. 'Yeah. Stupid question.'

'Good job, you two,' Ms Simon says, she and Mr Leavers inspecting the place, centimetres apart. 'How much did you raise?'

'We've not done the final count,' April says. 'Might be ten grand.'

Leavers whistles, impressed.

'That's fucking incredible,' Will says.

'Couldn't have done it without you.'

'Bullshit. You did this. You're amazing.'

April checks no one's earwigging their conversation. 'What you doing tonight?'

Will grins. 'I don't know. What *am* I doing tonight?'

Her cheeks flush pink. 'Bit cold for the Martello tower, innit?'

Will smirks. 'Yeah. And that place plays havoc with my . . . performance.'

'The altitude?'

'Yup, the altitude. That's it.'

April moves in close, laying her hand on the inside of Will's thigh. 'Come back to mine?'

Will nods.

'Stay the night?'

He can feel her fingers through his jeans. 'Yes, please.'

'It's gonna be just us tonight, yeah? No thinking about what's gone before, about other people . . .'

'Definitely.' Will nods. 'Just us.'

There are a series of taps on a distant window. Will scowls at the interruption.

'Jolly good!' April says. 'Well, that's sorted then.'

'Can't wait.' A gulp catches Will mid-sentence.

The noise is a full-on hammering now, someone rapping on the window from outside with a hard object.

'Somebody wants to get in,' Leavers shouts, but makes no effort to investigate.

'Gimme ten to sort a few bits here, yeah?' April says.

Kris jogs towards the closed main doors. 'I'll check it out,' he calls to April and Will.

Will looks deeply into April's eyes. 'Be quick.'

For a precious instant, their lips meet once more.

Kris is not yet outside when the pane is struck again, a rapid fire of hits, the last so hard it makes a dull crunch, the toughened glass shattering.

'For God's sake!' Leavers shouts, hurrying after Kris to see what's going on.

'Shit, nearly forgot,' April says to Will. 'You left your phone by the decks. It kept ringing after you disappeared at the end of your set. Leavers got the hump and put it on silent.'

'Fuck. Where is it?'

'By the mixer. Where you left it.'

Will dashes to the stage, the sickness from earlier returning suddenly.

Twenty missed calls. Some Danny, some his mum. And one text, from two minutes ago.

RING NOW NAIN GONE CRAZY WANTS TO SPEAK YOU RIGHT NOW PLEASE RING

'Fuck!' Will says again, storming towards the door.

'Will! Mate, stop!' Kris is back inside and heading for him.

'Not now,' Will says.

'Seriously, Will. Stop a minute.'

'What?'

'Mate, there's someone outside asking for you.'

'So what?'

A smirk seeps into Kris's expression. 'You ever seen that crazy old woman who's always walking round Ebbswick? The one with the pram with no baby in?'

'Yeah, seen her,' Will snaps.

'Well, she's just broken a window! Fucking screaming her head off to talk to you.'

'You OK, Will?' April asks. 'You've gone really white.' Her voice sounds distant.

'Leavers is threatening to drag her off the premises,' Kris says. 'She's having none of it, the batty old tart.'

'What the fuck?' Will whispers. 'What the fuck?'

'Sit down, Will,' April says. 'You look ill.'

He holds up both palms. 'Wait here.'

'What are you doing?'

'Gotta talk to her,' he says, running for the door.

'What the hell's going on, Will?' she shouts after him.

He stops at the door, grabbing his own hair. 'Haven't got a fucking clue.'

Will's feet slip on the compacted snow as he stamps towards the old lady. As he draws close, she is almost unrecognizable to him. Her features, ordinarily so soft and calming, are taut, angular in the glow of the white landscape.

'What?' Will asks, heartbeat thumping in his ears. 'What is it?'

'Talk to him,' she snaps. No hello, no niceties. 'Talk to him right now!'

'Who? Talk to who?'

'Now,' she screeches. 'Your place. The place where you meet.'

'The . . . the darkroom?'

She points a shaking finger into the building. 'Now! Before it's too late.'

Will asks no questions; her fear says everything.

He turns, and he does exactly as he's told.

Last Request

Will is breathless after his sprint along the darkened corridors. He flings the door open. The air inside the darkroom is stale and warm, sharp with developing chemicals.

He seals himself inside, takes a seat in this familiar blackened space.

Every shred of his willpower is in use to tame his breathing, to rein in his pulse.

His skin burns as his body bends to his will.

A tap drips somewhere. Heating pipes tick as they shrink. A drain gurgles.

In front of his face, the darkness starts to break like a dull kaleidoscope. Will relaxes his eyes and his ears, allowing them to become disconnected. He knows how this works now. These organs are no use to him.

The voice asks, 'You know who I am, don't you?'

'You are me,' Will replies.

The face is clear now. Like a mirror. Nodding back at him.

'Yes,' it says. 'Now listen to me. We are nearly out of time.'

So this is where it ends.

You and I are about to converge, to become *one* again. Your now and my now are about to meet. Are you about to join me, dying? Or am I going to join you, and together we live on?

I wish I knew.

But, finally, my memory has become crystal clear. How this day was for me.

Like you, I was at April's disco. Not DJing, of course. No chance. I was there because I was press-ganged by Calloway to help supervise. Even that scared the shit out of me, you know? Probably more than the DJ gig scared you. Crazy.

You've come a long way, you really have.

I'd have dodged the job if it hadn't been for April being there. I mean, I couldn't hold a conversation with her, let alone do the things you do. But it was a chance to see her, imagine how her skin feels, how her hair might smell.

You're so much less *weird* than you once were.

I visited Nain in the morning, like you. But, unlike you, I begged her to get well.

I visited Danny in the hospital too, no longer critical, but a long way from a full recovery from the stab wounds he sustained that night at the bowling alley. *Life-changing* – that's how they talked about Danny's injuries.

And when I turned up at school, a portrait of Alfie Lim stared back at me. Beneath it, flowers shivered in the icy breeze. A new poster boy for the Talk About It campaign, the subject of cautionary assemblies. Such a promising young man – dead by his own hand. I wasn't close to Alfie like you've become, but I missed his classroom antics all the same. I ached at the sight of that empty chair in photography.

This disco wasn't as good. April was right – your set really did make the night.

I didn't even say goodnight to her when I left. Didn't compliment her on her great job. Wanted to. Couldn't.

I waited up the road for the number 83. It was even later than it usually is. With six inches of snow on the ground and no salt on the road, the bus skidded along the kerb before it stopped.

It was packed out, that bus. Near on a hundred kids piled on in their rave get-up, all neon T-shirts and fading glow sticks. The windows were steamed up in seconds. I managed to get a seat next to some old boozer with a nicotine-stained beard. He had a hacking cough and he smelt of dishcloths.

It took ages to get through Ebbswick – there were cars stranded in the snow all over the place. Took more than half an hour to get near the seafront. I thought about getting out and walking, but it would've meant asking all those noisy kids in the aisle to move. So I didn't.

That's the sort of thing you used to be scared of. Why?

The traffic was nose to tail into Patten's Island. We were coming up to the level crossing. The car in front of the bus crossed the railway but wasn't going quick enough to get up the hill. He rolled backwards. But the bus driver was already on the crossing. He hit the brakes and all the kids standing up jerked forward.

So there we were, stopped over the railway line. Driver tried to back up but it was hopeless – wheels spinning, polishing the snow till it was a sheet of rock-hard ice.

The traffic lights right next to my window started flashing red to orange. The alarm started up. Most of the kids were still dicking around, oblivious.

The driver was revving the nuts off the engine by now. The back end of the bus was slewing left and right, but never backwards or forwards.

Up in front, the people in the car blocking the road were out pushing it. But the clear road ahead was no use to us now. This old, heavy, overloaded bus would not move.

A disaster is nothing more than several improbable events taking place at the same time – that's all it takes.

The sudden silence was somehow the most frightening part. One or two people saw it through the misted glass. They froze or pointed. And so, one by one, everyone else followed. Out of the right-hand windows of the bus, lights on the track. An express train. Full chat across the marshes.

Surely it would see us, we thought. But as those lights bore down, it was clear it hadn't.

The silence turned to screaming.

Time slowed almost to a stop.

Those monstrous lights gathered us in: so impossibly huge, so impossibly *fast*.

And it happened.

There was no sound. That's the strangest thing. Just this incredible pressure that swallowed everything, even noise.

Cubes of shattered glass hung motionless in the air, twinkling like the Milky Way.

There was a sense of moving fast, yet also being weightless, floating in this twisted, elongated capsule as it tumbled in the air.

We hit the ground. The shell of the bus burst open at one end like an over-squeezed toothpaste tube. Bodies smashed into me, head first, feet first. Others spilled out through the gaping hole where the driver once sat.

There was no pain, not that I remember anyway. There was an instant of hope that I was uninjured, as I was thrown from the bus, tumbling over torn steel.

I thumped into the freezing ground. I couldn't move. There appeared to be no arm where an arm should have been. My head was attached to my body wrong; I could see my own back in front of me. The snow turned red.

Bodies landed around me like they were falling from the sky. Small bodies mostly, some barely bouncing as the snow cushioned their fall.

Still no pain. No sense of the cold.

In the distance, I could see the train. Hundreds of metres from the track. Buckled and broken, carriages torn in half and turned upside down. Some people screamed for help. Most didn't.

How many people? I calmly wondered. Seventy, eighty on the bus perhaps? Hundreds on the train, surely.

A disaster. A tragedy.

I watched a while, but nothing much more happened.

And then it all just faded away. It was peaceful really.

I remember the sense of walls coming down. I remember colours like fireworks. A fitting of everything into place. Questions I'd never thought to ask being answered.

And then . . . And then . . .

Then there was you. With April and Danny. In the broken-down car.

And me. Confused. Disorientated. No idea who I was. Like I'd just woken from a dream and couldn't remember a single detail.

Following you.

Every time you've been near this level crossing, I've had this odd sense of being *home*. Now I know why. Because all this time, that's where I've been. Lying in the snow here. Broken. Alone. Dying.

The last throes of my consciousness, just minutes in the outside world, have felt like months to me. Months spent looking over your shoulder.

I'm still here, of course. In the snow. Death coming for me fast.

And now you've nearly caught up with me.

In your now, the number 83 bus will leave any moment, jam-packed with kids.

It'll get stuck on the level crossing at Patten's Island in about half an hour. And the coastal express, running behind time and fully subscribed, won't see the bus till it's too late.

Can you change something one last time? Can you stop this?

Not even I know the answer to that.

The Storm

Will leaves the school gates at a full sprint. As he turns on to the road, he slips in the snow. He goes over, skinning his knuckles on the kerb. There are piss-taking chants from the few kids still outside school as he scrabbles to right himself. Back on his feet, he veers from side to side like a speed-skater leaving the line.

The road rises to a brow, after which it's less than a hundred metres to the bus stop. It's a four-minute walk from the gates ordinarily. Will has it in sight in barely one. He stops at the crest of the hill.

He's too late. The number 83 is already leaving. He's just in time to watch it gingerly rounding the right-hander in the distance. Even from this far away he can see how overloaded it is, kids in neon sardined together in the back window.

'Stop!' Will yells. 'Fucking stop!' He knows there's no way he'll be heard, but it doesn't stop him screaming it. 'Someone stop that fucking bus! Please! Please!'

He hunches forward, out of breath. *How long have I got?* he asks himself. *How long before it happens?*

Ordinarily, the number 83 takes about fifteen minutes to reach the front. But on roads as bad as this it's sure to be much longer. How long, though?

He spins round. A group of three year eights walk slowly up the hill towards him.

'Do you know anyone on that bus?' he yells, pointing to a bus that has now disappeared from view.

'Have we missed the bus?' one of the girls whines.

Will blocks their path. 'Do you know anyone on the 83?'

They spend what feels like ages mulling the question over.

'Listen, right,' Will snaps. 'Can you please call anyone you know who might be on it?'

'Why?' the boy asks.

'Just fucking do it!' Will yells.

'And say what, angry man?'

'There's gonna be an accident.'

The kid grins. One of the girls sings *The Twilight Zone* music.

'Fuck's sake. I saw something when it left. The . . . the back wheel looks like it's gonna fall off any second.'

The lie is surprisingly effective. All three of them are listening now. 'Death trap, that thing,' a girl says. 'Always breaking down, innit.'

Will grabs the iPhone the boy's fiddling with. 'Who here is on that bus,' he says, scrolling through the contacts.

'Try Tommy D,' the boy says, finding the contact for Will and pressing call.

'Not answering,' Will snaps. 'Why isn't he fucking answering?'

The three of them look blankly. 'Never answers,' a girl says. 'Who answers voice calls at this time of night? Text him.'

Will chucks the phone back. He's wasted a minute of precious time already. Panic courses through him at the thought of the bus getting further and further away.

'Please, guys,' he says, holding out two shaking hands. 'Text everyone you know who might be on that bus. Call them too. Tell them they are in danger, yeah? Get them to tell the driver to stop. Tell them all to get off at the next stop. Yeah? You'll do that.'

Frightened by his tone, the three of them all agree. They tap at their phones, sharing sideways glances at each other.

Will faces the direction in which the bus disappeared. However fast he runs, however slow the traffic, he's not going to catch it. But he needs to get to it.

Or I could get to the front first . . .

He grabs his own phone. It bleeps *Low battery* at him. There's one cab firm saved on there, used occasionally for getting Nain a lift home.

'Outside Ebbswick Community Secondary,' Will barks before the controller is halfway through saying the firm's name. 'To the front at Ebbswick. Patten's Island.'

'The front, sir? Or Patten's Island?' His tone is condescending.

'Level crossing. You know the level crossing?'

'I do, sir.' The tapping of computer keyboard is hellishly slow.

There's no way Will can stand still. He's half walking, half jogging in the direction the bus disappeared. His free hand sinks nails into his forearm and draws blood.

'That'll be eleven pounds, sir.'

'Can you just send the cab?'

'With you in twenty to twenty-five minutes, sir.'

'Please! I need it now.'

'I'm afraid the weather —'

'Look, please just fucking listen. There's going to be a terrible accident. Down at the front. At the level crossing. Can you warn anyone? Send anyone? Please? Please? Anything.'

'Maybe you need the emergency services, sir?' the controller says, more patronizing than ever. 'Rather than a minicab?'

Will ends the call. The emergency services. Why didn't he call 999 to start with?

What does he say to them, though? That he's had a premonition hundreds of people are about to die? That a voice in his head tells him about things before they happen? What the *fuck* does he say?

'Which service do you require?'

'There's going to be a terrible accident.'

'Police, fire or ambulance?'

'Erm . . .'

'Or coast guard?'

'Police! Police, please.' Will continues to run, even though he has no idea where.

A different voice: 'What's your emergency?'

'There's about to be a massive accident.'

'Where are you?'

'I'm near ECS. Well, I was. Doesn't matter.'

'A road name, perhaps?'

'Look, listen. Something really bad's about to happen. At Patten's Island. A train.'

'Try to calm down, please. Now can you tell me what's happened.'

'Hasn't happened yet. There's going to be . . .' He stops himself, remembering the lie he told the kids a few minutes ago. 'The number 83 bus. Towards the seafront from ECS. You need to stop it. A wheel's about to fall off. There's loads of kids on board.'

Silence.

'Did you get that? The number 83, yeah?'

Nothing.

Will shakes his phone. He stares at the blank screen. He stabs at it till his finger buckles. 'No!' he shouts. 'Fucking no! Not fucking now!'

His phone's been ringing non-stop most of the afternoon and evening, and for an hour it was next to the decks with the torch switched on. And now the battery's flat.

Will stops himself just short of launching his phone into the night. Instead he punches it, cracks spidering across the black screen.

Did the police get the bit about the bus? Or did his phone die before he said it? It's impossible to know.

What now?

He could run back to school. Use someone else's phone. Try to raise the alarm. How long would that take? Five minutes maybe.

But that relies on one huge assumption: that the police will listen, believe him, and act in a matter of minutes to stop the bus before it reaches the level crossing. Will they do that? There's no guarantee, that's for sure. Running back to school, *away* from this impending disaster, it feels wrong.

Will stops for a second. How long has he got now? Twenty minutes at a push. No more than that.

The number 83 takes a tortuous diagonal path through Ebbswick, stopping every four hundred metres. The route it follows is far from the quickest way to reach the sea. He might not be able to catch the bus, Will knows, but that doesn't mean he can't get to the level crossing first. If he can do that, perhaps he can stop it before it pulls over the tracks.

The key is to make this journey as the crow flies. And that means not going through Ebbswick at all, but through the industrial estate on the outskirts of town and, from there, cross-country over the marshes. He'll reach the railway parallel to the shore. From there it's maybe eight hundred metres along the tracks to the level crossing.

How far is it? A good five-mile ride on the bus. But the route Will's planning can't be more than half that. Can he make it? Four kilometres in under twenty minutes? It should be doable. Right now, it's the best option.

The snow has become a blizzard. The landscape is utterly silent as Will sprints down a single-track lane. His vision is filled with the fuzz of snowflakes rushing into his face. Even his footfalls are muted; the only sound is his own heavy breathing folding back from the icy cocoon around him. Water runs down his arms, warm and crimson by the time it runs off his wrecked knuckles.

His feet skid across the ground as he reaches a left turn into a bridleway. He reaches out and grabs the rusted signpost that points to the industrial park and seafront, pivoting round it and launching himself downhill. Twice, he trips, but he loses no momentum, hands clawing along the rutted ground until he's able to right himself.

'Please. Please,' he repeats as he runs. 'Please let me make it.'

Every few minutes, he feels the onset of fatigue, of muscles crying enough. And then he visualizes them, the children, bent and broken, dead in the snow. And all those people on the train who'll never make it home. And he runs even faster.

The bridleway opens out on to a sweeping crescent-shaped road. It's lined with tall steel fences and gates secured by chains. Beyond, there are flat-roofed industrial units: a builders' merchant's, a tyre depot, a haulage firm. Will follows the line of the fence. Somewhere here there's an alley that cuts through the estate and on to the marshes beyond.

He hears footsteps running on the other side of the fence. He looks down. A flash of dripping pink mouth and wet fangs. The bark makes Will jump. He veers on to the road and almost goes over again, legs and arms flailing to keep himself upright. He looks back at the German shepherd through the steel bars, keeping pace with Will as he accelerates again.

'What's the big hurry, pal?' a gruff voice shouts from the forecourt of a metal stockholders.

Will's first instinct is to ignore the man, keep right on running. But this is the first human being he's encountered since his phone died. And he may be the last. He slows, enough so that he can speak.

'I need you to call the police,' Will says.

The night watchman looks puzzled.

'What's going on?'

'There's about to be a huge crash down at the front. The number 83 bus. Gonna get stuck on the level crossing. Train's gonna hit it. Gonna happen any minute now.'

'Aye,' the guy says, nodding, as if he receives such tip-offs regularly. 'Which level crossing?'

'Patten's Island. You know it?'

He steps closer to the fence so they can see each other clearly through the driving snow. 'Aye, I know it.'

'Tell the police, yeah?'

'I'll make the call. When did you say?'

'Any time now.'

'Righto.' He turns away and marches towards the site office.

Will doesn't dwell on how unremarkable the bloke found the suggestion. Instead, he redoubles his pace, spying the alleyway on the right up ahead.

The night watchman makes no call, circling the site instead for an imminent break-in, timed, no doubt, to coincide with the police racing to the front had he put the call in. 'Wasn't born yesterday, pal,' he mumbles.

The alley is overgrown and lined with fly-tipped rubbish disguised by the snow. Already a bramble has snagged Will's arm, gouging strips of skin away. He weaves from side to side down the obstacle course. Catching sight of some rubble bags only once he's upon them, he loses his balance as he tries to steer round them. Shoulder first, he ploughs into a fence. He doesn't see the barbed wire until it's ripping through his T-shirt. He shouts out, but it's in shock rather than pain. In fact, it doesn't really hurt at all. Instead, it feels like an ice-cold rake has been dragged down his torso. It helps, Will finds, once he's ripped himself free and begun to move again, to not look at the sheer volume of blood running down him.

By the time he's at the end of the alley, his jeans are soaked purple. His shoes squelch with every step. A dotted trail stretches behind him.

He's on the marshes now. White and unblemished in the moonlight, rolling gently down towards the sea, this landscape would be bleakly beautiful on a different day.

'Please,' he says again as he runs. 'Please . . .'

His feet thump out a rhythm. To his left, in the distance, an orange haze hangs over the town. Smoke rises from chimneys. Most people are safe and warm indoors, blissfully unaware of how their world will be shaken off its axis if Will doesn't fix this in time. He imagines for a second that he's watching himself from above, running bloodied and broken and crying across these fields.

Will's at the marsh road now. Almost at the very spot where Danny left April and him after the fight at the bowling alley. He can almost see the railway line. Without the snow, it would be in clear sight. Is there still time? It feels like he's been running for hours.

A minute later and he's there. He stops for a moment beside the rails. To his left, the tracks lead dead straight into Ebbswick, the level crossing half a mile away. To his right, the tracks begin to curve, following the coastline. That's the direction from which the express will come, racing at eighty miles per hour towards the town. Visibility is limited, but there's no sign or sound of it just yet.

The ground between the rails is the best for running on, flat and with no hazards lurking in the snow. Progress is good to start with. But then a foot lands wrong against the leading edge of a twisted sleeper. Will's momentum carries him five or more metres before he sprawls flat on his front.

He raises himself on to his hands and knees, takes a second to gather his breath. A stiff gust of wind kicks the falling snow clear of the ground. For a moment he can see along the straight tracks to the lit-up crossing five hundred metres away.

Initially the way is clear. And then, like a sliding door closing, the flank of the number 83 bus blocks the line. There's a delay in the noises reaching Will: metallic clanks as the chassis grounds, the squeal of skidding tyres, the panicked revving of a diesel engine.

'No,' Will whines. 'No!'

He's not yet back on his feet when he hears another sound from the distant level crossing. The alarm bleating, warning of an approaching train.

All Change

The face is close to Will's. They stare silently at each other in the middle of the tracks.

It's how calm he suddenly feels that surprises Will. How calm he feels for someone who's come face to face with, what, his own ghost?

Here he stands with his informer, his mystery messenger. His *guide*. Another version of himself. Himself, dying.

'I'm too late,' Will says.

On the wind is the screeching of the bus's belly against the cold steel tracks. Still the alarm sounds.

'You aren't too late,' his guide tells him. 'There's still a way.'

There's no urgency to how he says it.

The rails begin to hum under Will's feet. The coastal express is coming. How long has the bus been stuck now? Twenty seconds? In another twenty, the train will obliterate it.

'How?' Will says. He looks down the track behind him. No sign yet, but the rails hum harder. He steps to one side of the track. His guide takes the other side, looking across the rails at Will.

'You've come so far.'

Will nods. It's been a rollercoaster of a few months.

'I'm so proud of you. Of me.'

Will looks at the blood-dappled snow where he was standing a moment ago.

'I know how this ends,' his guide says. 'I haven't known long. But I know now.'

Will can see the lights of the train. It's rounding the bend, flat out through the driving snow. There's no way it'll see the bus. But he already knew that.

'We can't save them,' Will says. The guilt makes his organs feel like they're being wrung out. He should've been on that bus, with everyone else. Thanks to his guide, he isn't. But he's failed to change the course of history. They are all about to perish, just as they did before. As will so many people on the train. Will's only succeeded in saving himself. And he can't bear it.

'You can,' his guide says. 'I've seen it.'

Any second now, Will thinks, *that train is going to tear past us.* A moment later, it's going to hit the bus. Hundreds dead. An unimaginable tragedy.

'I don't understand,' Will says, the roar of the train's engine audible now. 'We can't move the bus. We can't get the people off. What do we do?'

'We can't move the bus. But we *can* stop the train.'

Will faces the direction it approaches from. The driving snow is blinding. He waves his arms frantically. But he knows how futile it is.

'How? Fucking how? Driver will never see me!' He's raising his voice now above the rush of the train.

'You stop the train,' his guide says. 'You *will* save them.'

Will stares blankly back at him.

'I don't understand.'

'You do,' his guide says. He sounds sad, resigned.

Will's about to demand more. But he doesn't. Because, just like that, he gets it. The answer to that question that's been bugging him. *Why me?*

Why is it that he, Will Parks, has been singled out to receive these messages, to grow as a person, to change the course of time? Because he can make the difference.

The train is nearly on him now.

It feels preordained. Like it was written in the stars all along. A circular series of events destined to link back on themselves. He wonders if he even has a choice now, or if the path of time has already made this final decision for him. If it wasn't going to end like this all along, surely none of what led him here would ever have happened.

Time, it seems, works in mysterious ways.

'You know, don't you?' his guide says.

'I do,' Will answers. He can feel the pressure from the train approaching now.

'You are a hero,' his guide says.

He smiles at the ridiculous concept. Will Parks, a hero.

Even in these last seconds, he thinks again of the shoe-licking incident. Of Mick Touch's words: *Not one for playing the hero . . . act a bit braver than that when you've got an audience.*

There's no audience here. No show to put on. No playing of the action hero.

Yet he is about to save the lives of hundreds of people. He is simply doing what must be done. No promise of applause. No status to be gained. No glory to bask in.

Will Parks. Wimp. Pussy. About to save the day.

'Even if no one knows what you did. Or why you did it. You *are* a hero.' His guide nods with the words. A Magician's Nod.

And he's gone.

For the first time in months, on these snow-covered marshes, Will is completely alone.

The train is unimaginably large.

Will loads up his left foot, sure it has good purchase on the slippery ground. The wind ramps. Snowflakes whip into tiny tornadoes. This is the last light to pass Will Parks' eyes.

Not yet.

Not yet.

Now.

Will jumps.

His final thoughts are of April. And of Nain. And, lastly, of Beppo. Dear old Beppo.

There's a fleeting instant when Will and the train driver are eye to eye through the windscreen.

The driver's arm reflexes up, as if to protect her own face. There is a dull thump.

Cracks shoot across the glass. Wipers paint the screen red. Emergency brakes are applied.

It is done.

A Narrow Escape

Most of the children on the bus don't even notice it coming. They're still too revved up from the evening they've had to realize the danger they're in. Just one or two, sitting nearest the right-hand windows, spooked by the sounding alarm, look along the tracks. Despite the snow, they see the distant lights.

'Try reverse,' a dog walker yells to the bus driver through the open window.

The driver obliges. A howl of wheel spin. The bus rocks half a metre backwards.

'Now forward,' she shouts. 'But gently. Gently this time.'

A year seven points through the window. He can see the train, distant but racing down on them. He's open-mouthed. Can't speak.

Some of the kids who stand in the aisle see it now. They fall quiet, too.

'It's OK,' the old boozer with the grubby beard and the hacking cough says. He looks along the tracks and nods. 'It's slowing. The brakes are on. We'll be all right.'

The panic dissolves into nervous giggling.

The rear wheels of the bus find some traction. Everyone on board rocks backwards as the bus powers out of the crossing.

Fifty metres away, the coastal express screeches to a stop.

The number 83 bus climbs the icy slope into Patten's Island.

'Shit a brick,' the bus driver says to himself. 'Shit a shitting brick.'

Behind him, the noise from his passengers rises, their revelry ramping up again.

An Inconvenient Delay

Under emergency braking, it takes just over four hundred metres for the coastal express to reach a stop from its eighty-two miles per hour.

In Carriage C, a couple, both in their early fifties, gather up belongings that have been hurled forward by the harsh braking. One mops her Bloody Mary off the table. Her wife scoops Kettle Chips back into their bag.

'I apologize for the delay,' the driver says over the PA. Everyone listens silently. The tremor in her voice is unmissable. 'I'm afraid we'll have to wait here . . .' A gulp. 'We've had something . . . someone . . .' She's quiet for a moment. 'Somebody has jumped in front of the train. Sorry.'

The carriage is quiet.

'Dreadful,' the woman whispers to her wife.

'Selfish bastard,' a voice mutters a few seats back.

The woman stands.

'Josephine, don't,' her wife says, but she doesn't listen.

'Somebody is dead,' the woman snaps. 'Would it hurt you to have a little empathy?'

'Sorry,' the young guy says. 'Gonna be stuck here ages though.'

'And that's the real tragedy, is it?'

'No. No. Sorry.' He looks at the woman and begins to smirk.

'Is something funny?'

'Ms Calloway?'

'Yes.'

'You taught me art at Kent Academy.'

'Oh, right. Yes, so I did. You've grown.'

'Never thought I'd still be getting bollockings from you at thirty!'

'Well, behave yourself then.' She wags her finger. 'You're not too old for a detention.'

'I wish you'd just leave things, Josephine,' her wife says as she retakes her seat.

Ms Calloway looks out of the window over the snow-covered marshes. 'Just outside Ebbswick,' she says. 'God forbid it's someone I know.'

Her wife squeezes her leg. 'Do you want to call it off? I know you've not been keen.'

She thinks about it for a moment. It's true, she's not been enthusiastic about this weekend away. In fact, she's had a distinct sense of unease whenever she's thought about it. A vague dread, the nature of which she's been unable to put her finger on. But as of these last few minutes that strange feeling has lifted like a fog.

Ms Calloway smiles. 'No. Let's go. I'm looking forward to it.'

No More Fighting

The ward is quiet now and almost in darkness, just a single desk lamp glowing at the nursing station.

The staff nurse begins her round of sleeping patients. In the first side room is the lady of seventy-nine they expected to lose a week ago, the one who is visited twice daily by the very tall boy who calls her Nain.

She is calm now, sleeping deeply after that episode earlier when she awoke so unexpectedly.

The nurse listens to her breathing. Slow. Irregular. A faint gurgling from the throat. A pulse is taken – barely there.

She takes a seat beside the bed and strokes that cold hand. She's done this job long enough to know.

'You go well, my sweet darling,' the nurse whispers. 'You go well.'

Level Crossing

The world around him tumbles and spins. Sky. Ground. Snow. Train. Ground. Sky. It feels like he's been airborne for many minutes. Will's landing, when it comes, is gentle. Like falling into a bed of feathers.

The night sky is clear. Inky black. No snow is falling on him.

There is no pain. No hint even of discomfort.

His eyes lose their focus.

His own weight melts away.

He has the very real sensation of his head opening like a butterfly. Of his mind being presented to the world.

No longer is what Will sees channelled through the constrictions of his eyes; nor is what he hears reduced by his ears. He is outside the cage. Outside the prison of himself.

The sky lights up above him like the most breathtaking firework display. The burble of voices he hears is like a lullaby.

Will begins to rise towards this incredible light show. Floating. Flying. The world, unfiltered by human experience, is more spectacular than anything any brain could imagine.

Will knows that this is it. Death. The end. But it doesn't seem to matter. His fading consciousness is taking him on a magical mystery tour, and he has no sense of wishing to be anywhere else.

Order to chaos.

Those words roll around his unlocked mind.

Hasn't he just disproved this very theory? Has his final act not made order where otherwise chaos would have reigned?

He is beginning to understand. This universe does move from order to chaos.

But is that, perhaps, why there has to be life? Is the very reason for the existence of life to disrupt this inevitable flow, to reverse the trend? Are we, in fact, here to make order out of chaos, sense from the senseless, something where there is nothing? Do we exist so that we might save the universe from itself?

Is that it, Will vaguely wonders, *is that the meaning of life?* To create order from chaos? How strange that the mystery of our own existence should only unravel as it comes to its end.

Time passes. Hours perhaps. Possibly days. Maybe a few seconds. Those bedazzling colours that had taken over Will's vision start to fade. The soothing voices are hushed. His mind begins to shrink once again, the philosophical questions silenced, their potential answers forgotten. Instead, he sees a dull light. Cool bluey-grey. Daylight. Evening in the early autumn, to be precise.

Will is way up high now. He has a Google Earth perspective over a town on the coast.

But, slowly, he's descending.

The sun is beginning to set. Like fire and smoke.

A line of cars queue below him at a level crossing. There's a small Fiat. With a huge stereo.

And Will knows. It's Danny. And April. And him. That night when it all began.

He's about to join them.

Do I get another chance? Will thinks. *Do I get another go at this? A chance to follow my old self again? To get messages across when I can?*

Is this another chance? To not just save everybody, but save myself too?

Please. Please let it be so.

He's almost with them now. Not that they can see him, of course.

His mind starts to empty, everything being filed away, far out of his reach.

By the time he's inside the car, it's gone. He has no idea who he is or what he's doing, only a nagging sense of purpose.

He's here for a reason. That's all he knows right now.

The Beginning

Will Parks is no longer alone.

This is the precise instant it begins. He is being watched. Followed. Everywhere.

Acknowledgements

Thank you first and foremost to Ben Horslen, whose editorial genius has made this book so much more than I imagined it could be.

Continued thanks to Harry Illingworth – agent, guru, dispenser of kind words when they are most needed.

Thanks to the terrific team at Penguin, especially Jennie Roman, Stephanie Barrett and Alice Todd.

Thank you to Mehreen Akhtar, who brought insight and wisdom to the sensitivity read.

I'm eternally indebted to the many family and friends who support my writing endeavours, especially my brothers Will and Sam, and Daniel Ross.

And, most of all, thank you to my wife Vikki my first reader, my greatest supporter, my reason.

About the Author

James Goodhand lives in Surrey with his wife and young son. A mechanic by day, much of his work has been written at an oil-stained workbench whilst ignoring a queue of broken cars in need of his attention. James's debut novel, *Last Lesson*, was nominated for the Branford Boase Award.

A boy. A bully. A bomb.
Read on for an excerpt from James Goodhand's
extraordinary debut novel
LAST LESSON

4.52 a.m.

I've slept for close to five hours. I almost congratulate myself. My sleep is black and it soaks the bedsheets, but it's a mechanical necessity for a mind that's screaming to rest. Being in constant fear for your life is every bit as tiring as you'd imagine.

I perch on the edge of the bed, clawing at the carpet with frozen toes. The first thoughts after waking are, of course, not to be trusted. Doubts have this way of worming themselves in during the small hours, leaving you to face each morning in the belief that you can't achieve anything above the ordinary.

Can I really do this?

As I do every morning, I squeeze my eyes closed and picture Aunty Kaye's face. Some days the image comes easily, sometimes so slow I panic that I've lost it. Today she appears with the clarity of a photograph almost immediately. My breathing steadies. Calm descends.

I begin my imaginary appeal to her; run through my reasons, one by one, as if we're just chatting over iced lattes at that jazz bar overlooking the marina – the one we hung out at last summer. I explain to her why this is the best solution. The only solution. She isn't fazed at all; her expression shows no judgement or shock. She just listens; she just understands. She always understood. I imagine her voice, still clear despite the time that's passed. It's the voice of birthdays, of Christmas Eve, the voice of the best memories.

'Well then, you have no choice,' she says, nodding, aware of just how huge the consequences will be.

Smearing my soles dry across the carpet, I stand and draw the faded floral curtains apart. A late May dawn has begun its rise over the slate roofs and chimneys that stagger down the hill from our house. The only hint of a woken world is the distant rush of a London-bound train. All the work vans are still parked in the shade. The place looks peaceful. You might even think it pretty in a rugged kind of way – pretty for the sort of estate people are born in and never leave.

For a moment, I can ignore thoughts of my fellow members of Class 11C, dotted about the town, enjoying the sleep they've long deprived me of. Instead, I think of Sophia.

Something close to a smile forms. She's due at work in an hour; she'll be leaving home soon. Is she as nervous as I am? It's hard to imagine. Does she even believe that I'm going to go through with it? She'll have her doubts, I'm sure of that. My stomach burns as I imagine our plans for tonight – for when this is over. For the first time today, I am certain.

This is happening.

5.11 a.m.

I'm halfway down the stairs when I see it. I stop dead. This is what I have to put up with.

Clinging to the banister holding my breath, I cock an ear up towards the landing. I listen for confirmation that Gramps is still asleep. There's a lengthy silence, then a desperate gasp for oxygen as his snore resumes its rattle. Relief – chronic back pain from a lifetime of laying lawns and patios makes him prone to unpredictable early risings. The thought of him stumbling on this doesn't bear thinking about.

I creep the rest of the way downstairs, shaking my head as I stare at the front door. My own jerky breathing seems deafening; the creak from each stair makes me wince. I'm certain I'll wake him any second.

On the mat, in the soft blue glow through the frosted glass, lies one unlit match. As I crouch, the now-familiar stench of lighter fuel fills my nostrils. Level with my eyes, a couple of tiny spheres of the liquid dangle from the sharp edge of the letterbox.

This is the third time. I'm furious that it still freaks me out so much; that my hand still trembles as I lay a palm on the bristles of the doormat and study the shiny coating it leaves on my fingers.

'Fuck you,' I hiss, my teeth digging into my bottom lip as I spit the words. The heat comes fast to my eyes; the floor becomes a blur. I swipe the sleeve of my dressing gown across my face. 'Why the fuck do you do this to me?' The words leave my mouth as a whining whisper. 'What did I ever do to you?'

It's not that they don't have the balls to light the match. They do. They will. This is just another warning shot, a little reminder of what's to come today. This is their game. Think of an executioner: when does he feel at his most powerful? As the axe slices through his victim's neck, or as he stands, wielding that axe far above his head?

This phase of their campaign is three weeks old now. Nate Mackie's whisper from behind me in that school assembly replays in my head. 'We're going to burn your house down, Morcombe,' his speech slow, no intonation to the words. 'We're going to burn it down when your grandad's asleep.' His hot breath was millimetres from my ear, the rancid waft of stale Marlboros curling round me. 'He's getting cremated, Ollie.'

The fight, once contained within the school's perimeter before sprawling out into the parks, alleys and pavements of my route home, had now reached my own front door.

I ease the key round in the lock, lean my shoulder into the door and noiselessly yank it clear of its frame. The mat bows under its sodden weight as I step outside, the dewy front lawn freezing beneath my bare feet. I angle it to dry in the low sun. Only a little of the solvent has spilled over on to the carpet, nothing a sheet of kitchen towel won't soak up. This brings me an odd sense of relief. The first time there'd been a lot more of the stuff. And the carpet was only laid a few months back. It's a brown-and-white swirly affair, like it was inspired by the icing on a vanilla slice. 'Won't show the dirt,' Gramps had enthused as he thumbed a musty book of samples the guy in the shop had taken ages to find.

I cried myself dry that first time – not out of fear, but out of concern for Gramps's new carpet. Why the hell was that the most upsetting thing? I fight an aching in my throat even now, as I massage at the pile, absorbing every last trace of lighter fluid.

The silent clean-up complete, I sit on the bottom stair with the unburnt match in my palm. An idea comes to me. It's perfect.

'Have it your way then,' I mouth, slipping it into my pocket. There's only one thing to be done with this little match. It's unnecessary, but I'll do it anyway. Because then I can tell Sophia that I did. She'll love it. And what matters more than that?

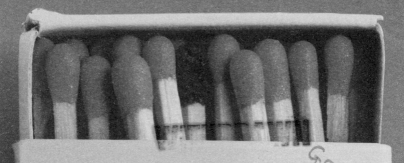

SCHOOL'S

LAST

OUT

LESSON

FOREVER